The
Himmler
Equation

Previous Books by William P. Kennedy

Toy Soldiers
The Masakado Lesson
Code Conquistador

The
HIMMLER

EQUATION

William P. Kennedy

ST. MARTIN'S PRESS NEW YORK

This novel is a work of fiction. No representation that any statement made in this novel is true or that any incident depicted in this novel actually occurred is intended or should be inferred by the reader.

Design by Judith Stagnitto

Library of Congress Cataloging-in-Publication Data

Kennedy, William P.
    The Himmler equation / William P. Kennedy.
        p.   cm.
    ISBN 0-312-03358-3
    I. Title.
PS3561.E429H56 1989
813'.54—dc20   89-32757
                                                                CIP

First Edition
10 9 8 7 6 5 4 3 2 1

To Rena and Marge
with gratitude for
Simple Words

WINTER

1944

By the end of 1943, giant cracks had appeared at the edges of the Third Reich. To the east, the advance into Russia had been reversed. German armies were in retreat from the Crimea, the siege of Leningrad had been relieved, and Russia's northern armies had reached the Baltic states. To the south, Rommel had abandoned Africa, and Sicily had fallen, giving the Allies control of the Mediterranean. American and British armies were in southern Italy, and the Italian government had withdrawn from the war. In the west, American convoys were sailing over the coffins of sunken U-boats, bringing supplies for the relentless air attacks that flew from English airfields. At every point of the compass, there was reason to hope that Germany would soon be defeated. But, still, Fortress Europa was intact. All of Eastern Europe stood between the Red Army and the German homeland. The western wall, facing the English Channel, seemed impregnable. There wasn't a single Allied soldier standing on German soil. Not one German-conquered state, from the Arctic reaches of Norway to the Mediterranean coast of France, had yet been liberated. Even in Italy, the Allied advance had been blunted by the German troops who replaced the *surrendered Italians. German threats of a massive spring counterattack seemed entirely plausible. And it was dangerous to ignore Hitler's boasts of secret new weapons that would smash the Allies in a flash.*

STOCKHOLM — *January 3*

Professor Nils Bergman wound the ornate pocket watch and pressed it to his ear. He smiled at the rhythmic ticking. It had been a year since he had carried the timepiece, yet somehow he had been certain that it would still work, just like the giant clock that ran the universe even though no one was listening to its sound. It wasn't that he expected to use the watch. Bergman carried it more as an accessory to his attire than for any practical purpose. Time, in his beloved field of physics, was measured in millenia. Except when you clocked the speed of the fast neutrons he had explored, and then time was reckoned in billionths of a second. His watch didn't measure either scale.

He slipped it into the vest pocket of his heavy tweed suit, smoothed the jacket, and then stepped back to examine himself in the full-length mirror. The suit, which he had worn only once before, matched his tall frame and settled comfortably across his broad shoulders. But it was pulled tight across his stomach. He sucked in his belly, and admired a physique that was more youthful than his forty-six years. Then he exhaled and watched the buttons tighten on the front of his vest.

"Ridiculous," he admitted, letting his shoulders slump in despair. "Why am I dressing to impress the Germans? It's Herr Diebner who should be dressing to impress me. Who the hell ever heard of Kurt Diebner?"

"All the German scientists will be there," Magda reminded him. She stepped up behind him so that he could see her in the mirror as she straightened his shirt collar. "They're very formal people. You should really have a dark suit."

"Or a uniform," he sneered. "I understand everyone in Germany is wearing a uniform these days. With riding boots. How do you think I would look in a uniform?"

He turned slowly and caught her lowering her face so that he wouldn't see the tears that had been in her eyes since he first received the invitation from Germany.

"Perhaps I shouldn't go," Bergman offered, taking Magda into his arms. But she pushed him away and turned back to the bed where his suitcase was half-packed.

"They have my work. My writings," he persisted. "What more do they need?"

"It's what you need," she reminded him for the hundredth time in the past week. "You need the chance to prove your theories. You deserve the chance." She lifted his heavy woolen sweater from the stack of clothes on the bed and held it over the suitcase. "This is all the uniform you need."

The sweater was his lab coat. When he worked at the laboratory he wore it over a pair of heavy corduroy slacks. When he worked at home—which was most of the time—he generally wore it over his pajama bottoms. Pads of paper. A few sharp pencils. And his sweater. That was all the laboratory equipment he had ever needed. But with those few tools he had postulated a theory of nuclear fission in heavy metals—a theory that Lise Meitner had proven mathematically before she had fled from Germany. With six pages of scribbled equations he had calculated the speed of a neutron and demonstrated the impossibility of neutrons striking a sufficient number of nuclei to cause a chain reaction. And then he had theorized the characteristics of the ideal moderator materials that would slow the neutrons, increasing the chances of a chain reaction.

Nominally, he was Professor of Theoretical Physics at the University of Stockholm. But he hadn't been near the school in almost five years. Instead, he worked at the "laboratory," a small office that the university provided for him in a building near his home, assisted by a secretary whose salary the university paid.

Professionally, he was a member of an international community of mathematicians and physicists who were beginning to unlock the secrets of matter. But he had never met most of its members. Like all the others, he worked alone, publishing his ideas in obscure journals that were intelligible only to a small fraternity, and reading the criticisms of his theories in the following months' editions. The scientists were all colleagues in the pursuit of truth. But they were all fierce rivals for professional acclaim.

He had heard that the Germans were pushing beyond theory. When they had marched into Belgium, they had captured half the world's supply of uranium, freshly delivered from Belgium's colony in the Congo. And when Norway surrendered, the world's only source of heavy water had fallen into their hands. As a result, they had the fissionable material, and they had an important moderator material. According to the Jewish physicists who fled the county, the Germans were actually going to build the reactor that would prove the theories he had developed with pencil and paper. Nils Bergman had felt left behind.

Then, just a month ago, he had received a letter from Kurt Diebner inviting him to join the effort. He had never heard of Diebner. Certainly the new Nazi Minister of Science wasn't a member of the fraternity. But the letter had mentioned Werner Heisenberg as part of the German team, and Bergman knew Heisenberg. Not that he had ever met the German genius. But he had read his work and admired his insights. If anyone could demonstrate a chain reaction, he was the one. But why should he let someone else—even someone as brilliant as Heisenberg—take credit for proving his theories? The Germans were offering him the opportunity to prove them himself.

"What time is it?" he asked, forgetting that he had just set his watch.

Magda laughed as she snapped the latches on his suitcase. "You have plenty of time. Birgit isn't due for another fifteen minutes. Even if she's late, as usual, you'll still catch your train."

He lifted the suitcase and followed her down the stairs to the small parlor that was dominated by his rolltop desk. There was no point in defending Birgit's lateness. Magda was critical of any woman who came near Nils, and since Birgit had become his secretary she was Nils's constant companion.

"Maybe you should come with me now," Bergman offered. It was a hollow gesture. He and Magda had discussed it many times and agreed that, if he thought there would be time for them to be together in Germany, he would send for her. But they were about to be parted for the first time in the four years since she had moved into his home. It was a sad moment for her, and he thought his expressions of need would make the parting easier.

"I'll come when you think it's wise," she answered. Then she forced a smile and opened her arms to embrace him. The sound of the Volvo's horn in the driveway interrupted their parting kiss.

Birgit swung the suitcase into the trunk while Magda and Nils whispered to one another on the front steps. She held the car door while the professor climbed into the front seat, and she waved to Magda as the car pulled out onto the winding road. Then she turned to Nils and began chattering about the arrangements.

"The train leaves at noon," she said, handing him the tickets that were resting on the dashboard. "You arrive at Halsingborg at nine. A car will meet you at the station and take you to the ferry. Herr Diebner will meet the ferry when it reaches Denmark."

Without taking her eyes from the road, Birgit reached into her purse, which was pressed between the seats. "Here are your ferry reservations." Again her hand was back into the purse. "And these are your hotel reservations in Berlin. You'll be staying there for a few nights while Diebner shows you some of the houses that are available near the Kaiser Wilhelm Institute. Now, about your bank account—"

"Birgit, if you don't slow down, I won't live long enough to reach the train, much less to reach Berlin."

She saw the speedometer needle touching 120 kilometers, much too fast for the country road that was spotted with ice. With a laugh, she backed off the accelerator pedal.

Bergman only half listened to the details of the personal bank accounts that she had opened for him in Berlin. Instead, he wondered how he was going to survive without her. She took care of all the professional details of his life. She had such energy, and focused it with such efficiency. Things seemed to get done before he had even decided to do them. If only he could take both of them with him. Birgit wouldn't mind. She seemed to accept her role as his assistant and secretary with no thought of a more personal relationship. But Magda would never stand for it. She saw Birgit as her rival for his time and attention.

He had thought of a romantic relationship with Birgit. It was a fantasy that was easy to nurture. She was several years younger than Magda, probably no more than thirty-five, and strikingly beautiful, at least to his taste. Long blond hair and deep blue eyes testified to her Nordic heritage. Her figure was slim and athletic, radiating the energy that was obvious in her work. And her small, pouty mouth seemed to invite a kiss.

She was also bright—a graduate mathematician who could understand most of his work. Certainly she could fill parts of his life that were beyond Magda, who had no idea what the language of symbols and numbers could possibly mean. Birgit had traveled. Several years in Germany, a year in the United States, and then two years in England. She had visited Columbia University where Fermi had moved his work since leaving Italy. And she had attended a series of lectures by Lindemann at the University of London. She could share his enthusiasm for ideas that no one else could begin to understand.

Why was he hesitating, he had sometimes wondered. He was a single man who had every right to change mistresses as his needs and desires changed. But the answer was apparent even while the question was being asked. He loved Magda. And she loved him, as she showed by every gesture in caring for him and his home. Birgit's beauty and brilliance were irrelevant. She was an excellent assistant. But she could never be Magda.

He felt the car slowing and squinted through the dirt-splattered windshield. A car—it looked like a Mercedes—was stretched across the road, its front end pressed against a tree. Two men in heavy overcoats were waving a warning.

"Damn," Birgit said, switching her foot to the brake. "We don't have time to stop." Nils Bergman shrugged his shoulders. They had no choice. They would have to help move the car so that they could get by.

He rolled down his window as they glided to a stop next to the two men. But before he could say a word, a gloved hand reached in and released the door lock, and the door was thrown open. He turned, bewildered, toward Birgit and saw that another hand was reaching in through her window and twisting the ignition key. When he looked back, he was greeted by the muzzle of a pistol.

It all happened without a spoken word. Birgit was led out of the car and toward the Mercedes that was stalled across the road. Her place was taken by a third man who slipped in behind the wheel of the Volvo and started the engine. The door next to Bergman was slammed shut, and the gunman who had been on his side climbed quickly into the backseat. The Volvo backed to one side, executed a tight U-turn, and accelerated in the direction it had come from.

Bergman turned and looked past the man in the backseat, ignoring the pistol that was still held unwaveringly toward his face. He watched the Mercedes back away from the tree and then turn to follow them.

"My name is Thomas Haller, Major, British First Airborne. Our driver is Sergeant Towers, also a Red Devil." The driver braced to attention in acknowledgment of the introduction.

"English?" Bergman asked, his confusion obvious. How did they know that he spoke English?

Haller gestured toward the gun. "I'm nervous around these damn things. I'll be happy to put it away if you'll promise . . . give me your word . . ." His eyes went to the door.

Bergman glanced out at the road, blurring by at better than 100 kilometers. "I'm not going to jump out, if that's what you mean."

"Good," Haller said with genuine relief. He opened his coat and slipped the gun into a holster that bulged under his jacket. "I know that all this is distressing for you. We'll try not to make it too unpleasant." He saw Bergman's eyes rise toward the back window and focus on the car that was following. "You have nothing to worry about," he said. "Your assistant is in good hands. I'm sure my people are doing their best not to frighten her."

Bergman was still too stunned to protest, and he was intimidated by the physical credentials of the man who slouched carelessly in the seat behind him. The major was making every effort to be polite. But his hands were strong and calloused, and even the hint of forearm that showed beneath his sleeves was thick and muscular. The eyes were friendly and the smile completely honest. But the wrinkles at the corners of his eyes suggested a habit of squinting into the sun rather than the onset of age, and his neck formed a straight line downward, the full width of his jaw. He was a pleasant man, probably enjoyable in conversation. But he was also a powerful man who could certainly be brutal in enforcing his will.

"I don't understand. What's this all about?"

Haller took a crumpled package of cigarettes from his coat pocket and offered one to Bergman. The professor shook his head.

"I won't go into all the details," Haller said as he searched his pockets for a match. "Some of our people want to talk with you before you go to Berlin. They asked me to pick you up."

"English soldiers? Here in Sweden? Where?"

The major found his matches and struck one in front of his cigarette. "No, not here in Sweden. They're in England. London, I suspect."

"In England?" Bergman knew he sounded foolish simply repeating Haller's words. But he was too confused to form logical conclusions.

"We're meeting a plane," Haller explained as he glanced casually out at the countryside. "You'll be in London tonight."

Bergman organized the pieces that he was beginning to understand. He had been stopped by British agents, kidnapped, and was being driven to a rendezvous with an airplane that would take him to England. This by a British officer whose attitude seemed to suggest that it was all in a day's work.

"No," he finally stammered through his mounting rage. "No, I am not going to England. I'm a Swedish citizen and we are a neutral country. You have no right to detain me. No right to take me anywhere that I don't want to go. And I don't want to go to England."

"You're right, of course," Haller agreed.

"Then turn this car around and take me back. I have to be in Stockholm in less than an hour." He tried to get control of himself and to match the arrogant calm of his kidnapper. "Some other time, perhaps. But right now I simply can't squeeze in a trip to England."

"Professor Bergman," Haller answered, leaning forward in his seat and fixing his narrowing eyes squarely on his target, "despite your neutrality, there's one hell of a war going on. I'm a soldier, and in wartime I don't question orders. I obey them. I'm ordered to deliver you to an airplane, and that's exactly what I'm going to do. I'm sure our governments will have a great deal to say to one another about this outrageous violation of your rights. But at this moment I don't give a damn about your privileges as a neutral. What I care about is getting you to England. Comfortably, I hope. But with my boot up your ass if that's what it takes."

Bergman turned away in retreat, intimidated by the change in Haller, whose suddenly menacing tone was more threatening than the gun he had brandished. He had no choice but to obey. There was an armed man behind him and a trained soldier seated beside him, so there was no hope of escaping from the car. And even if he could, he certainly wouldn't abandon Birgit. He was helpless— a British prisoner being transported westward toward a rendezvous with an English plane.

How had they captured him, he wondered? How had they known the road he would take and the exact time that he would be passing by? How did they know about Berlin, for that matter? He hadn't even told the university about his plans; just that he was taking a short leave of absence. He had recognized that the world had divided itself up into warring camps. Personally, he didn't give a damn about the war. Science didn't take sides and the development of his theories knew no politics. But he understood that the university had to be a disciple of his country's neutrality. So he had never informed them where he was going. Or why.

Yet the English knew. And apparently it was important to them that the Germans not be the first to demonstrate heavy-metal fission. Why? What in God's name did his rivalry with the other physicists have to do with the insane war that the English and the Germans were fighting?

"Can I have that cigarette?" he asked, turning meekly toward the British officer.

"Of course," Haller answered, his pleasant disposition returning. He offered the pack, and struck a match. Bergman could hardly steady the cigarette long enough to get it lit.

They waited in a small farmhouse at the edge of a frozen field, Bergman and Birgit alone at a linoleum-covered kitchen table while the British paced nervously in the parlor. The scientist reran all his questions, and Birgit's silence confirmed his sense of bewilderment. She didn't seem to understand how the English had known of his plans, or why they cared about his invitation to Berlin.

"Unless they believe that nonsense about a uranium bomb," he finally reasoned. He shook his head in despair. Some of his colleagues had postulated the possibility that the rapid fissioning of uranium could produce an explosion of enormous energy. But it would take thousands of tons of the material. Albert Einstein had calculated that a uranium bomb would be too heavy to transport in anything less than a battleship.

"My God," he suddenly realized, jumping up from the table. "If that's what they think, then they'll never let me go to Germany. They won't even let me return to Sweden. They'll keep me hidden for the entire war."

She had no answer for him.

"And you," he reasoned, pacing in a tight circle around the table. "They won't let you return either. They'll want to keep my disappearance a secret. They couldn't let you go free to tell our people where I was and what had happened to me."

He kept pacing, imagining possibilities that grew worse as the early twilight darkened the room. "They must want something from us. If they just wanted to keep me from working with the Germans, they could have shot me when they stopped the car. If they're bringing me to England, they must want me to work in England. You don't suppose that the English are trying to build a uranium bomb?"

But Birgit added nothing to his search for explanations. She sat motionless at the table, her face buried in her hands.

She looked up abruptly at the first sound of the engines, and turned to follow Bergman as he rushed to the window. The English had set up a few small flares, marking the corners of the field, and the airplane engines were circling, droning louder as they approached a landing. Bergman saw the shape of the plane flash over the bare treetops. "Look," he shouted, pointing it out for Birgit. But she turned away, her head sinking back into her hands.

"We've got to get away," he blurted, rushing toward the door. But the door opened in his face and Major Haller filled the opening.

"Time to go, Professor," he said pleasantly. He slipped his arm under Bergman's, and then the sergeant fell into line at the scientist's other side. He looked back and saw Birgit sitting at the table, her face still hidden. And then he understood.

"You're one of them," Bergman said, his voice hardly a whisper. But Birgit heard it as if she had been expecting the words. She looked up, and her face was smeared with her tears. She nodded just once.

He pulled his arm free from the sergeant's grasp and spun back toward her. "You planned this. You told them where I was going and where to find me." He hadn't yet found his anger. He was still struggling to believe his own words. "Why? Why would you do this to me?"

Birgit jumped up as if she were going to rush into his arms. But she stopped when she was still next to the table.

"I had to," she pleaded. "I had no choice."

"Why?" he demanded.

Her head shook slowly in her helplessness. "You dear, dear man. You still don't understand. You still don't know what they want, do you?"

"Why?" he screamed, struggling to break Haller's grasp.

"Because the Germans want you to build their bomb," she shouted back, her own buried anger coming to the surface. "Because they don't give a damn about your atomic theories. It's the atomic bomb that they want, and you were on your way to help them build it."

Bergman stepped back as if he had been slapped. "No . . . no," he began to explain. He looked to Haller, and then back to Birgit. "I have nothing to do with this war. I hate it. I would never build a bomb."

"You think they're scientists, just like you," Birgit said sympathetically. "But you don't know them. They're killers. Crazy killers. They need you to build their hell bomb so they can go on killing."

He was shaking his head in disbelief. Where could she get such ideas? He would never take part in killing. He was a scientist.

She reached her fingertips out to his cheek. "You just don't understand evil, do you? You can't even believe that it exists."

Bergman slapped her hand away.

"Don't touch me," he hissed.

"Please," Birgit begged. "Please understand. I had no choice."

He lunged toward her, and would have struck her if the sergeant hadn't grabbed his arm and wrestled it behind his back.

"Please," she whispered.

"You betrayed me," Bergman shouted, turning away from her. He pulled his arms free from his captors, and then began walking voluntarily between them.

"Please," she shouted after him. "I had no choice." But Bergman never looked back.

The three men hurried across the field toward the plane, a small twin-engined Blenheim bomber, with its propellers still turning and its bomb bay already opened. "Sorry about the accommodations," Haller quipped as he helped Bergman duck between the bomb bay doors and pushed him up into the belly of the plane. There was a small sling seat stretched at the front end of the bomb rack. The sergeant fastened the shoulder harness, then handed the scientist a leather helmet with an oxygen mask. "Put that on when the pilot tells you," Haller explained. "If he has to climb, you'll need the oxygen."

Bergman watched the major and the sergeant duck their heads and disappear behind one of the bomb bay doors. A second later he heard a motor start, and watched as the doors closed under him.

The pilot's voice came over a radio, telling him to put on the helmet and fasten the mask. Then the engines roared and the plane began to shake.

The Blenheim taxied to the end of the field, revved its engines, and then lurched forward. Its tail lifted and it gathered speed as it rushed toward the trees. At the last instant, it jumped into the air and banked over the treetops. Birgit watched from the window as it turned toward the west.

The pilot climbed to 5,000 feet, then leveled off and set the engines for maximum speed. The course drawn on the map that the navigator held in his lap was a straight line across Sweden and out over the Skagerrak, splitting the distance between German airfields on the southern coast of Norway and the northern tip of Denmark. The stripped-down Blenheim could make nearly 320 miles per hour, much faster than the seaplanes and timeworn Stukas that the Luftwaffe had assigned to patrol the northern sea lanes.

They broke out over the coastline. There was a high, scattered cloud cover, with enough moonlight filtering through to be dangerous. They would be easy to see, the pilot knew. But given the speed of the Blenheim, they should be impossible to catch.

The Skagen Cape slipped past their left wing tip, and far to the north, off the right wing, they could see the dark trace of the Kristiansand coastline. In another few minutes, the land would begin to open to the North Sea, giving them safe passage to their airfield in Blyth, near the Scottish border. The navigator reached to the radio, and began tuning in the Blyth frequency.

Suddenly there was a flash to their left. Before the pilot could turn his head, he felt the jolt against the fuselage. An instant later, a winged form rolled past the cockpit, its white-hot engine exhaust clearly visible.

"Sweet Jesus." The navigator ducked instinctively. There was a second flash of light, and then a second form roared by, only a few feet above the Blenheim. "What the Christ are they?"

"One-nineties," the pilot answered, already hitting the throttles and pulling back on the yoke.

Bergman had been struggling for a comfortable position in the sling seat when the metal wall behind him had been hit by a giant hammer. The blast seemed to set the whole world ringing, and the jolt had snapped his body like a whip. Now he was tossed forward toward the tail of the plane, hanging from his safety harness, as the plane began to climb. He called into the microphone that was attached to the flap of his leather helmet. But there was no response; not even the sound of his own voice traveling on the line.

"What in God's name are one-nineties doing up here!" the navigator screamed, his head spinning to follow the pair of German fighters that were rolling into a tight turn to line up another attack run.

"Looking for us, I suspect," the pilot said unemotionally. "They must have seen us come in and called the one-nineties to meet us on the way back. We better get into that cloud cover before they earn their Iron Cross."

The navigator was nearly standing out of his seat, watching the two planes that were lining up behind them. "Can we outclimb them?" he prayed.

"Fat chance," the pilot answered, twisting the propeller pitch controls for maximum power. The Focke-Wulf 190 had been an unpleasant surprise for the British when it appeared over the Channel. The stubby little German fighter was more than a match for the RAF's frontline Spitfires, and for the American Thunderbolts and Lightnings. The twin-engined Blenheim wouldn't stand a chance.

"Here they come," the navigator warned.

"Make sure our friend is on oxygen," the pilot answered.

The navigator called Bergman's name. "Damn line is dead," he reported.

The Focke-Wulfs quickly overtook the Blenheim, which was struggling in its steep climb, and began firing. Cannon rounds tore into the side of the body. Pieces of the left wing exploded and disappeared into the night. The glass canopy over the cockpit suddenly shattered, dropping glass shards on top of the cowering crew and letting the cold night air rush in. The two fighters roared by, then rolled into a climbing turn as they prepared for their next attack.

"The bastards are really enjoying themselves," the pilot shouted.

"Where in hell are those clouds?" the navigator answered.

Bergman had no hint of the second assault until the shells exploded against the side of his prison. The noise was deafening, and suddenly light flashed all around him. He squeezed his eyes shut, expecting the agony that would rip through his body. Instead, he was aware of a powerful blast of cold air. He looked, and was startled to see the shape of the wing. There were two gaping holes in the side of the fuselage. The bomb bay was full of smoke, but the airflow was quickly clearing it away. He searched his chest, and the long legs that were thrust out in front of him. He nearly laughed to find that he hadn't even been scratched.

They were climbing through 12,000 feet, but the cloud cover didn't seem to be getting any closer. And the German fighters were turning into another firing run. As they dove in from the left side, the pilot turned the Blenheim into a sharp turn toward them and pushed the nose down to increase his speed. The guns lighted on the wings of the fighters, but the Blenheim's sudden maneuver had surprised them. They flashed by on either side of the British plane without scoring a hit. Immediately, the Blenheim turned up, once again clawing for the cover of the clouds.

The sudden maneuver smashed Bergman back against the bulkhead. "What's happening!" he yelled into the microphone, and then understood that the connection had been destroyed. He braced himself against the structural frames of the body and waited, gasping for breath in his terror of the unknown.

They were up to 15,000 feet when the first traces of clouds covered the wings. The pilot eased the yoke forward. It was a thin cover, and he had to be careful not to fly out into the bright moonlight at the top.

"Have we lost them?"

The pilot shook his head. "They're still out there. And we're losing power on the left engine. I think it took a hit."

The two crewmen watched the left engine's oil pressure needle drop while the temperature began to climb. The pilot hit the controls to shut the engine down. With just one engine pulling, the bomber's speed dropped, and the altimeter began cranking down.

"If we come out of these clouds, we're finished," the pilot said, trying to keep the nose up without sacrificing the speed that the plane needed to fly.

Bergman couldn't breath. He swallowed hard, trying to suck oxygen from the mask but the dry pain in his chest didn't respond. He found the tube, made certain that it was connected to the mask, and traced it up toward the oxygen flask that hung overhead. But his mind was suddenly wandering in a giddy game. He couldn't make his eyes work. He blinked dumbly, trying to focus on the tube. And then he found it. It was trapped in a twisted structure over his head. The oxygen bottle had been shattered by the gunfire.

For several minutes, the Blenheim bounced inside the turbulent envelope formed by the clouds. But then it broke into the open again, into the faint moonlight.

"Where are they?" the navigator screamed, his head spinning around the full compass. "I can't see them."

"Maybe looking for us on top of the cover," the pilot shot back. But he wasn't looking for the Germans. All his attention was fixed on the controls as he labored to trim the ship for single-engine flight.

Bergman tore the mask from his face, and tried to stretch his head into the rushing airstream. He gulped at the air, forcing his chest through the mechanics of breathing. But the fire in his lungs grew worse, and the dizziness seemed to spin faster. He grasped at the riblike structures and dragged himself toward the top of the bomb bay. Then he screamed at the wall that separated him from the pilot. But there was no power in his voice. He was pleading for his life in a whisper.

"I don't see them," the navigator repeated. The pilot didn't answer. He had leveled the Blenheim at 14,000 feet, but he was making only half the plane's top speed. They were out in the open, and he didn't have enough power to climb or maneuver.

"Pray to God you don't see them. If you can see them, then they sure as hell can see us. And we're a sitting duck."

Bergman pounded his fist against the bulkhead. But there was no strength left in his blow. He screamed for help. But there was no sound. His limbs were heavy, and his head seemed to be falling backward. The whirlwind inside his brain made it impossible for him to think. He felt his grip weaken. When he swung his free hand toward the bulkhead, it fell short of the mark. He felt himself beginning to slip, and he tried to dig his fingernails into the metal. But it was no use. He was falling over backward.

He let his mind go blank. It was the only way to ease the pain that was spreading from his chest.

They searched the skies, but the Germans seemed to have vanished. And the Norwegian coast had disappeared along with them.

"Pull the hatch," the pilot ordered the navigator. "Better check on our passenger."

The navigator took one more cautious look at the sky around them, then unlatched his safety belt and turned in his seat. He levered open the cover that sealed the crew's compartment from the crawl space over the bomb bay. Then he leaned into the opening.

Below, he saw Nils Bergman swinging gently in space, his body hanging from the safety harness. The greatest mind in heavy-metal physics had been starved to death by lack of oxygen.

LONDON — *January 12*

The prime minister raised his eyes over his half glasses to the wall clock with its swinging pendulum, then returned his attention to the papers that waited beneath his pen. The three visitors understood. It was his way of telling them that his time was valuable, and that they had just a few seconds to earn his interest.

"Thank you, Prime Minister," Air Marshal Peter Ward said.

"You of course know Lord Cherwell." He gestured toward Frederick Lindemann, the empire's leading nuclear physicist, who had remained standing despite the title that his work had earned him. "And may I present Captain Emma Lloyd, who heads our photo reconnaissance section."

Churchill nodded toward Lindemann, and spared a glance toward the plump woman with cherubic features who wore RAF grays. She looked more like a charwoman than the head of the RAF photo reconnaissance service. He looked back at his papers.

"I'm afraid we have distressing information concerning the German development of a uranium weapon. I thought you should be briefed immediately."

The prime minister made a great show of screwing the cap back onto his fountain pen. The gesture was their permission to continue. But he did nothing to alter the displeasure that was written into the sagging corners of his mouth. When Air Marshal Ward had brought Lindemann into his office a few days earlier, it was to explain the botched rescue of a Swedish nuclear physicist. The rescue had turned out to be a kidnapping with potentially disastrous diplomatic consequences.

Captain Lloyd had raised a mounted aerial photograph onto an easel and taken an instructor's pose beside it. "These are photographs taken from ten thousand feet over a German airfield on the North Coast," the air marshal said. He nodded to Emma Lloyd, who pointed with a pencil as she talked.

"From ten thousand feet, we were able to make out two shapes that at first appeared to be amusement-park roller coasters—tracks supported on scaffolding. With a ten-times enlargement, we found this." She slid away the first photo, revealing another mounted print. It showed two ramps, beginning at ground level and then rising in graceful curves until they ended abruptly. "They are clearly launching ramps, designed to guide some sort of projectile into the air at a thirty-five degree angle of climb. Then here," she said, pointing her pencil to a dark corner of the photograph, "we noticed what appeared to be small airplanes. But as you can see, there was no detail. With further enlargement, the image broke up so that we could tell nothing."

"These were taken two weeks ago," Ward interrupted. He glanced at Emma Lloyd, who nodded in agreement.

"We wanted to know whether the aircraft were in some way connected with the launch ramps," the woman continued, "so we ordered a photo flight at three thousand feet. We got this picture just yesterday."

She slid away the second photo, to reveal a pale, grainy shot of two aircraft, parked side by side. Three small figures surrounded one of the planes, pulling on ropes that seemed to disappear into the surrounding foliage. Churchill gazed at the picture, his expression unchanged.

"You will notice several unusual characteristics of these aircraft," Emma Ward went on. "First, they have no propellers. They would appear to be gliders. But, then, here on top of the craft you will notice what appears to be a stovepipe. We have analyzed the shape of this pipe and we have concluded that it is a ramjet engine—a very simple type of power plant that our own engineers are experimenting with. It uses the rush of incoming air as a compressor. For that reason, it has to be moving at over four hundred knots in order to operate."

The prime minister nodded. Mrs. Lloyd clearly was not a charwoman.

"And, sir, you will also notice that there is no cockpit. No place for a pilot or crew. What we are looking at is a jet-powered, pilotless aircraft that can be fired along one of these launching ramps until it is airborne and then flown either remotely, or on internal guidance, towards a target at over four hundred knots."

"Why?" the prime minister interrupted.

"To deliver an explosive warhead," Captain Lloyd responded immediately. "We have done a thorough analysis of the craft based on known dimensional objects. For example, we are assuming that these men who are attempting to draw a camouflage netting over the aircraft are of average height. This gives us a very accurate guide to the size of the plane. We can also measure the length of shadows which, together with the angle of the sun at a specific time of day, indicate the size of the objects that cast the shadows. So we know the dimensions and the volumetric capacity of the craft. That tells us how much fuel it can carry, and with the known burn rate of a ramjet, we can then calculate the range of the plane. What we have concluded is that this particular aircraft can carry a one-metric-ton warhead from a launch site in western France to any target in England or in southern Scotland. It would cruise at about ten thousand feet and travel at over four hundred knots."

Churchill turned his head toward the air marshal. "Seems much ado about nothing," he offered.

"Precisely, Prime Minister," Air Marshal Ward said eagerly. "We asked ourselves the same question. Why go through all the pains of developing such an aircraft . . . of building launching ramps . . . simply to deliver one bomb. Surely, our friend Goering hasn't suddenly become concerned over the lives of his pilots. It just didn't make any sense, until . . ." He glanced uneasily toward Lindemann.

The scientist cleared his throat. "It so happens that my people have been assembling information from scientists who are familiar with the leading German physicists. Several factors have raised our curiosity.

"One was the Germans' interest in a Swedish physicist. You remember the unfortunate incident when we—"

The prime minister raised his hand.

"Yes, of course," Lindemann allowed. "Well, it so happens that the man's expertise was in chain reactions. He had done a great deal of work in the byproducts of chain reactions and had postulated the possibility of using a reactor to produce less stable . . . more fissionable types of uranium. It occurred to us that, if these variants of uranium could somehow be separated from the basic material, you would have a much more volatile explosive source. Then we determined that the Germans were building a rather sizable gaseous diffusion plant. We believe it is being built underground somewhere in the vicinity of Celle. The diffusion plant could, of course, be used to separate the more fissionable isotopes of uranium."

Churchill began unscrewing the cap from his pen. Lindemann was beginning to lose his attention.

"The scientists concluded," the air marshal interrupted, "that, by using these variants of uranium, it would be possible to construct a bomb of enormous power in a size much smaller than previously thought. They advised me that it might be possible to build a uranium weapon the size of our present one-thousand-pound bombs."

"We delivered a paper to Air Marshal Ward just yesterday," Lindemann added, "speculating on the potential yield of bombs of various sizes. One of the sizes we had considered was a weapon weighing one metric ton."

"The coincidence is uncanny," the air marshal said, taking up the explanation. "While we were pondering why the Germans would invest so much effort in a pilotless aircraft capable of carrying a metric-ton warhead, Cherwell discovers from entirely different sources that a one-metric-ton uranium bomb is feasible. A weapon of that power would certainly justify building a specialized aircraft. With a uranium warhead, one of these tiny planes would be worth all the bombers that we could build in a year."

"How much?" the prime minister asked. He saw that they didn't understand his question. "How much power would such a bomb have?"

"We can't be certain," Lord Cherwell began, as an introduction into one of his endless dissertations.

"Ten thousand to fifty thousand tons," the air marshal stated flatly. "They concluded that it would have the equivalent force of ten thousand to fifty thousand tons of dynamite. That means this one plane would be the equivalent of an air raid of four thousand Lancaster bombers. Each of these little drones would be more lethal than all the planes in Bomber Command."

Churchill set down his fountain pen. "When? When could such a weapon be ready?"

"We have no idea," Cherwell answered.

The prime minister's eyes locked on the air marshal.

"Our only clue," Ward said, "is the pilotless aircraft. These seem to be test models, so it is perfectly possible that the finished aircraft could have a different shape or different dimensions. But if these are close to the final product, then it would make sense that they would have been designed with a particular weapon in mind. Undoubtedly the two programs—the aircraft and the warhead—would be closely coordinated. So we have to assume that the uranium weapons would be ready approximately the same time as the airframe is ready for launching."

"And when will that be?" Churchill asked, his impatience at the endless speculations beginning to show.

"Given the present state of the aircraft and the launching facilities, we estimate in approximately one year."

"We have nothing more precise? No sources within the German program?"

"I'm afraid not, Prime Minister," the air marshal admitted. "We were hoping for some assistance from the Swedish physicist but . . ." He paused out of deference to their painful memories of the incident. "I'm afraid that, until now, we haven't taken the possibility of a uranium weapon as seriously as we might have."

"The scientific community is still quite divided on just how realistic a uranium weapon is," Lindemann added. "The calculations we presented to the air marshal are still quite speculative."

Churchill looked at the three faces in front of him. They weren't speculative. They were plainly frightened.

"I'd suggest you begin to take this very seriously," he said to the air marshal. "For starters, we might make additional efforts to infiltrate the German program. It would be good to know where the research and production facilities are so that we could recommend them to Bomber Command. Or perhaps, with the right agents, we might even be able to sabotage the German effort."

"We're already looking at agents," Ward said. "In fact, we've located a chap who seems quite promising." He signaled Captain Lloyd to gather up her photographs.

"Good," the prime minister said, picking up his fountain pen. "Keep me informed."

Churchill glanced up at the awkward efforts of his three guests to open his office door. Emma Lloyd was carrying the oversized photographs, so she couldn't reach the doorknob. Ward and Lindemann were used to having doors opened for them, so they both stood back. It was the scientist who finally analyzed the problem, pulled the door open, and then stepped back on Ward's shoes as he tried to clear the way for Captain Lloyd and her displays.

The prime minister glowered over his glasses until the photo reconnaissance expert and Lindemann had passed through the door. "Air Marshal," he ordered, and Ward turned back into the room. "Put a very small, trusted staff on this. I'd like to keep the number to an absolute minimum." The air marshal looked puzzled. "We don't want the entire general staff worrying about a super weapon that the Germans might not even be building," Churchill said. His face turned down toward the papers on his desk.

He tried to resume his work, but after a few moments, the prime minister brushed the papers aside. Ten thousand, 20,000, even 50,000 tons of dynamite in a single bomb. A bomb that the Germans might be ready to put into the air in a year. Lindemann was embarrassed because he couldn't be more precise. But Churchill could. He knew the Americans were hoping to have a uranium bomb within two years, and his ministers were suggesting that the Germans might get theirs first. They were alerting him that, with a single scientific stroke, the Nazis might be able to reverse the victory he was just beginning to glimpse.

The long years of painful and humiliating retreat had finally been stopped. For the first time, victory seemed more a possibility than just a patriotic slogan. But no alliance of countries could withstand the weapon that had just been suggested to him. A small, high-speed bomber on a one-way mission would be impossible to stop. And a warhead with the power of 20,000 tons of dynamite could flatten the entire West End, killing perhaps a million Englishmen in a single microsecond of inferno. A half dozen of these planes would bring England to its knees.

MADISON — January 20

As he crested the hill in front of his small, shingled house, Karl Anders saw the black sedan framed by the snowbanks that flanked the driveway. He touched his brakes and brought the old Ford to a stop. For an instant, he toyed with the idea of turning around and driving back to his offices at the University of Wisconsin. Or, even better, he could simply go straight ahead, past his house, and drive off into the lake country to the north. He could probably go hundreds of miles before they realized he had escaped.

But he knew there would be no escape. He had said no before, but the black sedans kept coming back. The United States Army needed his cooperation on a top secret project, and they couldn't understand how a patriotic American could refuse them. "The atomic bomb can save tens of thousands of our boys," they had argued. "It can cut a year off the war."

"It can also give us the power to devastate the planet," Karl Anders had countered. "I'm not sure we know how to live with such power."

They had appealed to his vanity. The Manhattan Project was the biggest scientific undertaking since the building of the pyramids. If he stayed out, he would fall hopelessly behind his colleagues. Anders answered that he had no desire to be in the vanguard of a community that was building weapons of mass slaughter. Then they had tried threats. They could have him drafted and shipped straight to the front lines. "Could you?" he had responded eagerly. "I've tried to volunteer twice, and they tell me I'm too old."

The military people saw the bomb as simply a bigger and more efficient explosive. But Anders saw it as the border of a new age that would be dominated by the threat of total destruction. It was a border that he had repeatedly refused to cross.

Now they were back again. Colonel Hamilton had called him at the university to ask for a meeting. Anders had replied that there was no point in a meeting. The colonel had volunteered to drop by at his office for a very brief chat. Anders had pleaded that his schedule was too crowded. But the army didn't take no as an answer. The black sedan had returned.

He shifted into gear and turned the car into his driveway, cutting around the parked car. A sudden movement of one of the living room curtains told him that his guests knew he was home.

"Professor Anders," the army colonel said, rising from the patterned sofa with a friendly handshake. Colonel Hamilton wore the fortress insignia of the corps of engineers. His bloated belly and broad seat were further evidence that he wasn't a combat officer. A pink-chinned, young captain stood when the colonel stood, but Hamilton did not introduce him. He was obviously an aide, whose function was to remain in the background. A rumpled civilian with brooding Semitic features waved the crushed fedora that he had held in his lap. But he made no effort to rise from the wingback chair.

"I hope you don't mind that we let ourselves in," the colonel apologized. "But it was cold waiting in the car with the engine off. And our gasoline is rationed, too."

"Did you make coffee?" Anders asked. They seemed embarrassed at the suggestion that they would have taken such liberties with his home, so Anders walked into the kitchen and put on a kettle. When he returned, the colonel was back in his place on the sofa. The aide was standing by the window.

"Let me introduce Doctor Simon Roth," the colonel said. "Unless you two have already met?"

Anders smiled, and crossed the room to offer his hand to the civilian. "We haven't. But I've read your work, Professor Roth. It's an honor."

"Thank you," said Roth, with a quick and self-conscious smile.

"I'm sorry the corps of engineers brought you all this way to pursuade me," Anders continued. "I hope you haven't been needlessly inconvenienced, because Colonel Hamilton and General Groves and everyone else at the Manhattan office already know my answer." He turned to the colonel. "How many times have we had this conversation."

"It's a different conversation," Hamilton said. "We've developed a problem in the past few weeks, and we think you're in an unusual position to help us."

"A problem?" Anders looked at Roth and than back at the colonel. "With Fermi and Roth working for you, you need me? Professor Roth has forgotten more about nuclear physics than I'll ever know. If he can't solve your problem, I sure as hell can't." He was smiling at the thought of Enrico Fermi and Simon Roth needing his help when he heard the kettle whistle.

Anders poured the water over the coffee, and paused in the hallway to hang his jacket on a peg. When he returned to the living room he was in a plaid shirt, separated from tan trousers by a thick leather belt. He looked more like a farmer than a nuclear physicist, which was half-true. He had been raised on a farm. The strong hands and the long cabled muscles of his arms and shoulders were the product of hard, physical labor. The freckled skin on his cheeks and high on his forehead were the result of days spent outdoors. He would still be a farmer, except for his love of machinery and his ability to fix any of the equipment on his family farm or the neighboring spreads. That ability had led him to study science, and that study had earned him a place in the university's physics curriculum. He had spent the last twenty years of his life in colleges and universities, studying phenomena so complex that they were restricted to a few hundred people on Earth. Yet even now, his idea of recreation was to go to his brother's farm and take apart the diesel engine of the tractor.

"Professor Anders." It was Roth's quiet voice. "Have you ever met Professor Nils Bergman . . . from Stockholm?"

"No," Anders said, after pausing in curiosity at the nonrelevance of the question. "I've read his work . . . or at least commentaries on his work. But I don't think I've ever met him. Not that I can recall, at any rate."

"You'd recall," Roth said, his eyes twinkling as if he had just thought of something funny. "You'd never forget, because you would think you were looking in a mirror."

Anders was lost at the turn in the conversation.

"You're both tall . . . same light hair . . . gray eyes . . . same Nordic coloring. Everything . . . the high cheekbones . . . the thin lips . . . even the way you show your teeth when you smile. It's all the same." He glanced around the room. "You even live in the same kind of house. And the countryside. It's just like the country near Stockholm."

"Bergman is older than I am," Anders reminded the professor. "I'm forty."

Roth shrugged. "It was several years ago when I met him. Then he was forty."

Karl Anders laughed at the absurdity of the logic, and Roth joined in with a chuckle. But in an instant Roth's dark face was once again solemn.

"You understand Bergman's work?"

"Well, I suppose so. I haven't studied him. I'm sure I haven't seen his latest papers. But what I've read, I've understood."

He saw that the colonel was studying him intently. "Look Colonel, if you need an expert on some theory of Bergman's, I'm certainly not your man. I've read some of his writings. But I'm sure there are other people who are up to speed on his ideas. Maybe his associates in Stockholm. Or Bergman himself."

"Sure," Colonel Hamilton agreed. "But the problem we have is a little different. It's a little more complicated that just understanding Bergman's work."

Anders caught himself before his curiosity could get the best of him. "Well, to be honest, I don't want to hear about your problem. We've talked about this before, and I think you know exactly how I feel about your Manhattan Project. I'm not an expert on Bergman. But even if I were, I wouldn't join your team." He turned to Roth. "With all respect to your own opinions, Professor Roth, I can't help with this project. I don't think for a moment that I have a higher ethical sense than you or any of your colleagues. But this is just something that I can't let myself get involved in."

"No one wants to get involved in a war," Colonel Hamilton agreed.

"This is a hell of a lot more than getting involved in a war," Anders corrected. He was suddenly distracted by the sound of the coffeepot rattling on the stove as the coffee began to boil. "Coffee?" he asked his guests.

"Sure," the colonel answered. Roth refused the offer with a wave of his hat. The captain simply shook his head.

Anders picked up his thought as he returned with two coffee mugs and set one down in front of Hamilton.

"The war is horrible enough. But at least the war will come to an end one day. There is *no* end to what you're doing. You're starting a chain reaction of madness, and you have no idea of how to control it."

Hamilton stared into his coffee. "I'm not a combat soldier. I've never even fired a gun. But I was out at Pearl Harbor rebuilding some of the seawalls. I've seen what ordinary bombs can do to buildings . . . and ships . . . and people. I'm not sure that anything we come up with can be a hell of a lot worse."

"It *can* be a hell of a lot worse," Anders snapped back. "Take my word for it. You have no idea just how much worse it can be."

"Worse if the Nazis have it before we do," Roth interjected.

Anders shook his head. "Worse if anyone has it. No matter who has it, it could destroy us all."

He sipped his coffee, then tried to put an end to the conversation. "I'm sorry, gentlemen. I don't question your principles. But I can't compromise my own. I don't want to hear about your problem, simply because I don't want to have anything to do with your work. There's nothing you can say that will get me to help you build your bomb."

Hamilton put down his coffee mug.

"Professor Anders, we don't want you to help us build the atomic bomb."

"Then what do you want?" Karl Anders asked.

"We want you to help us destroy it."

OXFORD — *January 25*

They met in an apartment at the university, a natural location for a visiting American professor, and an explainable destination for an assistant at the University of Stockholm. Haller wore a heavy tweed jacket, patched at the elbows, over a striped school tie—an academician except for the strong arms and broad shoulders that clearly hadn't been developed in the stacks of a library. Birgit had a drab sweater pulled over a shapeless woolen skirt, and Anders was in an open-collared sport shirt that was a distinctly New World touch. Gathered around a silver tea service, in a room walled with bound books, their meeting was invisible among the normal scholarly pursuits of the city.

The introductions, handled by Haller, were brief. He identified Birgit as a "scientist very familiar with Nils Bergman's work," and gave Anders's title as Professor of Theoretical Physics at the University of Wisconsin. His own résumé was simply, "Major, First Airborne, on special assignment," an understatement that brought a quick smile from Birgit.

But even before the introductions were completed, Haller knew there were possibilities. The moment that Birgit had entered the room, her eyes had locked on Anders, and she was still staring in amazement.

"You could be brothers . . . almost twins," she told Anders. "There's a difference in age," she admitted to Haller. "But he could be Nils five years ago. It's uncanny." Anders shrugged at the compliment. The only credential he offered that seemed to be of interest to anyone was his striking physical resemblance to someone he had never met.

Haller poured the tea, presided over the cream and sugar, and settled into his chair so that he and Birgit were facing their guest. He wasted only a few seconds on small talk about Anders' unusual journey as a passenger in a bomber being ferried to England, and then got into his subject—the struggle between Germany and the Allies to enlist the help of Professor Bergman.

"Will he be joining us?" Anders interrupted at a break in Haller's monologue. "I'd like to meet this twin brother that everyone keeps telling me about."

Haller's steady gaze faltered, and he stirred his tea unnecessarily. "Nils Bergman is dead," he finally admitted, "a tragedy of war for which I, I'm afraid, am fully responsible."

There was no shocked reaction from Anders, who knew of Bergman only through the scientist's books and papers. Instead, he glanced curiously from Haller to Birgit as if asking how the man's death could possibly involve him.

"We're both responsible," Birgit added softly.

Haller contradicted Birgit's confession with a detailed account of the kidnapping, and the impossible odds of a bullet severing an oxygen tube. "We simply couldn't let him join the German fission program," he concluded. "Frankly, if he had not agreed to work in the United States, we would have kept him under house arrest for the duration." He turned to Birgit. That was an element of the British plan that he had never shared with her. She had been told simply that they would try to pursuade Bergman to work for their side. "We had no choice," he told her, and he accepted the anger that she saw flash in her eyes. "Bergman would have put the Germans a year ahead."

He looked back at Anders. "It's absolutely essential that we have someone inside the German program. We need to know exactly how far along they are. We need to know where their facilities are located. And, if possible, we need to disrupt their efforts." He finished his tea, and leaned forward to pour another cup. "The problem, of course, is that there aren't any agents who could possibly infiltrate the program. It would require impeccable credentials in nuclear physics just to get through the door. And then, even if we could get someone inside, there aren't any agents who could even begin to understand what was going on. I'm sure you can see the problem. I mean, it's easy for us to put a man in an ammunition factory or in a railroad center. Anyone can look genuine in a role like that. But nuclear physics? How many people are there in the world who even understand the vocabulary? A few dozen perhaps?"

Anders was beginning to understand. "You want me to train one of your agents," he guessed.

Haller considered the suggestion. "That might be helpful," he allowed. "But actually, we have a much more promising opportunity. You see, the Germans have no idea that Nils Bergman is dead. They know that, for some reason, he decided at the last minute not to go to Germany. But they seem to have accepted the information provided by the University of Stockholm that he rushed off to a conference in London. Information that Birgit planted with the university. They're expecting him to return to Sweden in a month or so."

Anders' expression told Haller than he still didn't know where the conversation was leading.

"The Germans want him. In fact, they need him. He's the only scientist who understands graphite reactors who hasn't joined the Allies. Their heavy water program is falling behind because they don't have enough heavy water. And their graphite program needs a leader. So they have all their London agents searching for Nils Bergman."

"You want me to impersonate Bergman," Anders said, smiling at the ploy he was beginning to understand.

"Yes," Haller admitted.

"You brought me here so that I could be seen with the appropriate people in London. You want the Germans to go right on believing that Bergman is alive. That he may be coming to help them."

"Temporarily, yes," Haller agreed. "We'd rather have them waiting for Bergman than finding someone else. Someone who might just pull it off."

Anders nodded.

"And then, when you're ready," Haller continued almost as an afterthought, "we'd like you to accept their invitation and go into Germany to head their graphite program."

Anders' teacup paused short of his lips.

"You see, you're the absolutely perfect agent. You look like Bergman. You're a physicist. You speak Swedish, German and English, Bergman's languages."

"That's impossible," Anders started to protest. But Haller wasn't about to let his proposition be interrupted.

"What makes the idea workable is that no one in Germany has ever met Bergman. Oh, several years ago for a few hours at a scientific convention, perhaps. But Bergman was something of a recluse. He wouldn't even work at the university that payed his salary. Aside from a few people in Sweden, he was close to no one."

"But his work. His correspondence. There must be dozens of people he has exchanged letters with. And there have to be hundreds of personal details that I don't know about. Two minutes of conversation is all it would take. I'd say something that Bergman would never say. Or I'd miss something that Bergman would certainly know."

Haller was nodding all through Anders' argument. "Of course. But Birgit has spent two years working with the man. She has all his letters and papers. She knows what he has said to everyone he's been in contact with and what they said to him. She knows how Bergman thinks. How he talks. Even what he likes to eat. With her help, you could know more about Nils Bergman than anyone alive. Certainly enough to persuade people who have never met him."

Anders set the cup down, stood, and walked to the window. For a full minute he stared through the lace curtains at the casual activity in the streets outside. "It can't work," he concluded. He turned back to face Birgit and Haller. "A scientist . . . especially a theoretical scientist . . . has insights and intuitions that are unique. A way of approaching problems. Almost a personality." He watched Haller nod in agreement. "All I know about Bergman is what he wrote in one book and in about a dozen articles and papers."

"That's all anyone knows," Haller added.

"The Germans are expecting the world's leading thinker in graphite technology. That's certainly not me. How long will it take their scientists to realize that I don't know as much about it as they do?"

"They may realize it immediately. Or it may take them a year. The more you understand Bergman's work, the longer it will take them, I suppose. But even in a short time, you can learn things about their program that we need to know. And if you can send them in the wrong direction, even if only for a few months, it would be a few months that we desperately need."

Anders stared silently at Haller. Then he shifted his gaze to Birgit, who was looking vacantly away from the conversation. She seemed to want no part in his decision.

"Miss Zorn, do you think I could ever persuade you that I was Nils Bergman?"

She shook her head slowly. "No."

"Then you don't agree with this scheme?"

"You couldn't fool me, because I lived with Professor Bergman every day. Maybe you could fool a group of scientists who have only read his work. I don't know." She raised her eyes and looked directly into his. "I'm not a spy, Professor Anders. All I ever agreed to do was keep a close watch on one obscure scientist whom the Allies thought might turn out to be important. That was supposed to be my contribution to beating the Nazis."

Her attention shifted to Haller. "For important reasons I agreed to help put Nils Bergman into the hands of the British. In so doing, I helped kill a perfectly innocent man who had no interest whatsoever in the war."

She looked back at Anders. "But I won't do that again. I won't get involved with someone else's life. I've agreed to work with you to help you learn everything I know about Professor Bergman. To help you think like him. Sound like him. God knows, you already look like him. But if you do this, you'll be placing yourself in great danger. I don't want to have any part in your decision."

He nodded. "Thank you," he told her.

"I won't deny the danger," Haller said. "But I don't think I have to tell you what's at stake. You know more about the power of this bomb than I do. Nothing could be more dangerous than letting the Nazis get there first."

Anders sat down again, but this time on the very edge of his chair. "The Germans will just invite me to go into Germany and head one of their development programs?" he asked.

"They'll invite Professor Bergman. They already have invited him."

"That's how I get in. Now, how do I get out?"

"At the right time, we'll kidnap you," Haller answered. He flushed when he realized what he had just said. "We don't generally botch things the way we did with Bergman," he apologized. "But we'll agree on a letter that you can send us. Something totally innocent. It will be your recall letter. If you send it, we'll pick you up and get you out."

"And while I'm there?"

"We need to know where the reactors are being built. And we need your best estimate as to when their reactors will go critical. We'll teach you a simple letter-substitution code so that you can send us basic information with the correspondence you'll be sending to your office in Stockholm."

"They'll let me send letters out of the country?"

Haller nodded. "Sweden is a neutral country. They have normal relations with Germany. People come and go all the time. But they will be reading your mail. And they will have you under round-the-clock surveillance. So you can't get creative. All you can do is send us basic information on places and dates."

"And do whatever I can to misdirect their reactor program," Anders added.

"Exactly. Anything you can do that won't put you in danger. Your ideas and directives will have to be perfectly plausible. They'll have to seem logical to the best of their people, and their people are very good. But you may be able to demand additional testing. You may be able to insist on very difficult standards. That will slow them down. Or you may be able to start them down the wrong path and get them to waste time chasing unlikely approaches. You'll know better than I. But we don't want you tearing up formulas or burning down laboratories. No one expects you to be a saboteur. If they lose faith in you, they'll send you packing. But if they suspect you . . ."

Anders didn't need to be told the consequences. He started to pour himself another cup of tea, but then put the pot back down on the tray. "You don't happen to have any whiskey?" he asked.

Haller went to one of the bookshelves. "I'm told it's behind the King James Bible," he remembered. He slipped the book off the shelf and retrieved a bottle of Scotch. He searched for a glass, then decided to pour a generous measure into one of the teacups.

Anders toasted with the cup and then took a sip.

"How would you contact me?"

Haller shook his head. "We wouldn't. We don't want you playing secret agent, Professor Anders. You probably wouldn't be any good at it. So there will be no message drops, or anything like that. You just tell us where and when in a simple, one-time code. And then be a physicist who's perhaps a bit too cautious or a bit too careless."

"I'd be totally on my own?" Anders asked.

"It has to be that way," Haller said. "If you made contact with anyone they suspected of being on our side, or if we made contact with you, you could be in very serious trouble."

Anders took another sip of the whiskey. "When do you need to know?" he asked.

"Whenever you're comfortable with your decision. Obviously, time is the enemy. The sooner we get you in there, the better our chances."

"A day or two," Anders proposed.

"Certainly," Haller agreed. He poured some Scotch into his own cup and gestured the bottle toward Birgit, who shook her head. Then Haller raised his drink.

"To Siegfried."

"Siegfried?" Anders wondered.

"That's what we've named your operation. A character in German mythology."

Anders smiled at the symbolism. "Who was raised up by the gods to keep the power of the ring from falling into the hands of the evil dwarf."

"Except the uranium bomb is far more powerful than the ring," Haller corrected, "and when it comes to evil, Hitler doesn't take second place to any dwarf."

Birgit watched while the two men toasted.

LONDON — *January* 28

"Siegfried said yes."

It was Haller's voice over the telephone three days after their meeting, obviously delighted with the news. "We'll need him here in England for a week or so. Some cosmetics and a bit of tailoring. And some classroom time with our language people and code people."

He waited for Birgit's response, but none came.

"He seems very enthusiastic. I think he's going to do superbly."

"I'll train him," Birgit said, in a weary voice that in no way reflected Haller's enthusiasm.

"I knew I could count on you," he said, misunderstanding her meaning completely. He had taken her words as a promise of full cooperation. She had meant them to limit her involvement to nothing more than helping Anders become Bergman. He hung up the phone before she could correct his impression.

"Bastard," she said into the dead line before she put her own telephone back on the hook.

She walked straight into her bathroom and turned the bathtub water taps on full force, then pulled the sweater over her head and fired it through the door and onto the bedroom floor. Her skirt followed, and then her slip and underwear. She winced at the heat as she lowered herself into the caldron, then settled back to let the hot water envelope her body. Baths had become her emotional cleansing. She had spent night after night in the small tub of her Stockholm apartment after learning that she had delivered Nils Bergman to his death. And, years before, she had spent her last week in Berlin between her bed and her bath after she had seen what happened to Gunther.

She and Gunther had met in a Berlin that was still an intellectual center, drawing students from all over Europe, and artists from every corner of the world. Hitler had come into power, but still seemed to be the public fool made chancellor by the absurdities of Weimar democracy. His only true following were the beerhall lowlifes who found their pitiful identities by wearing ridiculous uniforms and carrying Roman flags. Street politics hadn't yet reached the universities, where the lectures in philosophy and science sought a purity of knowledge that was far above the lunatic ravings of generals and politicians.

Gunther, a native Berliner, was reading philosophy, specializing in the realists, which seemed out of place for his musical talents and unfailing sense of humor. Birgit's days were spent locked in the science laboratories, an odd setting for a woman at a time when most were majoring in poetry and letters. They had met at a student party, where Gunther was playing the piano and singing bawdy lyrics. Birgit had laughed when she was supposed to be shocked, a reaction that had made her a momentary favorite with the men. Gunther had seen her home at the end of the evening, and when she opened her door in the morning, he had fallen into the room, still sound asleep, along with the two bottles that had been left by the milkman. He stayed the day, and in the evening left only long enough to collect his clothes and his books.

For nearly a year they were everywhere together, so that friends never referred to Birgit, or Gunther, but always Birgit and Gunther. He sat cross-legged on the floor outside the university laboratories, reading his assignments while she finished experiments. They ate together, usually sausages and rolls, in the sidewalk cafés that surrounded the university. And they slept together, their lovemaking beginning as soon as one of them closed a textbook on the day's assignment and often continuing until the first hint of gray light sent the birds exploding out of the trees. They were so totally consumed in their work and in one another that neither noticed the nightly beatings that occurred in the doorways and the alleys of central Berlin. They weren't even alarmed when one of his professors was intercepted at the entrance to his lecture hall, and taken off to answer charges that he was agitating against the government. Then the racial laws were passed.

Their first awareness came from a fellow student, who slipped into a chair next to them at a café and announced that he was withdrawing from school.

"We're getting out," he whispered, his head turning to search the streets. "My family is going to Holland . . . to my father's business associates."

"Why?" Gunther asked, genuinely puzzled.

"We're Jews," the student said.

Gunther and Birgit had looked at each other as if nothing could be more irrelevant.

But the evidence mounted quickly. More students left, most simply vanishing out of the city during a night or over a weekend. The student populations of Poles, Slavs, and Jews thinned dramatically. Teachers vanished. Most were simply dismissed, but a philosophy professor who tried to return to his classroom was beaten badly by the police summoned to remove him.

The student body, once united in a brotherhood against faculty and administrators, against tavern keepers and rent collectors, was suddenly violently divided. Overnight, or so it seemed, half the students began echoing the absurdities that the Brownshirts chanted under their torchlights. "The superior races . . . the right to land for national expansion . . . the home-front betrayal that had cheated the German armies." Gunther was even assured by a fellow student that his relationship with Birgit was patriotic because she, too, was of the Aryan race.

"I think we have to get out of here," Birgit told him one night as she lay in his arms. But he was a Berliner. He had one more year to his degree, and nobody was threatening him. "It's just nonsense," he assured her. "In Germany, crazy ideas come and go like the seasons."

He had wanted to remain uninvolved, which probably would have saved his life. But she had tried to help a frail, young music student who had become the target of a Nazi prank, and that simple act of caring had gotten Gunther killed.

Sara was a violinist of no remarkable talent, burdened with a small, shapeless body and deprived of friends by a paralyzing shyness. She had come from Holland to study at a Berlin conservatory where her uncle was a faculty member. It was because of his arrest that she discovered the Jewish side of her family, and by her visits, she betrayed herself as half Jewish. The Brownshirts who were processing her uncle told her to leave the country, and she was making arrangements to withdraw at the end of the term.

Birgit knew her from a chance meeting in a university administration office and a shared table in a public cafeteria. She was amazed when Sara presented her with two tickets to her recital and referred to her as a dear friend. She brought Gunther, who found the recital enjoyable, and stayed for the refreshments. It was the only time he had ever spoken to Sara.

But he remembered the girl when Birgit told him that the Nazi students were planning to drive her from the university. She had heard three of the most vocal patriots howling over their plans to humiliate the girl the following evening, and then she had learned the details from a classmate who invited her to join in the fun.

"They've got a fool's cap and a white gown with a Star of David on the front and back. They're going to drag her out of her room, dress her in the costume, and parade her past the cafés. They've even given two of the Nazi district leaders the honor of leading the parade."

Gunther had shaken his head in despair, agreeing that the students were going too far.

"We've got to help her," Birgit had persisted. She had touched Gunther's face and turned his eyes up from the pages he was reading. "We've got to stop them. They could kill her."

"They won't hurt her," he had consoled. "It's just a bit more of their stupid games."

"But she'll be terrified. The bastards are planning to keep her in a circle until she plays the violin for them. Sara will just collapse. She's so timid she doesn't even look at you when she talks."

Gunther had sighed as he pushed his book aside. "What do you want me to do?"

There wasn't much they could do except put Sara on a train for

Holland before the Nazi leaders and their adoring students could get to her. Gunther went to the conservatory the next morning and got Sara's address. Birgit went to the train station and reserved a coach seat on an express to Antwerp, with a connection through to Amsterdam. She brought the tickets when she met Gunther, and then the two of them went to Sara's house. But when they knocked on the door, there was no answer.

They chased back and forth between the conservatory, the student lounges, and Sara's apartment, trying to find her. They could have simplified their chase by leaving messages, but they were afraid to arouse suspicion. It was late in the afternoon before they caught sight of her, climbing the steps to her front door.

At first she didn't believe them. She wasn't a German citizen and had never said a word about German politics. She knew the Nazis hated Jews, but she wasn't really a Jew; she had no religion at all. She had never even been inside a synagogue. Besides, she was leaving the country at the end of the term. And she had never done anything to offend any of her schoolmates. She didn't even know most of them.

Birgit tried to make her understand that her logic was no match for the madness that seemed to be growing up out of the German soil. The students had joined in the national game of harassing Jews without realizing that it wasn't a game to the Brownshirts whom they invited into their ranks. They wouldn't let the fact that she wasn't a Jew spoil their fun. And the Brownshirts wouldn't let her willingness to leave the country prevent them from doing their duty.

But there was no time for arguing. Gunther dragged Sara's suitcase down from the attic, and Birgit began packing it over Sara's protests. Gunther snapped it shut and carried it down to the street to get a taxi. Sara clutched her violin to her chest as Birgit nearly pushed her, step-by-step, down the stairs.

The students were already assembling across the street when Gunther reached the front door. The taxi hid him momentarily from their view, giving him time to get the suitcase inside, but there was a sudden shout when Sara appeared. Gunther hustled Birgit and Sara inside and dragged the taxi door from the clutches of the rushing students. He didn't even have time to pick up the violin that Sara had lost in the scramble, and there was hardly time to say good-bye when they pushed her onto the train.

Deprived of their victim, the students consoled themselves by smashing the violin and impaling it on the top of a fire hydrant. Then they broke into Sara's room and tossed her music out of her apartment window and into the street. But these gestures didn't satisfy the two Brownshirts' thirst for blood. If the Jew got away, they goaded the students, then it was their duty to find the Jew lovers who had helped in the escape and teach them a lesson. By the end of the night, the handful of students who were still drinking in the beerhall agreed that indeed it was their duty.

Birgit and Gunther were asleep when a heavy boot kicked open their door and a screaming mob rushed into their room. They were dragged naked from their bed and tossed back and forth in the center of a circle of students while the Nazi henchmen tore up their books, smashed furniture, and painted a dripping Jewish star on the wall over the bed. Then they were held still while the leftover paint was used to draw swastikas across Gunther's chest and, with howls of delight, across the curves of Birgit's breasts.

With a dozen students surrounding them, they were helpless to resist. But even as they endured the humiliation, they could see that they were in no serious danger. Their beer-soaked tormentors were tiring of their prank even as they were acting it out.

It was almost over when one of the Brownshirts decided that one more cruelty was needed. He pushed his way into the circle, seized Birgit, and wrestled her across his knee. Then he raised his swagger stick and snapped it across her buttocks. Birgit's scream of pain jolted the students into stunned silence. The only sounds were the horse laugh of the Nazi and the whistle of the stick through the air as he laid on another lash.

Gunther tore free from the relaxed grips of his schoolmates, and rushed two quick steps toward the Brownshirt, his fist already flying, powered by the full momentum of his body. It smashed squarely against the side of the man's face, sending him sprawling under the feet of the students. Gunther dove on top of him, his grip locking on the sweaty neck. He began choking the man, screaming into the face that was already bleeding through a yawning gash across the cheekbone. The students shouted, but no one reached to stop him.

It was the other Brownshirt who took action. Grabbing at the broken leg of a chair, he pushed the students aside until he was standing directly over Gunther. Then he raised the chair leg like an ax handle and smashed it down into the center of his skull. For an instant, Gunther seemed to rise up from his victim, his eyes panning the horrified faces that circled him until they rolled up into his head. He fell forward, a dead weight sprawled over the face of the Nazi.

There was a gasp, and then slowly the students backed away. Some of them were already through the door and out into the hall when the Brownshirt rolled Gunther off his comrade and helped the bloodied man to his feet. Then the two Nazis backed away from their victim, turned, and joined the flight down the stairs and into the street.

Birgit snatched up her robe and rushed into the hall screaming for help. Some of her neighbors hesitated, seeing the Star of David on the wall and fearing that they would become involved in helping a Jew. One finally used his telephone to call an ambulance, and then disappeared into his apartment as soon as the police appeared.

Gunther lived through the night. Birgit was at his side until his parents arrived, but then she was pushed into the background. They seemed to think that she, a foreigner, was more responsible for his destruction than the Nazis who had desecrated his body. She paced the corridors until a doctor told her that Gunther was dead. Then she walked home through the pale morning light, filled her bathtub, and tried to cleanse the filth that she felt covering her body. During the week before she left Germany, she spent hours in her bath, scrubbing at the swastika that was no longer visible.

She had felt the same terrible guilt when she learned that Nils Bergman had suffocated before he even reached England. She had helped plan his kidnapping and had even turned him over to his executioners.

Now the stench of guilt was with her again. But this time, she promised, she would not let herself become involved. She would have no hand in sending Karl Anders into danger. She would simply teach him everything she knew about Nils Bergman. She would not let herself become involved in his life.

BERLIN — *February 14*

The white-coated scientists treated the steel drum as if it were the Ark of the Covenant, almost afraid to touch it for fear of defiling the precious heavy water it contained.

"Tip it further," Werner Heisenberg ordered. He was monitoring the end of a rubber hose that led from the drum into a large metal sphere dominating the center of his laboratory. "Very good," he complimented sarcastically, his long face and the shock of blond hair nodding in approval as the colorless, odorless liquid began flowing again. "Just a few seconds more, gentlemen. We're nearly full."

The splashing sound rose in pitch until suddenly the heavy water overflowed and spilled out of the opening. Heisenberg clamped the hose and lifted it out of the sphere. Then he screwed the cover over the opening of his experimental fission reactor.

The sphere was only three feet in diameter, and its fuel load was only a few ounces of enriched uranium, divided into a hundred tiny pellets that were suspended throughout its interior. But the miniature laboratory setup had all the elements of the giant reactor that Heisenberg already had under construction in the south of Germany. A reactor that would convert several tons of uranium ore into a few kilograms of plutonium, the material that would become the German atomic bomb.

There was the spherical containment vessel, shaped so that neutrons flying in random directions from the uranium pellets at the center had the maximum opportunity of striking other uranium pellets.

There was the fuel itself. Uranium, like other heavy metals, had a complex nucleus with an unstable arrangement of protons and neutrons. When struck by a subatomic particle, the nucleus tended to shatter, releasing neutrons that flew off through the atom's field of electrons. In theories that had been demonstrated mathematically, each neutron could strike another nucleus, causing still more neutrons to be released. The resultant chain reaction would release tremendous energy in the form of heat.

There was the cadmium control rod that projected through a rubber gasket near the top of the sphere. Cadmium absorbed neutrons, which suggested that a chain reaction could be shut down by lowering the cadmium bar into the center of the activity.

Finally, there was the moderator—the heavy water that had just been poured into the sphere. The chances of a neutron striking another nucleus increased as the speed of the neutron was reduced. Neutrons moving through heavy water lost speed without being absorbed, thereby increasing the odds of their participating in a chain reaction.

The sealed sphere rested in the center of a large trough that was lined with sheets of hammered lead. Werner Heisenberg opened the faucet letting ordinary tap water run into the trough. He watched as the water quickly surrounded the sphere and closed over its top. Submerging the sphere was his final safety measure. There were a dozen pressure valves built into the surface of the vessel. If the cadmium rod didn't control the reaction, then the heavy water would boil, building up pressure. The pressure would blow the safety valves, venting the steam and allowing cold water from the trough to flow into the sphere and cool down the uranium.

Heisenberg moved quickly to the instruments that would record the neutron activity inside the sphere. Quietly, the other scientists gathered behind him, surrounding Kurt Diebner, who appeared from his office in his dark suit with the red armband the moment that the preparations were completed. The scientists needed no explanation of the steps that would follow or of the readings they should look for on the gauges. The one thing that they all shared in common was their faith in the possibility of a chain reaction. It was that faith that enabled them to work together. Without the reactor, Heisenberg, who regarded the Nazis as fools, couldn't have shared the same laboratory with Diebner, who believed that Hitler and his henchmen were the saviors of the world. Lauderbach, who had led the purge of Jewish professors from a university faculty, wouldn't have been able to speak with Fichter, who had found several Jewish colleagues positions on faculties outside the country.

For some of these men, the reactor had meant salvation from the concentration camps. Heisenberg himself had been denounced. On a worldwide tour, he had ridiculed the Nazi theory of Aryan physics, which held that all non-Aryan contributors to the literature should be ignored. No less a figure than Himmler had finally decided that Heisenberg's genius was essential and agreed to accept his apology.

Fichter had been rescued from the back of a truck that would have taken him to the boxcars. He had tried to protect a neighborhood shopkeeper who was being beaten by Nazi thugs. He was beaten himself, and thrown into the same cell as the shopkeeper. Only his knowledge of uranium fission had saved him. The shopkeeper had no similar ability to offer to the state.

For others, the reactor had meant instant power. Diebner had risen to the highest councils of the party because he promised to place the atomic sword in the hands of his superman leader. Lauderbach's ascent had been meteoric once he took possession of the work of the non-Aryan scientists he had purged.

But for all of them, the reactor provided a common language. The symbols and formulas that predicted its operations were bridges over the gulfs of political, religious, and social difference. They didn't understand one another. But they all understood the theory of the reactor.

Heisenberg threw the switch, energizing the neutron emitter at the center of the sphere. Immediately, the instruments detected the neutron activity, and the needles jumped on the gauges. But they leveled quickly, showing only the output of the emitter.

There were no neutrons breaking away from the uranium atoms in the tiny fuel pellets.

He turned up the power to the emitter and watched the indicator needles swing slowly. Neutrons were ricocheting around the inside of the sphere, but they were having no effect on the uranium fuel.

There were mumbles behind him as the scientists mouthed their disappointment. All were eager to see their theory proven. Yet Heisenberg knew that some of the sighs were faked. Many of his colleagues disagreed with his faith in heavy water as a moderator for a sustained chain reaction. They would be delighted to see this portion of his work discredited. Others simply envied his position of leadership in the international community of physicists. They wouldn't be grief stricken if Werner Heisenberg were taken down a peg or two. Even Kurt Diebner had mixed emotions. He needed Heisenberg's success if he were to deliver the reactor he had promised to Reichsfuehrer Himmler. But Heisenberg publicly ridiculed Diebner's ability and his politics. Diebner would certainly prefer if credit for the achievement went to a party member who had learned to show a little respect.

The needles jumped. Somewhere inside the sphere, the sensors had detected a burst of neutrons from a different source. They jumped again, and then began wagging from side to side, indicating sudden variations in the level of neutron activity.

"Look," said a voice, as a finger shot over Heisenberg's shoulder and pointed to the gauges. "They're climbing." The oscillations were beginning to dampen. The needles were climbing steadily.

"The popcorn is beginning to pop," Heisenberg laughed. He watched the arrows gather speed in their swing to the right. Then he began to turn down the energy to the neutron emitter. The needles immediately began to settle, indicating that the reaction within the sphere was still dependent on the artificial source of neutron energy. It wasn't yet self-sustaining.

He heard his audience suck in its breath as he continued to turn down the power to the emitter. Previous laboratory experiments in a half-dozen countries had gotten this far, proving that uranium fired neutrons out from its core when it was bombarded by neutrons. But more energy was used in sustaining the reaction than the reaction was able to produce. The theoretically limitless energy that bound together the parts of the elements remained locked in the uranium nucleus.

The needles steadied, indicating a constant level of neutron activity. Heisenberg continued to turn back the power to the emitter.

"It's running by itself," Diebner whispered.

Heisenberg nodded vigorously, his hair falling forward over his eyes. "The emitter is off," he said. "The reaction is self-sustaining."

The announcement was greeted with a moment of stunned silence as the scientists allowed themselves to comprehend the miracle they were witnessing. Millions of years ago, in the first microseconds of the universe, the energy of the Big Bang had been absorbed into the core of the elements as they were being created. Now that energy was being set free.

One of the physicists began to clap, and then another joined in. Diebner gave a spontaneous giggle, and then roared in delight. In the next instant, men who had reason to hate each other were shaking hands and then falling into one another's arms. For an instant, the joy of achievement belonged to all of them. The resentments and the jealousies were put aside.

"It's climbing," one of the scientists noticed. Heisenberg checked his gauges and confirmed that the needles were swinging slowly. He calculated the rate of increase, and compared it instantly to the conclusions of the formulas that filled his notebook.

"Too quickly," he answered. "Much too quickly." He threw a switch that started a simple worm-drive motor, pushing the cadmium bar into the sphere. In response, the needles flickered, dropping momentarily, then rising again. Heisenberg restarted the motor, driving the control rod further into the center of the reaction. Again, the gauges dipped, but after a few seconds resumed their accelerating climb.

"I can't control it," Heisenberg said.

"What's wrong?" Diebner demanded with more than a hint of fear. He pointed to the temperature gauges. The heavy water inside the sphere was approaching its boiling point. An instant later, the needle of the pressure gauge began to move.

"There's too much energy. Too much heat. Far more than we calculated!" Diebner screamed. Heisenberg recorded the readings in his notebook. "It might be wise if we all stepped outside. There will be some steam vented. It could be dangerous."

Diebner led the scientists as they filed out quickly, but Heisenberg lingered behind. Less fuel, he thought. Or perhaps several cadmium rods. Obviously, he had greatly overestimated the ability of cadmium to absorb neutrons. That was the next area where he would have to direct his attention.

He could see a layer of bubbles beginning to form on the outer surface of the sphere. The water in the trough was beginning to heat up and suddenly he felt afraid. The energy being released inside the sphere was enormous—far too much for the crude containers he had fashioned. Suppose the inward rush of cold water from the trough wasn't violent enough to scatter the fuel particles. Suppose the reaction continued, boiling off the water as fast as it entered the chamber. Was there any way to stop the reaction he had started?

A safety plug blew, and a jet of steam churned the water in the trough. Heisenberg ;umped back, slipped through the door, and closed it behind him. Through the wired glass window he watched as another jet of steam broke the surface, tossing a spray of water out of the trough. And then the entire room seemed to disappear in a fog of steam.

"Will it stop?" Diebner demanded, voicing the fear that Heisenberg was trying to keep in check.

"Of course it will stop," he snapped back, sounding much more certain than he felt. His calculations had already been overwhelmed by the furious energy of the tiny reactor. What if he had also miscalculated the limits of that energy?

The steam began to settle, and when the water in the trough became visible, its surface was perfectly calm. The gauges appeared, and their arrows had swung back to their stops. Temperature and pressure seemed to be down. There was no sign of neutron activity. But perhaps the sensors inside the sphere had been melted by the intense heat. Or perhaps the gauges had been destroyed by the rush of steam.

Heisenberg opened the door and stepped cautiously into the room, approaching the reactor as if it were a sleeping dragon that he was afraid to wake. He looked down through the murky water and found the crumpled remains of the sphere. The pressure had split the seams at its top, and the hot fuel pellets had burned through its bottom.

"Dear God," he prayed. The heat had been so intense that the uranium had burned like chips of wood. He was awestruck by the reality of metal burning even while it was submerged in water. "God save us all."

"A disaster," Kurt Diebner's voice said from the doorway. "What will I tell Reichsfuehrer Himmler? How should I explain?"

"Tell him you have just witnessed the first sustained nuclear reaction in the history of the world," Heisenberg suggested. "Tell him the energy released was at least twice what his scientists had calculated. Tell him there was enough heat to make steel burn like paper."

Diebner glanced at Heisenberg long enough to see that he was completely serious. He looked back at the ruins of the reactor. "Then it was a success?" he asked.

"A complete success, Herr Director. A success beyond anything we could have imagined. And tell Himmler that, when we examine those fuel pellets, we are going to find metals that have never existed before. Metals much more volatile than the uranium we started with. Metals that will fission much more rapidly, giving off energy greater by a dozen magnitudes."

Diebner took Heisenberg's hand between both his own and shook it vigorously. "Congratulations, Professor Heisenberg. A monumental achievement. I know the fuehrer will send his personal thanks along with the gratitude of the entire nation."

Heisenberg retrieved his hand. "Perhaps the fuehrer would send another hundred gallons of heavy water along with his gratitude, so that we could build one more experimental reactor."

Diebner was already backing toward the door, ready to dash to a telephone and report the good news.

"And for the full-scale reactor," Heisenberg continued, "perhaps another ten thousand gallons of heavy water. Enough so that we can cook a few tons of uranium instead of just a few pounds."

"I'm sure there will be no problem," Diebner said from the doorway. "Reichsfuehrer Himmler will be delighted." He disappeared into the hallway.

"I'm sure he will be," Heisenberg called after him. "He doesn't have enough brains to be frightened."

He stood for a few seconds staring out the empty doorway. Then he turned back to his colleagues. Some were walking away toward their offices, separating themselves from his ridicule of Himmler. Others were sharing his laughter. The common bond created by their work had been destroyed along with the reactor.

"Those fools in their jackboots will never understand what we've achieved," Heisenberg said to the small circle of friends that remained. "But we understand. And someday we'll be able to share our success with the other physicists all over the world. They will understand, and their congratulations will mean something. Something more important than anything we're likely to hear from our paperhanging fuehrer."

The scientists joined in his laughter until they noticed the grim expression on Otto Hahn's round face.

"Maybe no one will ever find out," Hahn said, to explain the terror he was suddenly feeling. "Maybe that paperhanging little shit will destroy us all."

STOCKHOLM — *F e b r u a r y   2 7*

"When you proposed graphite as a moderator, Doctor Bergman, you were very imprecise as to the effect of impurities. Are they of no concern?"

He looked up from the cold herring that he had been cutting with the edge of his fork.

When? When did I first write about graphite? For the Brussels meeting? No, wait. It was Paris, a year earlier. And I hadn't yet studied the effect of impurities.

"Not at first," he answered, forcing the Swedish words into a singsong cadence that was still strange to his tongue. "We were just beginning to think about moderators then. We were proposing everything. But in Brussels, when I presented my theory-of-games analysis of neutron behavior . . ."

"Paris," she interrupted.

"No, Brussels," he said.

She shook her head. "Brussels came before Paris. Your games theory paper was at the Paris meeting."

"Are you sure? Wasn't the Paris paper—" He stopped suddenly and looked at her, horrified, as he realized that he had responded in English.

"Christ," he cursed, dropping his fork on the plate. "This is never going to work."

"You're doing fine," Birgit said. "You've been talking about his work for half an hour. There were moments when even I thought you were Nils Bergman."

"Moments," Karl Anders sneered. "I can't keep it up for half an hour. And I'm supposed to live with the damn Nazis for a couple of months. It's insane. There isn't a chance in hell of their being fooled."

"Not now," Birgit fired back. "You're not ready yet. We still have a lot of work to do."

Anders jumped up from the table and grabbed his jacket from the coatrack near the front door. "It will take a lifetime," he told her. "That's what it takes to become someone. A lifetime."

He slammed the door behind him and pounded off through the snow-shrouded trees toward the lakes. Furious walks in the icy winds had become his escape. They were the only moments when he could save his own identity from the person he was supposed to become.

How could he become another person—even a person whose appearance was nearly identical to his own? In England, the doctors had taken care of the age difference, thinning his hair and stitching small wrinkles at the corners of his eyes. The tailors had cut his suits full across the waist and close across the shoulders to minimize his athletic physique, and a drama coach had rehearsed his posture into a slouch with his chin thrust forward until the resemblance to Bergman was uncanny.

Then a speech teacher had gone to work on the Swedish that he spoke fluently, rehearsing the cadence that was typical of Stockholm and pruning the North American immigrant corruptions until he sounded like Bergman.

Now, in a cottage by the Stockholm lakes, Bergman's secretary was taking him page by page through the physicist's work until he was even thinking like Bergman. The two personalities were being poured together into a common beaker. But, like oil and water, they kept forcing themselves apart.

There were millions of characteristics, learned over a lifetime, that defined a person. The ironies that caused a smile and the incongruities that caused a frown. Feelings that could be shared and feelings that were closely guarded. Reactions to colors and aromas. Pleasures in the harmony of sound. Reactions to cold and heat. The relish in approaching food—even the movement of the fingers that held a knife or lifted a wineglass. Each characteristic of Bergman's that Anders mastered suggested thousands of others that were entirely unknown. The more excited his teachers became at each of the mannerisms that brought the two men together, the more discouraged he became at all the mannerisms that kept them apart.

When Haller had first suggested the possibility of his substituting for the renowned scientist, Anders had been curious. And after a week in England, when he had looked into the mirror and seen the differences in their appearance vanish, he had been excited. Even in Sweden, when he had first begun working with Birgit and reviewing Bergman's work in its own idiom, the impersonation had seemed completely possible. But now, as he grew closer and closer to the man he was to become, the differences were widening into an impassible chasm. He was discouraged, and as the day of his journey to Germany grew closer, even frightened.

He had begun questioning every aspect of the plan. "How can

you be so damn sure that Bergman didn't have just one close friend in Germany who would know I wasn't Bergman?" he had demanded of Birgit.

"I was his secretary," she had reminded him. "I did his letters. I placed his phone calls. I've been through his records. There is no one close to him."

"What about people I know?" he had demanded in another moment of despair. "My students. I've worked with hundreds of people who could show up anywhere. People who would know in an instant exactly who I was."

"We've covered that," she had answered cooly. "Four of your students were with the American military in the European theater. They've all been reassigned back to the United States. There's only one professor who worked with you who's living in Europe, and he's in Italy. You'll never be within a thousand miles of one another."

They were all so damn certain that it would work—that he could be substituted for another person and that no one would question his new identity. Yet each time he became Bergman, he lapsed into damning errors within a matter of minutes. Like this morning, when he had confused two of his presentations to the scientific fraternity. Even people who had never met Nils Bergman would know when he had first raised questions about graphite moderators. And then, in his confusion, the momentary lapse into English. How would that have sounded over dinner with his German hosts?

"It's insane," he shouted into the wind that blasted against his face. "It can't work!" But even as he screamed his fears, he knew that he had to make it work. He knew better than any of the professionals who were coaching him exactly what the consequences would be if it didn't work.

"We know they're building a diffusion plant to separate plutonium from the reactor fuel," he remembered Professor Lindemann explaining over tea during one of his briefings in England. "It's being built underground, someplace in northern Germany. And we think we've identified the delivery vehicle." Lindemann had shown him the photos of the small, pilotless aircraft that had been taken at the German test facility at Peene-münde. "It can have no other purpose than to carry a very powerful warhead. So, if they can build the reactor to produce the plutonium . . ."

If they could, Anders knew, the war was over. Give England one experience with the energy of instantaneous atomic fission, and they would beg for peace. Fermi had calculated that a ton of fissioning uranium would be more powerful than all the chemicals that had ever been exploded. Teller had speculated that it might cause even the atmosphere to explode.

But the Germans weren't wasting time in scientific speculation. Heisenberg was already hard at work on a heavy water reactor. Or so the British surmised from the military guard that the Germans had thrown around their heavy water plant in Norway. And just to cover their bets, they had been about to lure Nils Bergman into Germany to begin work on a graphite reactor. If the Germans were serious about building a plutonium bomb, then the Allies had to be serious about stopping it. If the Germans were willing to take chances with the dangers of a chain reaction, than the Allies had to take chances. His impersonation of Bergman might be a long shot. But it was one of the few chances that they had.

Anders was ready to get back to work when he bounced up the steps to the porch and pushed open the front door of the cottage. But Birgit was wearing her coat and had her knit cap pulled down over the tops of her ears. She was gathering the files she had brought from Bergman's office for the day's lesson.

"I'm sorry," he said in his best Swedish. She ignored him as she continued slipping the folders into her briefcase. "It was childish of me to get annoyed. I'm sorry."

"You're right," she finally answered, using his language for the first time since he had arrived in Sweden. "This isn't your line of work. And God knows, it isn't mine." Birgit started for the door, but he moved to block her path.

"Let's give it another try," Anders offered. But when she turne' to him, he saw another person. She was no longer the ple encouraging teacher he had been working with.

"What do you think this is . . . one of your graduate courses?" Birgit demanded. "Do you have any idea what's at stake?"

"Of course, I do," he snapped back. "It's just that this whole idea is so risky. It's such a long shot . . ."

"Risky?" she fired back. "Let me tell you what's risky. Sometime in the next few days a team of British commandos is going to jump out of an airplane and take on a whole regiment of Germans just to get to their heavy water plant. That's risky. And long shot? Even if they manage to survive the Germans, their chances aren't very good because there's no way the English can pick them up and get them back to England. So if they live through the battle, they're going to have to find their way to the Norwegian Resistance and hope they can be smuggled across Norway to a seaport. That's a long shot."

"What are you talking about?" he asked defensively.

"Things I shouldn't be talking about. Things I don't even want to know about. I've seen enough good people die. Jesus, I've even helped to get them killed."

"Bergman?" he asked, intending to remind her that she couldn't blame herself for his improbable death.

"Yes, Bergman. And another before him."

Anders thought she was going to cry. He reached out a comforting hand, but she pushed it away.

"But no more," she said, her eyes rising defiantly. "I'm not gambling with other people's lives. Haller knows the odds on getting to the hydro plant in Norway. It's his call."

"Haller?" Anders was astonished. He had known that the academic garb was a disguise, but he had figured Haller for a deskbound planner.

"And you know the chances of convincing the Germans that you're Nils Bergman. That's your call and I'm not going to try to persuade you. I don't want to know if anything happens to Haller. And I don't want to be guilty if something happens to you."

She turned past Anders and pulled the door. But his arm shot across the opening. "I'm going into Germany," he said as a simple statement. "I'm going because I have to. Because I have more reason for going than Haller and his troops. There's something I know that none of those commandos can possibly know."

She stopped in the doorway and turned back to him.

"I know what it will be like if anyone ever explodes a fission bomb. I've calculated the possible shock force. And the heat. Those commandos wouldn't be able to even imagine what the numbers mean. I can't let that happen, no matter what it costs me. And I don't think you can let it happen no matter what it has already cost you."

Her eyes narrowed suspiciously. Then she stepped back into the room and closed the door behind her. "And I know something that you can't possibly know. I know the Nazis. I know the horror they can inflict with nothing more than a billy club and a bucket of paint, so I can guess what they could do with the bomb. I know how much they would enjoy dropping it into the center of London. So maybe we're a perfect team."

He tore off his jacket and tossed it toward a chair. "Let's get to work," he said, returning to his best Swedish.

"Your odds haven't gotten any better," Birgit reminded him, still speaking in English and still hesitating by the door.

"Neither have yours," he answered mischievously. "You'll have to take your chances on helping me get myself killed."

She stared at him for a long moment, then walked back to the dining room and set her files back on the table. She pulled off the knit hat and coat and carried them to the coatrack by the door.

"I'll make you one promise," she said, still in English, as she settled into the chair opposite him and opened the files. "When I think you're ready, I'll give you a test."

She saw the question in his eyes.

"I'll put you together with someone who knew Nils Bergman. Someone who knew him better than any German you're ever going to meet."

His eyes widened.

"If you don't pass for Bergman, I'll call the whole thing off."

He looked thoughtfully, then nodded. "It could save my life," he admitted.

"Mine, too," she said. Then she switched to Swedish. "When you proposed graphite as a moderator, Doctor Bergman . . ."

They picked up where they had been interrupted by his mistake.

RJUKAN — *March 2*

The four-engined Halifax that was towing them could easily have climbed above the weather. But the Horsa glider wasn't equipped with oxygen. If they went any higher, the Red Devils who were squeezed along the canvas slings that served as seats would quickly become disoriented, their brains starved for oxygen. And they would need all their judgment and cunning for the mission that was only minutes ahead.

The men had left the dirt strip in Scotland nearly three hours earlier, snatched forward with a jerk as the Halifax took all the slack out of the towrope. Almost immediately they were airborne, the light, wooden glider lifting even before its tow plane left the ground. And almost immediately, they were frozen as the winter air drafted through the cramped cabin.

They had been carried in a gentle arc out over the North Sea, locked in a lightless tomb where the creaking of the wings and force of their own breathing were the only sounds. Then they had climbed toward the north, not aiming at their target on the mountainous spine of southern Norway, but at the windswept sea on the country's western shore.

They couldn't approach the hydroelectric power plant at Rjukan in a straight line. That would take them over the Skagerrak where the German patrol planes might be flying, and inland over the southern Norwegian coast where the Germans had positioned anti-aircraft guns. Instead, they would stay out over the North Sea, turning inland well to the north of Bergen. They would follow a fjord right into the heart of the central mountains, and then turn south. A fast-flowing river would lead them down the steep slope of the mountain toward the hydroelectric station.

But when they reached the shoreline, they had run into thick clouds that were driving a blizzard of snow up against the mountains. Now they were being thrown about mercilessly by the force of the gale. Major Haller looked down the two lines of staring faces and knew that his mission was in trouble. He had anticipated the snowstorm as soon as he had seen the day's weather maps, but had traded the problems it might cause for the cover of the moonless sky—which would be lost if they delayed the raid. Now he wasn't sure he had gotten the best of the bargain. He hadn't foreseen the effects of the numbing cold that had turned the breath of his troops into ice that clung to their faces. He hadn't counted on the motion sickness that had filled the air with the stench of vomit. And he had certainly underestimated the physical beating they would take as they were bounced against the sides of the glider. They were already exhausted.

Still ahead was the landing, which, on unprepared terrain, was more like a crash. In training exercises, boulders had cut through the bellies of Horsa gliders, and tree branches had plunged like spears through their sides. How many of his two dozen raiders would walk away from the wreckage?

Then there was the forced march down the slope of the mountain to the plant. In the planning sessions they had called it "skiing down the slope," and each of his troops had rehearsed with a pair of shortened skis. But they had to follow the river with all its drops and turns. It was their only navigation aid. Haller knew that they wouldn't get much use out of the skis when they were climbing down the edge of a waterfall. He wondered how many of the men would still be with him at the end of the two-mile journey.

Then they had to fight their way through a regiment of German defenders and into the plant. They had to hold the buildings long enough for his sappers to set their explosive charges near the electrodes that collected heavy water molecules, and the storage tanks that held the product.

Finally, with all that done, they had to fight their way back out to survival.

It was a mission that demanded crack troops at the peak of condition. Instead, his men were already battered beyond recognition. Probably a little moonlight would have been less dangerous than the weather.

"We're crossing the peak now, sir." It was the glider pilot's voice coming over the sound-powered telephone. Haller acknowledged, then leaned forward, bracing his hands against the floor.

"We've made it," he told his men. "Five minutes to touch down. Tighten up." There were smiles of relief. Nothing the Germans could offer would be as bad as the flight they were about to complete. They pulled tight on the straps that fastened their equipment to their belt and backpacks.

The pilot leaned forward, wiping the icy frost from the windshield with the palm of his glove, and staring into the black sky to keep the dim taillight of the Halifax dead ahead. The tow plane was turning to the south and he couldn't let the glider drift by and wait for it to be jerked back into line. He had to fly his own turn, following precisely the arc inscribed by the Halifax. The tow plane was also beginning its descent, and the pilot had to dive the glider behind it, using the clumsy wooden air brakes to keep the towline taut.

"Jesus!" Haller cursed as the cabin pitched suddenly. The glider had caught a wind gust and nearly flipped, standing for an instant on its wingtip. Instead of looking *across* at his sergeant, he was looking straight *down* at him. Helmets dropped from the heads of men on one side of the plane and smashed into the faces across the narrow aisle.

"Get this fucking kite down!" Haller yelled into the phone.

"On our way, skipper," the pilot's voice said. "Only another minute."

The Halifax flashed a single white light. The pilot reached down next to his seat and pulled a metal ring. The towrope released, and the glider began to drop noiselessly toward the snow-covered mountain slope.

They could fly a long way. With the nose down only a few degrees, the airspeed held at over 100 miles per hour. At that speed, they could travel several miles before they would drop the

5,000 feet that separated them from the ground. But the time was short. The longest they could hope to stay airborne was five or six minutes. That was all the time they had to find the river.

If the release point were accurate, they should fly south, which was the heading that the pilot was trying to hold on his compass. They should reach the river in three minutes, with about 2,000 feet of altitude, and then follow it to the southeast toward the hydroelectric plant. They would swoop in noiselessly, landing on the riverbank, two miles above the plant, outside the perimeter patrols that the Germans maintained constantly.

The pilot strained against the windshield. The black sky that made him invisible also made it impossible for him to see the ground. He counted his seconds from the moment of release, compared the time with his altitude, and then turned blindly, assuming he had reached the river.

The altimeter cranked down: 1500 feet, then 1000. There was still no sign of the ground.

"Treeline," his copilot said, pointing out to the right. The pilot looked, and instantly eased into a turn. They were over a thick stand of trees that would tear the fragile glider to pieces. The break in the trees, which they assumed was the riverbed, was far to their right.

"Too goddamn low," the pilot answered. He pulled the nose up, trying to use the glider's speed to gain a bit of height. As his speed dropped, he pushed the nose lever, trying to nurse an extra few feet out of the plane's momentum.

"Brace yourself!" he shouted into the phone to alert the troops. "We're going to hit!" He could feel the tips of branches slapping against the belly. The Horsa skipped off a treetop, and for an instant it seemed to be gaining altitude. Then it started to drop. But at that moment, they crossed the edge of the forest, and shot out over the frozen bank of the river.

The pilot pushed the nose down, and as the plane gained speed, the wings began to lift. He banked the craft sharply to the left, turning tightly to keep from going out over the frozen river. Then, with the left wingtip about to hit, he banked sharply right. The plane flattened, lost speed, and buffeted into a stall. It dropped quickly, its wooden skid smashing against the ice.

There were screams from the cabin as the glider bounced back into the air. But it quickly hit again, this time more gently. And then it was skidding smoothly across the frozen river, its belly tracking like a sled.

The pilot tried to kill its speed with the air brakes, and used his rudder pedals to keep the plane pointing in a straight line. Gradually, the speed dropped and the Horsa slid to a gentle stop.

Eyes that had been squeezed shut in terror slowly opened. The commandos looked at one another, realized that they had landed, and then frozen lips parted in smiles.

"Let's move," Haller ordered, slipping out of his seat belt and throwing the release handle on the cabin door. The troops filed out onto the ice. "Get the equipment to the riverbank," the major said. The commandos formed a fire line between the plane and the edge of the river and passed their equipment to safety.

Haller held his map in front of the pilot. They weren't sure whether they had overshot the intended landing area or fallen short. But it didn't matter. All they had to do was follow the river to the southeast and it would lead them to the intake valves of the Rjukan hydroelectric plant.

The men had no idea what they were attacking. Certainly, they knew it was a power plant, but there were thousands of power plants in the German-occupied territories and none of them rated a personal visit from the Red Devils. In training, Haller had answered their questions by telling them that the plant made special chemicals that the Germans desperately needed, and that the chemicals were processed far underground in the viaducts that fed the turbines where they were protected from aerial bombing. He knew that his answer was only a half-truth. But there was no way he could ask the men to risk their lives just to spill a few thousand gallons of water back into the river. Unless he could make them understand the importance of the water, and that was impossible.

How could he explain a rare molecule of water that had an extra neutron freakishly attached to each of the hydrogen atoms? A molecule whose only value was its unusual ability to slow down the flight of an atomic particle that, in itself, had no function other than to add weight to a nucleus. And all this was occurring at the core of a metal so rare that they had certainly never held it in their hands, or even seen any of it for that matter.

Yet, if the heavy water reached Germany, the war was lost. With it, they could create a bomb that would vaporize London in a single flash. A second bomb would level Liverpool an instant later. By the time they dropped their tenth bomb, half the population of England would have been obliterated.

From water?

They could never understand.

It was better to lie. Major Haller knew that his men would willingly risk their lives to deny the Germans even a momentary advantage—to destroy a chemical that might power a few of their planes. But die for water? That would be asking too much.

They came to a long, gentle slope and tried their skis, gliding noiselessly for several hundred yards. But one by one they fell in the darkness, and the tight line began to stretch out. Haller ordered them to abandon the skis.

Ahead, they heard the roar of a rapid that warned them of a steep, rocky grade. They climbed down slowly, setting each footstep carefully into the frozen face of the rocks and then passing the spools of wire and the boxes of dynamite from hand to hand. They were exhausted when they reached the bottom but Haller was already falling behind his schedule so he ordered them to press on immediately, into a dense stand of forest that reached right to the bluff at the edge of the river. Now the protective darkness presented a new hazard as they stumbled in the dead underbrush and as unseen branches slashed at their hands and faces. Every yard of advance was painful, and the cold and fatigue were taking their toll. Haller pushed them harder, fearing that the forest might swallow up his attack force before it ever reached its target.

They were within a few hundred yards of the plant before they saw it, a large, square brick building with several small outbuildings, built into a hillside above the river. Next to the complex was the electrical switchyard, and the first poles of the power line that carried electricity east to Drammen and then to Oslo. The wire fence that protected the property was only a hundred yards ahead of them. German soldiers marched their sentry routes along the inside of the fence.

At the sight of the enemy, their fatigue vanished. The men moved instantly into the attack they had rehearsed countless times with a wood-frame model of the building. The three sappers, with six of the riflemen, crept down the slope toward the riverbed. Four of the commandos began to set up two mortars at the forest's edge. The remaining riflemen, under command of the sergeant, circled above the building. Haller watched the deployment, then dashed down the bank to join the sappers.

Haller's group reached the concrete island that was built into the water's edge. Steel gates in the island diverted the current into the viaduct that fed the turbines. They followed the duct until it disappeared into the foundations of the building. Then they climbed the steps to the steel doors that enclosed the generator floor. One of the sappers fixed a dynamite charge against the massive hinges. Then they crouched and waited.

Seconds later, they heard the distant "pop" as the first mortar round fired into its steep trajectory. In an instant, the other mortar fired.

There were shouted commands in German as the pacing guards turned toward the noise. Then the still, snowy night was shattered by a deafening explosion as the first mortar round hit close to the switchyard.

The sapper lit the fuse to the dynamite charge.

Haller could hear the screaming of the guards above him, and then the chatter of their guns as they fired blindly out into the night.

The second mortar shell exploded, and an instant later, another. He could picture the guards rushing madly in circles, trying to find protection from the shells and the gunfire that were coming from the empty darkness. His troops, he knew, held all the advantages, firing at fixed targets from the protection of the vast emptiness. But the advantage would be short-lived. The German troops in the garrison would assemble in seconds. They would spot the muzzle flashes of the British guns and then they would begin to return fire. It would take only a few minutes for their superior numbers to overwhelm the small force of attackers.

The charge exploded, and the steel door disappeared into the building. Haller jumped to his feet and led his small force through the opening. They rushed across the brightly lighted generator hall, dodging around the massive domed tops of the electrical generators that were being spun by the underground turbines.

A single guard posted at the door to the water-processing building recovered from the flash of the explosion in time to see the commandos rushing in and raised his rifle. But when he saw the English guns swinging toward him, he fled through the doorway. He was only halfway to the next doorway leading to the outside steps when a burst of fire from one of the invaders cut him down. He hurtled forward, sliding on his face across the immaculate tile floor and leaving bright streaks of fresh blood in his wake.

Haller ignored his death sounds. "Those," he said, directing the sappers to the row of tall metal tanks that could have come from a winery. "Then get these electrodes."

The huge electrodes, nearly two stories high, protruded from the top of a processing tank where the current they created broke ordinary water into its composite gasses. Galvanized ducts were positioned to carry off the hydrogen and oxygen, leaving behind water with a greater concentration of the freakish hydrogen atoms. By a slow and patient process of reducing the water to a hundred-thousandth of its original volume, heavy water was isolated.

Haller positioned his riflemen at the room's two doorways, one leading to the generator hall they had just crossed, the other opening to a flight of concrete steps that led up to the outside. Now, the battle was reversed. Instead of the attackers, the commandos had become the defenders. Their task was to keep the Germans out of the room until the sappers had done their work.

At first, the distraction of the mortar fire drew the Germans out into the grounds. But in a moment, the officers understood the prize that had to be protected. They stopped a company of soldiers who were rushing toward the perimeter fence, and led them down the steps toward the heavy-water processing room.

Haller's men caught them as they turned at the top of the stairs and cut down the first rank with automatic weapons fire. The second rank of Germans dove for cover and began pouring rifle fire into the doorway, driving the commandos back into the processing room. Haller knew they had only seconds left. He looked back at his explosive experts.

They had set charges against each of the storage tanks. One of the men was leading the wires toward the doorway that they had entered. The other two were fixing packages of dynamite sticks to the electrodes and to the gas ducts that led from the top of the electrolysis tank. Haller wanted to scream at them. They were running out of time. But they would never get another shot at the Rjukan plant. He had to buy them whatever time they needed.

There was a blast of gunfire from outside. The Germans had positioned a machine gun on the stairs. The sustained fire shattered the edges of the doorway, making it impossible for the commandos to return fire. Two of the British troops were hit, one turning toward Haller with only half a face. The other commandos were driven from their cover to new positions behind the processing tanks.

The Germans had to attack through a narrow doorway, which even the small British force could cover. As the first of the guards appeared in the doorway, he was cut open by a line of bullets, and he spun back out of sight as he fell. A second soldier appeared, but a hail of fire from inside drove him back for cover. It seemed to the British troops that they could hold the room indefinitely. But Haller knew that it would take the Germans only a minute to reposition the machine gun so that it was firing directly into the processing room. He also knew that it wouldn't take the German commander long to send troops around the building and cut off their escape.

"Let's go," Haller ordered. The sappers dropped the remaining charges on top of the processing tank and began to retreat, stringing the wires behind them.

Then there were gunshots from behind. German troops had entered the generator hall and now had both doors covered.

"Get out!" Haller screamed. He took the detonator with its

wooden-handled plunger from the sapper. "That way," he told the troops, pointing to the generator hall door. His troops charged back into the hall, firing at the Germans who had slipped in behind them. Then Haller began backing in their direction, the detonator under one arm, his automatic rifle under the other. He kept firing into the far doorway, holding off the German attackers. When he reached the escape door, he dropped to one knee and fell on the plunger.

There was a flash of light, a deafening blast, and then a hammer of air that drove him backwards, through the doorway, and out onto the generator floor.

The lights dimmed, throwing him into darkness. The only sound he could hear was the ringing in his head that the crash of the explosion had caused. There were flashes of light as the commandos and the German troops fired wildly in the darkness. Then, as the lights flickered on again, he saw the cascade of water that smashed against the doorway, and poured like a tidal wave out onto the floor of the generator hall. He struggled to his feet, and staggered toward the opening they had originally blown through the outer wall. But his escape was blocked by dark-uniformed Germans. The fleeing British were caught in the open and were being slaughtered by gunfire. Several of the Germans had locked the same commando in their sights, and his body jerked like a puppet as round after round pounded into him.

A brilliant light flashed behind Haller, followed by a shower of sparks. There was a crash as the rushing water poured into one of the generators and shorted its windings. Instantly, the overhead lights went out, giving the fleeing British a moment of cover.

Then the wave hit the backs of Haller's legs, knocking him down. It carried him toward the muzzles of the German guns that were flashing blindly in the dark. But as the water surged ahead, the Germans turned and tried to escape from its path. The wave smashed against them and pushed them over the slope and down toward the river below.

Haller crashed into his own men who were sliding ahead of him. He grasped for the edge of the door, but the force of the water tore his hands away. He fell into the stream of bodies, some living and some dead, that were tossed down the embankment.

The men who fell all the way to the river disappeared through the thin ice that was kept from setting by the surge of water entering the viaduct. One man—Haller couldn't tell whether he was English or German—fell into the viaduct, clawed at its edge for an instant, and then dropped screaming into the rushing stream that carried him underground and down into the churning blades of the turbines. Major Haller slid against a boulder just above the viaduct, and held on while the water rushed around him. He felt his fingers slipping across the wet rock and clung desperately, knowing the fate that waited below. There could be no escape from the rapids in the viaduct. If he were lucky, he would drown before he was sucked into the giant steel fans beneath the building that would cut him into a hundred pieces.

Miraculously, the cascade stopped. He spit the water out of his mouth and shook his head to clear his eyes. Then, carefully, he felt for a toehold, and began clawing his way back up the edge of glasslike boulder, leaving bloody handprints to mark his agonizing progress.

He pulled himself free, and crawled along the edge of the channel until it reached their reassembly point at the concrete island. Two of his commandos were waiting for him, one bleeding from a wound high in his chest that bubbled and hissed each time he took a breath. They huddled in the darkness until they were joined by one of the sappers, his face gashed from his fall.

"It was water . . . just fucking water," the sapper moaned deliriously. "We got the wrong tanks."

"They were the right tanks," Haller snapped. "That's what we came for."

"For water?" the sapper cried. "All these mates dead for a couple of tanks of fucking water?"

They began their retreat, along the riverbank, back toward the point where they had abandoned the glider. There, they would team up with what was left of the other half of their force, and begin a march across the frozen mountains, hoping to keep a rendezvous with agents of the Norwegian Resistance.

But from his own exhaustion and the battered condition of the three men with him, Haller knew that it wasn't much of a hope. Especially since he could already feel his clothes, soaked in the precious liquid, freezing against his skin.

STOCKHOLM — March 21

"The English have no program," Anders explained in the Swedish that had now become his most natural tongue. "They talk, but there is no substance. How can anyone hope to demonstrate uranium fission when they have no uranium?"

"But you spent several months in England," Birgit pressed, playing the role of a German interrogator.

"London is an exciting city, even in wartime," Anders answered. "And there are some very good people working there. You know that Otto Frisch is in London. And Samuel Goudsmit."

"Jews," Birgit hissed.

"Brilliant thinkers," Anders countered. "Even though I am Aryan, I have a great deal of difficulty with your Aryan physics. How can you simply ignore the work of Jewish physicists? I had several interesting discussions with Goudsmit. Discussions that will be very helpful in my work."

"But you chose not to stay there. You are, perhaps, more comfortable with the German cause?"

"I'm comfortable with progress," Anders answered. "Scientists should pursue truth, not national causes. If we are ever going to understand the atom, we will need reactors to change atomic structures and isolate atomic particles. The British will never have a reactor. Do you know that they have sent all their research notes to the Americans? They are letting the Americans build their reactor."

"The Americans?" Birgit tried to look surprised, even though they were certain that the Germans knew about the efforts in the

United States. They had agreed to tell the German scientists and Nazi officials anything that they probably knew already just to enhance Anders' credibility.

"Yes. With Canadian uranium. The English think that they are working with graphite. Enrico Fermi is there, and he and I have exchanged letters on graphite. He understands its possibilities. Can you believe an Italian running an English program in the United States?"

"You weren't offered the opportunity to work in America?"

"There were hints," he answered. "No one offered in so many words, but there were enough hints. I suppose I was never that impressed with Fermi. Certainly, there was no possibility of my working for his program. If I went to America it would have to be clearly understood that I was to be in charge."

"Then why do you think they asked you to come to England? If they have no program and they weren't trying to get you to America?"

Anders fingered his wineglass, and tipped his head in a rehearsed gesture. "I think probably just to keep me from coming here to Germany. You're their enemy, you know. I don't think the English can understand that pure science has nothing to do with war. And they can't stand the fact that we Swedes are neutral."

Birgit smiled and raised her glass in a toast. "God, but you're good. You make me forget that I'm not talking with Nils Bergman."

He joined her in the toast, and sipped the fruity German white wine.

"Now, shall we try it in German?" Birgit offered.

Anders groaned. "Could we order dinner first?"

The dinner was her idea, at a restaurant she had selected because Nils Bergman had liked it. They had been locked up for days on end in the small cottage, studying Bergman's writings and notes, paging through his correspondence and photo albums, and holding endless conversations about his social life as well as his professional interests. Anders sensed that he was becoming more convincing, and with the confidence he had become more daring. His progress over the past two weeks had been amazing, even to his own critical ear. In the morning when she arrived, Birgit had suggested that he return to Stockholm with her for a small celebration over dinner. Anders had forced back his momentary terror and agreed.

The waiter came with his pad and took their order. They both chose the whitefish with cold potato salad, Birgit because she liked it and Anders because he remembered that it was a favorite of Bergman's.

"Perhaps we could use our German to talk about you," Anders suggested. "We both know everything there is to know about Nils Bergman, and I'm sure you knew a great deal about me even before we met. But I'm at a disadvantage when it comes to you. Any secrets you've been holding back?" He tipped the wine bottle over her glass.

"Nothing that wine will ever get out of me," Birgit said suspiciously.

She had always dodged questions about herself. He knew she was Swedish from her mastery of the language and her occasional lapses into memories of her home and youth. Obviously, she was working for the British, and judging from her comments about correspondence she had with England, she was very important to them and enjoyed their confidence at the very highest levels. She had admitted to being a graduate of advanced university programs in mathematics and physics and she demonstrated great capabilities in the subjects. Her German and English were excellent, which she credited to having spent time in both countries. Her facial expressions each time they ventured into German politics convinced him of her hatred for the Nazis. But all these things were only the agenda of her life. He really knew very little about her person.

"Your work is obviously dangerous," he pressed on. "Was that why you teamed up with the British? Do you thrive on danger?"

She laughed. "Hardly. I don't think I would ever go into a dangerous country even if they asked me. I'm really just an advisor. A specialist, of sorts, I guess."

"But, you're not involved . . . in the war, I mean. If you were English, I could understand. But why is a Swede, and a woman at that, doing cloak-and-dagger work with British Military Intelligence?"

"It wasn't cloak-and-dagger," Birgit said, shaking her head at the absurdity. "I just volunteered to serve as a lookout. I knew from my studies what incredible power was locked up in the atom. I went to England to work with Lindemann. I was with him and Otto Frisch when they first postulated the possibility of an atomic bomb. Then the war broke out . . . the Nazis invaded Poland . . . and Lindemann began talking about the use of an atomic bomb in the war. I was horrified. But I decided that we would all be safer if the English had it instead of the Germans. So I asked the English if I could help. And eventually they found a use for me."

"With Bergman?"

"Yes. I was supposed to work with him, which is exactly what I would have wanted to do anyway, and keep them informed of whom he was talking with and what he was working on."

"Without him knowing that his ideas were being shipped to England?" Anders ventured.

"It really wouldn't have mattered. Nils Bergman had few secrets. He published everything he thought might be useful. So I really wasn't very important. But the war split the physics community, not so much along political lines as personal lines. Fermi went to America because his wife is Jewish and he was afraid for her safety. Frisch and Goudsmit were driven out of Germany because they were Jews. Heisenberg stayed in Germany because his wife wouldn't leave. So we had a group of the best people working for the Americans and the British and a group working for the Germans. Most of them didn't believe in causes. Oh, some of the Germans were pleased to learn that they belonged to the Master Race. But most of scientists on both sides didn't care about politics. They just went where they had to go and did the kind of work that they had to do.

"But Bergman was in the middle. And he was a major figure, every bit as important as Heisenberg or Fermi. He would have been a tremendous help to anyone he joined. So the English wanted to be warned if he seemed to be taking sides."

"Did he?" Anders asked.

The waiter appeared, placed their plates, and fussed for a moment with the table setting. Then he bowed and left them alone again.

"Did he take sides?" Birgit resumed. "No. He didn't really care about the war. He didn't want to know what was happening inside Germany. But the Germans had everything. The uranium. All the world's heavy water, once they captured Norway. And the Krupp works produces the world's purest graphite. When they invited him to prove his fission theories, he couldn't resist. It was his life's work."

"And you couldn't let him go," Karl Anders suggested.

She shook her head. "I was a student in Germany for over a year. I was there when the trains began to roll, carrying boxcars full of decent people off to slave camps. The Brownshirts were roaming the streets, humiliating and torturing people who disagreed with them. Old men and women. Children. Crippled people. They loved to beat the weak and the helpless because they couldn't fight back. They were crazy. It was as if the world had been turned inside out. As if the asylums had been emptied out and the mindless brutes were now in charge. The maddest person in the country had been elected its leader, because in a nation of madmen no one was more fit for command. I heard Hitler talk about his destiny to run the whole world and I was absolutely terrified. Then I watched them kill someone . . . a fellow student . . ."

Her mouth went dry and her voice choked.

"Someone you cared for," Anders knew.

Birgit nodded. "Believe me, the Nazis aren't dangerous because they're fascists. They're dangerous because they're crazy. I couldn't let Bergman help them. I knew exactly what they would do with his work. I had to stop him. I had no choice."

She turned away in shame as if she had just confessed some great sin. It was clear that she hated herself for having betrayed her mentor. Anders tried a new subject.

"Is your name really Birgit Zorn? Or is that some sort of a code name?"

Her eyes widened, and suddenly she began to laugh. As she

tried to stifle the laugh, food spilled from the corner of her mouth and she quickly covered her lips with her napkin.

"Of course it's my real name," she finally managed, and in the laughter, the guilt that had clouded her eyes disappeared.

"*Professor Bergman.*"

The voice came from over his shoulder and caught both of them off guard. Anders turned and saw a round man in a heavy woolen three-piece suit. His hands were folded in front of his ponderous belly, and he was bowing slightly over his hands.

He straightened as Anders turned and stared directly into his eyes. His face registered his confusion. "Excuse me. I thought . . ."

Anders fumbled with his napkin as he rose in order to buy an instant to remember. He had seen the man in pictures. The owner of the restaurant who had been bending over his guests in a photo of Bergman and his mistress. What was his name?

"Professor Bergman?" the owner said. This time it was a question.

The name came to Anders. "Of course, Mats. How good to see you again."

Mats still looked puzzled. "You're looking . . ." His hands gestured in circles to indicate his confusion. ". . . very well. Slimmer, perhaps. Have you lost weight? How long has it been?"

"I've been traveling," Anders answered. He patted both hands on his stomach. "And I have lost a bit of weight. That's why I came straight here for a decent meal." He pointed toward his plate.

"Ahh!" Mats's face glowed with recognition. "Your favorite whitefish. I always have some for you." And now he relaxed, perfectly at ease with an old friend. The surroundings, the food, they all identified Nils Bergman, even if the face had somehow changed.

"Have you met my assistant, Miss Zorn?"

"A pleasure," the man said, bowing formally toward Birgit. Then he looked questioningly back toward Anders.

"Magda is away with her family," Anders explained. "Miss Zorn was kind enough to keep me company."

Mats smiled, the suspicion replaced by a knowing wink.

"I hope I will see a great deal of you, Miss Zorn." Then he gestured Anders back into his chair. "Please, don't let me interrupt." He bowed, and moved to extend his greetings at the next table.

Anders reached for his wine, but he pulled his hand back when he noticed that it was shaking. "Jesus, that was close," he whispered to Birgit. "Do you think he suspects?"

"Absolutely," she smiled. "He suspects that I'm your new mistress and I think he was even pleased at your choice. But he doesn't suspect that you're not Nils Bergman. You did very well."

He shook his head in relief and managed to steady his hand long enough to gulp down a drink of the wine. When he looked back at Birgit, she was staring directly into his eyes.

"You're ready for Germany," she said simply.

He felt the shock register on his face.

"We'll write the German minister of physics tomorrow. I suspect he'll want you to come right away."

Anders looked helplessly toward the owner and then back to Birgit. "I'm not ready yet," he told her, his gesture suggesting that he had scarcely survived his encounter with a perfect stranger. "I don't think I'm even ready for the test you promised me."

"That was the test," she said.

He looked at her, then back at Mats, and then back to her. "Him?" he asked.

"Professor Bergman ate here two or three times a month. Mats always visits his guests. He even had his picture taken with Bergman."

"But, a restaurant owner. . . ?"

"He knows Bergman better than anyone you're going to meet in Germany. Karl, we never expected you to fool Bergman's mistress. But the Germans don't know Nils Bergman as well as Mats does. So if you can convince Mats, then there is no one in Germany who won't be convinced."

His appetite was gone. He pushed his plate away and concentrated on the wineglass.

"That's why you suggested a celebration? To test me?"

"I had to be sure," she answered.

"To protect the mission."

"No," Birgit snapped. "To protect you . . . and to protect myself."

"Yourself? You're not going into Germany."

She accepted his rebuke.

He sat in stoney silence until he felt her finger touch his hand that was resting against the wineglass.

"I said I wasn't a professional," Birgit reminded him. "I'm not. If this were my line of work, then all I would be interested in would be the mission. But I'm concerned about you. And about my own sanity."

His puzzled look told her that he didn't understand.

"I killed Nils Bergman," Birgit said. Anders started to protest, but she raised her hand to silence him. "Not with my own hand. But I made all the arrangements, and then I sent him to his death.

"Now I've made all the arrangements for you. But I have to be certain that I'm not sending you to your death. No matter what happens, I never want to be involved in killing another person. Can you understand that?"

He nodded that he could. "I'm sorry. I know you're not just shipping me off. I know you care what happens to me."

"I care very much," she answered. For a moment they stared at each other, the pale color of the wine reflecting in their faces.

"You don't have to go," Birgit whispered. "Just because you're able to do this, doesn't mean that you should. It's still dangerous. And it isn't your kind of work any more than it's mine."

He smiled ironically. "We made that decision at the cottage. Remember? I knew what the bomb could do, and you knew what the Nazis could do. That's what made us a team."

He raised his glass in a toast. For a moment Birgit just stared at him. Then she smiled and raised her own glass.

"To Germany," he said.

SPRING

1944

As the winter snows melted, the Russian advance came to a halt, blocked by swollen rivers and bogged down in miles of mud. All of Poland stood between the Red Army and Germany, and the Germans were using the respite to build up their reserves. No one knew which way the front would move when the land began to dry. In Italy, General Kesselring had surrounded the beaches of Anzio, threatening to throw the Allies back into the sea. The combined Allied armies were attempting to break through to the invasion forces. But they were being systematically slaughtered by German troops firing from the ruins of a medieval monastery called Monte Casino. And in England, the buildup for Overlord continued. General Eisenhower, still two armies short of the five armies he needed for the invasion, considered further postponements. But the Russians insisted that the second front not be delayed past spring. And American and British scientists warned that the Germans must be defeated before they could deploy their fantastic secret weapons. The most frightening of the new weapons was a uranium bomb.

HELSINGER — *April 13*

He was terrified by the sound of his own voice. Each gesture that he made threatened to betray him. And the German words that he had spoken since childhood seemed to scream that he was a fake.

Kurt Diebner, in a dark topcoat and precisely squared homburg, had met him at the ferry and escorted him through Danish passport control. Then he had led him to a black limousine and bantered pleasantries about the weather as they drove to the hotel that had become headquarters for the Nazi commission that ran Denmark.

"We've reserved the largest suite for you," Diebner oozed, as he led his guest through the lobby and joined him in the small open elevator. "Our flight to Berlin has been delayed a day or two. So, we'll stay here until it arrives. In the meantime, there are several officials of my government who are eager to meet you."

Anders understood their purpose. The Nazis wanted to be certain of their distinguished guest before they introduced him into their most secret research program. The officials who were anxious to meet him were probably from the Gestapo.

As soon as Diebner left him, he went straight to the bathroom, splashed cold water on his face, and blotted the beads of nervous sweat that had appeared at his hairline and across the top of his lip. He arranged the heavy woolen suit, making sure that the vest was pulled tight across his stomach, and rehearsed the slouch that tended to hide his physique. Then he stared into the mirror, mouthing German phrases until he thought they looked natural.

Diebner had believed him, he encouraged himself. The German had accepted his introduction and his few words of conversation as genuine. There had never been a flicker of doubt in the man's eyes. But Diebner wasn't the danger. He was Bergman's patron, anxious to add to his own prestige by associating himself with a world-renowned physicist.

The danger was the Nazi officials he would be meeting in a few moments. Men who questioned how foreigners could possibly lend anything to the brilliance of German thought, and who had been taught to be suspicious of everyone outside their closed circle of fanatics. Their joy would come from exposing him.

He started for the door, but stopped with his hand on the knob. The nauseous fear seemed to rise up from his stomach as he moved closer to the meeting. He breathed deeply, then opened the door and started toward the elevator.

As the car groaned slowly toward the lobby, Anders found himself half hoping that he would fail. It would be much easier to board the ferry back to Sweden than to climb onto an airplane headed into Germany. "I tried," he could tell Birgit in the security of the cottage where she had trained him. "It was a good idea and it almost worked." And later, when he was back in the United States, he could tell the Manhattan Project people, "I did what I could. What more can anyone ask?" But if he survived the scrutiny, then the terror would continue. It would build with each passing day, with each new person that he met and each new conversation he joined. And if they discovered him once they had brought him into the program and shared their secrets, they certainly wouldn't put him back on the ferry. He would probably disappear just as abruptly as the man he was impersonating.

Diebner was waiting in the lobby, and bubbled information as he led Anders to a small dining room that had been set with a buffet. "Herr Goetz works directly for Goebbels at the Ministry of Information," he said, explaining the dignitaries who had come to welcome Bergman. "He will want to prepare a story about you for our news services. And Colonel Hartmann is on Reichsfuehrer Himmler's staff. The reichsfuehrer only regrets that he could not be here to welcome you personally."

Now he was seated with them, while a waiter served wine and beer with their cold cuts and sausage. And as he responded to their casual questions, the words were sticking in his mouth. His movements felt wooden and his gestures contrived.

Their roles were obvious. Goebbels' man was conducting the interrogation, disguising the questions as polite table conversation. Diebner was trying to evaluate the scientific content of his remarks, while the colonel in his impeccable uniform was trying to judge his loyalties.

His comments to the scientific leads began to build his confidence. He could talk easily about nuclear physics, often using the exact words and phrases that he had rehearsed from Bergman's writings. The nausea began to subside as he realized that Diebner understood very little and would never dare to challenge his views.

"We believe there is great energy to be released from the atom," Herr Goetz tried. "Energy that will serve us well in war by giving our submarines an unlimited source of power. But energy that will also serve humanitarian needs once the war is over."

Anders nodded Bergman's agreement and began describing theories for controlling chain reactions. He could see Diebner's confusion when he began discussing the importance of accurate cross-section measurements of carbon, and when he seized a pencil and began scribbling equations on the tablecloth.

Diebner and Goetz beamed when he began calculating the volts of energy that could be released by the fission process and converting them into pounds of steam for the generation of electricity. He noticed that the hand that held the pencil was confident and steady, just as Bergman's would have been.

Then he made contact with Colonel Hartmann's narrow eyes, and read the suspicion that he had been dreading. The officer wasn't interested in theories. The eyes never drifted down to the numbers and diagrams on the tablecloth, but remained fixed on Anders' face.

"Do you believe in the possibility of a uranium bomb?" Hartmann suddenly interrupted. Goetz stopped posing as the leader of the discussion and Diebner pulled back nervously from the table.

Anders shrugged, Bergman's rehearsed gesture of indifference. "Possible . . . certainly. Anything is possible. But practical? It might be too heavy to move." He looked directly at his adversary and gave the answer that Bergman had often given to Birgit. "I haven't thought much about it. I'm not interested in bombs."

"You were in England," Hartmann said. "Are the English interested in bombs?"

Anders smiled, then gestured toward the colonel. "Like you, the soldiers are." He looked at Diebner. "The scientists aren't."

"Why didn't you stay in England?" Hartmann continued, not even acknowledging his previous answer.

Anders went into the conversation he had rehearsed with Birgit in the restaurant. The English had no uranium. They had turned their research over to the Americans. And he had no desire to work with Enrico Fermi.

"Then you don't care whose side you're on," Hartmann challenged.

It was the moment of truth that Birgit had anticipated. Anders took on a serious expression. "If you are asking whether I believe in your Master Race . . . no. I am Swedish, not German. If loyalty to Germany is a requirement for joining you, then I must sadly decline Dr. Diebner's invitation."

Hartmann's eyes widened slightly as he attempted to control his surprise. He was not accustomed to people who were not profuse in their loyalty to the fuehrer.

"I am a scientist," Anders said. "My loyalty is to facts and to truth. I am here because this is where science is making the greatest advances. So, I am on nobody's side. If English research was ahead of German research, then I would have stayed in England."

"Surely that is the proper attitude for a scientist—" Diebner began to offer. But Hartmann stopped him by simply raising his hand from the table.

"And knowing this, the English let you come here to Germany?" Hartmann challenged.

"My dear colonel, the English had no choice. I am a Swedish citizen, protected by the Swedish government. I had every right to go home from England. And I have every right to leave my home and visit here in Germany. Assuming, of course, that I am welcome here." He looked to Diebner for an answer.

"More than welcome," Diebner reassured. "We are delighted."
He looked to the colonel for an expression of agreement. But
Hartmann's cold eyes remained locked on Anders.

Goetz broke the uneasy silence with a trivial question about
Bergman's personal interests and the conversation quickly took a
less confrontational direction. But even in the small talk, the probing continued. There were references to Bergman's correspondence with German scientists. Anders remembered the letters.
There were recollections of scientific meetings that Bergman had
attended. Anders remembered the details. His German was fit-
tingly imprecise. And when he couldn't find the German word, he
slipped easily into Swedish, just as he had done in his conversations with Birgit.

He was convincing. And the more he responded, the more confident he became in his ability to handle their next question. The
terror left him, and the nausea vanished as his appetite returned.
"God, you're good," he remembered Birgit saying, as he realized
that Diebner and Goetz were now more interested in the food and
wine than they were in his words. He even noticed a change in
Hartmann's expression. The colonel had fallen into a gloomy silence, disappointed that he could find nothing to attack.

Diebner walked him to the elevator, repeating his delight in
having Bergman as a colleague. "I hope they can find a plane for
us so that we can get to Germany and begin working. I'm sure
we'll hear something in the morning."

As soon as he closed the door of his suite behind him, Anders
took a deep breath. It was over. Or was it just beginning? For the
moment, at least, he didn't really care.

He took off his jacket and walked to his closet. As soon as he
opened the closet door, he knew that his room had been searched.

He had left the sleeve of one jacket tucked into the pocket of
another. Now, it hung freely. He had left the zipper of his briefcase opened a fraction of an inch. Now it was pulled tightly shut.
In the bathroom, he had left the blade of his straight razor slightly
opened. Now it was pressed tightly into the handle. "People in a
hurry," one of his teachers in England had explained, "never put
things back exactly as they find them. So the trick is to remember
exactly how you leave them. They won't change by themselves."

They had interrogated him, and now they were probably verifying everything he had told them. They had searched him, and were probably discussing his papers, his clothing, even his choice of toothpaste and shaving soap with some master spy in Berlin. All he could do was wait for them to examine the evidence.

Whether he went back to Sweden or went on into Germany was their decision to make. And as he stretched out on his oversized bed, Anders could only wonder what the Germans wanted most.

Another sycophant to worship their fuehrer. Or the atomic bomb.

BERLIN — *April 15*

The three-engined Junkers climbed out over the Baltic and headed south, with Sweden quickly disappearing under the left wing and the coast of Denmark a constant reference to the right. The morning sun, low in the sky ahead, turned the drab water to silver and colored the thousand islands of Jutland. In the incredible beauty, it was possible to believe that all the world was at peace.

But the airfield near Berlin could have been the gates of hell. The air was heavy with black smoke that drifted from the fires of a bombed-out hangar. And there was a deafening cacophony of shouted commands and emergency sirens as the gray-coated soldiers rushed to battle the blaze.

"An unfortunate hit," Kurt Diebner said, dismissing the chaos as he rushed Anders to the waiting car. "We bring their bombers down by the hundreds, but I suppose it's inevitable that one or two get through."

The surroundings contradicted the boast. The runway apron further up the field was pockmarked with bomb craters. There were several piles of blackened debris that had the shape of airplanes. Behind them was the twisted steel skeleton of what had once been a building. It was obvious that the Allied bombers were paying regular visits.

Two motorcycles took position just ahead of the car's fenders, and then the entourage rushed from the airport and headed toward the silhouette of the city. Diebner took up the conversation that he had started on the plane, listing all the preparations that had been made for Bergman's arrival. But Anders wasn't listening. Instead, he was battling to control the fear that had returned to his gut, and to hide the tremor that seemed obvious in his hands.

It was his first realization of terrible loneliness. He was totally on his own, moving further away from any possibility of help with each mile the car traveled. In the past, the people who had challenged him, who had labored hour after hour in attempts to trip him up and expose the fraud, had been his friends—men and women who needed him to succeed. But as he moved into the heart of Germany, it was as if his friends had turned their backs and abandoned him. Now every face, every voice would belong to a potential enemy.

There was more fear waiting for him in the city. They turned from a tree-lined residential street into a block of apartment buildings that had been blighted by the bombers. To the left, the buildings stood majestically with only the empty holes of shattered windows hinting at the horror. But to the right, spires of jagged walls rose like ghosts from a rubble of pulverized bricks and splintered timbers. He could see the outlines of vanished buildings etched like a grid in the debris. He was entering a doomed city, being laid waste with workmanlike precision by Allied air forces. The allies he had left behind were reaching out into his new country and threatening his destruction.

"English bastards," he heard Diebner say, suddenly interrupting his monologue of preparations and arrangements. "They are helpless before our armies so they attack our women and children."

"I've been in London," Anders answered, asserting his neutrality and reminding his host that all the bastards weren't on the Allied side. He was pleased by the confidence of his own voice and relieved that his German had been convincing.

They turned to the southwest, entering a suburb of Dahlem,

and Anders was surprised by his sudden excitement. They were approaching the Kaiser Wilhelm Institute, the home of the gods of nuclear chemistry and the shrine of Germany's blind faith in science. Wilhelm, himself, had created the institute from the royal farmlands, signaling his intention to invent things rather than grow things. What he had hoped to invent were the impregnable steels and the hotter fuels that would turn his country into a vast engine. He had no way of knowing that its most important product would be a few scribbled equations that launched the atomic age.

But it was those equations that had brought the institute its world renown. Lise Meitner, an Austrian Jew, had worked here developing the theory of fission. Her ideas had created the discipline of nuclear physics, and had attracted promising students from all over the world to the Berlin suburb. Half of Anders' teachers had learned their trades at the Kaiser Wilhelm, and most of the books and papers he studied had been written here.

It was from the line drawings in his text books that he recognized the buildings as soon as they came into sight. Three stories of stone beneath gabled roofs surrounded a unique dome, shaped like the ridiculous spiked helmet that Wilhelm was rumored to wear even to bed. The institute was unmarked. As they turned toward the gates, Anders was reassured by the trappings of academia, an oasis in a desert of mindlessness, apparently spared by the Allies as a humanitarian gesture. But the illusion was instantly shattered. They stopped at a gate guarded by soldiers and, after an exchange of salutes to the fuehrer, drove to a steel-shrouded door. They entered a concrete corridor illuminated by wire-encased bulbs, and descended iron-railed stairs into the basement bunkers.

The scientists were waiting in a conference room and they rose as Anders entered, moving around the table to offer their greetings. The first three men introduced were complete strangers who weren't even mentioned in Bergman's notes. He recognized Otto Fichter's name as the short, round man was introduced. "I heard you in Paris," Fichter said, intending a compliment. "And I remember your paper on the dispersion of gasses," Anders answered in flawed German. "I have consulted it frequently." Fichter beamed.

"Professor Fritz Lauderbach," Diebner crowed, introducing a German who had earned a world reputation for his studies of the function of mass in fission reactions. Lauderbach clicked his heels, proud that he had adapted easily to the military mentality of his country.

Anders nodded to one after another, exchanging a greeting if he remembered the man's name or work from Bergman's correspondence. His casual performance covered the fear he felt as each man stepped before him and he searched the face for some hint of doubt—the narrowing of an eye or the sudden withdrawal of a hand. But the procession passed without incident. Birgit had been right. The German scientists didn't know Nils Bergman.

"And where is Werner?" Diebner demanded, looking over the gathering. "Surely Professor Bergman knows Werner Heisenberg?"

Anders stiffened. The hardest of tests was now at hand. Heisenberg was world-famous, winner of the Nobel Prize when he was only thirty. Twice he had shared the stage of physics seminars with Nils Bergman.

"His office," one of the scientists explained. "He asked to be summoned when Professor Bergman arrived."

"Don't disturb him," Anders asked. But Diebner had already taken his elbow and was steering him out of the conference room and down the corridor. "Nonsense. He would be offended if he missed your arrival. You and he must have a great deal to talk about," Diebner promised as they approached the closed door.

Heisenberg was seated at his cluttered desk when they entered his office, a Brandenberg Concerto turning on the phonograph behind him. He rose slowly, ignoring the elaborate introductions that Diebner was offering and stared directly into Anders' eyes.

"Leave us," he told Diebner, without even sparing him a glance. His face stayed locked in Anders' direction.

Diebner bristled at the affront to his position. But if he were ever to deliver the chain reaction he had promised Himmler, these were the two men who would make it happen.

"You'll join us in the conference room?" he asked.

"In a few moments," Heisenberg answered. "Professor Bergman

comes to us from the outside world. There are many old friends I've lost track of. He may be able to tell me what they're all up to." Diebner was careful to close the door behind him.

"Ass," Heisenberg said. His severe expression softened and he shook his head in despair as he gestured his guest to a chair. "Before the war he couldn't have found work sharpening our pencils."

"What has he written?" Anders asked, suddenly aware that Heisenberg was smiling in genuine acceptance.

"Nothing more profound than notes to his milkman."

Werner Heisenberg lifted a bottle of Rhine wine from the drawer of his desk. "Will you join me?" Anders noticed Heisenberg's half-filled wineglass buried in the papers on his desk.

"Not before dinner," Anders said. Heisenberg nodded his approval.

"Do you like Bach?" the German genius wondered.

Anders shrugged his shoulders and shook his head from side to side in the gesture he had learned from Birgit. Heisenberg understood its meaning. Professor Bergman didn't care much about music.

"He's an incredible mathematician," Heisenberg continued. "I wrote a formula for one of his fugues. I gave each note a value. Then I could put in any ten notes in sequence and the formula would predict the next note. It was right about ninety percent of the time. Everything in order. Everything very precise. A perfect mathematician. He would have been marvelous in theoretical physics."

"Perhaps you'll lend me some of your records," Anders said. "As long as we will be working together, maybe we can develop a formula that will write an entire fugue."

Heisenberg didn't answer. His mind had already changed subjects. Instead he stared over the rim of his wineglass, analyzing his guest the way he had analyzed the progressions in Bach. He seemed to be weighing a question, and Anders felt his mouth go dry as he tried to compose a thousand possible answers. But once again, Heisenberg's thoughts skipped, this time backward to polite banter.

"Was your trip pleasant?"

"Denmark was beautiful," Anders said, relieved to have found safe ground. "We only stayed a day while we waited for a plane. But the flight was . . ." He fumbled for the German idiom, and then substituted, ". . . not so comfortable. It was a military plane. Very drafty. And noisy."

"And the ride through Berlin?" Heisenberg asked mischievously.

"Frightening," Anders said. "There is so much destruction. So much bombing."

Heisenberg put his finger across his lips. "Not so loud. We're not supposed to notice the bomb destruction. We have to pretend that all the buildings are still standing."

Anders didn't understand.

"So that we don't hurt Goering's feelings. He has assured us that the Luftwaffe commands the skies. So we all pretend that there are no Allied planes flying over our cities. It's a national game of the Emperor's New Clothes. Like the heavy water reactor we have built. Himmler says that we will have heavy water, so we pretend that it is going to run."

"There is no heavy water?" Anders said, trying to sound shocked.

"Not a cupful." Heisenberg laughed cynically. "But we try not to notice that either. It would offend Himmler."

"But . . . your work. How can you produce a chain reaction?"

"I can't," the German scientist said. He drained his wineglass. "But we have plenty of graphite. Germany is made out of graphite. So it will be your reactor that will go critical. Not mine."

"But I haven't even started," Anders protested.

Heisenberg waved away the objection. "I have started for you, Professor Bergman. I'm having them enlarge the cave so that you can build your reactor right next to mine. The cooling water that we pump up from the river can be directed to your project simply by turning a few valves. The construction workers are waiting for your plans."

"It will be built in a cave," Anders pressed.

Again Heisenberg raised his finger to his lips. "Very secret. We shouldn't be talking about this. It's called 'Castle Church.' But it's really a cave. Nothing in Germany is what it seems."

The German reached back to the record player and moved the tone arm back to the beginning of the disk. He waited for the music to begin before continuing.

"You've met Hartmann, Himmler's adviser on science?"

"Yes, in Denmark. But he didn't seem interested in our conversation. I didn't suspect that he was a scientist."

"A scientist?" Heisenberg sneered. "The man catches his cock in his zipper. But if you have spoken with him, then you know what this is all about. You understand, of course, that these idiots haven't suddenly become interested in pure theoretical physics. They brought you here to help them build their nuclear bomb."

Anders shrugged and waved his head. Bergman, he indicated, is no more interested in bombs than he is in classical music. "I'm not sure a bomb is even possible," he explained. "I'm interested in a reactor. If the generals can turn a reactor into a bomb, that's their affair. They seem to be able to turn almost any scientific discovery into a weapon. Scientists invented the lever to lessen mankind's burdens. But the generals turned it into a catapult so they could throw bigger stones. There's really nothing we can do about the uses they make of our work."

"A bomb is possible," Heisenberg said softly. "It's really quite simple. They use a shaped explosive to compact the heavy metal into a critical mass, and a neutron gun as a fuse. All they need is the plutonium. And to make the plutonium, all they need is your reactor."

Anders feigned indifference. "In theory, perhaps," he conceded. "But will the bomb have enough energy to be worth the effort? We're really only guessing on the energy potential of fission. Even very rapid fission. Perhaps, even if it works, it will be no more than a firecracker."

"I've seen the energy," Heisenberg said. "Right here in the basement of the institute. We started a small chain reaction two months ago—"

"You have succeeded," Anders interrupted. "You have sustained a chain reaction." His surprise was genuine. Fermi's success in Chicago had been rumored, but no one connected with the American program had confirmed to him that Bergman's idea of a self-sustaining chain reaction had been actually demonstrated. No one in England seemed even to know what Fermi was up to.

"Yes," Heisenberg said, with no hint of satisfaction. "But just for a few moments. We couldn't control it, so we had to destroy it. But in those few moments . . ." He shook his head slowly. "Dear God, in just those few moments, the energy released was enormous. Incredible. I had just a few kilograms of uranium. No more than you could hold in your hand. In just a few moments, the energy boiled off perhaps a hundred gallons of water. The metal itself caught fire. And that was only slightly enriched uranium. If it had been plutonium, that handful of metal would have brought down the entire university. Think of it. A weapon no bigger than a hand grenade with the power of a thousand-pound bomb. In the hands of madmen who can pretend there are no airplanes flying over their heads."

Now it was Anders who was staring across the desk, trying to find the words for a question. "Then why are you helping them?" he finally asked.

Heisenberg's long, blond hair fell across his eyes as his head slumped into his hands. "Because this time there will be no armistice. This is a fight to the death. One side will totally destroy the other." His reddened eyes looked longingly toward the narcotic in his glass. "Nazis or not, I'm a German. I don't want my country to be the one destroyed."

Slowly, he focused on Anders. "That's the question I need to ask you. I'm here because I'm a German. But why are you here, Professor Bergman? You are not German. Or English. Why are you going to build a fission reactor?"

"Because I'm a scientist," Anders said. The words came with great difficulty because they were not his words. But it was the answer that Bergman would have given.

They sat quietly, the silence filled by the mathematical precision of the Bach music. Werner Heisenberg stared at the wineglass. Anders stared at Heisenberg. Neither had a solution to the riddle that held them prisoners.

LONDON — *April 24*

Major Haller turned up the hot water tap, raising the temperature of his shower water until it was nearly scalding, and filling the glassed enclosure with steam. He groped for the soap, then lifted the pink-colored bar to his nose and inhaled the flowery fragrance.

"Bloody marvelous!" he screamed out into the bedroom. "What's keeping you?"

The glass door slid open cautiously, and Eleanor's towel-clad figure leaned into sight.

"Get in here," Haller ordered. "Let's see how long it takes your ivory ass to turn pink."

She waved ineffectively at the hot clouds, then pulled her head back out of the caldron. "Have you lost your compass, Major?" she screamed over the roar of the water. "It's hot enough in there to cook potatoes. I'd have no skin left."

"I want your body pressed against mine," he demanded.

"Then come to bed like a gentleman," Eleanor answered. "I can't make love while I'm being boiled like beef!"

The bathroom door slammed behind her, and Haller roared with delight. Eleanor was marvelous. The shower was marvelous. The hotel was marvelous. His senses were warming to the realization of being alive.

Only four of them were alive.

Of the twenty-five men who had climbed into the Horsa glider for the attack on the hydroelectric plant, only four had returned to England; Haller himself, his sapper, one of his riflemen, and one of the soldiers who had been with Sergeant Towers' group. The sergeant had been alive, too, when the remnants of the raid had reached their rendezvous near the wreckage of the glider. He had walked out of the forest carrying a wounded man across his back, not realizing the man was dead until he tried to make him comfortable next to the dying soldier that Haller had carried from the river. It was Towers who scratched the shallow grave in the snow where both men were left.

Then, late in the morning, as they were climbing a sloped meadow, a German patrol plane had caught them out in the open. With their woolen hats pulled down, and deafened by the sound of their own breathing, none of them had heard the engine until the bullets were kicking up the snow all around them. They dove for cover, watched the plane turn away, and then climbed slowly to their feet. But Sergeant Towers never moved. He lay perfectly still in snow that was turning crimson beneath his body. There wasn't even time for a shallow grave. The plane was turning back to begin another strafing run.

They marched all day, climbing higher into the mountain ridge that they had flown over in their glider. At night, they burrowed into the snow for protection from the wind and used flares to thaw some kindling so that they could build a fire. The next day they crested the range, and started down the western slope, twice rushing for the cover of the forests when German patrol planes approached. That night, they saw a blinking signal light from a farmhouse that had been described in their escape briefings. They moved forward cautiously and fell into the arms of the Norwegian Resistance force.

The men had hidden for three days in a root cellar beneath the farmhouse while enemy patrols scoured the countryside. The Germans, who had learned the number of men in the raiding party from two prisoners they had stood naked in the freezing river, claimed to be looking for seven Englishmen. Then they found the grave near the glider and narrowed their search to five. The local SS commander had taken twenty-five civilians as hostages and promised to kill them all unless the English commandos were handed over. Haller and his men told the Resistance leader that they would surrender to save the hostages, but he wouldn't hear of it. "We are all fighting the Germans," he explained, and then he loaded the attackers into truck beds and covered them with cut wood. They were driven north, away from the lands patrolled by the Germans.

For two weeks they were moved from house to house, delivered each morning into the keeping of a stone-faced farmer or trades-man who grunted when he received his instructions, and showed them silently to a cellar or an attic. They spent their days like prisoners, huddled together against the numbing cold and waiting for the tin of hot soup, and perhaps a few biscuits that would be delivered, usually by a weathered old woman, but occasionally by a pink-faced child. At night, they were moved again.

"Not a friendly lot, these Norskis," the sapper had said as they were being rushed out of a house into a waiting truck in the mid-dle of a frigid night.

"We're their death warrant," Haller had reminded his ragged band of survivors. "The only reason they take us is that they're more afraid of the Resistance than they are of the Nazis."

It was three weeks after the raid when they were delivered into the keeping of a leather-skinned fisherman who gave them a place at his table next to a roaring hearth.

"You lads must be damned important," he said in excellent En-glish while he served them a feast of pan-fried fish. "The Germans came through here the day before yesterday and turned the village inside out. Even climbed into the holds of the boats, and mucked about in fish up to their knees."

"Just a raiding party," Haller had explained, but his host knew it was more important than that. The Germans really wanted these men. They had forced the twenty-five hostages—ten of them women—to dig a mass grave. Then they had left them standing by the grave's edge for an entire day, waiting for the English soldiers to be handed over. At the end of the day they had methodically executed them, one after the other, with a bullet through the back of the neck.

The next night, they boarded a fishing boat and headed out into the fjord, flashing a light skyward every five minutes. Haller was the first to hear the sound of the airplane's engines.

"A Sunderland," he told the others, a smile showing through the overgrowth of beard as he recognized the distinctive sound of the flying boat's four radial engines. The soldiers scampered out on deck, searched the sky in the direction of the approaching sound, and cheered when they saw the flashes from the plane's signal lamp.

The Sunderland dropped down onto the choppy water and cruised up next to the fishing boat. They were transferred in a rubber raft, and four hours later they were lying in hospital beds at a navy base in the Orkney Islands.

Haller lost two toes to frostbite, the only permanent injury that any of the four sustained. The scars were the third combat decoration that had been affixed to his body since the beginning of the war, joining the round indentation in his left shoulder from a bullet he had taken at Dunkirk, and the colorless flesh on his forearms from a phosphorous grenade he had smothered during the Dieppe raid. He was sent to a hospital in Wales to rest and recuperate.

But Haller chose his own prescription for recovery, based less on rest than on frequent draughts of gin and the constant companionship of attractive women. He had begun with a sympathetic nurse at the hospital who climbed into his bed on the night of his arrival and was making daytime visits as well by the time he was discharged. There was a buxom naval coding clerk, who had the questionable fortune of being booked into the same compartment with Haller on the train returning to London. She had overstayed her pass for a night at the small village where the train made its first stop. And now there was Eleanor, the daughter of the proprietor of the first pub that Haller had visited upon his return to the city. They were beginning their third day in one of the most expensive hotel rooms on Park Lane. Haller had no idea how he was going to handle the bill.

"What's keeping you, love?" It was Eleanor, now wrapped in the quilted bedspread. "You didn't find someone else in there, did you?"

Haller laughed. "No one like you," he sang. "I'll be right there." And he turned to let the scalding water run down his back one last time.

The heat eased the torture of the cold, which still made the marrow of his bones feel like ice. The soap seemed to bleach away the persistent stain from the blood of his dead comrades. The touch of the women stirred all the senses that he had gladly let die during the weeks in Norway. And the gin? Sometimes it helped him forget about the Norwegian hostages in their mass grave.

"What's the matter?" Eleanor complained as Haller charged past her bed, his naked body still dripping. He tore open the door of the closet and lifted his freshly pressed uniform from its wooden hanger.

"Won't be more than an hour," he promised her. "Two at the most. It's a very important meeting."

"You're going out? Now?"

"Can't be helped," he said as he hopped in circles, trying to get his foot into the leg of his trousers. He stopped, posed on one leg like a flamingo when she pushed the quilt back from her breasts. "I really have to go," he insisted.

"I suppose the prime minister is waiting," Eleanor teased.

"No. It's General Eisenhower," Haller said, as he pulled the cardboard out of the folds of his shirt.

Eleanor laughed hysterically. "General Eisenhower," she mocked. "What would he want with the likes of you?"

"He needs me to tell him when to attack the Germans," Haller said. Eleanor was still laughing when he closed the door behind him.

General Bedell Smith apologized for Eisenhower's absence, mentioning the sudden changes that were inevitable in his schedule. The words were polite, but the meaning was clear. Some information simply fell beneath the supreme commander's threshold of interest. Discussions of German secret weapons fit into that category.

Air Marshal Ward delivered the latest intelligence on the German unmanned rockets. Frederick Lindemann spoke of the potential devastation of a uranium warhead. Then Haller delivered the best information they had on the progress of the German uranium bomb.

"We believe their heavy-water work is at a standstill. They were counting on the production of the Rjukan plant, and that won't be available to them for quite some time."

"A nice piece of work," Bedell Smith complimented, suddenly

realizing where he had heard the name of Thomas Haller. "That was your show, wasn't it?"

"There were several of us," Haller said, "but the important point is that heavy water was only half their effort. They're moving very seriously to graphite, which, we understand, is what you Americans are pursuing. They have some fine people, and God knows they have all the uranium and all the graphite they could possibly need. So, I'm afraid we can't rule out a German uranium bomb."

"Frightening!" General Smith allowed. "You think it's a real possibility?"

"Definitely," Haller answered. "It's simply a question of time."

Smith scribbled a few words and then closed his notebook. "Anything else I should pass on to the supreme commander?" he asked, as he rose to his feet and slipped his pen into his pocket.

Haller suddenly realized that secret weapons were below General Smith's threshhold of interest as well. He could hear Smith reciting the details of the day to his boss with a chuckled comment about "some Brits, and more of that big-bomb nonsense."

"Well," Haller suggested, "you might tell him that there's a time limit on how long he can take to win the war. Time is on the side of the Germans."

Smith's eyes flashed. The invasion of Europe had been considered for 1943, then planned for the spring of this year. But even now, Eisenhower and Montgomery weren't sure they had all the troops and all the supply ships they needed. There were hints of further postponements, and criticism was coming from every corner.

"General Eisenhower is well aware of the need for speed," Smith answered icily. "And if he weren't, there would certainly be enough people to remind him." He paused with his stare fixed on Haller. "But he is also acutely aware of what it takes to move an army from England to the coast of France. And what it takes to hold a beachhead. I think that has to be his prime concern, don't you?"

Air Marshal Ward and Frederick Lindemann nodded their agreement. Haller didn't.

"General Smith," he said, not faltering for an instant under the senior officer's gaze, "perhaps the supreme commander should know that once the Germans have their uranium bomb, there won't be any England to move an army from. Any of our lads who aren't on the Continent by that date, won't be going at all. I don't have the foggiest idea of how many ships or how many soldiers General Eisenhower thinks he needs. But if he doesn't get a few of our men to the German reactors before those reactors begin running, there won't be enough men in the world."

It was Smith who broke the eye contact. He looked from one of his guests to the other. Then he settled back into his chair and opened his notebook once again.

"How long?" he asked.

There was no response.

"How long have we got and where do we have to get to?"

"Less than a year," Haller answered quickly. "They'll demonstrate a graphite reactor in three months. It will take them six more to build one. Then another month—maybe two—to fabricate a bomb from the processed metal."

"Where?" Bedell Smith persisted.

"We're not sure. The development work is going on in Berlin. We know the separation plant is being built underground, near Celle. But we don't know where the reactor is."

"Can we find out?"

"We've got a man on the inside," Haller said. "That's how we know their timetable. He gave us the code name for the reactor, 'Castle Church,' but he doesn't know what it means. We'll be looking for 'Castle Church' in German radio traffic. That may give us a clue. And sooner or later our agent should be able to find out where it is."

"Let's hope it's sooner," Smith answered. He closed his notebook once more. "I'll talk to General Eisenhower as soon as he's free." He tapped the notebook against his hand. "This isn't going to make his job any easier, but I think he has to take it into account. And please, keep us up to the minute on anything you learn."

They all stood together, Haller braced at attention while the two senior officers shook hands. Then Bedell Smith turned to Haller. "I suppose you'll be going back in there to make contact with your agent."

"As soon as he's had time to learn something," the major answered.

"Don't push it," Smith advised. "You've already been through enough war for one lifetime."

Haller nodded his appreciation for the general's concern. "I've been working my way back slowly," he said. "In fact, now that we're finished, I'm going straight home to bed."

BERLIN — May 10

To escape from the terrifying loneliness, Anders hid behind his work.

During the days, he labored in the caverns beneath the Kaiser Wilhelm Institute, beginning the development of the graphite reactor. He covered the blackboards that were fastened to the whitewashed blocks of his office walls with the equations that described the chain reaction. Then he converted those equations from speculative theory into pounds of uranium, tons of graphite, and thousands of gallons of water per hour.

He carried his figures out of his office and down the intersecting passages to a room filled with Comptometers, where a dozen actuaries worked day and night clanking out probability curves. He rushed in and out of the chemistry laboratory where white-coated technicians analyzed and reanalyzed the purity of graphite samples and the composition of uranium ore. He sat through meetings where his colleagues explained the results of their work and fit their efforts like interlocking pieces into the giant puzzle.

He was always busy, and was always surrounded by people who would have gladly shared his fears. But still he was lonely, kept separate not so much by a language barrier or cultural chasm as by the fear that his next conversation, however brief, might be the one to give him away.

At night, he packed his work into a thick briefcase, secured by a heavy lock, and brought it home to protect against the emptiness of his house. Diebner had suggested an apartment in the institute. It was an academic environment that he would find familiar, and it was close to his work.

But Anders chose a small house just a few blocks from the institute that had become government property when it was seized from a Jewish family. "I like to work late," he explained. That much was true, although it omitted his fear of the free conversations among the scientists at the end of the workday, and his dread even of things that he might say in his sleep. It was exhausting to keep his defenses at the ready for all the minutes of the day. He couldn't carry his pretense into the evenings.

Yet even in his house he was afraid to be himself. The men whom he saw entering and leaving the attached apartment next door looked menacingly official. On two occasions, there were signs that his rooms had been searched—a book left opened to the wrong page, and papers stacked too neatly at the corner of his desk. So he lived the externals of his lie. He tuned to Swedish broadcasts on his radio and kept them playing in the background while he worked. He left correspondence forwarded from Stockholm and drafts of articles that Bergman had been reviewing in plain sight. Even the refrigerator was stocked with foods that Birgit had served him as being Bergman's favorites.

Anders' truly free moments were the brief walks he took in the mornings before the official car arrived at his door. The spring had come quickly after a winter of bitter cold, and it seemed that all the Berliners had burst out of their apartments at once. Men walked purposefully, but nodded cheerfully to the strangers they passed. Women chatted as they formed precise lines at the doorways of stores that were not yet opened. Somehow, the Berliners had found a way to turn their eyes away from the black scars that the bombers had inflicted throughout the city. Somehow, they had found the courage to ignore the soldiers who were at every street corner, holding their own country under siege.

In the warm spring mornings there was an atmosphere of normalcy, a zest for life despite the triumph of death that was closing in from all sides. Anders could breathe deeply and let his mind roam freely. He could enjoy his own thoughts, his own memories, safe from suspicious eyes. He could return the greetings of his neighbors without measuring his words and gestures, and without looking for puzzled expressions that would be the first hint of doubt. He could forget for the moment the horrors that his colleagues were envisioning in the basement bunkers and the plans he was developing to slow their progress and frustrate their efforts.

His first step had been to order the reevaluation of the work that had already been done on a graphite reactor. There had been a few murmurs of protest, but then a general appreciation that it was a prudent investment of time. How could Professor Bergman bring his genius to bear on a program until he fully understood it? Why plunge ahead only to have the master show them that their work had been flawed at its foundations? They anticipated losing perhaps a week. But Anders had stretched the review for three weeks, challenging even the simplest conclusions and demanding that they be proven again.

Then he had suggested a more detailed analysis of the materials they would use. All their conclusions, he reasoned, were based on the properties of the materials. They had to know with certainty exactly what those properties were.

He counted each moment of delay in the program as a significant victory. And he used the time for his own education. Like Bergman's, all Anders' work had been in theory. He had labored in an imaginary world where an equation that simulated an event was as important as the event itself. He had never built anything based on theory. But the German scientists had gone beyond theory. In solving the practical problems of material and density, of weight and size, they had crossed frontiers that he had not yet reached. They were ahead of him, even ahead of the Bergman work that he had committed to memory. He had to catch up before he could lead. And he needed to be accepted as the program's leader before he could aim it in the wrong direction.

Now he was about to impose another barrier to progress that

would delay the reactor certainly for weeks or perhaps even months. He had summoned the experts from the Krupp factories that supplied the graphite, and was about to tell them that all their work was flawed. He was going to demand that they begin again. He could visualize the outrage that would inflame the faces of Diebner, and Lauderbach and Heisenberg. He could hear the screamed protests of the Krupp people. His proposal would unite all the Germans against the presumptions of this foreign academician. There would be an awful moment when they would stand toe-to-toe and join battle. It would be a battle that he could not allow himself to lose.

They were all waiting when he entered the conference room adjacent to his office. The scientists, in their sweaters and lab coats, were down one side of a massive table, the darkly dressed businessmen down the other. Werner Heisenberg sat like a judge at the end of the table, lighting a new cigarette while the old one still burned in the ashtray at his elbow. It was Heisenberg that he would have to convince.

"We have to replace the graphite," he said, shaking his head in despair. Then he listened for the roar of protest that he felt would certainly follow. Instead, his announcement was received in stunned silence.

"It's a matter of uniformity," Anders continued, filling the quiet. "We can tolerate almost any known level of impurity. But we need absolute uniformity. Otherwise, there can be no predictability. And without predictability . . ." He waved his hands to indicate confusion while he groped for the German phrases that would indicate a reaction that was out of control.

"But that's impossible," one of the Krupp representatives finally challenged. "There can't be complete consistency. Even within the same vein of the raw coke there are wide variances . . ."

"And unnecessary," Lauderbach added, punching his fingertip against the tabletop. "In your own writings, Professor Bergman, you give no weight to uniformity."

Industrialists nodded in agreement with scientific arguments that they didn't understand, and scientists were suddenly sympathetic with the difficulties faced by the industrialists. They all began talking at once, and then from both sides of the table, hostile faces shouted toward Anders.

He turned away from the assault, stepped to the blackboard, and shattered a piece of chalk as he circled one of the equations. "And what value shall we put here?" he shouted back at his adversaries. "What value shall we use for the moderation effect?" He ran back to the table, lifted the reports of laboratory tests one at a time and tossed the pages toward his audience. "This one? Or perhaps this one?" Each graphite sample had demonstrated slightly different properties under test.

"Use an average!" Fichter shouted, and then he jumped to the blackboard and began plugging values into the probability calculations. "What difference can it make?" he concluded. "We are looking to the probabilities of neutron collisions across the entire reactor, not in each molecule. It's just as you wrote five years ago, Professor Bergman. What has changed?"

Anders strode back to the blackboard and took up the argument, erasing figures and symbols and substituting other figures and symbols. "And what good is an average value here, at the control rod, if the actual value is this?"

There were screams of disapproval from the scientists, who roared their disagreements as they pointed toward offending equations. But Anders battled back, compromising the theories of Bergman, with which he was more familiar than anyone in the room, in order to reach a conclusion that Bergman would never have supported.

The industrialists watched the tennis match in awe, their uncomprehending faces swinging from Anders to his opponents and then back to Anders as each took his turn with the chalk. They watched the equations as if they were the notations of a chess match, meaningless to those unable to visualize the broad concept of the board. Kurt Diebner turned from side to side as well, looking from Anders to his own scientists and then to Heisenberg, to see which way the master was tilting.

Heisenberg alone remained motionless, the soft blue eyes fixed on Anders. He was evaluating the arguments not in their mathematical perfection, but in the impact each point seemed to have on Anders' expression. The equations could give him facts. It was in Anders' eyes that he searched for truth. And Anders could feel his gaze. From his position at the head of the table, he could look on all the Germans as if they were characters on a stage. Heisenberg commanded his attention because, in all the hysteria and shouting, he alone was calm and silent.

"This is a fraud," Anders heard, and he swung his attention to Lauderbach, who was becoming red-faced as he stuck his finger into one of the formulas. "This is not what you wrote, Professor Bergman. It is completely inconsistent with your writings. Why have you reversed your theories?"

"It is a refinement," Anders defended, recognizing that his position was cracking like old plaster.

"More than a refinement," a voice from the group challenged.

"Much more," Lauderbach pressed, sensing he had found a rallying point for the other Germans. "It is the complete negation of your whole approach to graphite moderators. You bring us no clarity or insight. If we take this path, you will bring us nothing but endless delays."

All pretense of academic debate had vanished. The Germans had broken through his defenses and were mounting a blitzkreig. Anders' hopes of delaying the German reactor were about to be routed. In desperation, he raised his hands and shouted above the din.

"Gentlemen . . . gentlemen . . . it is your program. Your reactor. It is your decision."

Lauderbach seemed startled by the suddenness of the surrender.

"I came as your guest," Anders continued. "I have studied your approach, and I have given you my opinion."

"An erroneous opinion," Fichter chided.

"An honest opinion," Anders corrected. "But the choice is yours. You can ignore my warning and build your reactor with the material you have on hand. It will be completely uncontrollable. You will have to shut down the moment it goes critical. So, you will have to start all over again, perhaps after a year of failure.

"Or, you can take the time now to assure your success. I recommend the latter as the prudent course. But if you choose to go

ahead with the present materials, you have my best wishes. I'll
return immediately to Sweden where I won't be in your way."

"That won't be necessary." It was Heisenberg, who had finally
broken his icy silence. He crushed his cigarette into the overflowing ashtray, stood, and walked away from the blackboards that had
been the center of the argument toward boards on the opposite side
of the room that had gone unnoticed. He tapped his knuckles
against one of the equations.

"Right here. You've revised your theories of cross sections,
haven't you, Professor Bergman?"

Anders sensed a trap about to spring. "Revised from what?"

"From what you held four or five years ago."

"Of course my ideas have changed. Doesn't our knowledge
grow?"

Heisenberg sneered. "Not here in Germany, where we have
burned all the books," he said, glancing back at his colleagues. "I
think we are arguing what Professor Bergman knew five years ago
in opposition to what he knows right now. I prefer his current
thinking."

"But the loss of time," Kurt Diebner pleaded.

Heisenberg tapped again on the blackboard and then pointed
across the room at the equations that had been hotly debated.
"Professor Bergman has shown us that what we are doing now
won't work. We have no choice."

"What will Reichsfuehrer Himmler say?" Diebner worried.

"Himmler has no choice, either. He'll get his reactor much
faster if we do it right than if we lose a year doing it wrong."

"But this equation is wrong," Lauderbach insisted, trying to re-
gain the advantage that was vanishing in Heisenberg's comments.

"It's wrong if you start there," Heisenberg admitted, pointing to
the blackboard that Lauderbach was fondling. "But that's where
our guest was five years ago." Heisenberg touched the board he
was standing near. "This is where Professor Bergman is now. If
you start here, I think you'll see that he is correct."

Diebner searched for a consensus. Bergman and Heisenberg
seemed confident in their position. The rest of the scientists, so
aggressive only moments before, were now uncertain. He looked

to the Krupp representatives who were plainly stunned by the sudden turn of events that had just occurred. "How long will it take?" he demanded.

The ranking executive patted his neck with an oversized handkerchief as he calculated. "To return all the graphite, grind it, and then reprocess it in small batches . . . then randomly mix the batches and reprocess, to let's say one-tenth percent maximum variation?" He looked toward Anders for confirmation.

"One-hundredth percent," Anders answered.

The Krupp man seemed shocked as he balled up the handkerchief and then rolled it in the palms of his hands. "Two months," he ventured.

Diebner gasped.

Perhaps less, the executive answered, with a further allocation of labor and additional charges.

"Anything," Diebner promised.

"Then, maybe a month," the Krupp official conceded, already calculating the enormous profit to be made from processing the same material over again.

BERLIN — *May 13*

The double doors were thrown open on a darkened office, vaguely illuminated by a single point of light in the distance. Diebner stared momentarily, then made out the hands that were folded on the desk. Cautiously, he stepped into the silent space and was immediately conscious of the explosions that his leather heels caused on the hardwood floor. He shifted his weight to his toes and moved softly for fear of disturbing the pale face that was barely visible in the yellow glow of the desk lamp.

Heinrich Himmler raised his head and the light flashed from his rimless glasses. But still, the features remained indistinct. Diebner could see the hands and a soft chin that seemed to have no mouth, and the two burning electric lamps where the eyes should be.

He stepped onto a carpet, then moved the last dozen paces toward the desk, his fear mounting with each step he took. He could make out the white linen cuffs above the folded hands that could deliver death with a gesture. He noticed the reflections from the ravens and the lightning bolt insignia that marked the uniforms of the torturers and the assassins. But even when he reached the edge of the desk, there was still no face.

Diebner snapped his heels together and thrust his right arm out in a Roman greeting. "Heil Hitler!"

There was no reply. Just the sound of breathing.

"Good afternoon, Reichsfuehrer Himmler," he tried. "It is good of you to see me."

"You are behind schedule." The voice from the darkness was without feeling, metallic as if reproduced through a cheap speaker.

"Unfortunately yes, Reichsfuehrer. But happily, to good purpose." There was only silence, so he continued. "Professor Bergman has asked us to pause so that we can correct . . . certain inaccuracies. Overall, it promises an enormous saving of time."

"Saving?" The word sounded curious rather than critical. "Aren't we reprocessing some of the graphite?"

"Yes, Reichsfuehrer."

"How much are we reprocessing?"

Diebner was afraid to disguise the truth. "All of it," he admitted.

"Saving?" the voice wondered aloud. "And the time?"

"One month," Diebner said boldly, and then less declaratively, "not more than two."

"And this is the second schedule," the voice recalled. "The first schedule is also months behind, I seem to remember."

"It is awaiting the arrival of the heavy water," Diebner said, reciting the official position.

The hands moved, and manicured fingers reached out and drew a file into the pool of light from the lamp. But still the face remained in the darkness, animated only by the flickering reflections across the surface of the glasses.

"You agree with this . . . reprocessing?"

"Most certainly, Reichsfuehrer."

"But your colleagues disagree. Lauderbach . . . Fichter."

Diebner was stunned to realize that Himmler had infiltrated his staff. Did he know everything? The open disrespect of some of the scientists. The mockery of Nazi doctrines. Diebner hoped that the trembling in his knees wasn't obvious to the reichsfuehrer.

"Heisenberg agrees with me," he defended.

Himmler ignored the prestigious name. "Lauderbach is outraged," he countered. "He isn't even certain that this man is actually Professor Bergman."

"Absurd," Diebner ridiculed.

"Then you are certain," Himmler's voice prompted.

"Of course, Reichsfuehrer."

Suddenly the face moved into the light, small, soft, with a mouth that would be nearly invisible were it not outlined with a mustache. Narrow eyes appeared over the tops of the glasses. "Then you will certainly have nothing to fear from a little test."

"A test?" Diebner heard his voice crack in apprehension.

"Yes. A test of Bergman's identity. And, therefore, also a test of your judgment."

Diebner forced down the nausea that was beginning to bubble up from his stomach. "I'm afraid I don't understand."

"A scientist unknown to any of our people joins us after a visit to England. The first decision he makes puts us months behind schedule. And then one of our scientists suggests that the man's work isn't authentic. That perhaps he is a British substitute for Professor Bergman. I think you can appreciate my concerns."

"But, Reichsfuehrer—" Diebner's words were cut off by the raising of one of the hands from the surface of the desk.

"The fuehrer is counting on this program. I think you can imagine, Doctor Diebner, how disappointed I would be if you should fail our fuehrer."

Diebner thought he was going to wet his trousers. "Whatever you suggest, Reichsfuehrer Himmler."

The face faded back into the darkness, leaving just the hands that rested on the file.

"I suggest that we make certain of this man's identity. In fact, I have an appropriate test in mind. One that I think you will enjoy . . . assuming that your protégé passes."

"Most certainly," Diebner said. "And may I ask when this test will occur?"

"Very soon," said the voice. And then, barely audibly, "Heil Hitler!"

Diebner clicked his heels and turned away smartly. His pace quickened as he rushed for the door.

NORDHAUSEN — May 20

The day had begun badly.

They started from Berlin early in the morning, Kurt Diebner driving the Mercedes sedan, Anders beside him, and Werner Heisenberg lounging in the backseat. Just after they escaped the city, they ran into the smoldering rubble of the night's bombing. The Lancasters, flying blindly in the dark, had wandered far from their target, and had simply disgorged better than 100 tons of high explosives. Sleeping beneath them was a grid of small houses, surrounding a stone church. It was the stones of the church and the bricks of the houses that were strewn across the roadway.

Diebner had stopped at a soldier's command, cursing the delay as he made a great show of examining his watch. He demanded to see the ranking officer, and then insisted on an escort to lead him around the town on back roads. But as the single motorcycle pulled into position, he noticed that his passenger seat was empty.

Anders had climbed from the car in a trance as if hypnotized by the gray smoke that wisped above the debris. He was walking away from the road, into the lines of broken brick that marked what had been streets only hours ago. Ahead of him, people were digging frantically, dragging rafters and tossing bricks aside as they attempted to reach a sound that someone thought might be a voice.

But Anders wasn't rushing to help. Instead, he walked in the deliberate half step of a funeral procession, his head turning as if to look into the windows of shops that were no longer there.

"Where's he going?" Diebner snapped at Heisenberg. The scientist didn't answer. Instead, he opened the back door of the sedan and started after Anders.

It had been a street, and there had been shops. Anders could see a charred window frame, collapsed onto the pieces of what had once been a china serving on display. There were hardware implements behind another wooden window frame. And there had been apartments above the shops. Bed frames and headboards, tables and chairs had fallen through into the stores below, and then the roof rafters and tiles had settled in a new layer on top.

The buildings had been flattened until the roofs were only up to Anders' waist, the brick facades blown out into the craters that an instant before had been a paved street. And then there had been fire, probably ignited spontaneously by the heat of the explosion and then fed by gas seeping from the stoves and the space heaters. There were still pale flames dancing across some of the broken wooden beams, and columns of smoke-marked infernos still burning beneath the rubble.

"Help me," a small woman begged, but Anders passed without seeming to notice. She was trying to lift a rafter that was pinned under tons of broken mortar. There was no hint of life anywhere in the pile.

"Professor Bergman."

Anders turned to find Heisenberg by his side. "Where are the people?" he asked.

Heisenberg closed his eyes and shook his head. "Don't look. There is nothing to save. Flesh burns away faster than stone."

"There are no people?"

"Just the dead. There is no point in digging them up just to bury them again."

Anders turned slowly, looking out to every side. "What was this?" he asked.

"A town. I forget the name. Most of the people worked in the city. Government workers, I suppose."

"My God," was all that Anders could manage in his disbelief. "They never knew what was happening," Werner Heisenberg promised. "It was over as soon as it started. The English drop their bombs all at once. The last one leaves the plane only a few seconds after the first one. So no one had any time to be frightened. The whole place . . . just exploded."

Anders nodded. He felt Heisenberg's hand on his arm, and he allowed himself to be steered back toward the car where Diebner was waving frantically.

Diebner began cursing the British as soon as the car was moving again. "Barbarism," he hissed, and he speculated on the savage joy of the English bombadiers as they locked the sleeping village in their cross hairs. "They won't challenge the Luftwaffe. They won't attempt to fight their way through to military targets. Instead, they slaughter defenseless villages."

But Anders wasn't listening. His senses were still filled with the smell of smoke and with the screams of the rescuers tossing hopelessly through the shattered stones to retrieve the splinters of furniture and the other relics of human life. He still saw destruction reaching out in every direction. And this was, what? A hundred tons of nitrates? That pitifully small cargo had generated a shock that had shaken century-old buildings to dust. It had generated heat that had flashed timbers as if they were kindling, and consumed oxygen until not a single cell was left living.

The cargo he was building would pack thousands of tons of destruction into a single warhead. Its shock wave would rage like a storm over hundreds of miles. And the heat! There were no instruments on Earth that could even measure its intensity.

"They'll pay," Diebner was promising. "For every German, we'll kill a hundred of them. For this village, we'll level a city . . . their entire country."

"Herr Diebner, please shut up!" It was Heisenberg's voice from the backseat, speaking softly, more in disgust than in anger. Diebner glared back through the rearview mirror.

"Our guest comes from a country that isn't given to killing," Heisenberg explained. "I think he's had all the slaughter he can handle for one day."

They continued in silence, and after a few moments, in the freshness of the spring countryside, the gruesome carnage was left behind. Anders' head cleared, and the gradually became aware of the blessed quiet and the cold smell of fresh, uncontaminated air.

They slowed as they passed through villages, small clusters of sloping houses that faced the road, with broad fields rolling away into the hills behind them. People looked up to stare curiously at the car, and then turned back to their chores.

"It's a beautiful country," Anders said absently.

"A great country," Diebner corrected, as if beauty were not enough. "In a few minutes, you will see just how great Germany will be."

The road signs announced Nordhausen, but before they reached the city, Diebner turned off the main road and followed a narrow macadam path to the north. He slowed as they approached a wire fence that cut like a scar through freshly planted fields, and rolled to a stop at a guardhouse. A black-uniformed officer stepped out to greet them, scrutinized the papers that Diebner presented, and then waved them ahead.

They drove cautiously past a barricade of sandbags, topped with another row of coiled wire. And then they swung into a parking area that was covered with a netting of foliage. A small, concrete blockhouse was the only structure they could see in any direction.

"Where are we?" Anders asked.

Diebner smiled broadly. "In the future, Professor Bergman. In the present, you see the English and the Americans laying waste to our country. Now I want you to see the future."

"In a blockhouse?" Heisenberg said cynically.

Diebner nodded, still smiling at his delicious secret. "Just follow me, gentlemen. You will see."

The blockhouse covered the top of a shaft and held the machinery that raised and lowered a mine elevator. While Anders and Heisenberg leaned over the railing to peer into the bottomless pit, another SS officer rechecked Diebner's papers. Then they stepped into the mesh-enclosed car and began their descent toward the center of the Earth.

Diebner shouted above the rattle of the guide rails and the rush of wind around the falling elevator. "This is a personnel entrance. There is a railroad entrance nearly two miles from here. And then there is another equipment entrance in Nordhausen. The city underground is bigger than the city on the surface." He was as proud of the achievement as if he had built it himself.

"An underground city?" Heisenberg asked, looking up at the spot of light that was disappearing at the top of the shaft.

"An industrial city," Diebner corrected. "A new Ruhr, built underground, completely safe from air attack. Even if the Allies could find it, there is nothing they could do about it. The fuehrer ordered it built in 1941. It has been operating for nearly six months, building weapons that the Allies can't even imagine."

"How deep are we going?" Heisenberg begged, realizing that they had been in free-fall for nearly a minute.

"Three hundred feet, here. One hundred twenty feet at the other elevator. There are over a thousand men working below us. And then there are the managers and the engineers."

The elevator slowed and dropped into a pool of light. When the wire gate swung open, they entered a concrete office, totally sealed except for the whistling air that was forced in through louvers high on the walls. Once again, Diebner presented his credentials to an SS guard who made a confirming telephone call, and then slid open a steel door.

They were greeted by a flood of blue electric light, and the screech of metal being cut by machine tools. Then they stepped into Diebner's future, an underground factory half a mile wide that converged to a horizon that seemed miles away.

The floor and the walls were white concrete, and the roof, nearly forty feet above, was the uneven gray of freshly cut rock. Wire-encased lights blazed in perfectly even rows along the ceiling, separated by the rails of overhead cranes that merged like the tracks in a switchyard.

They began walking, and with each step they took, the products of the future began to take shape. Cut strips of shiny metal were drawn past teams of welders and emerged from the showers of dancing sparks in the shapes of wings and tails. Deafening rivet guns fastened thin steel plates to gracefully curved frames, yielding the cylindrical shapes of aircraft bodies. Thin, colored wires were bound together in cable trunks, connecting the sockets that would hold the glass tubes of radios and instruments. Small pumps were connected to power hydraulic systems, and servos were fitted into the levered arms of control surfaces.

Everywhere there was frantic activity, directed by voices that shouted in the dozens of languages of all the European people. The workers, intense in their efforts, were the slaves gathered from conquered nations that reached from the Atlantic to the Urals. Overseeing each group was a conquering soldier, armed with the instruments of authority, the billy club and the bludgeon.

Diebner stopped his tour at every station to gloat with pride as he explained each step in the process. The guidance controls were the most precise ever conceived; so accurate that they could lead a plane to a specific street corner within a target city. The radars were incredible, capable of detecting the movements of an enemy plane within a knot of speed and a degree of direction, and instantly calculating the lead angles for firing. All the scientific knowledge of Europe had been gathered in one place and focused on a single purpose—the annihilation of the Allies.

In the blinding glare of the overhead lights, the cowering workers suddenly seemed like shadows and the deafening noise became a chorus of anvils. They had descended into a Nibelheim, where a race of slaves was fashioning, from the materials of the earth, the riches that would give power to the evil dwarf. Madness had risen beyond legend and become reality.

They reached the end of one production line where dozens of small, winged craft stood in a row like vultures perched together on a dead branch. "You have heard of jet propulsion?" Diebner challenged, pointing up to the long thin pipe that sat atop the plane's rudder. They had, as a futuristic type of engine that required no propeller or other drive mechanics. "We have perfected it. These craft fly so fast that nothing the Allies have can catch them. They fly to an exact target and then suddenly dive to deliver their bomb."

"There is no pilot," Heisenberg added, noting the absence of a cockpit. Diebner simply laughed in response.

"These will be attacking England in a matter of days. Yet even before they are launched, we have already made them obsolete. Look over here!"

He turned them into another area where enormous, projectile-shaped air bodies were lying on their sides. "Rockets," he announced in near-reverent tones. "They climb to a height of sixty miles. Then they plunge back down through the atmosphere at nearly two thousand miles an hour. There is no conceivable defense. The enemy will be helpless."

Anders hunched his shoulders in Bergman's familiar posture of indifference. "And then the Allies will invent one that falls at three thousand miles per hour for which you will have no defense. It's a lunatic's game. It can never end."

"It will end," Diebner contradicted, "and very soon. These weapons will soon be in the hands of our soldiers. Then we will be on the offensive."

Heisenberg's glance swung slowly, taking in the expanse of the underground factory. It was a huge cavern, with frantic activity spreading to every corner. But at the end of the lines, the output was hardly enough to turn the tide of a war. Heisenberg could count the number of pilotless bombers and rockets, and there were only a few rows of the silvery fighters with the jet engines under their wings. "It may not be enough," he whispered.

"It doesn't have to be," Diebner teased. He enjoyed the confusion in the faces of the two physicists. "There are more factories just like this. Three more, working day and night, and still another one that is nearing completion. All producing weapons that are beyond belief."

He noticed that Anders seemed stunned by the news, his jaw slackening as he looked again at the size of the underground city. "A great country, Professor Bergman," he said, reminding the men of his comment during the drive. "A victorious country. I wanted you to see this so there will be no doubt as to who is going to win this war. I wanted you to know that you are on the winning side."

Diebner gathered them under his arms as he started back toward the elevator, pointing out once again the wonders that were surrounding them. But Anders was sickened by what he had already heard. All the scientists and all the engineers of Germany had moved underground, abandoning the sunlight to the Allied planes. Beneath the earth, they were fashioning a new generation of weapons, to be built by an endless supply of slaves. Far from being beaten, they were fawning over their brainchildren, eager to turn them loose on the best that the Allied scientists had been able to develop. The war wasn't nearly over. It was simply entering a new phase that promised to be infinitely more destructive than the war he had visited just hours earlier in the small town at the edge of Berlin.

"Congratulations, Professor Bergman," Heisenberg mocked. "You have chosen the winning side."

Anders shook his head. "There can be no winners. When the scientists are working for the generals, all there can be is more destruction."

STOCKHOLM — *June 10*

Birgit was suddenly aware that she was being watched again. And with the realization came an awful fear that something was terribly wrong inside of Germany.

Months earlier, when she had sent Bergman's expression of renewed interest to Kurt Diebner, the Germans had closed in around her. A balding man in a long leather coat had followed her from Bergman's laboratory, then reappeared the next morning at the small café where she took her coffee. He showed up at several points of her daily itinerary, and within a few days had become her constant companion. Then, when Anders was in Denmark, there had been a clumsy attempt to confirm that Bergman was really out of the country. A young man who identified himself as an editor for a scientific magazine had shown up at her office bearing a manuscript that he claimed Bergman had submitted.

"If the Professor could spare me just a few moments of his time, I'm sure we can clear up these inconsistencies," the editor tried.

Birgit knew that Bergman had no interest in the article's subject, and no respect for the journal. "I'm sorry, but the professor is out of the country and cannot be reached," she answered truthfully. But even though she was pleased to have seen through the ruse, she was frightened by its implications. Someone was less than certain that the Bergman who had presented himself in Denmark was authentic.

Her office telephone had been tapped, a fact discovered by a telephone repairman who had answered her complaint about a noisy line. This had made her suspicious of the clicks on her home telephone, and led her to locate a tap that she left in place, feeding her listeners a steady diet of technical conversations and the delivery orders that she called into her grocer.

But then the man in the leather coat had disappeared. Birgit wasn't sure exactly when. She had simply become aware that she hadn't seen him in days. The tap disappeared from her phone. Weeks went by without any unexpected inquiries as to Professor Bergman's whereabouts. In the privacy of her apartment, she smiled at the thought that Anders had been accepted for Bergman. And that triumph was confirmed in her office by the regular correspondence she began to receive from Germany, signed with Bergman's careful signature.

They had expected the Germans to intercept all of Bergman's mail, and the correspondence Birgit received, through a Danish mail drop that the Germans had established, had certainly been scrutinized. The hair she had taught Anders to seal under the envelope flap was missing from all the letters she received. But nothing about their guest or his letters seemed to have aroused their suspicions. Coded sequence numbers showed that nothing was being withheld, including the letter that had told her that the German scientists were working in Berlin and revealed the code name "Castle Church" for the reactor.

It figured that the Germans were also reading the correspondence that she was forwarding through the same mail drop. So she sent letters addressed to Bergman from colleagues all over the world, along with the huge stacks of journals that he received on a regular basis. As she brought each package to the post office, she smiled at the frustration of the German security officers who would have to wade through hundreds of pages of material that they couldn't begin to understand. And in her own disdain for the Nazis' simple precautions, she realized how thoroughly she and Anders had succeeded.

And then, without warning, they were watching her again.

On two consecutive mornings, she bumped into a bespectacled little man by the open baskets that served as mailboxes for the tenants in her office building. Birgit had offered a friendly greeting and been startled by the perfunctory, evasive response. Later, she realized that the same man was lingering at the windows of the shops across the street. She watched him carefully as he waited for the arrival of the mail man and followed him into the building.

Birgit placed her own arrangement of business and personal letters in the laboratory's mail basket. The gnomelike figure followed the postal delivery and, when he left, Birgit's letters had been rearranged.

It didn't make sense to her. The Germans had complete control of all correspondence between Bergman and the institute when it passed through their Danish mail drop. What were they looking for? What did they expect to find in Bergman's other correspondence?

When she went to Bergman's house to retrieve some of his papers, she found more evidence of their presence. The rolltop desk was continually sticking in its track, so she had gotten into the habit of leaving it open the width of her fingertips. As she struggled to free it, she realized that someone had slammed it tight. She searched carefully and found that the drawer where Bergman kept his personal correspondence was badly disarranged. Apparently it wasn't Bergman, the scientist, that they were interested in, but rather Bergman, the man. For some reason, the Germans had suddenly become interested in his personal life.

Then, as she left the house, a car had fallen in behind her. Birgit made a few careful turns; enough to assure that the car was attached to her, but nothing sudden that might signal that she had caught on. She was followed back into the city, right up to the front door of her own apartment.

Why, she wondered? They could find her at the laboratory every day. Why should they lock on to her just because she visited Bergman's house?

Suddenly, she wanted help. She needed to talk with Haller, or with one of his people who would know how to read the tea leaves. She needed to know why she was being watched. But precisely because she was being watched, help was out of the question. Any link, no matter how fragile, between Bergman's office and British agents, would indict Anders and quickly uncover the fraud. So she set the blinds in her office windows to the agreed-upon pattern that would warn Haller's people that they shouldn't attempt to contact her.

Then the answer came.

Birgit remembered Paul Rasmussen's name as soon as she heard it over the telephone. He was one of the German physicists, a minor luminary whom Bergman had once described as "gifted in analyzing the obvious." They had exchanged letters several years back, his a congratulatory note in fawning phrases over one of Bergman's articles, and Bergman's response a simple acknowledgment.

He called in the morning and explained that he had just arrived from Germany for some business dealings in Stockholm. "I have been working with Professor Bergman. Such an honor. His insights are staggering." Then he got to the purpose of his call. He had some messages to deliver. He wondered if he might stop by at the laboratory?

Birgit was bewildered. Nowhere in their plan was there any provision for Anders to contact her. To the contrary, they had all agreed that any such attempt would be ridiculously dangerous. Rasmussen was a fake. Or, if he were genuine, then something was happening in Germany that was so important that Anders had decided to risk his entire mission to get the information to her.

Rasmussen wore a near-black, three-button suit with a high boiled collar that was long out of style. He chose a straight-back chair and sat on its edge, his knees together and a hat resting in his lap. Birgit made coffee, and joined in small talk about the challenge of working with a genius like Bergman while she waited for Rasmussen to find his way to his subject.

"There was a woman that Professor Bergman originally hoped to bring to Germany," Rasmussen said, as a jarring change of topic. He paused, expecting Birgit to fill in the name. Instead, she feigned surprise.

"We are anxious to locate her and extend our invitation," Rasmussen continued. "Professor Bergman speaks of her so often."

He was proving his own lie. In their briefings, Haller, Anders, and she had agreed that Anders would make no mention of Magda. If asked, he would simply refer to an unfortunate end to the affair. In order to cover Bergman's disappearance, Birgit had told Magda that Nils had decided to work in England. And when her letters had gone unanswered, Magda had sadly gathered her things and returned to her family home in the country. There was no possible way of introducing her into Bergman's fabricated new life.

"Since you work so closely with Professor Bergman," Rasmussen persisted, when his obvious question had gone unanswered, "we thought you might know where she can be reached. Naturally, we could simply ask him to extend the invitation directly. But with my schedule bringing me to Stockholm, we thought we might arrange a surprise for him."

In Birgit's mind, the pieces of the puzzle locked together. The Nazis were beginning to have doubts about the foreign genius they had invited into their most secret program. They needed to find someone who could positively identify Nils Bergman.

That was the reason for the mail watch at the institute and then the search of Bergman's private correspondence. They were trying to identify Magda, and that was why she had been followed. They were watching Bergman's house, waiting for his mistress to appear. The people at the house weren't the same ones that were covering the laboratory, so they didn't recognize Bergman's assistant. They simply covered any woman who had free entry to the house.

"Perhaps it sounds childish to you," Rasmussen said, with his face coloring in embarrassment.

"Where is Professor Bergman?" Birgit asked, testing her adversary.

Rasmussen rearranged his homburg on his lap. "In Germany, of course. But I can't be more specific. I'm sure you understand. With the war . . . secrecy."

She understood. They couldn't simply give Magda an address and ask her to stop by. She would have to be taken into Germany. And they couldn't let someone who knew the location of their atomic research leave Germany. They couldn't risk having that information fall into the hands of the Allies. So, Rasmussen was just a messenger; someone assigned to deliver Bergman's mistress into the hands of people who knew where the professor was working. His problem was that the German agents who had been sent ahead hadn't been able to find her. In fact, if Rasmussen had exhausted his questions, they didn't even know her name.

But they would, and probably very soon. When they despaired of Bergman's home and his workplace, they would widen their search. There were stores where Bergman shopped. There were his physician and his dentist. There were repairmen who worked on his house. There were hundreds of people like Mats, the proprietor of his favorite restaurant, who had seen Bergman and Magda together and who had been introduced to her by name.

Of course they would find her. It was only a question of time. And when they did she would rush into Germany and answer the one question that had brought spies to her country and Paul Rasmussen to her desk. "Was this really Nils Bergman?"

Magda was the one person on Earth who would know the answer in an instant. Somehow, Birgit knew, she had to keep the Germans from finding her.

"I may be able to help," she finally decided.

Rasmussen reached for the briefcase by his heel.

Then she added, "Perhaps you can call again tomorrow."

He looked confused, his hand poised over the open flap of the briefcase, uncertain whether it should continue reaching for a pen and paper.

"I should determine whether the lady wants to be identified," Birgit reasoned.

Rasmussen nodded. "Yes, most certainly. That would be the proper way." He lifted the briefcase under one arm and held the homburg cradled in the other. "This is most kind of you." He bowed stiffly from the waist. "I will call again tomorrow. And thank you for your trouble."

She followed Rasmussen to the door and then stepped to the window so that she could watch him walk toward the corner. When he had disappeared, Birgit looked carefully at the shops across the street. There was no sign of the man who awaited each day's postal delivery.

She reached for the window shade, but then pulled her hand away. It was too dangerous to make contact with the British when the Germans had agents covering her movements. But it was even more dangerous to do nothing. Once the Nazis found Magda, Anders was as good as dead. She paced the room weighing her alternatives. And as she argued the sparse choices that were left to her, Birgit realized that the walls she had constructed to protect herself from involvement were crumbling around her.

She had blamed herself for Gunther. If only she hadn't involved herself with Sara, Gunther wouldn't have been killed. But could she have protected her own peace by ignoring the pain of another? And if she had, what kind of peace would she have been protecting?

She had blamed herself for the destruction of Nils Bergman. He would still be alive if she had let him join the Germans. But could she have ignored the millions of other lives that his work would have put in jeopardy?

Then she had determined to be nothing more than Karl Anders' teacher and correspondent, a simple carrier of information between him and his British controllers. But now she was facing choices that would determine whether he would live or die.

She wanted to run, not from any danger threatening her, but from the responsibility of involvement. If she made the decision, then Anders' life was in her hands. To shore up her barriers, she wanted to set the window shades. She wanted to summon Haller and his people and let them decide how to keep the Germans away from Magda. And if they made the wrong decision, then Anders was another one of their victims, not another one of hers.

But she couldn't call them. Simply by being seen with them she would link Bergman's imposter to the enemy and write his death sentence. She couldn't call for the help she desperately wanted. She couldn't avoid the possibility of making another fatal error.

When Paul Rasmussen called the next day, she alone would put into motion the forces that would either save Anders or destroy him.

Birgit left the shades just as they were when she closed the office and went home for the night.

LONDON — *June 12*

Haller was in the second row, one of the staff officers seated behind Air Marshal Ward. To either side of Ward, in chairs pulled up to the sprawling conference table, were ranking officers of other British services, as well as the top commanders of American, Canadian, French, and Polish forces. Flanking Haller, in a second ring that surrounded the table, were adjutants and aides in almost regimental strength. All were leaning toward the words of an American colonel from Eisenhower's staff, who was standing in front of a giant map of Normandy. All were slowly becoming aware that the great invasion they called Overlord was in serious trouble.

They had brought the euphoria of Eisenhower's press releases into the room with them. Twice a day, for the past week, the Supreme Headquarters for the Allied Expeditionary Forces (SHAEF) had published figures on the number of troops and the tons of material that had been put ashore at Normandy. News releases tallied the number of tanks on the ground and planes in the air, the explosive equivalent of artillery rounds fired and bombs dropped, the gallons of fuel burned by the troop ships and cargo ships that were stretched bow to stern from southern England to northern France. The impression was of a tidal wave that had swept in from the Atlantic and was rolling in full fury all the way to the Alps. Now, at the end of the American colonel's pointer, they could see exactly how much of Fortress Europa the Allies had managed to conquer.

"Caen," the American said, pointing to a dot at the east end of the invasion beaches, "remains in German hands. Without it, we can't bring our forces from the beachhead around toward the east." The pointer moved. "Saint-Lô has yet to be taken. It remains a danger to the flank of the Utah force that is moving toward Cherbourg. And here, in the middle, we are still having a hell of time getting off the beaches."

The map was frightening. The British and Canadians had broken inland at the easternmost point of the invasion, only to be stopped in their tracks at Caen. The Americans at the western end had moved inland, and were marching west toward the port of Cherbourg. But with each mile they advanced, the German force on their left flank became more dangerous. In the center, the invaders had hardly gotten out of the water. At some points, the strip of land they held was less than a mile wide.

"If the Germans break through in the center . . ." It was the beginning of a question by the ranking British naval officer.

"We will continue to land troops and material at both flanks," the American answered.

"And if the Germans attack out of Caen?" asked an American rear admiral.

"We think we can hold our position," the colonel said confidently. And then, in a softer voice, "Or, we can transfer troops over to the Utah side to strengthen our hold on Cherbourg, SHAEF regards capturing and holding Cherbourg as the absolute minimum for the invasion. We need a major port to build up our forces."

There was an irreverent snicker from a Polish officer that faded into the solemn silence of the room. The invasion had already disembarked enormous forces on a beachhead that the Allies might not be able to hold. If they abandoned those beaches, what forces would be left to bring in through the port of Cherbourg?

"What reserves do the Germans have?" an American air corps

colonel asked. It was the most threatening question. The Allied and German forces at Normandy had reached a standoff. With the Allies constantly landing men and material, it seemed that the battle should inevitably tip in their favor. But if the Germans could bring up reserve forces quickly, then they would seize the upper hand.

The American colonel brought the tip of his pointer to an area just north of Paris. "Our best information is that there are two panzer divisions here, halfway between Normandy and Pas de Calais."

"Whose divisions?" an English field officer fired.

The American acknowledged the question with a nod. "Rommel's divisions," he answered.

Haller could taste his own bile. The sick fear that had been growing all during the briefing had suddenly overflowed. The Allies still had their heels in the channel, and Rommel had two panzer divisions less than a hundred miles away. The German general's tanks had covered that much African sand in five hours. Given the French roads that were available to them, they could hit the British at Caen early the next morning. Or the Americans at Saint-Lô by lunchtime tomorrow.

In his mind, he transformed the giant wall map into a calendar. Normandy was June. Paris was August. The Rhine was the fall. Breach the Rhine before winter set in, and Germany would be out of business by March. There was an even chance that they couldn't have a reactor running by December, which meant that they probably couldn't build a bomb by March. So according to that calendar, the Allies were going to survive the war.

But the American colonel was changing the dates. At best, Normandy was going to drag on into August. Which meant Paris in the fall, and no chance to reach the Rhine before winter. Germany could last another year. Or, at worst, the Normandy assault was going to fail, which meant a second invasion, probably in southern Brittany, late in the fall. Either way, atomic bombs would be falling on England long before the Nazis surrendered. And once they had the bomb, why would the Nazis even think of surrendering?

He pushed his chair back, stood slowly and slipped out into the hallway, the beaches of Normandy growing silent behind him. Haller didn't need to hear any more. He didn't have much patience for staff briefings in which military units were indentified by numbers, and front lines were named after the towns and cities they passed through. Haller had been in the front lines and knew exactly what was happening to the men.

They were lying out in the open, hiding behind their helmets with their clothes still wet from the sea. In front of them were concrete bunkers, with cannons and machine guns peeking out through slotted windows. There were rows of barbed wire stretched over fields that were seeded with mines. There were fortifications that had been strengthened day after day for five long years. It was suicidal to even think of attack.

But that was exactly what they had to do. Despite the slaughter that was inevitable, Haller would have commanded them to stand up and charge if he were leading them. He couldn't tell them why. They couldn't begin to understand. But they had to attack because there was no time for delay. Certainly no time for a second invasion. They had to attack because they had to be over the Rhine by winter. Otherwise, they would face a devastation far more terrible than anything that could be aimed at them from the German bunkers.

He stepped out into warm spring air, the evening sunlight just beginning to fail behind the shapes of the buildings. In the civility of the West End, it was almost possible to forget the war. The sandbags packed at intersections and street entrances were more an obstacle than a defense. No one seriously considered the possibility of a German raid across the Channel. And the lookout posts on top of the buildings had become a curiosity. The Germans hadn't even attempted a serious air attack in more than a year. The shops were open and the streets were bustling with relaxed activity. All that remained of the early war terror were the blackened tops of the automobile headlamps, and the uniformed wardens beginning their search for unshaded windows. The open, smiling faces he passed showed no trace of fear.

When Haller heard the sound, it was behind him and he turned to search the sky for it. He knew it was a plane, and by the uneven rumble of the engine, he knew the plane was in trouble. The rising volume told him it was coming closer, but he couldn't find it above the high sightline of the rooftops.

"Doesn't sound like one of our lads." It was a warden who had heard the sound and stopped in the street beside him.

Haller shook his head. "Doesn't sound like one of theirs either."

The warden saw it first and jabbed a finger toward the sky. "It's on fire!" he shouted.

It broke into the clear above the buildings, a small, square-winged fighter, traveling level, at high speed, and trailing beads of smoke.

"It has to be a Jerry," Haller said calmly. There were no landing patterns over the West End, and he knew that no Allied pilot would ever bring a crippled plane over the city.

The two men turned slowly as they followed the flight out over the open sky. "What is it?" the warden asked. Once again, Haller shook his head in response. He knew most of the German aircraft by the sounds of their engines. There wasn't one that he couldn't identify by sight. But he had never seen anything like this before. The engine seemed to be faltering and there was clearly a trail of smoke. But the plane didn't seem to be having any difficulties.

"Jesus," he said in sudden recognition. "It's a jet. It's a German jet." The warden look bewildered, but Haller didn't bother to explain. He had heard reports of the new German jet fighters that had appeared over the Continent, far faster than the best Allied fighters. Two of them had run wild through a formation of American bombers, bringing down three of the Fortresses, and running rings around their escorts. But what in God's name was one of them doing cruising over London?

The sound stopped, and just as suddenly the trail of smoke disappeared.

"He's had it," the warden observed factually. But the plane continued for several seconds, still holding in level flight. Then the nose began to dip, aiming the craft into a dive. As the dive steepened, the wings began to roll, throwing the falling shape into a fatal spin.

At that instant, Haller knew what he was seeing. He remembered the small, pilotless bombers that had been photographed beside the launch ramps and Peenemünde. He remembered the detailed analysis of their range, their potential speed and their one-ton bombload. He remembered the inescapable conclusion of what bomb they had been built to carry.

Haller stood paralyzed. He wanted to scream a warning to the hundreds of people in the streets, many of whom had stopped and were watching the falling bomb curiously. He wanted to trigger the sirens that would howl over the entire city and send all London diving for cover. But it was too late. The bomb was seconds from impact, and even with hours of preparation, there could be no escape.

He knew he should dive for the ground to escape the brutal impact. Turn his eyes away so that they wouldn't be burned in their sockets by the white-hot flash. But he was drawn like a moth in his fatal fascination for the awesome power that was about to be unleashed.

The winged bomb was still clearly visible, its spin quickening as it plunged. And then it disappeared, perhaps half a mile away, behind the tops of the buildings. He waited an eternity. And then he saw the flash.

It was like a flicker of lightning. A quick whitening of the sky that began to dim the instant it became visible. It brought a scream from those around him, but the air that rushed up from his own chest was a sigh of relief. He had seen hundreds of bomb blasts like this one. The city would survive.

The shock wave reached him. It was a slight tremor of the ground, senses uncertainly through his legs, that confirmed what his eyes had just told him. A huge bomb with enormous destructive power. But an ordinary bomb.

He heard the crash, followed by a decaying rumble, and saw the plume of black smoke that climbed over the rooftops, carrying traces of yellow and orange from the fires that were suddenly blazing below.

The warden rushed away in the direction of the blast, joined by men and women on the street who had learned over the years to run toward danger in order to help. But Haller turned slowly away, the sickness he had felt during the Normandy briefing once again rising in his throat.

The Germans had their missiles. The little jet-propelled drone, even with its feeble explosive, had proven its point. It could take off from the sanctuary of the German-held Continent. It could travel across the Channel, fly too fast to be intercepted and navigate itself into the heart of London. And, at precisely the right moment, it could shut off its engine and dive down on its target.

All they needed was their uranium warhead. That would take time. But the Germans had time. More than enough time if the Overlord invasion couldn't hurry the calendar.

BERLIN — *June 21*

Rumors of the invasion had been circulating at the institute for several days, sending the scientists to consult their maps. Normandy, they saw, was a remote coastline nearly 200 kilometers south of Pas de Calais, where the invasion was expected, separated from the nearest point of England by 150 kilometers of open sea.

It was a diversion, they agreed as they shared their coffee. The Allies certainly wouldn't attempt a major attack across so much open water, to seize a beach so far from Paris. "It would put them twice as far from the Rhine," Lauderbach pointed out, in arguing that it couldn't be a major invasion. "Even the English aren't that stupid."

Diebner discounted the attack entirely. The Luftwaffe, he argued with certainty, would never let the English and the Americans set foot on the beaches. And the U-boats would decimate any fleet that approached the Continent. One of the laboratory chemists politely took issue. The SS officer who commanded the guards had told him that the English and American troops had, indeed, landed in Normandy. "But there are panzer divisions rushing to meet them," he had assured the scientists. "They are already being driven back into the sea."

Anders' spirits rose and fell with each variation on the theme. If it were the invasion, and if it were successful, then there was a chance that the Allies could be in Germany before his reactor was completed. But if it were just a diversion or, worse, if it were unsuccessful, then the reactor would be producing plutonium before the Allies could cross France.

The evidence was in front of him. He held the laboratory analysis of the new graphite which, according to the tests, exceeded his specifications. And he held his equations for an atomic pile which, when constructed with the pure graphite, seemed certain to achieve a chain reaction. There was little he could do to keep the Germans from building their bomb.

He had delayed them. His initial review had cost them a few weeks, and his insistence on new graphite had stopped the program in its tracks for more than a month. But now, instead of hindering them, he was actually helping them in their efforts.

The delays he had imposed had aroused the suspicions of his German colleagues. As he had worked out the equations for the reactor design, they had looked carefully over his shoulder leaving him no room for misdirection. There was no fooling them. Even though they might not be as imaginative nor as gifted as Nils Bergman, they were certainly the equal of Karl Anders. There was no fatal flaw he could have introduced that wouldn't have been immediately apparent to them.

To the contrary, he had been forced to deliver his best work. And, as they followed the elegance of his equations, their hostile sneers had turned into appreciative smiles. The distance they had imposed between themselves and this disruptive foreigner had narrowed. The stiff, formal reviews they had held on each of his proposals had turned into cooperative, friendly gatherings. Even his bitterly fought decision to reprocess the graphite had turned to their advantage. Lauderbach, his most outspoken critic, saw how much simpler the control formulas were with the new material. "Professor Bergman," he had said while sharing a morning cup of coffee, "I hope you will accept my apology. You were right, of course. In the long run, I think your idea will even save us time."

His credibility was rising. Enthusiasm for the reactor he was designing was growing. But in the process, his own purpose was being destroyed. To keep from being discovered, he had to make contributions. And the contributions he was making were bringing the German atomic bomb closer to reality. He couldn't delay them unless they had complete confidence in his ideas. But to win their confidence, he had to help them to succeed.

He needed help. Someone with a clear picture of the Allied invasion plan had to weigh the dilemma and decide what he should do. Should he risk discovery by offering a catastrophic misdirection? Or should he bide his time, waiting for a less conspicuous opportunity to destroy their program? He needed to know how much time he had to work with. If the Normandy invasion were real . . . if the Americans and British were actually charging into France . . . then even a month's delay might be all that would be needed to frustrate the Germans. In that case, he should misdirect them even at the risk of discovery. But if Normandy were just a diversion, or if the attack were stalled, then he would need to delay the Nazi scientists by much more than a month. Then he should do everything possible to remain at the center of their efforts. But there was no one who could tell him. He was by himself, locked inside a hostile country with no way to reach to the outside. All he could do was use the simple coded messages to tell Birgit where he was and how the program was progressing.

Probably he shouldn't risk discovery until he had learned at least where the reactor was being built. Heisenberg had mentioned "Castle Church." But that told him nothing.

His loneliness was terrifying. But the terror was not for his own safety, as it had been during his first weeks in Berlin. Now the fear that was paralyzing him was the fear of a miscalculation. He had to decide how to destroy the German atomic bomb. He had to decide by himself. And each of the choices he weighed had just as much chance of insuring the Germans' success as it did of destroying their super weapon. He had come into Germany with a simple mission. Now that mission was hopelessly complicated.

"Professor Bergman."

Anders looked up into the beaming face of Kurt Diebner. He was wearing a dark gray suit, with the red band and black swastika over his sleeve. He held a binder with Anders' preliminary equations clutched in both hands.

"Brilliant work," he complimented. "Simply brilliant. And your calculations of plutonium yield are spectacular. We never dreamed that such a high percentage of the uranium could be converted."

"It's only speculation," Anders cautioned, even though he was confident that his optimistic figures for the reactor's output were correct. "And it assumes ideal conditions. It's unlikely that we can achieve those figures in actual operation."

Diebner waved away the apparent modesty. "Even if we reach only half your estimates, we will still achieve our production goals." He leaned forward and whispered confidentially. "Guess where I am going this afternoon?"

Anders shook his head.

"I have an appointment with Reichsfuehrer Himmler. I told him we were ready and he wants to see the work immediately. And he has telephoned the fuehrer. The fuehrer himself!" Visions of medals danced in his head. "Professor Bergman, you have brought honor on all your colleagues. I'm sure Himmler will want to thank you personally. Perhaps even the fuehrer!"

"Those are just theories," Anders corrected, pointing to the binder. "There is still a great deal to be done."

Diebner smiled at the modesty. "Of course. But now we know it can be done." He gestured with the papers. "What you have given us is a clear path to success. The rest is just details."

"We should check everything again," Anders tried. "We should be absolutely certain before we create any false hopes."

Diebner laughed. "You are too cautious, Professor Bergman. All your colleagues agree with this work. Even Doctor Heisenberg says it is brilliant. 'Beyond my own capabilities.' Those were his exact words. No, our theoretical effort is completed. Now we are ready to build a prototype."

Anders stopped protesting. "And where will that be? I assume we will all be moving to the construction site." He held his breath as he waited for the answer.

"In due time," Diebner agreed. "For the present, you will supervise construction of the model, here in Berlin. The production reactor will simply be an upscale version of your model."

Anders was alarmed. He had never even considered the possibility that he wouldn't be part of the reactor team. "Herr Diebner," he challenged, "we still have great difficulties before us. I think I belong at the construction site. We should build our test model right where the production reactor will be built."

"In peacetime, of course," Diebner countered, explaining the official position just as it had been explained to him by Himmler. "But in war, there is need for secrecy. How could we keep people from becoming curious if half the scientists in Germany were suddenly to arrive in a small town? No, I'm afraid this has already been decided. You will remain here with our main design effort. Others will be responsible for beginning construction of the production reactor."

Anders was on his feet in protest. "May I remind you, Herr Diebner, whose design it is that you are building. I have the right to be there."

Diebner held out a hand defensively. "Of course. And you will be there. Just as soon as your model has been completed and tested we will move you to the site. Have no fear, Professor Bergman. No one will take your reactor critical but you. You will have the honor."

"I am not concerned about the honor," Anders shot back. "I am concerned about the results. I think I know better than anyone else exactly where I should be when my design is being built."

"Out of the question," Diebner said, shaking his head defiantly. "It has already been decided."

Anders played the only card he had left.

"I have no interest in toying with a model while the real reactor is being built somewhere else," he said coldly. "If that is your decision, then I have nothing further to contribute to your efforts." He held out his hand. "May I have my work back?"

Diebner's eyes widened in shock, and he clutched the binder to his chest. He had no intention of returning the work. But how could he explain to Himmler that the man whose brilliance he had praised so highly would no longer be available to the Germans. In response to Himmler's suspicions and implied criticism of his judgment, Diebner had made Bergman's contribution sound even more essential than it actually was. He couldn't now tell Himmler that Bergman's departure was of little consequence.

He backed toward the door and pushed it closed with his elbow. "Of course I agree with you, Professor Bergman. As a scientist, I understand your position perfectly. I will do everything in my power to have you transferred to the reactor site at the earliest possible moment. But you must understand the need for caution."

"I am not concerned with military secrets," Anders continued, pressing the advantage that seemed to be proving more valuable than he had expected. "My concern is with results." His hand was still extended for his papers.

Diebner's eyes darted around the room as if to be certain that no one else was present. "Please, I will do my best," he promised again. "Besides, we are bringing someone to join you here in Berlin. Someone very important to you. We are doing everything we can to make the delay as pleasant for you as possible."

Anders' breath caught in his chest. They had found someone who knew Nils Bergman.

"Please trust me," Diebner said.

"Who?" Anders demanded.

"I shouldn't tell you," Diebner countered. "I have said too much already. But it is someone who cares for you very much. We are bringing her here to Germany to share in your triumph. She will be with you while you work on the model. And then, as soon as possible, she will be able to join you at the reactor site."

Magda, Anders knew. They had found Magda and were bringing her to Berlin. The one person in all the world who would immediately know he was a fraud was rushing to be with him.

Diebner continued with his pleading, telling Anders that everything would work out perfectly if he would only cooperate. But Anders didn't hear his words. Instead, he sank slowly back into his chair as his worst fears turned to cold panic.

When was she coming? Perhaps within a week. A few weeks at the most. It wouldn't be long. And that was all the time he had left to do his work and send the message that would have him kidnapped out of Germany. They weren't going to tell him where "Castle Church" was. So he had to make certain that no matter where they built their reactor, it would never produce the plutonium that they desperately needed. And then he had to get out. All within a few weeks.

But how could he destroy their reactor when the best minds in nuclear physics were watching his every move?

SUMMER

1944

Victory seemed assured. The Allied invaders had pushed inland from the Normandy beaches despite the German counterattacks. Behind them, the largest fleet ever assembled landed more tanks, trucks, and guns than the Germans had been able to build since the beginning of the war. In the south, Kesselring fell back to still a new defensive line, and the American troops marched into Rome. In the east, the Red Army split the German defenses and stormed into Warsaw. It was only a matter of time. But time remained the most dangerous enemy. The German boasts of secret weapons were becoming a reality. New jet fighters flew circles around the suddenly obsolete Allied airplanes, and rocket-powered interceptors dove freely through the British and American bomber squadrons. Pilotless drones began falling like raindrops on England, carrying cargos of explosives. If they could be built in sufficient numbers, they could stem the flow of the war. But more important, each new weapon gave greater credibility to the secret weapon yet to come. The one weapon that could make Germany victorious.

BERLIN — *July 12*

Werner Heisenberg had provided the answer.

"It's the damn heat," he had told Anders. "We can't even calculate it. But if you don't have a way to control it, the reactor will generate enough heat to destroy itself."

He was slouched behind his desk, the smoldering ashtray and the glass of white wine buried in a disarray of papers. The precise scales of a Brandenberg Concerto were rattling from the phonograph behind him. Heisenberg found the bound copy of Anders' reactor calculations and lifted it above the rubble of his own notes. "Your work is beautiful. But double the flow of cooling water. Hell, triple it. Even that may not be enough."

Anders had opened the plan to his calculations of the heat that would be generated during the reaction. "I've checked the equations over and over—" he started to explain.

"Screw the equations," Heisenberg said with a wave of his hand. "I had equations." He pulled open a desk drawer and rummaged through his notebooks. "They're here someplace," he muttered, and finally located a black-covered tablet that he tossed casually toward Anders. "Those are every bit as good as yours. And just as useless. The problem is that we don't have any idea what we're dealing with. We're writing equations where all the known values are really unknown."

Anders began to turn through the pages of calculations that described Heisenberg's experimental heavy water reactor.

"Study them carefully," Heisenberg offered. "They'll tell you that the temperature of the water around the reactor should have risen only a few degrees. But the whole damn tank boiled off in less than a minute. I don't know what the exact heat output was. All the instruments I was using melted in a matter of seconds."

He reached for the wine and held it to his lips, his words sounding hollow across the top of the glass. "We're playing a dangerous game, and we're going so fast that we're not bothering to learn the rules."

Anders rose, taking Heisenberg's notes along with his own plan. "I'll do as you suggest. I'll study these carefully."

Heisenberg nodded and then swung his chair around so that he could turn the record. Anders started for the door.

"Professor Bergman."

When he turned, Heisenberg's back was still toward him as the German genius set the needle precisely into the groove. The music resumed, and then Heisenberg turned back toward his colleague.

"Maybe we should stop. Maybe we're not ready to build a reactor."

Anders was stunned by the suggestion. "Would they let us stop?" he asked. "Aren't we in a race?"

"A race to where?" Heisenberg said.

Anders settled back into his chair.

"Suppose you can't control the heat. What happens to your graphite?"

He had no answer.

"I saw uranium burning like paper," Heisenberg continued. "Perhaps all your graphite goes up in flames. And if it does, what happens to the uranium you are processing? Wouldn't it melt together into a more dense mass, accelerating the chain reaction?"

Anders nodded at the possibility.

"Which would, of course, increase the heat still further. And that, in turn, would increase the reaction. The process would continue feeding on itself. How would you stop it?"

Anders stared back blankly. Nothing would stop it.

"So, perhaps we shouldn't start it," Heisenberg suggested, "at least until we understand all the rules."

He had left the thought hanging as he leaned back in his chair and slipped quietly under the spell of his music.

Anders had plunged into Heisenberg's calculations as soon as he closed the door of his own office. It was the answer he was looking for—the certain way to destroy the German uranium bomb before it was ever built. He would design a reactor that would destroy itself.

As he studied the notes, his plan began to take shape. He would use Heisenberg's calculations to develop a cooling system that none of the German scientists could challenge. A design that was mathematically correct but inadequate to the experience that Heisenberg had documented with his test reactor. And the Germans, as Diebner had explained, would invest their resources in building a production reactor according to his laboratory designs. When his prototype self-destructed they would be left with a pile of graphite that would be much too dangerous to even attempt to operate.

But was there time? He needed to escape before Magda was brought into the country to join him. Once she exposed the fraud, then all his work would be discredited. And he needed to have his plans for the prototype completed before he vanished so that they could guide the German scientists to their own self-destruction.

His escape was in the hands of the British. Haller had assured him that they would always be close at hand. All he had to do was send the prearranged message to Birgit—a complaining letter that a Swiss scientific journal had not published an article that he felt was important. Haller's people would kidnap him and bring him out of Germany, leaving behind the impression that his work was so valuable that the English had gone to great lengths to silence him. But he had to be exact on the timing of the message. Once he sent it, his kidnapping would happen quickly. He had to give himself enough time to complete the plan for the prototype.

He had worked day and night, living in the bunker. He took his meals, usually a roll and a pot of coffee, at his desk and collapsed in a heap on his sofa when he could no longer think. "You need rest," Lauderbach had told him with genuine concern as they reviewed the specifications for the fuel rods. Anders responded with a nod as he pressed his fingertips into eyes that would no longer focus. "Yes, soon. We're so close."

"Too close to lose you now," Lauderbach had said. "We can't afford to have you taken ill."

Diebner had been giddy with the progress, rushing out of each meeting to deliver his reports to Himmler. "Our test reactor will be running in just a few months," he promised. "We'll be switching to the production reactor early in the fall." The only cloud in his childlike optimism was his fear for Bergman's health. "A heroic effort," he had told Himmler. "Professor Bergman is achieving in weeks what we would have expected to take months. But I'm not sure he can continue much longer."

"We are all making sacrifices," Himmler had reminded his protégé in a cold voice.

It had been three weeks since Diebner had hinted that Magda would be coming to Germany when Anders was finally able to assemble the drawings for the prototype. All his theories and all his calculations had been magically changed by the engineers and draftsmen into a reactor blueprint. The sizes and shapes of the graphite blocks had been specified. The locations of the fuel rods and the control rods had been precisely fixed. The convoluted path of the stainless steel piping that would carry the cooling water had been traced. Now, he downed one last cup of black coffee before entering the final review meeting with the physicists and engineers who would construct the reactor.

It was more of a celebration than a meeting. Each of the scientists seated along the sides of the enormous conference table presented the sector of the reactor for which he was responsible, gloating over the precision with which theory had been changed to fact. Each presentation was concluded with absolute assurances and given curtain calls of applause by the group. Diebner conferred the fuehrer's blessings on each of the teams as it finished and then introduced the head scientist for the next team with words of praise and gratitude. For the next thousand years, citizens of the Reich would reverence their achievements.

But Anders heard nothing. His attention was fixed on Werner Heisenberg, who sat at the far end of the table, exempting himself from the celebration. Instead, he gathered the pages of the blueprints as they were presented, set them next to his overflowing ashtray, and studied them from the corner of his eye. He said nothing and applauded no one.

Anders studied his face, hoping for some clue of Heisenberg's reaction. But his face remained bored and noncommittal. Surely, he would have no quarrel with the fuel system and the graphite moderator. The plans simply confirmed the calculations that he had already approved and praised. And he wouldn't take issue with the mechanics of construction. They were pedestrian concerns that fell far beneath his level of interest. But now his eyes were roving over the plans for the cooling system. He would be mentally calculating the water capacity of the reactor and the rate of water flow made possible by the pumps that would be used. His mind would be totalling the calories of heat that the cooling system could absorb.

He would see instantly that it was more than adequate for the heat output predicted for the reactor. But he would remember the calculations he had worked for his own reactor and he would be making his own estimates of the heat that Anders would have to contend with. "It's the damn heat," he had told Anders. "Double the flow of cooling water." How long would it take him to realize that while the flow had been increased, it had by no means been doubled? And when he realized it, how would he weigh the illogical results he had witnessed in his own laboratory against the elegant logic of Anders' calculations.

"Then we are all agreed," Diebner's voice suddenly announced, breaking Anders' concentration on Heisenberg. But even as he pronounced the victory, Diebner looked uncertainly toward the silent monk at the end of the table.

"Professor Heisenberg?"

Heisenberg said nothing, but continued to stare at the blueprints. Anders felt himself lifting slowly out of his chair.

"You have no problems?" Diebner said hopefully.

Heisenberg crushed his cigarette. Then he looked down the table toward Anders.

"Very nice," he offered with a congratulatory nod. He scooped up the blueprints. "May I borrow these for a few hours? I'd like to spend some time with them in my office where it's quiet enough to think."

Diebner's head snapped toward Anders. "Professor Bergman?"

"I'd be honored," Anders said directly to Heisenberg.

"Well, I'm sure we can spare a few hours . . ." Diebner started to explain. But Werner Heisenberg was already out the door with the blueprints under his arm.

It didn't matter. There was nothing more that Anders could do. If Heisenberg accepted the plans, then the Germans would begin building a reactor that would destroy their uranium bomb program. If he took issue with the plans, then the scientists would begin fighting among themselves and lose weeks, perhaps even months while they salvaged their egos and revised the drawings. But his time was up. He had to leave Germany before Magda arrived or all his efforts would count for nothing. It was time to send his message to Birgit. He returned to his office and began drafting the letter.

Diebner knocked, but opened the door without waiting for an answer.

"Magnificent," he said as he rushed across the room and seized Anders' hand in both of his.

"Professor Bergman, there are no words to express our gratitude. The entire Aryan race owes you an enormous debt."

Anders tried to retrieve the hand that Diebner was shaking like a pump handle. "And I must express my gratitude to you, Herr Diebner, for giving me the opportunity to demonstrate my work. But now I must sleep." He gestured to the half-written letter on his desk. "I have a few details to finish and then I think I will go home to my apartment."

"There's no time," Diebner sang sweetly. He picked up the fountain pen from Anders' desk and replaced the cap. "We must go right away. Reichsfuehrer Himmler is waiting to receive us."

"Now?" Anders asked. "But I can't . . ."

Diebner darted across the room and retrieved Anders' suit jacket from its hanger. He held it out like a valet, ready to slip it over Anders' arms.

"Of course, now. The reichsfuehrer has been waiting a year for this moment. He wishes personally to convey the thanks of the German people."

Anders shook his head. "Not now. I'm exhausted. Tell him how grateful I am for the opportunity."

But Diebner was back across the room, trying to slip the jacket sleeve over Anders' protesting arm.

"There's more. He has a surprise for you. Something that will make your well-earned vacation much more pleasant."

His smile was conspiratorial, and suddenly Anders understood. He had waited too long. It had taken him a few days too many to complete his work.

"She's here?" he whispered softly.

Diebner nodded. "Here in Berlin. Waiting to see you."

"She's with Himmler?"

"Of course. He wants to be present for the moment when you are reunited."

Anders went numb. He stood like a rag doll while Diebner fitted the jacket over his shoulders and turned him around so that he could smooth the lapels.

"You will be together in less than an hour," Diebner smirked. "And then you will have a few days together before we have to get back to work."

Anders was being steered toward the door before his mind began to work again. And as they started down the corridor toward the bunker steps he began to plot his desperate escape.

He couldn't allow himself to be brought to a meeting with Magda. She might smile when she first saw him and start across the room to greet him. But as she drew close, she would stop abruptly and her openmouthed shock would bring down the whole British plan. Or, if she reached him, her first touch would knock her backward in horror. He could see her instant of confusion, and watch her turn toward Himmler mumbling, "But . . . this isn't . . ."

The Germans would need no further explanation. If he wasn't Bergman, then it didn't matter who he was. His work would be immediately discredited. He and Diebner would be hanging from meat hooks within an hour, and the rest of the scientists would be thrown in with them before nightfall.

As he started up the bunker stairs, his foot froze on the bottom step. There were two black-uniformed SS guards who were waiting to escort him at the top of the stairs. He knew that once he was walking between them there could be no escape. For an instant, he weighed the chances of bolting away from Diebner and back into the labyrinth of bunker tunnels. But to where? There were guards at every entrance and it would take only minutes to search the bunker. He climbed wearily up the steps with Diebner at his heels.

One guard held the door of the Mercedes sedan, then climbed into the backseat so that Anders was squeezed between himself and Diebner. The other guard climbed into the front seat next to the driver. The soldiers at the entrance to the Kaiser Wilhelm Institute snapped to attention as the car sped past and out into the streets of Berlin.

The only miracle Karl Anders could hope for was his own death. The evidence of the bombers was everywhere, from the craters in the streets that the car swerved to avoid to the skeletons of buildings that they passed on every block. If only they would come now. If only, by some chance, they would place their strings of deadly explosives down the center of the street they were traveling and obliterate the car with all its passengers. Then his fraud would never be discovered.

But the sky was clear, and the city was resting in the peace of a warm summer day. There would be no miracle. He would live to meet the all-powerful Himmler. He would live to be introduced to Magda.

Werner Heisenberg stretched the reactor blueprints across the rubble of his desk, pinning one corner down with a heavy glass ashtray, and another with the wineglass that he promptly filled with colorless Mosel. Then he bent over his record collection, found a disk of Bach selections for the harpsichord, and set it on the turntable. He lit still another cigarette while the opening bars filled his small office. Then he dropped into his chair and spared the plans only a momentary glance.

He knew what the blueprints said. If a technical evaluation were all that was needed, he could give it in an instant. But much more was at stake. With a uranium bomb, the Germans could win the war in one blinding flash. Without it, Germany would be crushed to death in an iron vise, between the Allies closing from the west and the Bolsheviks coming from the east. An insane god was giving him the power to decide which of the alternatives he preferred.

Heisenberg knew what his family would say. His mother was an aristocrat, prosperous even during the wild inflations of the early thirties, blessed with the racial purity that modern Germany worshipped. She was certainly not a Nazi. She was openly critical of the lowlife types that the Nazis dressed in tasteless uniforms and turned loose in the streets. But you did have to give that ridiculous housepainter his due. He had restored German pride, he did stand for hard currency, and he had made the trains run on time. Certainly she was appalled by the wanton destruction that the war had brought to her country. But that was British doing. Why couldn't they stay on their damned island and stop meddling with affairs on the Continent?

His wife was totally ignorant of the war. She had her modest house in Bavaria, in the wooded foothills of the Alps. The air was clear, the streams as cold as diamonds and the trees tall and strong. Of course Germany had to survive! Where was there a more beautiful land or a more spirited people? She didn't care about the events that were colliding all around her. All she needed was to be assured that her lovely, pastoral life would never change.

But everything was changed, even the very nature of knowledge, which was Heisenberg's only vital interest. He had studied the structure of matter simply to understand it, with no thought of ever altering it. His original systems of mathematical logic were almost a plaything, a way to arrive at firm conclusions for topics that had no particular importance. In the rarified academic air that he loved to breathe, an interesting question was far more important than a definitive answer. The international commerce in ideas that pitted American scientists against Russian thinkers, and German mathematicians against Swedish physicists was exciting—a mental Olympics in which the medals were awarded by the learned journals and the well-endowed foundations. No sensible man could take it all very seriously.

But those days were gone forever. Now knowledge was a machine. Every thought had to lead toward a particular conclusion.

And every conclusion had to lead toward a product. No one asked, what does it mean? The only question was, what can we build with it? Or in wartime, how many people can we kill with it? Scientists were no longer thinkers. They were manufacturers. Ideas were no longer shared. They were developed in bunkers, their existence guarded as a national secret.

There was a new era coming when everything that could be imagined would be built. Never mind if it was needed. Why be concerned with its consequences? Simply build it, in unlimited quantities, before someone else does. Ideas would clutter the Earth, trample over the trees, pollute the oceans, blacken the sky. Ideas would kill. Most of them slowly and almost imperceptibly. Some of them, like the one cast on the desk before him, instantly and grossly.

He had no desire to see the coming era when scientists and thinkers would be the stooges of the generals and the industrialists. It would hold no place for him, and certainly none for his wife. All he could do was hope that whichever nation controlled the mad world that was dawning might quickly come to its senses. And where should he invest that hope? In the Bolsheviks? In the Nazis? In the British imperialists? Who would be most likely to spare the world the secret horrors that its best minds could conjure? Was there any reason to hope? Was there any reason to care?

Heisenberg felt the heat of the cigarette searing his fingers. He heard the phonograph needle clicking monotonously at the center of the disk.

He looked down at the plans, then picked up a grease pencil and scribbled "Approved—Heisenberg" across the center of each page.

It wasn't an encouraging choice. But he had made his decision.

SPREEWALD — *July 12*

They had driven past the boundaries of Berlin, well into the open country to the south that was still untouched by the war. The farms along the banks of the Spree were green with the ripeness of summer, and the great houses set into the countryside were standing tall and proud. The battlefronts to the east and the west were still hundreds of miles away. Only occasionally did the planes circle overhead on their way back from distant targets. And the only soldiers to be found were the few uniformed guards who stood idly at the road intersections.

Diebner babbled like a tour guide, identifying each house by the names of the important Nazi leaders or the work of the essential government bureaus that had taken it over. "Luftwaffe staff," he said, as they passed a timbered mansion that had once been the manor house of a great agricultural estate. "Goering, himself, has apartments there." He pointed to another sprawling building, a collage of structures that appeared to have been assembled over a century. "Ministry of Information," he explained, and then listed all the news and publishing services that had been uprooted from Berlin to safeguard their critical work from the danger of a stray bomb.

But Anders was studying the open countryside. If, somehow, he could get out of the car and disappear into the fields, they might never find him. With his fluent German and a change of clothes, he could blend in with the farm workers who bolstered the populations of the towns and villages during the summer.

He had to act now before he was delivered to his meeting with Magda. Now, he wasn't being watched. The officers riding with him were relaxed, concerned with nothing more than delivering an important person to a national leader. Once he became their prisoner, they would never turn their eyes away from him.

"Can we stop?" he interrupted Diebner. "I could use the privacy of a few tall bushes."

Diebner blushed, then leaned forward to the officer in the front seat. "No need," he said turning back to Anders. "We'll be there in another minute."

Anders looked uneasily from side to side, weighing his chances of lunging over Diebner and forcing open the door. His panicked thoughts were interrupted by a sudden change in the engine noise, and he watched hopelessly while the car swung through a stone gate and onto a driveway. The house, probably once a small hotel, was directly ahead.

"It's a residence for important guests of the government," Diebner said. "And today, Doctor Bergman, our government has no more important guest than you."

The two SS officers walked on either side of him as he climbed the steps and entered through the front door into a small lobby. Two more officers, in their black-and-silver uniforms, flanked the entrance to a dining room to his left. They snapped to attention as Anders passed between them.

Himmler was waiting, his slight figure silhouetted against the bright windows at the end of the room. His cap, turned over to hold his gloves, rested on the long dining table, but he still held his riding crop, slightly bowed, between his hands. Anders felt his legs begin to tremble with the first edge of terror.

"Ah, Professor Bergman," Himmler sighed. "How good to meet you at last." But he made no move toward his guest. Instead, he waited until Anders had crossed the entire room and presented himself before him.

"Herr Himmler," Anders said. He started to offer his hand, but it was obvious that the German leader had no intention of relaxing his grip on the crop. "A pleasure to meet you," Anders added, his hand dropping slowly back to his side.

"I have followed your work carefully," Himmler continued. "You have done a great service to Germany."

"To scientists everywhere, I hope," Anders responded, surprised at the confident tone of his own voice.

Himmler nodded, his features still indistinct in the shadows of the window. "Perhaps," he said. "Time will tell." He lifted the crop and gestured toward the door. "We have persuaded someone from your home country to come and join you in your work. I think she will be able to make the time pass more quickly."

In response to his gesture, one of the officers marched away from the door. Anders turned toward the opening and heard the tap of approaching high heels. The only other sound was the wheezy breathing of the man who waited behind him. "I hope you'll be pleased," Himmler said as the footsteps grew louder. "I wanted to be here to enjoy your reaction." But Anders knew there would be no reaction. He was frozen in fear as the woman's form suddenly filled the doorway.

It was Birgit Zorn.

She stopped long enough to see Anders and let her face fill with a smile. Then she ran across the room toward him and threw herself into his arms, whispering "Nils" as she disappeared into his embrace.

Anders' arms clutched her, but he said nothing. He was bewildered, totally unsure of what his reaction should be. Who was she? What kind of trick were they playing? Did the Germans think that she was Magda? Was she pretending to be Magda? He didn't even know what name to call her. And Himmler was standing only inches away, certainly measuring his reaction.

She pushed back from him and showed a hint of embarrassment for her display of affection. "I won't interfere," she promised Himmler. "I'll help Professor Bergman with his work just as I do in Stockholm." His mind groped for an image. What was she trying to tell him. That she was herself? His assistant? But Diebner had suggested that Magda would be coming to him. And Birgit was in his arms, playing the role of a lover. Was she Birgit? Or was she Magda?

"We should all have such assistants," Kurt Diebner volunteered from the doorway. And then Anders understood. They had gone looking for his mistress. Somehow, Birgit had persuaded them that being Nils Bergman's lover was another part of the role she played in his life. So, as far as the Germans knew, there was no Magda.

There was just Birgit, the one woman on Earth who would confirm his assumed identity. He felt the breath return to his lungs.

Himmler's colorless hand moved into Anders' view and retrieved the gloves from the military cap. "We have prepared an apartment for you here," his voice explained. "I think you will find it most suitable for your reunion." A gloved hand picked up the cap, and then Himmler stepped around the table setting the visor low over his eyes. It was only half a face that confronted Birgit and Anders. "Enjoy the few days you have before returning to Berlin. Then we must resume our work. Time is short." He walked toward the door and disappeared between the two guards, leaving Birgit and Anders alone with Diebner.

They followed the head of German science as he walked backward like a concierge, gesturing toward the stairs that led to their apartment. "What in God's name—" Anders started to whisper as they crossed the small lobby, but she silenced him with a sudden squeeze of his hand.

"They can watch us inside the apartment. They can hear everything we say," she whispered in return. Then she smiled toward Diebner who was waiting on the landing. "Nils, wait until you see our rooms," she said in a loud voice. Diebner darted ahead of them to open the door.

The instant they were alone, Birgit drew him into a close embrace and whispered a quick instruction into his ear. "They're watching. You have to be Nils Bergman." Then she pulled away, and in a full voice said, "I have so much to tell you."

She chattered continuously, first about the spread of meats and cheeses and the bottle of chilled wine that had been left for them and then, as they ate, about the affairs of the university. He listened attentively, resisting the urge to let his eyes search the room for the microphones and peepholes that he was beginning to understand were surrounding them. As he ate, he tried to reconstruct what had just happened.

The Germans must have accepted Birgit in the role she had played for almost two years as Nils Bergman's confidante. And she must have taken on the additional role of his mistress to keep the

Germans from identifying Magda. She had brought those two identities with her, and her embrace in the dining room had shown Himmler that he was, indeed, Nils Bergman.

It had been a test. They were suspicious enough of him to want confirmation. And Birgit's warning about their watching and listening meant that the test was not over. He was under a microscope, now even during the hours when he was away from the bunker. They were watching for an expression, listening for a word that would be out of character for the man he was pretending to be. His fear had relaxed for an instant when Himmler had gathered his gloves and cap and left the dining room. But now it returned, and the food turned to paste in his mouth.

He realized that Birgit was still chatting, filling every moment of silence so that he wouldn't have to speak until he understood the situation. Even when the soldier, wearing a white jacket over his military trousers, came to retrieve the food trays, she continued to talk about events in Sweden that had no meaning to him. He responded only with nods or with quick expressions of surprise and distress. He was hesitant to launch into any conversation for fear of the direction that it might lead.

She was suddenly quiet, and even the brief instant of silence seemed threatening to him. But then she rose, stepped around the table, and rested her hands on his shoulders. She leaned forward and kissed his cheek. "I'll get ready for bed," she said with a perfect hint of mischief in her voice. He watched silently as she gathered a few things from the dresser drawer and disappeared into the bathroom. For the first time, Anders realized where their impersonation was leading.

They could be watching from anywhere, Birgit thought as she stood in front of the mirror that was fixed into the tile wall above the bathroom sink. She had to force herself to ignore the eyes that might be looking back out at her. She unhooked her necklace and carefully placed it with her bracelets and rings in a satin case, keeping her attention riveted on each piece of jewelry as she removed it. Then she began undressing, fighting back the fear that her most natural movements were looking rehearsed. Did she usually remove her blouse before her skirt? Did she struggle with all the buttons on the back of her blouse or simply pull it over her head? Was it easier to remove her slip before she manipulated the garter clasps that held her stockings? The most insignificant procedures now seemed critical.

She lifted the slip over her head and felt suddenly chilled even though the air that touched her skin was warm. She folded the slip on top of the skirt and blouse that she had placed on the dressing table, then crossed the small room so that she could rest her foot against the edge of the bathtub while she rolled down her stockings. As she unhooked her garter belt and returned to the dressing table, she was terribly aware of the mirror and the leering eyes that it might conceal. She knew it would be impossible for her to stand naked before it.

The dressing table was off to one side. She would be completely visible, but she would be looking away from the mirror when she stripped. Somehow, the fact that she wouldn't be looking into their hidden faces made their violation less unbearable. She slipped the bra off her shoulders, forcing herself to take the time to fold it carefully. Then she pushed her pants down over her thighs, stepped out of them, and stood naked while she reached for her nightgown and struggled it over her head. She was surprised that her hands were steady, revealing nothing of the frightening torture that she was undergoing.

It was a modest black gown with full shoulder straps, revealing only the outlines of her figure. Once she straightened it, she had no trouble facing into the mirror as she touched a brush to her hair. She leaned forward as she smoothed her lipstick, her face only inches from the face that she sensed at the other side of the glass. Now her efforts were to disguise the smug triumph she was feeling for having endured their brutal examination.

When she stepped out into the bedrooms, Anders was waiting. He had changed into the pajamas that Himmler's men had included when they packed a suitcase at his apartment. He had opened the French door that served as the bedroom window and was standing half outside on the small balcony.

"You look lovely," he said in greeting, and then when she crossed the room to join him, he added, "God, how I've missed you." Birgit felt a surge of confidence. He had sorted through his paralyzing confusion that had numbed him since her arrival and grasped the outline of the plot. He knew who she was, why she had come, and what they had to do to persuade their hosts. He was now her ally instead of being the most dangerous part of her plan.

Birgit welcomed him into their bed beside her and fell easily into his embrace prepared to pantomime the rituals of lovemaking. The room was dark, except for the trace of moonlight that illuminated the outlines of the French door. Their guards couldn't see them distinctly and probably wouldn't be able to record their murmurings.

Anders, too, gathered his first hint of security from the darkness. The hand that he slid gently down the small of her back was strong and reassuring. He didn't hesitate to bring his lips close to hers and then to brush them in a kiss.

But as he held her, the months of lonely terror welled up inside him. He pulled her closer, suddenly needing assurance that he was no longer alone. Birgit was the first person in this strange, foreign world that he could completely trust. She was the only person in the insane Nazi empire who knew who he really was.

He needed to be himself, even for only a few moments. He needed to confess his terror. Like a child awakening in the darkness from a frightening nightmare, he needed to be held and stroked. He needed someone he loved to tell him that he was safe.

Anders was nearly crying with joy as he drew her body against his. He wanted to be close, so close that their persons would merge and all the space and time that separated them would disappear. His kiss grew violent, probing for a parting of her lips.

Birgit wasn't surprised. She understood his need because it was identical to her own. Since the moment in Stockholm when she had offered herself to the Nazis as Nils Bergman's mistress, she had felt her own dread of discovery taking hold of her. She had traced Anders' steps into a hostile land, breaking her links with the British agents who knew her work. She had immersed herself in a danger that she could share with no one. Now, she was in the arms of the one person who knew her secret. She needed to feel the protection of his strength and love.

Her response was genuine and even hurried. She pressed back at his kiss, her mouth open and her tongue darting. Her leg wrapped over his body to draw him even nearer. As his hand pushed the strap of her nightgown down from her shoulder, she arched her back to offer her breast.

Suddenly, the thought of peering eyes became exciting. The danger that surrounded them became erotic. Instead of inhibiting their lovemaking, the knowledge that they were being tested made them more daring. Their nakedness became a scream of defiance hurled into the faces of their murderous captors. Death suddenly held no terror for them. It was simply the promise of eternity for the love that was quenching their agonizing needs.

Anders pushed her away for the instant it took to pull her nightgown up over her head. As he tossed the gown aside, Birgit was pulling apart the buttons of his pajama and pushing the top back from his shoulders. And as he slipped his arms free, she pushed the pants down along his legs. She kicked the blankets back furiously, then spread her knees to receive him. Her excitement was obvious in the ease with which she felt him enter her.

Birgit thrust herself to him, matching his uncontrolled drive. She could feel his pleasure swelling and her own growing wildly along with his. She had only an instant to enjoy his orgasm before she was lost in the explosion of her own.

They clung to each other motionlessly, sharing their strength without words. Only their breathing, diminishing as the pledge they were offering to one another was understood, broke the silence of the summer night. They were lying side by side, holding hands, when the first graying of dawn crept into the bedroom.

They were still hand in hand when they walked down the stairs, nodding politely to the two soldiers who snapped to attention as they passed. Were they the ones who were watching, Birgit wondered as she studied their faces. Probably not. The Germans would have assigned that task to a high-ranking medical quack—someone who could render a learned judgment as to the authenticity of their relationship. Either that, or to some sick ideologue. Perhaps the demented Himmler himself.

They walked down the path and out into the empty fields, feeling their freedom grow as the house disappeared behind them. They had much to discuss. Anders needed to tell her about the status of the reactor. He needed to know the progress of the Allied invasion, and get her accurate estimates of the time that the Nazis had left to perfect their uranium bomb. They would have few moments alone, and they had to make the best use of every second of privacy that was given to them. But they walked in silence, each afraid to break the spell that lingered from the night. Each unwilling to give up the security they had found and plunge back into the loneliness of the pretense they shared.

"Last night," Karl Anders suddenly said. He wasn't looking at her, but rather out over the rolling grain fields with their faded golden color. "Last night was real. I needed you more than I have ever needed anyone in my life. I know I should apologize. But that would be a lie."

Birgit said nothing for a few moments. Then she told him, "I know. It was real for me, too. It's real for me now."

He squeezed her hand in acknowledgment.

"Karl, be very careful," she said. She stopped walking and waited until he had turned to face her.

"I loved a young man before. Here in Germany, under the eyes of the Nazis. Our love destroyed him. If he hadn't loved me . . . if he hadn't tried to protect me . . . he might still be alive. But he did love me. And that's what got him murdered."

He tried to take her in his arms even though he wasn't sure exactly what she was telling him. But Birgit pushed him away.

"Be careful," she said. "Don't let your guard down. I'm frightened that the same thing may happen to you."

BERLIN — *July 15*

Kurt Diebner stood stiffly, trying to imitate the braced posture of the young officer who stood at attention beside him. Both of them looked over the top of the desk lamp that illuminated half of Heinrich Himmler's face and focused on his pale, frail hands. To look directly at the man would be an unforgivable sacrilege. And it would be unnecessary. They could feel his presence without the evidence of their eyes.

"You witnessed all this personally?" Himmler wondered as he turned the pages of an official report.

"Yes, Reichsfuehrer. Most certainly," the officer responded, almost in a marching cadence.

The hands tossed the pages, and the fingertips glided lightly over the typewritten lines of the report.

"Then there is no doubt that she knows him quite intimately . . . and that he is equally familiar with her."

"None whatsoever, Reichsfuehrer," the officer snapped.

Himmler read further, turning another page almost idly.

"Apparently neither of them showed any signs of suspecting your presence," he commented.

"None at all." The response was delivered in the same military precision.

"And there are no doubts as to the authenticity of the woman?" Himmler said, confirming the information he was reading.

"None," Diebner said, now trying to imitate the officer's tone of voice. "She has been an employee of the university for two years, assigned to assist Professor Bergman. She has been handling all his official correspondence while he has been with us in Germany. We have even authenticated her birth certificate."

The hands closed the last page of the report. "Then we appear to have struck gold," he said. And then wearily, "That will be all."

Diebner watched in awe as the officer executed a routine that began with a snap of his heels, the fixing of his cap down over his eyes, and a quick forward thrust of his right arm.

"Heil Hitler!" the young man chanted.

Himmler's hand raised slightly to return the salute.

The officer spun on his toes, clicked his heels, and marched smartly toward the door. Diebner raised his own arm awkwardly. "Heil Hitler," he said, almost as a question. But Himmler did not return the salute. He waited until the young officer had closed the door behind him.

"My congratulations, Herr Diebner," the whispery voice said from behind the wall of the lamplight. "It appears that your Swedish genius is genuine."

"Thank you, Reichsfuehrer. I am most humbly grateful for your confidence."

"I was half convinced that he was a fraud," Himmler continued, "and half convinced, therefore, that you were a fool."

Diebner swallowed hard.

"But his reactor design, according to our experts, is brilliant. And his credentials seem impeccable. So I suppose that I am the fool and that you are a hero of the Reich."

"Hardly a hero," Diebner said nervously. Flattery from Himmler was known to be a death warrant.

"No," Himmler corrected, "certainly a hero. You have given us victory in a struggle where the outcome was in doubt. The fuehrer sees your work as a sign of favor from the gods."

"I'm overwhelmed," Diebner whispered.

"But I wonder, Herr Diebner, if you can satisfy me on one point. I wonder if you can tell me why the British have not simply assassinated Professor Bergman? Why are they allowing him to deliver this great victory into our hands?"

Diebner was stunned. "Perhaps," he speculated defensively, "they don't know he is here."

The soft hand waved away the suggestion. "Hardly. You could dress all the women in Europe with the silk of the British parachutes we find each morning. Their agents are everywhere. They know Professor Bergman is in Berlin. And he walks back and forth to his apartment everyday. He has romantic liaisons in a country house. He even . . ." The hands turned the pages of the report and rested on a specific paragraph. ". . . walks after breakfast through the wheat fields."

"Perhaps they don't understand his value," Diebner tried.

"But he is world-renowned," Himmler's voice countered. "And he spent several months in England before he came to us. Surely they appreciated his value as much as you did. Yet they let him return to his home when they knew he was interested in joining us. And they make no effort to interfere with him working for us. They haven't even bombed his laboratories. Can you tell me why the British are so unconcerned about the one man on Earth that can certainly destroy them?"

Diebner raised his sweat-soaked palms. "Perhaps they think his work is pointless. Perhaps they believe the physicists who insist that a uranium bomb is impossible."

Himmler's fingers toyed with the pages of the report. "Perhaps," he agreed. "Certainly he appears to be genuine. And his work, according to our best scientists, is correct. But I would be more certain if the British seemed concerned. I think that we should be cautious of anything that comes too easily."

"I will exercise every caution, Reichsfuehrer," Diebner agreed.

"Please do," the voice said, and the hand flapped in imitation of a salute. "Heil Hitler."

"Heil Hitler!" Diebner responded, his arm flying out. Then he turned precisely, copying what he had learned from the young officer, and beat a hasty retreat from the dreaded office.

SPREEWALD — *August 15*

It was no longer just an impersonation. In the love of a woman who knew his assumed identity far better than the man he once was, Karl Anders became Nils Bergman.

She called him Nils with no sense of stage play. At first it had been a conscious decision—a critical part of their charade in case the Nazis were still watching and listening. But then it had become his real name. The name she whispered at night when he held her close and that she gasped when he brought her to ecstasy.

She spoke of Bergman's work as if it were his own, complimenting him on the results of past decisions and expressing genuine sorrow at professional disappointments.

"The smug little bastard!" she had screamed as she read the review of one of Bergman's papers in a Swiss journal. "Who is this fool, to criticize you? What has he ever written?" And Anders had found himself consoling her. "Don't worry, Birgit. The important people will understand. The poor simpleton is just trying to make a name for himself. Wait until you see what Bohr has to say. Or ask Heisenberg." Then he had read the review and felt the sting of rejected work just as if it had actually been his own.

With Birgit near, he was comfortable with Bergman's mannerisms. The gestures and expressions that had once been forced now came as natural reactions. He selected his neckties with Bergman's eyes, and ordered his food with Bergman's palate. And as he did, he realized that his most ordinary choices brought her pleasure.

The intimacy of their relationship became routine to the Nazi agents who had been cautioned to watch their every move. They became ashamed of their voyeurism as they looked through the back of a mirror that hung in the bedroom. They turned away in boredom from the daily rituals in the kitchen and dining room. Sometimes they even forgot to start the tapes that recorded the conversations. The pages of their notebooks became fewer and the entries less detailed.

"They are who they are," an officer reported to Himmler with a shrug of his shoulders. "They talk about friends in Sweden. They talk about themselves. Most of the time they talk about science. They laugh at each other. They become annoyed with each other. They are normal people, except that they are both geniuses."

Himmler's fingers flicked the pages of Diebner's reports, documenting the incredible progress with the reactor.

"So it would seem," he allowed. But there was still a tone of reluctance in his admission.

As a scientist, Anders had actually become heir to the other man's mind. Bergman's ideas had reached the limits of theory. But Anders had tested those theories in the crucible of the bunker. He had amended them in the face of persuasive arguments and expanded them with the results of experiments. He could understand why Bergman had decided to travel into Germany. The Germans had the materials and the determination to move far beyond abstract suppositions. Bergman must have known that he needed to be tested if he were to continue to grow. Instead, it was Anders who was tested and had been allowed to see what Bergman had only imagined.

Even when Anders was working in the bunker and watching the shaped blocks of graphite being assembled, he had felt an identity with Nils Bergman. It wasn't just that it was Bergman's ideas that were being turned into reality. Rather, he was convinced that Bergman would have shared his intentions. Anders was working to make the reactor fail. His hope was that, with the unmeasured heat it would generate, it would boil away its coolant and distort itself beyond recognition. And that, he was sure, was exactly what Bergman would have planned. Certainly, by now, the evidence of Nazi evil would have cut through the intellectual indifference of the man whose life he was living. Bergman would no longer be so casual as to the uses to which the generals would put his work. He would fully understand the awesome energy that his fission theory was about to unleash. And he would be certain of the insane use that his German colleagues planned for that energy. He would realize that he held the power of deciding whether the madness that captured the Continent should now be extended to the entire globe. And he would decide that the devil he had brought to life had to be destroyed. Then, the Germans had moved their Swedish guests out of the city, to a small cottage in the Spreewald, not far from the guest house where they had been reunited. "For your comfort and privacy," Diebner had beamed in making the announcement. Anders nearly laughed. The head of Aryan physics still couldn't bring himself to mention the bombers that had made Berlin too dangerous a place to house their prize scientist.

Their cottage was a farmhouse, a small, stone-walled structure with two small bedrooms and a crude kitchen. A massive fireplace, facing the one common room, was the only source of heat. Because of the confined space and the solid walls, there was no place where Himmler's spies could be hidden. And the two soldiers who escorted their car back and forth from the institute remained posted at the roadside far from the house and clearly in view. For the first time since Birgit's arrival, they were sure that they were alone.

Still, they had saved their secret conversations for the long walks they took through the fields. And now, when they had climbed a rising pasture and could look down on the house with its two guards posted at the gate, Anders raised the question that had been torturing him. He asked Birgit to return to Sweden.

She was stunned by the suggestion, but he began arguing his case before she had time to protest.

"You've done all that you can," he said. "You came here to give me credibility. And you succeeded. You saved the whole plan. You probably saved my life. But that's over. The Germans love Nils Bergman. Christ, Diebner thinks I might even get a medal."

"Then why make them suspicious?" she started to argue.

"They won't," he interrupted. "I've given this a lot of thought. What could be more natural than you going back to the university? I'm an important name there. I'm responsible for important work. My trusted assistant should be there, handling my affairs, not here writing instructions to administrators and students. They're more apt to begin wondering just how important I am in Stockholm if I don't have any representative at the university."

He was right, of course. Their impersonation was fine just as it had originally been planned. She wanted to argue with him, but she couldn't find the words.

"You came here. You visited with me. And then you had to get back to work. It's completely plausible. It's exactly what they should expect."

"And I just leave you here. Alone, and in terrible danger. Is that what you think I should do?"

"The danger is the same whether you are here or there," Anders countered. "And I can still use the escape message. If things seem to be closing in, I can still ask the British to take me out. It would be even easier now. Driving down a country road each day, with two guards and a driver! I'll be an easy kidnap victim."

"If you can get the message out in time. And if Haller can find you in time," she reminded. "You still don't know where they will be taking you."

He nodded. Haller's glib suggestion had never been foolproof. "But your being here with me doesn't make it any more certain. And if it fails, why should both of us be left here with the Nazis?"

"It's my safety that you're worried about, isn't it?" she challenged. He was going to deny it, but the answer was too obvious.

"Why shouldn't I be worried about your safety? I love you more than anything else in my life."

"And I love you," she stated as a fact. "That's why you have to let me stay. For my sake. It's important to me."

"But you can't protect me," Anders insisted.

Birgit turned to look directly into his eyes. "And I can't leave you either. Can you understand that."

He stared back at her while he fumbled for an answer. Then he simply nodded and took her hand. He led her further up the meadow where even more of the open countryside came into view.

"I've been thinking about what the Germans will do," he began again. "In a few days I'm going to start up their test reactor. If I've figured correctly, it's going to overheat. It's going to start to melt and then to burn, and no one will be able to stop it. What they'll be left with is the half-built production reactor that they'll know isn't going to work, and with not enough time to fix it. In a few days even these madmen are going to know that they're finished. And Nils Bergman is going to be the one man they can all point their fingers at. Not a likely candidate for the medal that Diebner keeps hinting at."

"What can they do to you? You're a Swedish citizen. And a world-respected figure."

He smiled at the simplicity of the notion. "Aren't you the one who warned me that they're insane? Do you think, when it finally dawns on them that all is lost, they're going to be very concerned about the niceties of international relations? A foreign saboteur will make a very handy scapegoat."

Birgit had run the same line of logic many times herself. In Sweden, when Anders had simply been a courageous operative, when she was determined to remain uninvolved, she had stopped short of imagining the consequences that he would face. Now in Germany, when he had become the reason for her life, she hadn't even allowed herself to think of the danger. But it was true. Every word that he had spoken was perfectly reasoned. The closer he came to destroying their bomb, the closer he came to his own destruction. And now that moment was only a few days away.

"We'll both leave," she suddenly shouted. "Right now. We'll send the letter in the morning. And you can delay the tests. Just a few days. Just to give the English enough time to come for us."

He pulled her into his arms, and as he held her close she knew that his embrace was her answer. He couldn't leave. His mission was too important. And she couldn't stay. He wouldn't let her put herself at risk. He was saying good-bye.

"I won't leave you," Birgit vowed.

He didn't challenge her decision. Instead, he lifted her chin from his chest and kissed her softly. But her response was fierce. She kissed him wildly, blending their bodies so that they couldn't be separated. In the brutal strength of her embrace, he realized his own need for Birgit. He was telling her to go, and yet he was terrified at the thought of being left alone again. Despite his real concern for her safety, he knew he couldn't bear the sham life he had been living before she joined him.

They settled toward the ground, never relaxing their embrace, already probing into each other's clothing before they reached the thick, moist grass. "Wait," she whispered, and even as she was pulling away she began pushing down her skirt and her underclothes. He threw his own shirt over his head without attempting the buttons, watched greedily as Birgit followed his example and lifted her blouse frantically through the tumbles of her hair. Still on his knees he began tugging on his belt, watching her as she fell back on the rumpled spread of her skirt and blouse.

"The damn thing is stuck," he realized. He tugged at the belt and pushed against the buckle. "It's jammed. The damn buckle is broken."

And suddenly she was laughing, lying nearly naked in the grass and laughing uncontrollably through the tears that had stained her face only moments before. Anders looked at her, and then down at the long end of his belt that was knotted through the simple metal clasp.

"I don't suppose Diebner will ever give me that medal," he teased sheepishly, making her laugh even harder.

"One of the great minds of Europe," she managed to say, and then he was laughing with her.

"How could they think that I was a saboteur?" he asked, shaking his head in disbelief.

She finished his thought even though she could hardly catch her breath. "They'll just think that you're stupid!"

"Stupid!" he protested in mock indignation. He leaped on top of her, pinning her to the ground, and began tickling her. She screamed, pushed him off, and then rolled on top of him. They thrashed about the grass in childish horseplay, threatening one another with outrageous punishments and laughing together at the absurdity of their antics. At one moment, when they had nearly composed themselves, they saw that the two guards far below had heard their private screams. They were staring up the hill in confusion, trying to decide whether they should be coming to someone's rescue.

"See if one of them has a knife, so you can cut your belt," Birgit teased, which sent him pouncing on her once again for another round of tickling.

The wrestling ended in a gentle embrace, and in the calm moment Anders found that that his belt unbuckled quite easily. They finished their lovemaking tenderly, free from the frantic urgency in which they had begun. Then they lay side by side, for the moment unconcerned with the dangers that were closing in around them.

It had been in their laughter more than in their passion that they had realized that they shared a world of their own. Their childlike innocence was an act of defiance, hurled in the faces of the jackbooted madmen who were putting all of Europe to the torch. You can kill us, they seemed to be saying, but you can't destroy us. When you've built all your bombs, and salted the earth with their fire, our love will still be here. And the sound of our laughter will still mock all your pretense of power.

They held hands as they walked slowly down the hill, hardly noticing the two guards who watched them pass. Neither said a word about the possibility of Birgit's leaving.

BERLIN — *August 2 3*

Everything was ready.

The only sound was the hum of the electric motors that had begun pumping the cooling water through the labyrinth of pipes that were buried inside the six-foot-high pile of graphite blocks. The uranium fuel was already in place, pressed into rods that had been carefully inserted into the pile. The cadmium control rods, suspended from pulleys anchored to the ceiling, were ready to be lowered.

"Herr Diebner," Anders said, indicating the switch that would energize the neutron emitter, "will you do me the honor?"

Kurt Diebner flexed his fingers as if he were a surgeon about to take the scalpel. Then he reached out and touched the switch.

The scientists pushed together, peering down at the control panel instruments that would begin to record the neutron activity within the reactor. But Anders wasn't yet interested in the gauges. He was still obsessed with the consequences of the unimagined energy, locked in the atoms of matter since time began, that he was about to release.

It was entirely possible that neither he nor any of the scientists would leave the bunker alive. If the energy multiplied itself quickly enough, then the graphite could begin to burn with the heat of the sun. It could become a fireball feeding on itself and, as Heisenberg had once asked him, what could stop it? Perhaps it would have the power to flash the entire building into flames.

His calculations had shown that the radiation produced by the reaction wouldn't escape from the graphite. And he had added the precaution of a hammered lead shield that separated the pile from the control room. But if the graphite was shattered and the reaction was accelerated, what good were a few microns of lead? Wasn't it possible that the intense radiation would kill life right to the bone marrow?

Diebner had thrown the switch leading to an unknown world, and there were no maps to guide their journey. He had pulled the cork on an all-powerful genie who might not be obedient to their commands, who might not even understand their language. And if it did obey, whose orders would it follow? Hitler's? Himmler's? All the consequences were terrifying.

"We have neutron activity."

It was Lauderbach, giving words to the first movements of a needle.

Anders nodded. It was simply the activity of the energized neutron source. Nothing was yet happening within the dead stillness of the graphite. But soon the self-destruction would begin.

It had to fail. No matter what the dangers of the meltdown, nothing could be as destructive as its success. Give the Nazis the plutonium for their bombs and there would be a hundred meltdowns.

"It's rising."

Diebner's voice had an edge of fear as he pointed an unsteady finger toward the gauge. He looked toward Anders, waiting for the next step. Anders did nothing. A simple tip of his chin acknowledged a result he clearly expected.

"The control rods," Diebner nearly begged.

"Not yet," Anders said.

The level of the needle indicated that fission had begun. Deep within the pile, unstable uranium atoms were shattering, firing off neutron bullets that were splitting other atoms.

Werner Heisenberg recognized the moment from his own test reactor. There was a reaction, but it was not yet self-sustaining. If they turned off the emitter, the needle would quiver and then settle back. He knew that Nils Bergman still had time to cancel the test. If his colleague had any flicker of doubt, this was the time for him to act. But all he could read in Bergman's eyes was icy determination. The man was going on.

"It's accelerating," Lauderbach announced. The rate of increase in fission activity was beginning to rise. Now the neutrons produced by the explosion of atoms were outnumbering those produced by the controllable emitter.

"It's running. It's self-sustaining," Diebner shouted.

Anders nodded. "Just a few more seconds," he said.

Diebner's hand reached toward the switch. His eyes darted toward Anders for instruction.

"All right," Anders advised. Instantly, Diebner threw the toggle. The gauges never faltered. The needles kept climbing.

"We're showing a temperature rise," Heisenberg advised calmly. "It's up to eighty degrees."

There was no response from Anders.

"The reaction is still increasing," Lauderbach reported.

"Ninety degrees," Heisenberg observed, watching the rapid rise in the water temperature.

Anders touched a button. From overhead, the clattering sound of the pulleys responded. The cadmium control rods began lowering into their channels, absorbing neutrons and slowing the chain reaction. He released the button when the rods had dropped a third of their length into the graphite.

"One hundred ten degrees," Heisenberg intoned.

Diebner suddenly looked frantic. "It's running too fast."

Again Anders pushed the control rod button. The rods dropped further into the pile.

"The reaction is still accelerating," Lauderbach shouted. He, too, was beginning to show panic.

Heisenberg's reports were now coming more quickly. "One hundred thirty," he snapped.

The scientists knew that Bergman was working to achieve a delicate balance. The cadmium control rods had to absorb just enough neutrons to stabilize the speed of the reaction. A constant number of neutrons had to be allowed to reach their uranium atom targets, splitting them to release the same number of neutrons. And at that level of activity, the cooling water flow had to be sufficient to carry off the heat that the reaction generated. Both parameters seemed to be failing. The reaction was accelerating, and the water temperature was continuing to climb toward its boiling point.

"One hundred fifty degrees," Heisenberg announced.

Anders responded by once again pressing the button. The control rods lowered further into the graphite blocks. Involuntarily, some of the scientists began backing away from the control console.

"It's slowing," Diebner shouted hopefully. The needle indicating the rate of the reaction was still climbing, but its speed across the face of the dial was lessening. Anders flashed a hair-trigger smile. All his calculations had indicated that the reactor would stabilize itself, and all the work of his colleagues had come to the same conclusion. His test was proceeding exactly on schedule.

"One seventy-five," Heisenberg said of the water temperature. Anders shifted nervously. This was to be the reactor's downfall. The heat that had amazed Heisenberg would continue to climb until the cooling water would prove inadequate.

"It's stable," Diebner gasped. "It's stable. We have complete control of the reaction." Some of the Germans shouted in joy. But others were becoming aware that the water temperature was still rising. Their margin of safety was being cooked away.

"One ninety," Heisenberg said. Now there was an edge of nervousness in his voice. He looked at Bergman, although he understood that there was nothing that the Swedish genius could do. The reaction was stabilized. The control rods were nearly fully inserted. There was no time to begin pulling the fuel rods. And the radiation danger of such an emergency procedure was incalculable.

Anders had reached the moment. In the next twenty seconds, the water temperature would slip past the boiling point. Its ability to carry off heat would be diminished. He would close the control rods to their full effectiveness. The rate of fission would begin to drop, but not quickly enough to compensate for the loss of coolant. Nazi hopes for a super weapon, like the graphite in the pile, would begin to burn away.

"Two hundred," Heisenberg said.

"There's not enough water," Diebner understood. Now he began backing slowly away from the controls.

Anders stretched his fingers toward the control rod button. He was about to announce a shutdown. The test was a failure. But only he knew how catastrophic the failure would be.

"Wait!" the command came from Heisenberg.

He and Anders were the only ones left leaning over the control console. Heisenberg was staring at the water temperature dial, holding one hand in the air as if to block any action by Anders.

"I think we may be all right, Professor Bergman," Heisenberg said cautiously. Anders slipped along the console until he was pressing against Heisenberg. He could see the water temperature gauge hesitating near the boiling mark.

"Too close," Anders said. "We should begin shutdown."

Heisenberg shook his head. "Look, it's in balance. It's right on the edge, but it's in balance."

Anders ran his eyes quickly over the dials. The rate of fission was steady. The water temperature was holding just a few degrees below boiling.

"At this rate of water flow," Heisenberg said, "you could sustain the reaction for a year."

"There's no safety margin," Anders cautioned. But once again, Heisenberg's hand was in the air.

"Just another minute. All we need is enough time to measure the conversion rate. Then we'll be able to check the plutonium yield figures."

Lauderbach led his colleagues in step back to the console.

"It's a success," he whispered.

Anders was stunned. His reactor was running perfectly.

Diebner began to scream with delight. "We've done it! We've done it!" He rushed to Anders. "Professor Bergman, you've done it. A chain reaction. The first ever."

Anders looked past Diebner. "Another minute," he said to Heisenberg. "Any change in the flow rate . . ."

Heisenberg nodded his agreement. They were flirting with disaster. Even a momentary fluctuation in the water pressure could send the heat soaring. But the longer they let it run, the more information they would have for the production reactor.

They all stood in silence. Once again, the only sound was the humming of the electric pumps. The seconds slipped by with all the needles steady in their gauges.

There was nothing that Anders could do. To avoid suspicion he had kept all his calculations as close to legitimate values as possible. He had counted on the runaway heat that Heisenberg had experienced to do the damage. And that heat had failed him by only a few degrees. But that was enough. His design was a success. And with the experience he had gathered, there would be even more safety margins built into the production system.

He had given the Germans their bomb.

"That should be sufficient," Heisenberg finally said.

Anders touched the button. The control rods lowered by their final measure. A few seconds later, the neutron level began to drop. The control rods were absorbing more neutrons than were being released. And the water temperature slowly followed.

Heisenberg turned to his colleague, his face lighted by a broad smile. "The victory is yours, Professor Bergman. I congratulate you. I wanted to be the first. But at least I will always be able to say that I was present when Nils Bergman demonstrated a controlled chain reaction. When he established himself as the leading figure in the world of physics."

"A triumph. A total triumph!" Diebner shouted, leading the scientists in enthusiastic applause. "And look at him. Nils Bergman's moment of triumph, and he looks bewildered."

He grabbed Anders' hand and pumped it enthusiastically.

Anders stood numb. In his coded correspondence, he had assured Haller that his reactor would fail. Now he had to rush a warning to him. The Germans had taken a giant step closer to their bomb.

As the scientists around him shouted their congratulations, his mind was already racing ahead. There was still time. There would still be opportunities to build fatal flaws into the production reactor. He had to assure Haller that, as long as he was on the inside, the Germans might still be stopped.

But the time was short and the opportunities would be few.

LONDON — September 5

Air Marshal Ward paced back and forth, glancing up at the huge aerial photographs that were hanging from the wall, pausing in front of each one as if to give it time to speak. He had been examining them for nearly half an hour, interrupted only by the comments of the technical experts who were watching him. He seemed no closer to reaching a decision.

"We'd have to hit *all* the buildings," he said, echoing the point that Major Haller had made at the outset. "Several direct hits on each building."

"I think so," Haller repeated. "It's the only way to be absolutely certain."

"So it should be during daylight, and from a low altitude."

No one responded to the point on which they had all agreed, so Ward resumed his pacing.

The photos of the Kaiser Wilhelm Institute had been taken months earlier, when Siegfried had first identified the institute as the Nazis' center of uranium research and when they had first weighed the possibility of bombing it to oblivion. A pair of Mosquito bombers, equipped with high-resolution cameras, had photographed the institute as they turned away from another target in order to disguise their interest in the undamaged academic buildings.

"We'd take frightful losses," he concluded, putting into words the obvious fact that no one had wanted to mention.

"Very high," a squadron commander agreed. "We'd want a low speed to give the bombs a vertical drop. The antiaircraft gunners should certainly enjoy themselves."

"And you're not at all certain of the results," Ward said, repeating an earlier comment of the squadron commander.

"By no means. We could certainly rough the place up, but I doubt if we could drop all of the buildings into their cellars. We'd need two or three trips at a minimum."

Ward nodded his agreement with the comment, then turned back to the photographs. There was little doubt left in his mind. What Haller was asking was nearly impossible.

"Thank you, gentlemen," he said without looking back at the airmen he had assembled. "I think you've told me all that I need to know."

The RAF officers rose and filed from the room, leaving Ward alone with Major Haller. Haller's eyes seemed to be pleading as he looked toward the air marshal for his answer.

"I'm afraid I agree with them, Tom. The conditions you put on the raid are quite impossible. There's simply no way we could guarantee to destroy your bunker in one raid. If a single raid is absolutely essential, then I think we'd be risking our chaps needlessly."

Haller nodded. He had listened to the technical comments on the problems posed by the tall, stone buildings. And he had heard the evaluations of the pilots. He had already concluded that he was asking for a great deal.

"We would have to get the reactor in one shot. If we missed it, they would simply move it somewhere else. I think we're better off knowing where it is, with our people on the inside."

Haller had been stunned to learn from Birgit's coded message that the reactor test had been successful. "Design proven," she had written into Bergman's correspondence. "Will scale up to production plant already under construction. Location unknown."

Lindemann had been shocked by the news. To Britain's leading nuclear physicist, the test reactor was the major milestone. If it worked, then a large-scale reactor, producing plutonium in weapons quantities, wouldn't be far behind. "They could certainly run into difficulties," he had told Haller, grasping hopefully for straws. "But a successful pilot reactor would solve the practical problems. You have to assume, if they are ready to run tests, that they have the theoretical problems well in hand. And they would probably be well along with the construction of their production pile."

"How long?" Haller had begged, cutting through the rambling speculations.

Lindemann had looked toward the ceiling for guidance, then thrown up his hands hopelessly. "Impossible to say. Perhaps a few months. Certainly within a year."

"Could they do it in six months?" Haller had pressed.

Lindemann's head had wagged from side to side. "No reason why they couldn't, if they were well along with construction. Once they had the information from the prototype, they might need nothing more than a few refinements."

Haller had turned to his maps, and once again used them as a calendar. Lindemann was speculating that the Germans could be running a production reactor in February, perhaps even in January. That meant full-scale plutonium production in February or March, which put atomic warheads on the V-2 rockets by April. And the maps told him that they would probably have all the time they needed. The Allies were still well short of the German border, their advance, which had liberated Paris in a whirlwind, now slowed by a lack of supplies. Patton's tanks, charging toward the Saar, had simply run out of fuel. Montgomery refused to move on the Schelde estuary until his ammunition was fully replenished. The trucks bringing supplies up from the beaches of Normandy and Calais simply couldn't keep up with the advance, and the front had slowed to a crawl, waiting for them to catch up.

They would reach the German border in December, at the earliest, Haller had concluded from a study of the maps. Across the Rhine in, perhaps, February. Unless the Germans surrendered, they would have their bomb at least two months before the Allies could overrun the fatherland. And why would they surrender when they were about to bolt their victory on the noses of their incredible drones?

"We've got to get their prototype reactor," he had told Air Marhall Ward. "It's the only way we can slow them down." In response, Ward had reviewed the aerial photos of the Kaiser Wilhelm, and assembled his top airmen to evaluate the raid. But the problems they had just presented seemed insurmountable.

"Perhaps," Ward said, "we should settle for a night raid. We could send a few Mosquitos in first to light the entire area with flares. Then the heavy bombers could attack in force. We could certainly make the place uninhabitable. And we might get lucky."

But Haller was already shaking his head. "We would have to be absolutely positive. If we missed, and they moved the reactor, we might lose all contact with their program. If we can't be certain that we've destroyed it, then I think we're better off knowing where it is and what they're up to."

Ward pursed his lips. "It's risky, letting them go ahead."

"It's risky either way," Haller said. "Right now, our best chance is to find a way to get our troops into Germany sooner." He pulled his red beret from his pocket and set it on an angle over his ear. "I'll pay a visit to our friends on the Continent. Maybe we'll be able to light a fire under them. And if that fails, then maybe we'll talk about your night raid. It may be the only hope we have left."

He was nearly to the door when Ward suddenly asked, "What about Siegfried?"

Haller didn't understand the question.

"You never mentioned him . . . or the young woman . . . when you were asking about the bombing. A daylight raid? Wouldn't they be working in the bunker during the day? If we could give you direct hits on all the buildings, their chances of survival would be slim. You must have thought about that."

Haller stepped back into the room. He nodded slowly. "I did think about it. But only for a few seconds. It's not the kind of thing we can let ourselves think about."

Ward was staring directly at him.

"Damn it," Haller snapped, "I know how it sounds. But if your pilots could give me direct hits, I'd ask for the mission no matter how many of them might get killed. I'd trade lives if I could stop this thing. A lot of lives, even civilians. And if I could succeed, I'd think I got a hell of a bargain."

Ward's gaze relaxed. "You're right, of course. Let's hope it doesn't have to come to that."

"Let's hope," Haller said.

BERLIN — *September 7*

The changes were minute; fractional alterations in the design as he transposed his test reactor into the blueprints for the full-scale machine. But cumulatively they would cause the neutrons to travel at even slower speed, and cause the reaction to accelerate beyond the limits of control.

Anders had been working alone. Heisenberg and most of the scientists had been moved to the production reactor site, wherever that was. Their papers and records had been packed in the middle of a night, and the next morning they had been given just a few seconds to gather their personal belongings. A few days later, half the engineering staff had vanished along with all of the chemists. Anders was left behind at the institute, with a few scientists to assist him and the draftsmen who would transform his calculations and rescale his design into plans for the production reactor.

"Am I not trusted?" he had screamed at Diebner. "Are there to be only Germans present when my ideas are fully proven?"

"Of course not, Professor Bergman," Diebner had insisted. "We will be moving you and Miss Zorn immediately. But for now, you are needed here, with the reactor, to supervise the preparation of the plans. It has to be this way. The others are needed at the production site to begin construction. As soon as your work is completed, you will be joining them."

Diebner had cajoled and flattered. To demonstrate his affection he had offered Anders and Birgit a more luxurious house. And when they refused, he had stocked their small cottage with wines that had been looted from France and with delicacies from all the conquered countries. He had even presented Birgit with a coat made from soft Russian sables. "You are world heroes," he told Anders. And then he discussed the plans that were being made for publishing Bergman's work as soon as the war was ended. "All the world's scientists will learn exactly what you have achieved," he promised over and over.

The procedure made sense. The scientists and engineers weren't needed for the work he was doing. They would be better utilized in building the new reactor. But still, there was evidence everywhere that the Nazis might be suspicious of his loyalty. Diebner still refused to tell him where the reactor was being built, pleading the necessity for military security every time the question was raised. Elaborate procedures had been put in place to deny him any direct contact with the colleagues who had gone ahead. As each drawing was completed, the pages were snatched from the drafting board and handed to a courier in an SS uniform. The same courier brought back questions and suggestions concerning the plans from the other scientists.

"It would be easier if we spoke by telephone," Anders complained to Diebner whenever he had visited the bunker. "We waste time when it takes two or three days for me to hear their opinions on the work I am doing."

"Anyone can listen in on telephone lines," Diebner countered. On another occasion he had claimed that some of the phone lines had been destroyed by Allied saboteurs.

But despite his near paranoia, Anders was well aware that it was only because of his isolation that he had been able to work his nearly inperceptible changes into the reactor design. He would not have been able to alter his calculations if Heisenberg or Lauderbach were looking over his shoulder. Or, if they were doing parts of the redesign, then the inconsistencies would have become apparent as soon as they tried to put the pieces together. Instead, they were accepting the drawings he sent as perfect extensions of his already proven design.

At first, his scheme had seemed obvious and dangerous. Wouldn't Heisenberg recognize that the new drawings did not match the proven calculations the instant he ran his eyes over the first page of blueprints? Wouldn't Lauderbach go running to Diebner with the first hint of sabotage? After the courier had left with the first parcel for the construction site, Anders had sat up all night staring aimlessly into the smoldering embers in the fireplace.

"I've given them all the evidence they need to take us out and shoot us," he admitted to Birgit when she left their bed to join him. "All someone has to do is work backward. Take the plans and recalculate the equations that they represent."

"Is anyone capable of doing that?" she asked. "It's all so theoretical. There's so much room for judgment."

He nodded. "Heisenberg. Heisenberg would see through it in a minute if he had any reason to be suspicious. And perhaps Lauderbach. If anyone raises a question to either of them, they'll see what I'm up to."

She moved closer to him and leaned against his shoulder. "We have to risk it," she said, indicating that she was more than willing to share his fate. "There's no other way."

He felt her shivering in the cold, and he pushed two fresh logs into the embers. In an instant, the cherry red coals had become bright yellow flames. Then they sat silently, sharing the warmth, each realizing that the time they had left together would probably be counted in hours.

But there had been no protest from the reactor site. The courier arrived to gather the next few drawings as soon as they were completed, and when he returned, the questions that he brought from the scientists had nothing to do with the flaws he had introduced.

With each new day, Anders had become more confident that his destructive work would go undetected. New pages were rushed from the bunker, and the comments that came back indicated that the reactor was being built precisely according to his calculations. Diebner, during his visits, was bubbling with enthusiasm over the spectacular progress they were making.

Each night, he and Birgit had found new reasons for hope. Rumors had the Allies already at the German border. If, as it seemed, the Germans were investing everything in his doomed design, then it would take them several months to recover. And if the Allies were already at the Rhine, then the reactor wouldn't be ready soon enough. As they huddled in front of their fire, late into the nights, they were tempted to think of a future that only weeks before was beyond their imagination.

But he had to be certain. Before he could send a coded message to Haller, he had to be positive that the changes he had made would end any chance of a German atomic bomb. He would start again and recheck every equation, every calculation. Only then would he let himself think about a future.

GATWICK — *September 8*

The radar screens at Fighter Command were alive.

Captain Davey Jones stood in the darkness, staring over the shoulders of the two men and two women who sat before the glowing tubes, watching the abrupt spikes that indicated approaching buzz bombs.

"Jerry is keeping busy this morning," he commented idly. The line of flying bombs that were cruising across the Channel seemed endless.

"Five in the past hour," Sergeant Tony Maginnis answered above the chatter of communications between the radar specialists and the Fighter Command pilots who were on station over the Channel. Maginnis was the senior operator, a slight and bespectacled young man who had been rejected for military service until his genius for electronics had made him essential to national defense.

The radars detected the V-1 bombs before they crossed the Dutch coastline. The operators locked on with antennas located several hundred miles apart along the British side of the Channel and used the two ranges to fix the precise position of the target.

Then they directed the high-speed Typhoons that were on patrol toward an intercept point.

The propeller-driven Typhoons couldn't match the speed of the jet-propelled buzz bombs. So as they headed toward the intercept, they climbed high above the approaching target. Then they dove down, building up the speed they needed for one firing pass. The tactic was highly effective on clear days when the bomb, with its telltale trail of black smoke, was easily seen. It was less effective at night when the red glow at the jet engine's exhaust was the only visible target.

The German drones, despite their deadly cargo, had become routine. Out over the Channel, the Typhoon pilots had grown used to flying the vectors that the radar operators assigned. They had learned that the flying bombs, unlike manned aircraft, couldn't take evasive maneuvers and couldn't fire back at them. So they pulled in close, steadied their fighters to bring all their guns to bear, and hammered away until the buzz bomb broke into pieces, or pulled away out of the range of their guns. In London, the populace had learned to ignore the sputtering sound of the jet engines. It was only when they heard the engine stop that they dove for cover.

Captain Jones had stepped away from the radar screens to fix the third pot of tea of his watch, when he heard Maginnis scream over the normal murmur of conversation, "Good God, what the hell is this?"

He scarcely looked up from the steaming kettle that he was pouring into the porcelain pot.

"I've got one coming in at two thousand miles per hour."

Jones laughed. "What you've got is a burned-out capacitor," he quipped. "You better switch to another monitor." He put the kettle back on the stove and carefully placed the cover onto the teapot.

"I've got it too," one of the women operators called. "Speed, two thousand. Altitude . . . I can't tell. It's climbing right off the scale."

He shook his head as he walked back toward the radar screens. "Nothing flies at two thousand miles an hour," he chastised. But Jones could see the spike on the electronic trace that indicated a target reflecting the radar signal. It was moving so quickly that he could actually see its progression across the screen.

"I can't even get a fix on it," Maginnis said, panic beginning to creep into his voice. "By the time I switch from one antenna to the other, the damn thing has already moved."

"Twenty-two hundred miles per hour. Altitude over sixty thousand feet," the woman operator said factually, elaborating on her previous report.

"Goddamn it," Jones barked. "Nothing travels that fast. And nothing flies that high. Check your equipment."

He watched while Maginnis switched his radar monitor into the test mode. The anticipated values immediately appeared.

"Set is okay," Maginnis reported. He switched back to the target display. The spike had moved a third of the way across the screen in the few seconds it had taken to run the test.

"What the hell is that thing?" Jones demanded. "It must be a bloody meteorite."

"But it was climbing . . . not falling,"the young woman corrected.

"It can't be," Jones snapped. He reached over her shoulder to the control dials and began checking her calculations.

"I've got a fix," Maginnis interrupted. "It's on the same course as the buzz bombs. It's heading toward London."

Jones stared bewildered at the displays as his own calculations confirmed what his operators were reporting.

"Should we give the target to Fighter Command?" Maginnis asked.

Jones shook his head. "They wouldn't believe it. They'd think we were all drinking."

"It's a real target," Maginnis reminded. "We've got it on both antennas. Maybe it's some kind of artillery shell."

"There's no such thing," Jones snapped. "What kind of cannon can fire from Holland to England?"

"Range, two hundred miles," the woman said. "Time to London . . . six minutes."

Jones stared at the spike, now halfway across the radar display.

"Why tell Fighter Command?" he asked absently. "If it's real, there isn't a damn thing they can do about it."

"It's gaining speed," the woman's voice announced. "Twenty-four hundred."

"And it's coming down," Maginnis added. "The damn thing climbed off the screen and now it's back on."

"Tell them," Jones said.

Maginnis keyed his handset. "Errand Boy, this is Palace. We have a target bearing zero eight five, range two hundred, speed twenty-four hundred, altitude sixty. Unidentified."

The speaker responded immediately. "Say again, Palace. Understood speed twenty-four hundred. Is that two forty?"

"Negative," Maginnis answered. "Speed twenty-four hundred."

There was a pause. Then the voice came back through the speaker. "Are you chaps quite all right? It can't be twenty-four hundred."

"Speed still twenty-four hundred," the woman intoned. "Arrival at London, five minutes."

Jones snatched up a telephone that connected him with the air defense commander for the London district. He identified himself, paused for an instant, and then screamed into the phone, "Get him out of his bloody meeting right now. This is an emergency." He looked back at the screen while he waited. The identifying spike was now two-thirds of the way across the display. "Jones, here," he suddenly barked, his eyes riveted to the target. "We have something new coming at us from Holland. It's traveling at twenty-four hundred miles an hour, descending from something like eighty thousand feet. It should hit down in . . ."

"Four minutes," the woman told him.

"Four minutes," he repeated into the phone.

He listened for a moment, his face expressionless. Then he hung up the handset. Maginnis was waiting for his instructions.

"He told me to pray," Jones mumbled. He leaned over his operators and watched the spike as it slid steadily closer to the end of the display screen.

No one saw it. The German's first operational V-2 rocket broke through a murky sky in a vertical dive at over 2,000 miles an hour.

Four seconds later, it blasted through the top of a four-story building and ripped through its foundations. It was twenty feet below street level when its ton of high explosives ignited.

From the deep cavern it had dug for itself, the blast had little effect. Its energy was directed upward, vaporizing the building it had already cut through, and shaking the surrounding buildings from their foundations. Less than half a block was destroyed. People only a few streets away had no idea that there had even been an explosion.

But Haller knew what warhead the incredible rocket had been designed to carry. And if the British had learned to defend themselves against the buzz bombs, then the Germans had gone them one better. There was no possible defense against a rocket that climbed out of the atmosphere and plunged down on its target at three times the speed of sound. There could never be a defense against such a weapon.

The report that he held in his hands proved that the Nazis had already achieved half their victory. They had demonstrated the precision with which they could place their atomic bomb in the heart of London, even announced that it was coming, for all the chance that the British had of stopping it. All they needed was their warhead.

"Production reactor will suffer catastrophic failure," Anders had assured in his coded message. It was the only hope left to Haller. If the amateur agent, isolated in Germany, was wrong, then the Nazis would soon achieve the other half of their victory.

BERLIN — *September 10*

"It will mean our annihilation," General von Rundstedt pleaded. "We are in no condition to hold the line. We must reconsider."

But the half-lighted face behind the giant desk remained silent. The hands kept fingering through the papers as if to demonstrate that Himmler wasn't even paying attention.

"If we fall back to the Rhine, we will have a chance. We can regroup. Resupply our divisions. Then, with the Rhine as a barrier, we may be able to hold."

It was the same logic von Rundstedt had laid out before the fuehrer when he had been summoned to the labyrinthine command bunker. Hitler had taken away his command only a month before, furious that the Allied invasion had succeeded. Now the great leader was ordering him back to the western front to stem the onslaught that seemed to be gaining momentum. But his orders were ridiculous.

"How can I hold Holland without bringing in more armor? And if I do, the allies will simply bypass Holland, cutting off the armor I have supplied and leaving me with that much less to build a defensive perimeter."

He waited for a counterargument, but none came. Himmler continued to busy himself with the files on his desk.

"And then counterattack!" Von Rundstedt threw up his hands. "With what? If I were going to counterattack, why would I leave armored divisions to be cut off in Holland? Don't you see? I'd be destroying our entire western force just to gain a few weeks. Perhaps a month. But after that month, the Reich would be left defenseless."

The hands came to rest, and then the whispered voice spoke from behind the glow of the desk lamp. "I would assume that the fuehrer considers time to be more important than your armies."

"Are there new armies being raised?" von Rundstedt asked sarcastically. "Armies I don't know about? Perhaps manned by the children and old men that we are now pouring into the ranks?"

"The fuehrer has his reasons," the disembodied voice said softly.

"But if you would speak with him, Reichsfuehrer. He has the highest regard for your opinion."

"And I for his," the voice snapped back, this time with a menacing edge of anger. "He has always been right, even when our general officers couldn't understand his wisdom."

Von Rundstedt felt his muscles tightening. It took all his effort to keep from hurling himself over the desk and choking the frail neck until it snapped in two. He had seen the fuehrer's genius firsthand when Hitler had withheld Rommel's panzers from attacking the Normandy invasion. "It couldn't be the invasion," Hitler had insisted, because it was not where he had predicted the invasion would come. So he had kept Rommel guarding Pas de Calais until the Allies had won the beachheads of Normandy. If von Rundstedt had been giving the orders instead of the fuehrer, the forces that were now charging through Belgium would have been thrown back into the Atlantic.

"Herr Himmler," he said, refusing to speak the detestable little bastard's lofty title, "for all his genius, the fuehrer cannot possibly know the condition of the troops he is asking to mount a counterattack."

"Not asking," Himmler responded in an almost singsong tone. "Ordering. The fuehrer is ordering them to attack. And may I suggest, Herr Rundstedt, that you cannot possibly know the weapons that we will have ready for our enemies in just a few months. Weapons that will crush them completely. He orders the attack because that is what the Reich needs of its armies. Not victories! Just time. Enough time to prepare the ultimate victory."

The general felt his strength crumbling under a tremendous weight of despair. They were all mad with their super weapons. Their scientific wonders made great propaganda for battered civilians. But they did nothing for his soldiers in the trenches.

"We will be slaughtered," he begged. "There will be no one left to fire the new weapons."

There was a moment of silence, and then an insulting snicker came from behind the desk. "With our new weapons, we will have no need of soldiers," Himmler said. "Let me assure you, General von Rundstedt, that if you can hold the western front until February, then the Allies will surrender in March."

Von Rundstedt was stunned at the audaciousness of the suggestion. Were they all crazy? Did they honestly think that the massed Allied armies, now dwarfing the German forces in both men and material, would surrender before a doomed counterattack?

"Reichsfuehrer Himmler," he tried patiently, "I fully appreciate the importance of our new rockets and of the new jet fighters that are being delivered to the Luftwaffe. I share your belief that with these weapons, and a little time, we may be able to make a stand. But even with all these weapons, how can we hope to make a stand if all our divisions are either dead, or penned into prison camps? If we are to make a stand during the winter, we should rescue what is left of our armies now."

"The rockets and the jet fighters are only the beginning," Himmler's voice responded. "We have a new weapon that will be ready in a few months, and that will destroy our enemies in a day. I'm afraid, General, that our armies must die where they stand. There can be no retreat." The voice paused for a moment, letting the death sentence register with Germany's highest-ranking military leader. "That is the sacrifice that the Reich demands. By that sacrifice, your soldiers will buy us the time we need to deliver the final blow to our enemies. They will be fully responsible for our total victory."

Von Rundstedt stared blindly into the light. He reached out to the top of the desk and retrieved the orders that Himmler hadn't bothered to examine. He had started to turn away from the desk when he thought of an alternative that might spare some of his troops from the slaughter that was inevitable.

"Perhaps I could buy all the time you need by a carefully staged retreat. If we fell back in stages, holding a line and then retreating to the next line."

"I would suggest, General von Rundstedt, that you put your trust in the fuehrer's judgment," Himmler answered softly. "I would advise you to follow his orders."

He was in his command car, speading from Berlin toward the Belgian frontier, before he had the courage to examine his orders again. "Hold Holland at the line of the Waal River. Prepare a counterattack from the Belgian frontier toward Namur, isolating the Allied armies that were pressing toward the Ruhr." It was insane. Holland was of little value, except as a launch site for their useless rockets. And his armies should be falling back to defend the Rhine, not charging forward and leaving the center of German heavy industry totally undefended.

Why? To buy time for another of the super weapons that Goebbels kept promising? What kind of super weapon could stop Patton's tanks? What kind of sick minds thought that there was any weapon that could make the British surrender?

EINDHOVEN — September 22

Haller's information had been decisive.

He had arrived on the Continent as the furious debate was raging between Montgomery, leading the northern armies into Holland, and Eisenhower, who commanded all the Allied armies. Montgomery was proposing a massive airborne assault to seize all the bridges through Holland and across the lower Rhine. He planned to drive his armor in a lightning assault across the bridges and into the heart of Germany, hastening the Nazi collapse by months. Eisenhower had decided that the plan couldn't work. To equip the headstrong British field commander, he would have to steal supplies from all the other Allied forces, causing the entire front to grind to a halt. And even if Montgomery's force did make it into Germany, its entire supply would have to be carried across the series of bridges he had seized. If the Germans succeeded in destroying just one bridge, the attacking army would be stranded with no avenue of retreat.

Bedell Smith was negotiating between the two generals, trying to keep Montgomery pacified so that he wouldn't take his complaints public. The hero of El Alamein had become a legend to the English people, and his constant demands to be put in charge were threatening the entire structure of the unified command. Smith was on his guard when Haller was saluted into his office. The last thing he needed was another English officer who had been carefully rehearsed to plead Montgomery's case.

Haller knew nothing of the controversy. There were just two facts that he wanted to bring to the attention of Eisenhower, and he had no way of knowing that they would prove to be the levers that Montgomery needed. One was the German's new V-2 rocket. "The damn things are range critical," he told Smith. "They're designed to fly from Holland. We can cripple the whole concept if we push north into the launching areas instead of east into Germany." He made the same case for the buzz bombs. Several of them had failed to explode on landing, and the English had found that their fuel tanks were empty. "They don't shut off their engines. They simply run out of gas," he explained. "Move the Germans back out of Holland and they won't be able to reach England."

His second point was the timetable for the uranium warhead that the two guided missiles would be able to carry. The Germans had already proven their prototype design, and he couldn't rely on Siegfried's assurances that their production reactor would be any less successful. The Germans could be producing plutonium in less than six months. "We're talking about atomic bombs falling in England by spring," he explained patiently, hoping that Smith would react with the same panic that he himself had been feeling since Anders had told him of the successful reactor test. "The bastards can still win this thing."

But Smith had played his poker hand, his face expressionless as he made notes of the meeting. He had tried to console Haller by pointing to rapid advances that the Allies were making all across the front. "If we can open Antwerp, we'll triple our supply capabilities," he said, echoing the logistic strategy that Eisenhower had explained repeatedly. "We should be at the Rhine, from Switzerland to the North Sea, by Christmas."

"That won't be soon enough," Haller had finally snapped, running around Bedell Smith's desk to get to the wall map. "The Germans will still hold all of northern Holland. They'll still have safe launching pads for their rockets. And they'll be building their uranium bombs here . . ." His finger jabbed toward Nordhausen. "That's still two hundred miles beyond the Rhine." He spread his fingers from Holland to southern England, and then swung an arc down through France. "They'll be able to obliterate any targets in this entire area, and that covers all the territory we'll be holding at Christmas. Christ, you keep saying that Antwerp is the key to the war. The Germans will be able to make Antwerp disappear once they have their bomb."

Smith had nodded, then closed his notebook. There was no arguing with the case Haller was making. Speed was essential. They had to get into Germany before the Nazis could fabricate their bomb. And they had to take out the rocket launching pads.

"I'll review this with Ike," he had promised Haller. But he already knew the advice he would give to the supreme commander. Montgomery's dash across the bridges was the best chance they had, even though it wasn't much of a chance at all.

Now Haller paced back and forth in a battered house near Eindhoven that the British had converted to a command post. Through the empty window frames he could see the trucks rushing supplies up the road toward Nijmegen where the Americans were assaulting one of the bridges. Over the field radio, he was listening to reports from Arnhem, where his own regiment had parachuted onto another of the bridges. The news wasn't good.

Von Rundstedt's war-worn divisions were fighting for Holland as if it were Germany itself. They weren't even attempting to blow the bridges, which was what Montgomery had feared the most. Instead they were using the bridges themselves to rush troops into the area. Just north of Eindhoven, they were attacking both sides of the corridor, trying to shut down the supply road that the British armor at the front desperately needed. At the Waal River, they were battling the American paratroopers in the streets that led up to the bridge. And at the Rhine crossing, the Red Devils were being slaughtered in buildings that were a half mile from their target.

"We're still in the game," Bedell Smith said, trying to sound optimistic despite the reports that were spread across the kitchen table that was serving as a desk. "The Poles are dropping into Arnhem this afternoon to reinforce your guys. And our people are going to try to force the Waal right here." He pointed to the shoreline west of the Nijmegen bridge where the American paratroopers were mounting an invasion in rubber rafts. "If we get Nijmegen, then we have a clear road for the armor right up to Arnhem. We'll be hitting the Germans from three sides."

Haller nodded without enthusiasm. His thoughts had drifted far beyond the tactics of the battle.

"I think they're on to us," he reasoned. "I think they know exactly what we're after. They know that this is the battle that decides the war. Why else would they be throwing everything they've got into Holland?"

Smith didn't understand.

"What does von Rundstedt gain by attacking in Holland?" Haller pursued. "He's taking troops and armor that he needs to defend his side of the Rhine, and wasting them on our side. Why? What is he gaining?"

"A glorious victory for the fuehrer?" General Smith speculated sarcastically.

"Time," Haller said in answer to his own question. "He's trading troops for time. Which means that, unless he's crazy, he knows that time is more important than armies. He knows that if he can buy enough time, he won't need the armies."

Smith looked puzzled. "Maybe," he allowed. "But maybe you're giving them too much credit. Arnhem is a bridge over the Rhine. It could be simply that a good offense is their best defense."

Haller walked to the window and stared at the trucks that were now stalled along the road outside. "Possible," he admitted. "But it ties in with their schedule. We know they've taken a reactor critical. And we know they have a production plant under construction. All they need is a few months. My guess is that they see this attack as a frantic attempt to deny them the time they need. I think that's why they've marched half their army into Holland. They're fighting for time . . . not for territory."

Throughout the day, the two men monitored the messages coming from the battles that were raging up the road. Repeatedly, Smith picked up a secure phone and talked with Eisenhower, giving him an accurate recitation of the facts uncolored by his emotional swings from hope to despair.

He was drained by reports that German fighters and antiaircraft fire were slaughtering the transports that carried the Polish parachute regiment. Then he was lifted by a message from the American airborne troops reporting that they were across the Waal.

Spirits plunged when communications were lost with the Red Devils who were pinned down near the Arnhem bridge, but rose when he learned that the Americans had taken the Nijmegen bridge intact, and that British tanks were starting across.

"One more bridge," he told Eisenhower. "It's only eight miles, but von Rundstedt wants it just as much as we do."

He listened for several seconds before he hung up, then turned to Haller. "Ike has told Montgomery that he has to decide by morning whether he's going ahead or pulling back. He's afraid that, even if we take the bridges, we won't be able to keep the road open."

"Christ," Haller cursed. "We've got to keep going."

Bedell Smith shook his head. "How, if we can't move supplies and reinforcements?" He gestured toward the window. The supply trucks were still stalled outside.

It was nearly midnight when the verdict came in. Montgomery's tanks were stopped dead, five miles from the Arnhem bridge. The Red Devils were pulling out of the city, moving in small groups across the Rhine and escaping southward. German troops had cut the road at two points, and the Americans had scarcely been able to push them back. Montgomery was ordering a retreat as far as Eindhoven.

For some reason, Bedell Smith felt that he had personally let Haller down, and apologized for the failure of the attack. "What's your next move?" he asked.

"Berlin, I suppose," Haller answered wearily. "As far as we know, they're still getting information from their prototype reactor. Maybe we can slow them down a bit. It's not much. But right now, it looks like the only play we can make."

BERLIN — *September 27*

They were driving through the streets, headed out of the city toward their farmhouse, when the sirens crashed through the still darkness. Their driver slowed as he weighed his options. He could dash back toward the safety of the Kaiser Wilhelm, which the bombers seemed to regard as privileged ground. Or he could accelerate toward the south, hoping to clear the target area before the bombs began to fall.

He turned in his seat. "Herr Professor Bergman, I think we should return. We can be back at the institute in just a few minutes."

"We're nearly out of the city," Anders answered.

"It's risky," the driver reminded. "The bombs could fall anywhere."

He looked at Birgit, who seemed unconcerned by the fear that the sirens were causing all around them. People who had been walking in the streets were suddenly running toward doorways. Others were fleeing out of the buildings and crowding toward the protection of the basement doors.

"I think it's best to keep going," she said. "The further away from the center of the city, the better."

Anders nodded his agreement to the driver, who immediately shifted and began to accelerate. But his speed was limited. There were no lights, other than the pale glow of his half-painted headlamps, and there were shadowy forms darting across his path to find shelter. His horn was useless, drowned in the wail of the sirens and ignored by people whose attention was focused on more threatening dangers. The intersections passed slowly, and he counted each one as if it were a milestone.

"We'll never make it," he finally shouted without taking his eyes from the road. "I think I should stop so that you can get into a basement shelter."

"Keep driving," Anders decided. "They could be attacking anywhere. We'll be safe."

But even as he was speaking, their escape path was blocked. Two military trucks had pulled to the side of the street. Soldiers, young boys in mismatched uniforms, were pouring out of the cloth-covered cargo bays. Some were diving for shelter between the wheels. Others were attempting to set up machine guns in the street and on top of the truck.

The driver braked and then backed into a U-turn, the wheels jumping up onto the sidewalk. "I think you should take shelter, Herr Professor."

"Can we try another route?" Anders asked. The driver hunched his shoulders. Nothing was certain. And they were losing time. The bombs could begin falling any second.

Suddenly, the sky ahead of them burst into brilliant blue light, silhouetting the skeletons of wasted buildings. It was as if a star had suddenly fallen on top of them.

"My God," Anders shouted. He felt Birgit's grip tighten around his arm.

"Flares," the driver yelled back. "They're dropping flares to light up their target."

Anders could see the light source, an intense flame like the cutting heat of an acetylene torch, descending slowly through the night.

"They're attached to parachutes, so they hang in the air like searchlights."

The shape of a small bomber flew into the glow, and behind it another point of light exploded. And then there were more planes, perhaps a dozen, seeding the sky with flares until the noon sun seemed to be shining over the Dahlem suburb.

"It's over the institute," the driver shouted. "They're bombing near the institute." He braked the car, and started to open his door when a crash of cannon fire paralyzed him. Brilliant red flashes leaped up from the ground. An instant later, the sky seemed to explode, in white bursts where the sky was dark and in ugly black smears where the night had been illuminated by the flares.

"We'll get to a shelter," the driver ordered, finally climbing out of his door and throwing open the passenger door. Anders scampered out, pulling Birgit behind him. But he stopped dead in the street between the abandoned car and the safety of the buildings. He was aware of a new sound, growing steadily in intensity and rising above the chatter of the antiaircraft guns. It was the drone of airplane engines, rising in a crescendo like a drumroll in an overture.

"The shelter!" their driver yelled, but his voice was scarcely noticed over the howl of the engines. Anders didn't respond. He was transfixed by the unleashed violence that was shattering the sky. He pulled Birgit close as if to protect her, but he remained frozen in place, his eyes searching for the armada of bombers still hidden in the darkness above the glowing globe created by the flares.

The driver tugged at his sleeve, but Anders didn't notice. Birgit stood pressed against him, looking up in disbelief at the deafening power that was assembling overhead. And then the planet began to explode.

Shocks of fiery light belched up from behind the roof lines of the buildings. At first they were separate clusters, but then new blasts filled in the voids until the horizon ahead was raging. Before the flashes could dim, swirling columns of fire rose up to take their place. And then the fires were split by new explosions of yellow and red.

The sound struck them like the crack of a whip. Birgit and Anders felt its impact on their faces an instant before it set their heads ringing. Then the ground under their feet began to tremble. They could see the dark shapes of the buildings vibrate against the crimson sky and could feel the clouds of dust that were shaken from the rooftops.

The cataclysm grew worse as new waves of bombers emptied their bellies over the same target. They had no need of the flares that by now had burned out. The fires from the first raiders had turned the target into a giant incandescent lamp. New spears of light were followed by even more brilliant towers of flame. The crashing of the explosives was blended into a constant, head-splitting roar.

Anders realized that he and Birgit were not alone. The people who had rushed into the basements had realized that the attack was in another part of the city. Slowly, they had climbed from their holes back up to the street. They were staring dumbstruck, the parchment of their faces colored with the bloodred glow of the fires. The center of their eternal Reich was vanishing before their eyes.

The explosions stopped, and Anders could once again hear the drone of the engines, now diminishing as the planes moved away. But the fires grew more intense, spreading as they found new fuel in the rubble of the target buildings. Columns of fire intertwined, building into tornados of flame that seemed to climb endlessly. Pieces of charred debris rose with them, dancing in their climb as if to the score of a mad symphony.

A man standing next to them began to cry. He pulled two small boys into his embrace, buried his face in their bodies and shook them with his sobs. Another man stepped toward him, reached out a consoling hand but then turned away in despair. He had no words. He knew they were all doomed.

The stilled crowd began to move in slow processions toward their houses. But their faces remained fixed on the fires, filled with the realization of the hell that awaited them all. They had been gods, with power over all men. Now the Valhalla of their scientists was being offered up to a greater god in a giant immolation.

Anders felt Birgit's body trembling. He broke his fixation with the flames and turned his face toward hers, finding her cheeks streaked with tears.

"It's over. We're safe," he assured her.

But she shook her head. "It isn't over," she whispered. "It's just beginning. The madness is just beginning."

The driver pushed them back into the car and headed away from the inferno, weaving carefully through the clusters of frightened faces that couldn't turn their gaze away from their fate. He crept past the army trucks with their cargos of uniformed children, and through other streets that were lighted with the reflections of dancing flames. They were well out into the country, with Birgit and Anders still huddled together in silence, before the driver spoke.

"Perhaps you should return to your own country, Professor Bergman."

Anders made no reply.

"That was the institute sector that was bombed. I don't think there is anything left to go back to."

Anders caught the driver's eye in the rearview mirror. He nodded in agreement. There couldn't be anything left.

"I think," the man continued, "that things here will only get worse. If I weren't German . . . if this weren't my home, I would try to get out."

"Perhaps," Anders conceded. But he knew he couldn't leave yet. There was a greater horror yet to come. A horror that he had to prevent if the madness were ever to stop.

FALL

1944

The Allied attack that had liberated France during the summer suddenly ground to a halt. The British and American armies had outrun their supplies, and somehow the battered Germans had thrown together a defensive wall. Montgomery seemed to pitch camp at the Dutch border, and Bradley's troops were caught in a killing ground called the Ardennes. Even the Russians were stopped. The whirlwind that had driven the Germans out of the Ukraine and across Poland was funnelled into the narrow space between the Alps and the North Sea. The compact German lines proved impossible to penetrate. In England, the silent, invisible rockets were falling like rain. No one doubted the eventual victory. It was just a matter of time. But, as a few men knew, time was running out.

BERLIN — *October 1*

Heinrich Himmler stood beside his staff car, pressed and polished as if he were reviewing a parade. The black cap, with its silver raven, was squared low over his bespectacled eyes. The lightning bolts gleamed on the lapels of his fitted jacket. The black pants, with their silver trim, were tucked into leather boots that were soft with fresh oil. His riding crop was tucked under his left arm and he held a pair of gloves in his right hand.

"Everything," he whispered more to himself than to Kurt Diebner who was standing to his left and a half pace behind him. "Everything is destroyed."

In front of them were the blighted remains of the Kaiser Wilhelm Institute, truncated stone walls outlining the foundations of buildings, protruding through a desert of black ash. Only the steel frame of the domed tower remained. The debris contained within the shape of the great library was still smoldering. Two hundred thousand volumes had fallen through shattered floors into the basement. It would take days for all the pages to burn themselves into vapor.

The first bombs had crashed through the timbered roofs, smashing their way to the foundations before they exploded. The thick stone walls had contained the blast impact, forcing the energy up through the buildings and turning each structure into a blast furnace. Then subsequent hailstorms of bombs had pounded the walls to rubble.

"We were finished with our experiments," Diebner consoled. "We had learned everything there was to learn. We were ready to move on to the production site."

"Then there will be no delay?" Himmler asked, as he began to pull the gloves over his fingers.

"None whatsoever, Reichsfuehrer," Diebner chanted.

Himmler walked out into the wreckage, stepping around the huge blocks of stone that had scattered from the falling walls. Diebner followed in his footsteps, stopping whenever his leader stopped and looking wherever he looked.

The reichsfuehrer stepped into a space that had once been the huge double doors of the main building. His head swung slowly, taking in the remembered details of the lobby with its two curved staircases rising to the upper floors. He raised his riding crop and pointed toward a marble wall that was no longer there.

"Wilhelm's statue. It was right here, wasn't it?"

Diebner nodded. "Yes, Reichsfuehrer."

Himmler leaned down and began searching the black dust with the tip of his crop. From the ashes he lifted a metal coffee mug by its circular handle.

"Wilhelm is gone, but look what remains."

He led Diebner from building to building, poking in the debris and retrieving the curious survivors of the blitz. There was a metal balance scale from one of the laboratories, its arm and hanging pans intact but its wooden base vanished. A pair of iron bookends marked the edges of a rectangular stack of feathery ashes. A metal globe stand was undisturbed, but its replica of the planet had been burned away.

"A barbaric atrocity," Diebner offered when they stood before the library and looked up at piles of smoldering ash.

Himmler nodded. Then he braced himself and marched quickly back toward the car.

He stood with one foot on the running board while his driver wiped the gritty film from his boot.

"Curious, isn't it?" he commented for Diebner's hearing. "None of the other schools has been touched. The cathedrals still stand. Only the institute was destroyed."

Diebner looked back at the ruins.

"First they dropped flares," Himmler continued, moving the other foot to the running board so that the chauffeur could continue his work. "They lighted up the entire region so that they could see their target. The British don't generally do that. They don't seem to care where their bombs fall. But this time they cared."

Diebner was puzzled. It was obvious that the bombers had meant to hit the institute.

"And the number of bombs. Wave after wave dropping their bombs on the same target. They were determined utterly to destroy the buildings."

Diebner suddenly understood. "You think they knew about our work?"

Himmler stepped back while his driver opened the door. Then he slid into the backseat and waited for Diebner to join him.

"Of course they knew. I believe, Herr Diebner, that they even knew we were working in the cellars. I believe they knew that it wouldn't be sufficient to simply destroy the buildings, but that they had to reach down into the foundations. No other part of the city has ever been bombed with this precision or with this intensity."

"But how could they know, Reichsfuehrer?" Diebner blurted. "It's our most closely guarded secret."

"Not guarded closely enough, apparently," Himmler responded, his disinterested gaze turned toward the window.

Diebner felt himself shiver. The security of the nuclear program was certainly one of his responsibilities. Himmler was implying a grievous failure.

"I suppose there are many ways that we could be compromised," Himmler speculated almost idly. "Any scientist in the institute could know the reputations of men on your team and make a decent guess about the nature of the project. All it would take would be an idle comment by someone who wanted to make himself appear important."

Diebner nodded eagerly. It certainly didn't have to be a mistake on his part.

"Or a telephone operator could hear things that weren't supposed to be heard."

Again, Diebner agreed that the possibilities were endless.

"But isn't the timing curious?" the reichsfuehrer continued. "While we were laboring and falling behind schedule, the institute was given sanctuary. But when we succeed, when we finally have our reactor running, it is suddenly destroyed. Utterly destroyed. It would almost seem that the British know our day-to-day activities."

"A coincidence, I'm sure," Diebner offered. "The only people with that detailed a knowledge of our progress are our own scientists. It would be unthinkable—"

"Nothing is unthinkable," Himmler interrupted. "And I have never trusted in coincidence. Things happen for a reason. When our reactor is attacked just as it begins operating, then we have to look for a reason."

Diebner accepted the admonishment and leaned back into the seat, putting as much space as he could between himself and Himmler.

"Who in your group might not be completely enthusiastic with our success?" the reichsfuehrer wondered aloud. "Who might have an opportunity to discuss our activities with the British?"

"But there is no one, Reichsfuehrer. All our people are under constant surveillance. There are no visitors . . . no telephones."

"Professor Bergman corresponds with colleagues all over Europe," Himmler remembered aloud. "He wouldn't need a telephone. We deliver his mail for him."

"But we read everything he sends. It is all highly theoretical. There are no specifics about his work. He has been meticulous in observing our security requirements. He has never mentioned Berlin or the institute."

Himmler reached a gloved hand across the car and patted Diebner on the knee. "I'm sure you are right, Herr Diebner. But humor me with one small favor."

"Anything, Reichsfuehrer!"

"For the few months that it will take to assure our success, please see that none of his correspondence leaves the country. I would hate to hear that British bombers had suddenly taken a similar interest in the 'Castle Church.'"

"I will arrange it," Diebner promised.

"And in return, I will do a favor for Professor Bergman. I will arrange for him to receive a medal as a token of our esteem. Perhaps even the Iron Cross."

Diebner's face lighted with joy. "He will be stunned by the news, Reichsfuehrer."

Himmler nodded and returned a thin smile toward Diebner. Then he turned back to the window.

He wondered if the British would also be stunned by the news.

HAIGERLOCH — *October 3*

Even in the darkness, Anders knew they were heading to the southwest. He had found the North Star through the small, rectangular window of the ancient Junkers trimotor, and had kept it in view as the plane bounced over the grass-covered country field. The star had been off the right-wing tip as the plane climbed toward the west, and then had moved to the edge of the rear stabilizer when the plane turned to its left. It was still there, indicating that the nose was pointing slightly to the west of due south.

"Bavaria," one of the scientists guessed, above the uneven drone of the plane's engines. "I'll bet it's buried so deeply in the Alps that the British will never find it."

There were ten of them aboard—three scientists, two with their wives; a draftsman with his wife and a daughter of grade-school age; Anders and Birgit. They wore warm clothes and woolen army caps to protect against the cold air that drafted through the metal fuselage. The rear seats of the plane had been removed to make room for the scant luggage that each was allowed to bring, and for paper cartons of personal records that had been removed from the institute before the bombing.

"Not the Alps," Anders volunteered. "Perhaps the Swabian Mountains." He indicated the star that stood alone in the clear black sky over his shoulder. "Closer to the Swiss frontier than to Austria."

"So close to France?" the draftsman asked. "Why would we put our most secret project within sight of the French border? It doesn't make sense." Anders shrugged his shoulders and leaned back into his seat. It would be daylight within an hour and then there would be no need to speculate.

Birgit was the first to see the rolling hills below in the first pale light. She leaned back toward Anders and pointed down through the window. He wiped away the frost with his gloved hand. "Certainly not the Alps," he announced, and in response all the passengers pressed against the windows began debating where they might be. They were at low altitude, passing over the western foothills of gentle mountains. Ahead, there was dense green forest as far as they could see.

"No war here," the mother whispered to the little girl who was kneeling in one of the seats, staring down in amazement.

"I'm just like a bird," the child answered, more thrilled at seeing the world from an airplane than interested in what part of the world it was.

A river appeared through a break in the forest below.

"The Rhine?" a scientist asked.

"No, the Danube. The upper Danube," a colleague responded. "And that would be the Black Forest ahead." He turned toward Anders. "You were right, Professor Bergman. We have crossed the Swabian range. We're near the Swiss frontier and the French border."

"Why?" the draftsman asked again. "Why do such importanat work in such a dangerous place?"

Anders smiled. "Dangerous? Look at it. Mountains, forests, and rivers. No cities. No factories. There is no war down there. What could be safer?"

The plane banked steeply, dropping down below the tops of the hills.

"Get back into your seats and put on the seat belts," the uniformed pilot ordered through the open door to the cockpit. "We're landing."

The Junkers dropped down through the trees, its engine sounds dying. And then it was bouncing across a dirt landing strip and rolling to an easy stop.

They were met by three cars, all unmarked French sedans with civilian drivers, and a small truck that was loaded with their luggage and papers. Then they drove on a narrow, limb-covered road until they reached the bank of a river.

"The Danube?" one of the scientists in the car with Anders and Birgit asked.

"The Eyach," the driver answered as if the small river were a famous landmark. No one spoke as the cars rolled south until they came suddenly into a village made up of a few streets of rustic homes pressed against the river's bank. The cars stopped in the square in front of an old inn that overlooked the only significant crossroad in Hechingen.

They found their luggage waiting in the living room, a large space with leaded windows on three sides, furnished with fat chairs and heavy tables, and decorated with the stuffed carcasses of foxes and birds. Logs crackled in a cavernous stone fireplace to take the edge off the fall air. Birgit and Anders carried their bags up the wooden stairs to a large, sunlit room on the second floor. They smiled at the huge bed with giant corner posts supporting a white lace canopy, and at the porcelain chamber pot that rested underneath. There was a dresser and a chest of drawers; two straight chairs that flanked a round, three-legged table; and a washbasin and pitcher that rested on a wooden stand in front of the room's only mirror.

"Hardly the setting for a great breakthrough in theoretical physics," Anders joked.

"It will be just perfect," Birgit answered.

They found the bathroom at the end of the hall—a toilet with a wooden water tank suspended above it, a bathtub held off the tile floor by four large animal paws and a round sink with enormous brass fixtures.

"Have we traveled backward in time?" he asked.

Birgit nodded. "To a peaceful time."

They returned to the room, and Anders lifted the suitcases up onto the bed. Then, as Birgit began unpacking, he ran down the stairs and took his overcoat from the rack near the door. Outside, a car was waiting to take him to the reactor.

The road followed the river, matching the tight turns of the shoreline and climbing up onto the limestone cliffs that were cut along the eastern bank. In the clear, cold air, the sunlight set the river sparkling, reflecting against the low trees on the opposite shore. Anders was overwhelmed by the pastoral beauty. In one short night, he had traveled an infinite distance, leaving far behind the skeletons of scorched buildings, the incessant whine of the air raid sirens, the smoke and the fires, the convoys of camouflaged trucks, the terrified faces peering from cellars, the dull eyes of beaten soldiers. He had passed through time, arriving in an age when nature was still in command. When arrogance had not yet leveled the forests, polluted the rivers, and clogged the air. He sensed the possessive fear abandoning his body and, for the first moment in over a year, felt the freedom of his boyhood in the fields of America. Madness had not yet triumphed. It was still reasonable to hope.

Suddenly the castle church of Haigerloch broke into the skyline ahead, and he nearly laughed with his pleasure. It was so simple. "Castle Church" wasn't a code. It was real. The reactor was built in a cave near a real castle church.

It was a relic of the Teutonic knights, a cathedral built within a fortress, high above a turn in the river where it gave some ancient warlord total control of the only world he knew. In his destructive rage, the knight could fire rocks, or perhaps even iron shots down on the barges below to enforce his toll. But his greed was limited to one small bend in one insignificant river. Then, with the crude tools of the time, his madness was insignificant. It was science—mathematics, physics, chemistry—that had enabled madness to take on global ambitions.

The car crept through the tight turns of the narrow street that climbed to the church, then braked in front of the massive wooden door. Anders didn't wait for the driver. He pushed the car door open, jumped out and bolted up the church steps. But then he stopped abruptly, suddenly aware of a sound that had been hidden by the wind. An organ was playing. He smiled as he recognized the barely audible staccato of the sounds. It was a Bach fugue. Heisenberg. He pulled open the wooden door and rushed into the building.

The inside was alive with the cascading melody. Rushes of

sound echoed from the gilded and painted walls and vibrated against the elaborate stained-glass windows. He charged to the center of the long aisle and turned so that he could look up into the choir loft, dominated by columns of tarnished metal pipes. There was Heisenberg, his blond hair bobbing as he danced happily along the bench in front of the curved tiers of keys.

Anders found the circular stairs to the loft and rushed up the steps until his breath began to come in gasps. He stopped in the doorway and leaned against the frame, watching Heisenberg in his ecstasy.

Werner's eyes were closed, and a nearly angelic smile played across his lips. His head fell back as his fingers danced lightly across the keys, and then plunged forward as his hands pounded the tempo. His toes darted across the wooden pedals, setting his entire body into a melodic motion so that the music seemed to come from within him instead of from the giant windpipes that reached to the peaked roof of the building. Anders recognized the melody—one of the recordings that Heisenberg played constantly on the phonograph in his bunker office.

The sound stopped, and Heisenberg's eyes opened slowly. He smiled when he saw Anders standing beside him, and then gestured broadly toward the giant instrument.

"Magnificent, isn't it?"

"You play it beautifully," Anders said.

Heisenberg patted the edge of the keyboard. "It keeps me sane," he allowed.

"Where are we?"

Heisenberg laughed. "In Haigerloch, of course. In the castle church of Haigerloch. Didn't anyone tell you where they were taking you?"

"They said we were going to the reactor site. Where's the reactor?"

Heisenberg stretched out his arm and pointed his finger toward the floor. "Straight down. About a hundred feet."

"Here? In the church? Why here?"

"There were several sites," Heisenberg said. "The Nazis asked me to choose the one that was most appropriate. This was the only one that had an organ." He paused for a moment to enjoy Anders' confusion. Then he jumped off the bench and started toward the door.

"Come, Professor Bergman, I'll show you."

They charged down the steps and then up the main aisle to the nave of the church. Heisenberg led Anders around the marble altar and through a door at the back of the nave. In an instant, they were outside, crossing toward the edge of the cliff that commanded a bend in the river.

Heisenberg seemed not to notice the cold wind as he started down the open steps that descended the face of the cliff. "It's a fortress," he shouted back over his shoulder. "You remember the narrow street you used to reach the door of the church? One tank could hold off a regiment in that street." He pointed up to the ledge they had just left. "And one gunner on that ledge could keep an army from climbing this cliff."

At the bottom of the stairs they walked out onto a rocky beach that slid slowly into the water. Heisenberg pointed back up at the face of the cliff.

"Fifty feet of limestone," he shouted over the wind. "They could bomb the church to rubble. But down here, under the rock, you wouldn't even feel the vibration."

Anders followed Heisenberg around a turn and then saw the opening that had been cut in the face of the limestone. "This will be sealed up as soon as the diesel pumps are brought inside. They'll pump the cooling water from the river into the reactor. We brought all the graphite in this way. It came down the river from Stuttgart on barges and then we brought it in through the opening."

Anders nodded his approval at the simplicity of the scheme, then followed Heisenberg into the cave that had been dug under the church.

"The Allies would never think of looking here," Heisenberg continued like a tour guide. "The only things we make in this part of Germany are cuckoo clocks. It's hardly a center of munitions factories. And even if they did find it, what can they do? Send in a few commandos? They'd never be able to get close to the place."

The entrance widened into a huge cave that had been jackhammered out of the limestone. The strings of overhead lights in wire cages reminded Anders of the underground rocket factory at Nordhausen. But this cave was much smaller. There were just two rooms. The space to his right was empty, an echoing vault with its floor hollowed out into a giant cistern.

"That was the first reactor. My reactor," Heisenberg said with a gesture of dismissal. "The well is supposed to be filled with the heavy water that Diebner promises will be arriving any day. We've pirated all the equipment for your reactor, so God knows what we'll do with the heavy water if it ever gets here." They both laughed at the thought that the Nazis were still talking about heavy water.

Then, in the second vaulted area, Anders saw the top of the huge mountain of graphite that was being shaped into the reactor he had designed. They had dug a square hole, sixty feet on each side and forty feet deep. The graphite blocks began at the bottom, and were piled to a height that reached to his eye level as he stood at the edge and peered down. Far below, at the base of the pile, and army of workers were connecting the water pipes that disappeared into the graphite wall.

"It looks nearly finished," Anders said in surprise. He had expected that the construction would still be in its preliminary stages.

"We've been busy," Heisenberg said. He pointed to the rows of metal cylinders that hung like stalactites from the ceiling above the reactor. "An addition I made. I hope you don't mind."

Anders was puzzled.

"Lead containers," Heisenberg explained. "When we pull the fuel rods out of the reactor, we'll raise them right into the containers. And we'll ship the sealed containers. That will eliminate the radiation from the fuel rods."

Anders nodded his approval.

"We don't want to radiate the balls of the Master Race," Heisenberg allowed. "Otherwise, there wouldn't be any little Master Race to grow up and take our places."

Anders shook his head at the absurdity.

He followed Heisenberg around the perimeter of the pile while the German explained the details of construction. Then they entered a shielded control room that was built into one of the walls. The controls and the instruments were all in place, waiting to manage the nuclear activity that would occur inside the graphite mountain.

"When will it be ready?" Anders asked.

"We're planning on being in production by the end of February," Heisenberg said casually. "I don't see any reason why we shouldn't be ready by then."

"Production in February." Anders heard the shock in his own voice. "That doesn't allow any time for testing."

Heisenberg shook his head. "We did our testing at the institute. Your machine will go right into production."

LONDON — October 25

"Siegfried is alive," Haller told Air Marshal Ward the instant he had closed the office door.

Ward jumped up from behind his desk. "You've heard from him?" he asked.

Haller tossed the decoded message onto the desk and waited while Ward adjusted his wire-rimmed spectacles.

"Production reactor being built to my specification," the air marshal read, and then his voice rose as he completed the message, "Design cannot—repeat—cannot sustain reaction."

He smiled broadly as he removed the glasses. "Thank God," he told Haller. But then his smile narrowed. "When did this come in?" he asked.

"Into Stockholm yesterday," Haller said. "It was dated the twenty-sixth of September. Siegfried got it out the day before the raid."

"Then we can't be sure he's alive," the air marshal began to speculate out loud. "He may have still been working at the institute when we hit it."

"We can be sure," Haller smiled. "We picked up another lead on him. From Geneva of all places."

"Geneva?" Ward said as he watched Haller toss his beret on the desk and fall casually into a chair. "What's he doing in Geneva?"

"He's not in Geneva. He's still in Germany. But a German attaché in Switzerland was bragging about him to his French mistress who happens to be working for us. It seems our friend Siegfried has become something of a celebrity. The Germans have given him a medal."

Ward's mouth dropped open, causing Haller's mischievous grin to break into laughter. "It's true, I swear. They've given him a fucking medal! For services to German science. According to the attaché, Nils Bergman has scored an incredible scientific breakthrough, and has been selected to head up a major program that will make Germany invincible. He's still alive, and still on the inside."

Ward looked skeptical. "Do you believe it?" he asked.

Haller nodded. "It figures. The medal and the announcement are obviously pure propaganda to pump up any Germans who might be thinking of jumping ship. They've been announcing a new secret weapon every day. But why use Nils Bergman for credibility if he's already dead? He must be alive, or they wouldn't dare wave his name in front of the scientific community."

Ward weighed Haller's reasoning and seemed to accept it. "Thank God he wasn't in the institute," he said, gesturing toward the aerial photos that were pinned to his bulletin board. "No one could have lived through that."

They had reviewed the photos when they first came in, two days after the air raid. The ones taken from directly overhead showed a scorched field with vague outlines of buildings that seemed to have been drawn with a dull pencil. The ones taken at an angle showed the skeleton of the tower, and the indentations in the ground that had once been the foundations of the stone structures. It was clear that anyone who had been working underground had been buried in tons of debris.

They had looked at the photos again a few days later when no communications from Siegfried had arrived. "Something is wrong," their agents in Stockholm had reported. "There have been no mail pouches from Berlin. Siegfried may be compromised." Haller had ordered that the agents keep checking the mail at the university. But he feared that no more would be coming. When he had ordered the attack, he had evaluated the risk that Anders and Birgit might be in the buildings. The instant and utter destruction of the target, reported by the Bomber Command pilots and confirmed in the aerial photos, could well explain why Siegfried wasn't corresponding anymore.

Haller and Ward had fallen into panic, afraid that they had lost track of the German program. True, they had succeeded in destroying the prototype reactor. Hopefully, essential documents and drawings had been vaporized in the process. But there was still the chance that the Germans were far enough along with their production reactor so that the prototype was no longer important. And if they had lost Siegfried, there was little possibility of their locating the construction site.

Now they were nearly euphoric. "They'll be moving him to wherever they're building," Ward speculated. "And you'll be hearing from him as soon as he's relocated."

"I certainly hope so," Haller answered. "It's the easiest way for us to find out where the new reactor is."

"Is there any other way? We haven't learned anything from our radio watches. If he doesn't contact us, we're left pretty much in the dark."

Haller smiled. "We would have been. But the Germans have solved that problem for us." He enjoyed the puzzled look on Ward's face for a moment before he explained. "Up until now, we couldn't show any interest in Nils Bergman without running the risk of compromising him. But now that the Germans have given him a medal, he's fair game. I mean, if they're going to tell the world that Nils Bergman is their great hope for victory, they would have to expect that we would try to find out what he's up to. So I think we can tell our agents to find Nils Bergman. And even if the Germans should learn that we're looking for him, they would have no reason to suspect our motives. After all, they're the ones who made a public announcement about how important he is."

"And if we can't find him?" Ward asked.

"Then we'd have to hope that he knew what he was talking about when he coded that message and said the production reactor wouldn't run. My guess is that, as long as the Germans believe in him, they'll follow his design. And he seems certain that the design will give them problems."

"Risky," the air marshal mumbled. "Siegfried was sure that the prototype would fail. He's obviously working with very thin margins."

"I think we'll hear from him," Haller said. "And if we don't, I'm pretty sure we'll be able to find him. Either way, he'll lead us to castle church, and we may be able to bury it just like the Kaiser Wilhelm Institute. But even if that fails, we still have hope. I'm sure we set back their timetable by destroying the institute. And with Siegfried still on the inside, we may be able to set them back a bit further. God knows, we're in better shape than we were yesterday when we thought that Siegfried might be under one of those photos."

Ward rose from his desk and walked to the window that looked out into a courtyard. There were piles of sandbags by two of the doors into the basements of the buildings, set up to protect the entrances to the bomb shelters. Like most of Britain's defensive measures, London's network of shelters had been rendered useless by the buzz bombs and the V-2 rockets. The winged glide-bombs came over with such frequency that people would be running in and out of shelters all day long. Londoners had learned to ignore them until they heard the engine stop. Then they dove for cover. There was no time to look for an air raid shelter.

They were even more defenseless against the rockets. They simply hit and exploded without even a second's warning. The sandbags were relics of a past war that had been fought with outdated technology. In the new war that the scientists had invented, sandbags and shelters served no purpose.

"There is another possibility," Ward finally offered. Haller turned his head toward the window.

"It's possible," the air marshal speculated, "that the Germans are on to him. Or at least suspicious of him. That would certainly explain the interruption in his communications."

"But not the medal," Haller countered. "If they thought Nils Bergman might be doing them in, they'd hardly make him a national hero. They'd certainly never tell the world how much they loved him if they thought they might have to shoot him."

"That's what puzzles me," Ward said. "Would we tell the world who the top man in our most secret military program was? Would we parade him out in public and give him the Victoria Cross?" He turned his eyes away from the window so that he could measure Haller's reaction.

"No," Haller admitted.

Ward walked quickly back to his desk and confronted Haller like a prosecutor badgering a witness.

"Why not?"

"Security, I suppose," Haller answered. "Why tell the Germans who they should shoot if they want to knock us back a peg?"

"Then why are they telling us who to shoot?"

Haller squirmed under the question. "Well, they do need all the propaganda they can put out. Maybe they need to make all this talk of secret weapons credible."

Ward shook his head. The answer wasn't good enough. "I don't think so. They never told us who was building their rockets. And God knows, their rockets certainly have enough credibility!"

"So why are they telling us?" Haller wondered.

"Maybe to see if he's genuine," Ward offered. "The way they tested for devils in the Middle Ages. If someone was suspected of being possessed, they tied him up and threw him in a river. If he floated to the top, he was a devil. If he didn't come up, then he wasn't possessed. The only way you could prove you weren't working for Lucifer, unfortunately, was to drown."

Haller didn't grasp the analogy.

"If Nils Bergman is working for us, we wouldn't do anything. But if he is really helping the Germans win the war, then it would be reasonable for us to take very strong measures to stop him.

More than likely, we'd either try to steal him or, if that proved to be too difficult . . ."

"We'd kill him," Haller said, finishing the sentence.

Ward nodded. "To prove he's genuine . . . that he's not a devil in their midst . . . we have to make one very convincing effort to do the old boy in."

Now it was Haller's turn to pace to the window.

"Maybe I'm reaching," Ward allowed. "Maybe it is just another propaganda campaign. But I'm certainly not comfortable when the Nazis begin putting out press releases on their top secret program."

Haller shook his head. "No, you're not reaching, Air Marshal. They know that their top secret isn't a secret. They know we're on to them. I felt sure that they knew exactly what we were after when they threw all their troops into Holland. And God knows they couldn't have missed our intentions when we hit the institute. They're not telling us anything that they aren't sure we know already. Except the name of the man that's running their program. It could very well be that what they are trying to find out is how well we know Nils Bergman."

"Bit of a dilemma, isn't it?" Ward said. "We need him alive inside the program. But we have to try to kill him in order to keep him there."

"Unless," Haller continued, "the damn reactor is out in the open where our bombers can get at it. I'd feel a lot more comfortable blowing the son of a bitch to hell instead of waiting for some scientific theory to run its course. I won't sleep nights until I have pictures like those." He pointed to the photos that recorded the destruction of the institute.

But Ward looked skeptical. "That's not likely. My guess is that when we find it, it will be at the bottom of a mine shaft. Siegfried says he's built a time bomb into the design. I think we have to make sure that his time bomb keeps ticking. If the Germans are suspicious of him, then they'll be suspicious of his work. They'll check every detail of the production reactor. To keep them moving down the path that Siegfried has set, I think we have to make sure that the man stays a German hero."

Haller looked shocked at the implication of Ward's thinking.

The air marshal was telling him that a dead Siegfried, with an unmistakably British bullet in his chest, was their best chance.

"Let's wait until we locate the reactor," he asked.

Ward nodded. Then he added, "But let's not wait too long."

There was a quick rush of anger into Haller's eyes as he squared the red beret over his ear. "But let's give the poor bastard every chance that we can," he snapped.

"It just has to be convincing," the air marshal said, his voice more authoritative than friendly. "The Germans have to believe that we are afraid of what Nils Bergman is building."

"And dead is very convincing," Haller shot back.

Ward turned back toward the window, no longer able to match Haller's furious stare. "You called it," he said softly, "when you first argued for the bombing raid. You said you would trade my pilots for the reactor. I wasn't happy with the idea. But I knew you were right."

Haller stood stunned for a moment. Then his hand raised slowly and slipped the beret from his head. "And you're right now, Air Marshal," he sighed. "If it comes down to it . . . if we can't get at their reactor . . . then we'll have to do something very convincing."

"Let's hope it doesn't come down to it," Ward concluded.

HECHINGEN — *November 5*

"They can do it. The bastards can still do it," Anders insisted to Birgit as they took their evening walk around the periphery of the Hechingen square. The intersection in front of the inn had been sealed off by soldiers, setting it aside as a private courtyard for the scientists. It was the one place where Anders and Birgit could talk together without the lingering fear of microphones buried in the walls or cameras behind the mirror.

"But with so little time," she argued. "It's such a complex process and everything is so uncertain."

"They've been preparing for years," he reminded her. "All the pieces are in place."

During the weeks at the reactor site, Anders had assessed the Nazi preparations for their super weapon, and had come grudgingly to respect their dark determination. They had begun over a year ago—probably while Heisenberg was working on his heavy water prototype—to dig a cave under the castle church. He could only guess how many slave workers, from how many countries, had entered the cave never again to see daylight. They had carried hundreds of tons of rock on their backs and loaded it into small, inconspicuous barges that would carry it down the river. Then, with the loss of their heavy water supply, they had enlarged the space to accommodate the new graphite reactor.

They had built an equally impregnable underground factory near Celle to separate the plutonium from the fuel rods. And he had personally toured the enormous underground slave labor camp at Nordhausen that manufactured their super rockets.

Years earlier, even while their victorious armies were extending the borders of the Reich, someone had seen the possibility of an Allied attack on the homeland. Someone had conceived the designs of a super weapon that would assure Germany's total victory. And someone had directed the massive construction efforts that would make that super weapon a reality.

"The reactor could be producing plutonium even while the RAF was leveling the church above it," he explained to Birgit. "Then the fuel rods with the plutonium can be barged up the river to Stuttgart and taken from there by train, or maybe by truck to Celle. The Celle plant is underground, too, so they can be separating the plutonium no matter how many bombs the Allies are dropping. And then the plutonium bombs are taken to Nordhausen—again underground—and installed on the rockets. Don't you see? They can be losing the war up above, but underground they're winning. Their production is unaffected. When they come out of their holes, they could be masters of the world."

They broke their conversation as they passed close to one of the soldiers. He snapped to attention, and Anders acknowledged his salute with a tip of his hat. Then Birgit took up the argument.

"But it's all unproven. You said yourself that separating the plutonium was possible only in theory. How will they deal with the radiation?"

"By using workers who have never heard of radiation," he fired back. "Slave workers who won't understand why their skin is red and blistered, or why they're coughing up blood. You don't think they gave a damn about the workers who dug the cave in Haigerloch?"

She realized that he was right. They already had the rockets. It was all that the scientists talked about when they gathered around the dining table at the inn. And if the reactor kept on schedule, they would have the plutonium by the end of February.

"Can the Allies get here in time?" she asked.

He raised his hands helplessly. The Nazis were boasting to have slaughtered the British in Holland. And they claimed to have the Americans stopped short of the Maas. Yet the British broadcasts they picked up reported a steady advance through the Saar valley only eighty miles away.

"Then it's up to you," Birgit concluded. "And you're sure the reactor will fail."

But he wasn't sure. The closer the reactor came to completion, the more Anders doubted the effectiveness of the destructive changes he had worked into the design.

He had no reason to suspect that he had failed. As the mountain of graphite grew with each day's construction, he checked each weight, each dimension, each measure of density. He took core samples to evaluate the consistency of the moderator material. He tested and retested the chemical composition of the fuel rods. The purity of the uranium oxide was accurate to the thousandth part. The workmanship of the clad metal cylinders, fabricated in the strongly defended German Ruhr, was a study in perfection. Everything was exactly according to the plans he had prepared in the bunker.

He ordered the pumps started and took physical measurements of the amount and temperature of the water delivered. He tried the mechanical controls that would insert the fuel rods and the control rods into the graphite. Again, they matched his design.

At night, he sat atop the huge bed in his room, his knees pulled up under him to make room for the papers that were scattered around him. He checked and rechecked each of the calculations that had led to each step in the construction. If his numbers were right, then the reactor that the Germans were building was doomed. He had no reason for doubt.

But there was no hint of doubt by any of the physicists and chemists who surrounded him each day. They were brilliant men. Heisenberg was Bergman's equal, which put his abilities well beyond those with which Anders could credit himself. Lauderbach had much more experience than Anders. If men of that caliber seemed certain that the reactor would work, how could he be certain that it would fail?

Each morning, beginning at the breakfast table that they all shared, he studied their faces for some hint of suspicion. He was relieved that they continued to accept him unquestioningly. But his fear built as they also seemed to accept his design. If they were right, then he was wrong. And if he were wrong, then he was building a Nazi victory.

As they worked in the cave, he listened for some sound of dismay. He found himself longing for a comment that questioned the accuracy of his calculations. Each time Heisenberg picked up a plan and then scribbled an equation in its margin, he looked anxiously for a narrowing of his eyes or a tightening of his lips that might indicate even a moment of confusion. He had no idea of how he would defend a conclusion that Heisenberg would challenge. But as Heisenberg seemed to become more and more convinced that the reactor would run, his own conviction that it would fail became less certain.

At the dinner table back at the inn, and in the conversations around the fire, the growing mood of optimism only increased his secret despair. The confident talk about the glorious future of science after the war convinced him that there would be no future at all.

At night, when he walked with Birgit in the square, he poured out his fears. "How can Heisenberg not know?" he asked over and over. "He was doing the calculations for uranium fission when I was still doing my thesis. How can Lauderbach miss the chemistry errors? What is he? The number one . . . maybe the number two expert in electron chemistry in the world?"

"Who's good enough to challenge Nils Bergman?" she answered. "Especially when they were present at the institute to see Nils Bergman's success."

"Damn it, I'm not Nils Bergman," he once snapped at her. "I'm good. Good enough to work with these people. But not good enough to fool them."

"You are Nils Bergman," she corrected sternly. "It's your reactor that they're building. Not Heisenberg's. Not Lauderbach's. Yours."

"I've played it too cautiously," he castigated himself. "The changes aren't significant enough. The damn thing is going to work!"

During one night, Birgit had awakened to find him standing by their bedroom window, staring absently out over the shallow river. She put on her robe and stood beside him, touching her fingertips to the back of his hand.

"I was thinking about the BBC broadcast," he told her in a whisper. The scientists had heard an unjammed portion of the news broadcast from London, announcing the American victory at Metz. Lauderbach had dismissed it as English propaganda.

"I'm sure it's true," Birgit answered, hoping to be encouraging.

"It is true," he said. "That's what frightens me. They're still fighting in France. I stand here hoping to see American soldiers coming across the river. Christ, they're still six months away."

His voice was rising with emotion, and she moved a finger to his lips. It was her reminder that they shouldn't speak out of character, even in the privacy of their own room.

At the construction site, he tried the delaying tactics that had served him well when he first entered Germany. He demanded stress tests on the overhead structures that supported the fuel rods and the control rods. The engineers cheerfully agreed, arranged the tests, and completed them in a matter of hours. He rejected a box of instruments that had been carelessly dropped, insisting that they might have suffered internal damage. New instruments were delivered two days later. He wanted pressure tests made on the piping that fed cooling water to the pile. A construction foreman opened a file drawer and produced records to show that the test had already been performed. It was quickly obvious that he was working on the highest-priority project in all of Germany. His most outrageous demands were met immediately, without causing even a momentary pause in the construction effort.

There was still another reason for his growing panic. Since they had been moved to Haigerloch, he had received no communications from the university. In Berlin, his correspondence and papers had been delivered like clockwork, reassuring that his own letters to Stockholm were also being delivered. Now nothing was being received, despite Kurt Diebner's assurance that it was nothing more than a bureaucratic error that would be corrected immediately. If mail couldn't get in, wasn't it likely that his own letters weren't getting out? And if that was the case, then perhaps Haller had never received his coded message indicating where they were.

He had lost confidence that the reactor would fail and had given up hope of delaying its completion. The liberating armies were still hundreds of miles away, and he and Birgit were cut off from all contact with the outside world. They could expect no help. If the German atomic bomb was to be stopped, they were the ones who would have to stop it.

STRASBOURG — *November 20*

It was a stroke of luck that brought Haller the location of the reactor. And the information, he could hardly believe, had come from the French. Allied intercepts of the German Ultra code, interrogation of Nazi prisoners, and even the meticulous reports of the hundreds of British agents who were scattered all across Germany had yielded nothing. Instead, the first news of the production reactor had come from a French school teacher who was serving as a translator with the Free French Army.

The U.S. Sixth Army had taken Strasbourg, and the honor of liberating the city had been given to the Free French. German civilians in the city, who could see which way the war was turning, and French collaborators in dread of reprisals were trying to win favor with the French liberators. They were all talking, trying to pass off any rumors they had heard as valuable intelligence on German plans. Most of the information was worthless, but a French translator, interviewing a German businessman, was struck with a story about a huge cave in Haigerloch that the Germans were filling with graphite. He asked a British liaison officer if he knew of any reason why the Nazis would be hoarding graphite.

Haller flew to Strasbourg the next day, kidnapped the man from the hands of the French, and interrogated him in the back of a commandeered truck. The terrified German provided a sketchy description of construction that resembled the building of a reactor. Haller was put off when the man couldn't identify photographs of Nils Bergman, but he knew he had struck gold when the German pointed to an old photo of Werner Heisenberg. "This one looks like the organist in the church," he offered hopefully.

Haller pushed his prisoner into the backseat of a single-engined Lysander and took him back to England. Two days later, a Mosquito bomber made a low altitude run up the Eyach valley and continued due north so as not to display any particular interest in the Haigerloch area. That night, Haller sat his German down in front of clear photographs of the castle church and had him pinpoint the entrance to the cave.

"We can't bomb it," he now told Air Marshal Ward. "Bombs would bounce off that rock."

"Are we positive it's the reactor?" Ward asked, looking skeptically at the photos of an ancient church on a hill that overlooked an insignificant village.

"They brought in dozens of barges loaded with graphite blocks," Haller answered. "And look at these pipes coming up from the river. They're three feet in diameter. They can handle thousands of gallons a minute. So we've got graphite and cooling water and Werner Heisenberg all in one place. It has to be the reactor."

"But no sign of Siegfried," Ward reminded.

"He was still in Berlin when our source was in Haigerloch. But I'll bet my mother he's there now."

Ward looked up from the photos. "I'm sure the ¿erries had no way of knowing this, but they couldn't have picked a safer place. The Eyach valley isn't even on our maps."

Haller looked puzzled.

"No one's going to Haigerloch," Ward continued. "Not us. Not the Americans. Right now the plan is to jump the Rhine in Holland. The big push is going to be across northern Germany. Our troops will be in Berlin before anyone gets close to your church."

"Any chance of changing that?" Haller asked.

Ward shook his head wearily. "Not at any time soon. All our forces have their hands full in the north. We won't reach the Rhine until the spring."

Haller picked up the photographs and studied them again. "Maybe if we hit it with a small force. Something fast that wouldn't alert the Germans. If we dropped down right on top of the damn church . . ." But even as he spoke, he could see the problems. It would have to be a perfect drop. Miss by just a few feet, and his men would land in the narrow streets where they wouldn't have a prayer.

Ward recognized the problem. Their attack on the reactor would have to be a full-scale assault prepared to cope with heavy losses. Or else it would have to be an undercover action involving a few men who could approach the site unnoticed. Given the problems that the Allies were facing all along the German border, there was no possibility of mounting a major assault in the near future.

"Study it, Tom," he concluded. "If you think there's a way we can get into that church, then that's our best bet. If not, then the best we can do is fall back to our second alternative."

Haller's head snapped up from the photos.

"If you're sure Siegfried is in the area, then find him," Ward continued, "and give him credibility. It may be easier to get at him that to get at his reactor."

HECHINGEN — *December 24*

"No, no. Toward the left. More toward the window," Lauderbach said, leaning his body in the direction that he wanted the tree tilted. Kurt Diebner, who was nearly hidden by the branches of the evergreen, pulled the tree's trunk with him as he took a half step toward the window.

"Too much," Fichter shouted. "Come toward me just a bit." Diebner did.

"It's still not straight," Lauderbach complained. "And there's a bare spot facing toward me. Try twisting it forty-five degrees to the right."

Their theoretical instincts were useless. Placing the Christmas tree demanded a designer's eye more than a mathematician's precision. They had spent half an hour moving the eight-foot evergreen around a small circle at the side of the fireplace and they still couldn't agree on exactly where it looked best.

"There! That's perfect," Fichter said. Diebner stepped back to examine his work. "Too close to the window," he concluded, causing Heisenberg to double over with laughter. "You just said it was too far from the window!" he shouted.

"We won't have any time to decorate it," Anders warned, "if you don't make up your mind."

Birgit had been put in charge of the decorations, and she had prepared dozens of pieces of fruit, each tied with a bright red ribbon. Then she had sat up for half a night tying ribbons to small candles so that they could be attached to the branches of the tree. She began passing the ornaments to the scientists. Heisenberg stepped forward to help, but Diebner ordered him to the piano.

"Play some Christmas carols," he pleaded. "We can't decorate a tree without Christmas carols."

It was their first day of rest from the demands of constructing the reactor. The work planned for the day involved the installation of valves to the cooling system.

"We'll leave it to the plumbers," Heisenberg had decreed and declared a holiday so that they could decorate the inn for Christmas a week away. Two of the scientists and the innkeeper had spent the morning on a search through the countryside for the perfect Christmas tree. The others had bound evergreen branches with ribbons and hung them throughout the room. Anders had helped Birgit finish with her tree trimmings. Now, they were giggling like children as they tied the colorful decorations to the branches.

Heisenberg began playing the carols, and the men began to sing. Within a moment they were all laughing at their off-key renditions.

"My mother had a wonderful voice," Fichter remembered. "All year she sang in the church. But at Christmas, she sang all the carols for us. I always think of her when I see a Christmas tree."

"I always think of a red wagon," another added. "It was my favorite Christmas gift."

And then they were reminiscing over Christmasses past, filled with sentiment as each treasure was recalled.

Did they have any idea where they were, Anders wondered. Did they really understand what it was that they were building? How could they turn so easily from the production of massive death and fix delicate ribbons to a symbol of life?

They were decent men. Ask any one of them to design a furnace in which a whole generation could be murdered, and he would recoil in horror. But ask him to calculate the exact temperature at which a human body would vaporize and he would rush to be the first with the calculation. Ask one of them to build a bomb that could flash an entire city into fire and he would become enraged at the suggestion. But ask him to create an element that would release the energy of the sun and he would labor day and night. They could leave their Christmas tree to watch the first atomic bomb explode over London. And then they could return to their carols in celebration of the precision with which they had been able to calculate its heat.

What testimony would he give when the Allies finally marched into Haigerloch and rounded up its population of scientists? Were they war criminals? Or were they fools? "Your honor," he heard himself say to the head of the tribunal, "these men simply didn't care what use was made of their discoveries. They were pursuing knowledge for its own sake without any regard for its consequences. Can we take them out and shoot them simply because they didn't care?" He thought of Nils Bergman's answer when Birgit had cautioned him about traveling into Germany. "They want you to build weapons," she had cautioned. And Bergman had hunched his shoulders and wagged his head. "Should we not have invented the lever just because some general might use it as a catapult?" he had asked in return.

And what would they say if he succeeded in destroying their reactor? At the moment when three years of study, of experiments, and finally of construction were melting before their eyes, what would they do to him? Their rage would have nothing to do with the lost reactor's impact on the war. Instead they would be furious that he had deprived them of being the first to fashion a new element.

They were back into their singing, joined in a song that announced glad tidings to the Earth. The yellow pears and bright red apples were hanging cheerfully from the branches and the thin tapered candles were positioned up the face of the tree.

"Werner," they called to Heisenberg, who looked up from his Christmas carols. "Come, light the first candle!"

But Heisenberg reached out towards to Birgit. "In my home," he said, "the honor always belongs to the lady of the house." Birgit smiled, completely caught up in the happiness of the moment. She took a burning twig from the edge of the fireplace and was about to touch it to one of the candles.

"Victory!" came a scream from another part of the house. The door to the gathering room flew open. "Victory!" screamed the owner of the inn as he rushed in. "We have broken through. Our armies are advancing all along the front."

They abandoned the tree and charged toward the owner, who was delirious with his news. "In Belgium. In France. A massive attack," he shouted. "It's on the radio. The Americans are in flight."

He pushed past the scientists to the radio and with trembling fingers dialed into the German broadcast. The announcer was even more ecstatic. Von Rundstedt's armies had broken out of the Ardennes and split the American lines. German divisions were driving toward the Meuse. The British armies were cut off in Holland and were faced with another Dunkirk.

Lauderbach pounded his fist into his palm. "I knew it," he announced. "We've lured them into a trap." He led the charge away from the radio to the rolled-up map that was consulted each evening as they listened to official broadcasts or the BBC news. Quickly, he located the Ardennes, and ran his finger westward to the Meuse River.

"Look," he lectured. "Brussels will be ours in a few days. We'll be back to the Channel by New Year's."

He traced the split that would isolate the British in Holland, where they could be chewed to pieces, and turned the northern flank of the American advance. "Brilliant," he announced. "Our strategy is brilliant."

They listened anxiously as the BBC confirmed the turn of events, minimizing its importance. "What else can they say," Lauderbach exalted. "They have to pretend it's of little consequence. But look at the map. Anyone can see that they have been cut in half."

Anders stared hard at the map. He had no idea how many men were in the German divisions. And clearly the Meuse was a long way from the Channel. The Allies were by no means "cut in half."

But they were giving ground at a time when he had assumed they would be charging forward. He had expected to hear that they had broken through to the Rhine, not that they were falling back to the Meuse. Even if they were able to regroup, how much time would be lost? How many weeks would it take to recapture the land that they now seemed to be surrendering to the German onlsaught?

The madmen would have their plutonium months before the Allies even entered Germany. Their bombs would be ready for launching. The Third Reich might, indeed, last a thousand years. Unless he could stop it.

"What a wonderful Christmas present," Fichter said, turning his attention back to the tree. "Werner, play us another carol so that we can all sing." He turned to Birgit and handed her a burning twig so that she could light the first candle on the tree.

WÜRTTEMBERG — *December 28*

The parachutes fell silently through the black December night, and dropped like feathers on the fresh white snow.

Haller landed on his feet and began pulling in on the cords even before the gray silk umbrella touched the ground. He looked around as he worked. He and his three companions had settled in a straight line, each no more than 100 yards from another. It was a perfect jump.

The equipment chute had gone only slightly off course, dropping into the edge of the trees on the soft slope of the Swabian mountains. That would be their first task—find the chute and recover the weapons and explosives that it carried.

He gathered his parachute into a bundle against his chest and ran toward the tree line. One of the men reached him immediately and the other two were already rushing toward them.

"Did you see it?" he asked the last arrival.

The young man pointed back in the direction he had come from. "In the trees. Back there. We'll have to climb a bit, but it's no problem."

They dug with their hands until they were turning over rich, black soil. Then they buried the parachutes and ran along the edge of the forest until they found the canvas-covered pallet that was dangling awkwardly twenty feet above their heads. Without exchanging a word, two of the men boosted a third up to the lower limbs, and he climbed quickly into the tree. The pallet dropped lower as he cut the cords, then suddenly tore free and came crashing down.

Haller paid no attention as his men began to untie the bundle. He was studing the small map he had taken from his breast pocket in the light of a pencil-sized flashlight.

They were in their military uniforms, except that they wore ordinary working shoes instead of their commando boots. The most dangerous part of their jump would be the next few hours when, if their plane had been spotted, German patrols would be searching for them. If they were going to be captured, they wanted the protection that their status as soldiers would afford them. But before dawn, if they were sure they weren't being pursued, they would change to civilian clothes.

To do that, they had to reach their first rendezvous, a battered farmhouse that was two miles away from their drop zone. The house had been taken over by British agents who had stocked it with food and left a small Italian panel truck hidden in the barn. The truck would contain electricians' tools and spools of telephone wire. Under the dashboard were identification papers and work permits for four Italian nationals who had been brought into Germany to repair communications facilities. One of the paratroopers spoke fluent Italian and halting German. Haller and the other two had rehearsed enough Italian phrases to identify themselves.

They buried the equipment parachute and broke up the pallet. Then they each shouldered a heavy knapsack and began walking in file on the open ground at the edge of the trees. Within a mile as Haller figured it, they would reach a small stream. Then they would follow its flow, downhill into open country until the abandoned farm appeared on their left.

They felt protected while they marched along the forest's edge. The trees obscured the faint skyline, so there was no chance of their being seen from the open fields below. At the same time, they had a commanding view of the countryside, enabling them to see anyone who moved toward them out of the darkness.

But when they reached the stream, they left their protection behind. Now they moved painfully, crouched low into the shallow channel that the running water had etched through the flat ground. They alternated the point role, sending one man a hundred yards ahead while the others clung to the ground until he signalled that the way was clear. They saw lights in the window of a small house that wasn't indicated on their map, and spent several minutes with the icy water brushing their feet, deciding whether they should leave the stream and swing out across open ground to keep away from the house.

"If we stay low, no one will see us," one of the soldiers argued.

"Suppose the bastard has a dog," the Italian-speaking soldier warned.

"Then we'll use these," his companion returned, lifting the small carbine that he carried.

"And wake up half of Germany!"

It was Haller's call, and his most important concern was time. He didn't want to be seen near their rendezvous house because it was supposed to be abandoned. Four strangers moving into a deserted farm would certainly arouse interest. His plan was to change their clothes, pick up the panel truck, and be on the road before daylight.

"We'll keep going," he ordered. "If there's a dog, we'll let the mutt come to us. Then we'll use these."

He patted the trench knife that hung from his belt.

They moved cautiously, past the lighted window, breathing easier when there was no sound, nor any movement that they could see through the window.

Further down the stream, they were stopped by distant headlights that seemed to be moving in their direction. Haller ordered them to spread out and take positions against the slope of the bank, facing an open road that the car would be using. They heard engine sounds as it drew closer and the half-masked headlamps grew brighter. It was an open military car with three uniformed passengers barely visible. They heard sounds of laughter as the car sped past.

"Christ, they're patrolling the roads," one said as soon as they reassembled.

"Home guards," Haller answered. "If we get stopped, let's hope those are the ones that stop us."

The sky would begin to lighten in less than an hour, and still the house was nowhere in sight. Haller checked the map. They should have reached it by now but he couldn't be sure how far they had traveled. He couldn't afford to keep moving at their slow, cautious pace.

"Double time, lads," he said. "Keep a sharp eye, but keep moving."

They broke into a trot, the heavy packs bouncing against their shoulders with each step.

They had almost run past it when the tottering barn appeared at the edge of a stand of trees. They rested for a few moments, stretched out in the hay that was wet with snow that had come through the open roof. Then they pushed some of the hay aside, and rolled the small truck out into the open. It was still dark when the group, dressed in workmen's coveralls, pulled out onto the road, and headed toward the Eyach River.

Haller stopped the truck when a flat wooden bridge, six miles below Haigerloch, came into view. One of the men worked his way down to the water's edge, climbed a telephone pole, and cut the phone wire. Then they drove to the bridge and presented their papers to the two uniformed home guardsmen who stepped out of a windowless shed.

The guards looked at the papers, then glanced at the equipment in the back of the truck. They understood enough of the Italian words and gestures, which were mixed with mispronounced German phrases, to figure out that the Italians had been sent to repair phone lines. And when they tried to call their headquarters for instructions, the story became credible. The makeshift wooden barrier was lifted, and Haller's party crossed to the west side of the river.

They drove north, with the river several hundred yards to their right, separated from the road by heavy woods. Their guns were close at hand. It made sense that the Germans would be patrolling the entire area around Haigerloch, and they couldn't be sure that their workmen's masquerade would stand up to the scrutiny of regular soldiers. When they reached a point across from the town, they pulled their truck up next to a telephone pole. The three soldiers unloaded the equipment, and one climbed the pole to begin stringing wire. Haller broke straight into the woods and made his way to the river's edge.

He saw the castle church, high on its stone bluff, while he was still a long way from the shore. Through his field glasses, he could see uniformed figures at the top of the cliff, and machine-gun emplacements that had not been there when the aerial photos were taken. The Germans had brought in reinforcements to protect their prize.

He pushed closer, suddenly aware of the sound of the river. He had to be careful not to break out into the open. The guards who were facing him had probably spent days staring across the water at an uninhabited shoreline. Any movement would certainly attract their attention. He stopped when he could see the water through the trees, dropped down on his belly, and began searching through the glasses.

At first, he couldn't find the cave entrance. In the photographs it had been at the waterline, directly beneath the cross that was mounted to the top of the church spire. But now all he could see was the blank face of the limestone cliff. It was the lighting, he thought. The sun was behind the church and the wall beneath it was still in shadow. Slowly, he began to crawl toward another vantage point further down the stream.

"Sweet Jesus," he cursed, when he looked again. He could see the lighter color and the regular corners of the stone patch that had replaced the cave's opening. The entrance had been sealed. The Germans had no more need for a doorway to the river. The attack plans they had rehearsed were completely useless.

They had learned two things from the aerial photographs. The first was that the castle church was lightly defended. Nowhere in the pictures had they seen a gun emplacement, a military vehicle, or a structure that could serve as a barracks. They had assumed that a quick, light assault against a scarcely defended target would certainly succeed. Now, with soldiers and machine guns on the top of the cliff, that assumption no longer held.

They had planned to cross the river under cover of darkness in a small raft and then rush the opening to the cave. The security guards and the few workmen who might be inside would pose little barrier to their surprise attack. They would set their charges around critical equipment and be back across the river when the inside of the cave exploded into a fiery inferno. Now, with the cave sealed at the waterline, that plan had to be abandoned.

He searched the top of the cliff. The entrance to the reactor had to be large enough to bring equipment and fuel in, and to bring the processed fuel rods out. Haller guessed a shaft somewhere inside the church, or perhaps leading down from the grounds around the church. There was no way his small raiding party could scale the cliffs under the eyes of the guards who now seemed to be looking back toward him. And there was little chance that his group of conscripted Italian workers would ever be allowed to pass through the streets that led to the church from the other side.

He reviewed some of the plans they had considered and discarded. A parachute drop onto the church grounds seemed even more fantastic now, with the actual target in front of him, than it had when he studied the photos. And the height of the stone wall made a bombing raid seem even more futile. The damn place was invulnerable to anything but a full-scale invasion.

He saw just two choices. One was to bomb the bluff incessantly, leveling the church, destroying the streets that led to it, and perhaps even closing the entrance to the cave. That could at least make it more difficult for the Germans to bring fuel in and processed uranium out. It might buy time. The other was to drop a regiment into the open fields to the east of town. The losses in men who would have to fight their way through the narrow streets would be frightful. But once they reached their target, they could put the German atomic bomb out of business permanently.

He slipped the field glasses back into their case, and moved carefully back into the woods.

Haller heard commands being shouted in German even before he saw the patrol car that had pulled up behind his panel truck. Two soldiers had their rifles pointing at his three companions who were standing against the truck with their hands folded across the tops of their heads. A German officer in a leather jacket was waving the work papers in their faces and screaming at them in German.

Haller raised his carbine and moved cautiously until he had a close and clear shot. Then he squeezed a quick burst into the back of each of the soldiers.

The officer wheeled in confusion, openmouthed as he watched his two men topple. His hand snapped toward his sidearm, but his prisoners were on him before the Luger cleared the holster. They tossed him on face, bending his arms up behind his back.

"Stand clear," Haller ordered. Before the German officer could roll over, Haller shot him twice between the shoulders.

"Get rid of them," he said. "Well back in the woods and out of sight." Each of his men took the arms of one of the fallen Germans. While they began dragging them off the road, Haller jumped into the patrol car, started the engine, and drove it carefully through the spaces between the trees. Then he joined his soldiers at the panel truck, and helped them toss the telephone equipment through the back door.

"Let's get rolling. They had to hear those shots across the river. They'll be coming over to take a look."

"Where to, skipper?"

"Head south." Haller answered. The truck backed into a U-turn. "We'll cross back over the same bridge. I want to take a look for some possible drop zones on the other side."

"We're not going to attack it?" one of the soldiers asked, sounding genuinely disappointed.

"Not a chance," Haller answered, looking back over his shoulder to make sure there were no cars on the road. "We'd never get near the place. It's a bloody fortress."

"Then we're getting out?" another soldier asked.

Haller nodded. "But not right away. First we have to find two of the people who work under that church. It may take us a day or so."

"Are we taking them out with us?" The question came from the back of the truck.

"If we can," Haller said. "If not, we'll have to leave them behind."

WINTER

1 9 4 5

The vise was crushing in from both sides. Mile by mile the Russians were squeezing in from the east, scorching the fields that had been the estates of the Prussian military leaders. The German armies fought desperately, but they were being forced back by the sheer weight of Russian steel. In the west, the Allies were back on the offensive. The German bulge into Belgium had been eliminated, and the Americans had outflanked the Siegfried Line. Von Rundstedt had fallen back to the Reich's last line of defense, the River Rhine. But to the German leaders, land was expendable. Instead, they were fighting for time. If they could keep the vise from closing for just a few months, their atomic bomb would be ready. And then the vise could be destroyed.

HAIGERLOCH — *January* 5

The attack came so suddenly that Anders didn't recognize the danger. When the lead car exploded, he was sure that it was accidental. And when the automatic weapons began to fire, he tried to walk out into the open so that both sides could see they were making a terrible mistake.

Birgit had decided to spend the day with him at the reactor site. In the early morning, when the scientists had been climbing into the waiting cars, a telephone call had summoned him back into the inn. There was a long series of connections, linking operators from Stuttgart and then Weimar to an operator in Berlin. Then he was told to wait while his party was connected. He waved the motorcade ahead, indicating that he and Birgit would follow. When he returned to the telephone, he listened to more operators passing messages as they attempted to link him with the caller. And then, just as his patience was exhausted, the line went dead.

His car, and a single escort car, were the only ones waiting when he charged down the steps. As they pulled away, another escort car, with its three armed soldiers, fell into line behind them.

"All these guards," he said to Birgit in Swedish. "Are they protecting us, or are they holding us prisoner?"

She laughed. Over the past few weeks, the size of the German garrison at Hechingen had grown dramatically. The castle church had been converted into a medieval fortress. The uniforms and the guns seemed obscene against the restful countryside with its pure white blanket of Christmas snow.

The motorcade rolled quickly down the river road, climbing the limestone ledge just as Anders had done on his first morning in Hechingen. Anders leaned back in the seat, composing his thoughts for the tasks that lay ahead. They would be pumping cooling water from the river through the graphite mass of the reactor in a test of the new valves that had been installed. Birgit was staring idly out over the river at the snow-covered trees on the opposite bank. Time, she thought morbidly, was the enemy. No matter what the outcome of Anders' plans to scuttle the reactor, the time they had left together was growing short. Their brief honeymoon, shared though it was with the other scientists and the demands of their mission, had been perfectly placed in a beautiful setting. But now it was nearly over.

Suddenly, an explosion shattered the morning, its echo ricocheting off the walls of the valley like a bullet. Their attention snapped forward just in time to see the bright fireball envelope the car ahead of them. Then the concussion shock hit their car like a hammer.

The driver cursed as the automobile swung toward the side of the road. For a second, he battled furiously, trying to bring it back under control. But the front wheel caught the soft ground on the shoulder and the car swerved violently. It slammed to a stop with its radiator crushed into the trunk of a small tree, three wheels carved into the muddy shoulder, and one wheel suspended in air over the road they had been driving on. Only a few feet ahead of the car was the edge of the limestone cliff that dropped abruptly forty feet into the river below.

Anders had been thrown violently against the door. Birgit had fired forward, first smashing against the front seat and then dropping to the floor.

He reached down toward Birgit and helped her to her knees. Then he pushed on the door handle and lifted the door open, struggling to climb free while he pulled Birgit behind him.

"Get down." The command came from the driver who had worked his own door open and rolled out onto the ground.

"Give me a hand," Anders ordered, still intent on helping Birgit out of the wreckage.

"Down!" the driver screamed, this time pushing Anders violently so that he fell on the road and rolled under the rear fender. He tried to pull himself back up, but the driver had scampered along the side of the car and was crouching beside him.

"Take cover," he ordered, and he pushed Anders over the edge of the road and sent him rolling down the slope of the shoulder.

Anders screamed a curse at the driver who was now crawling around the corner of the car toward the edge of the road. But his voice was drowned in a sudden explosion of gunfire. The driver yelled in pain and bounced forward, rolling past Anders and into the bushes below. He looked down in confusion at the crumpled form and saw blood spouting from the precise row of holes that were etched across the man's back.

What was happening? Why were the guards suddenly firing at one another? Anders was struggling to his feet, when the second patrol car screeched to a halt directly above him. The soldiers dove out of the car and rolled over the edge of the embankment. In an instant, they were positioned on their bellies, their rifles aimed under the car they had just abandoned.

"Stop," Anders ordered. "There's a mistake."

His ears were pounded by the impact of another explosion up on the road. The patrol car rocked, but held its position. His own car broke its precarious hold on the tree that had stopped its fall. The radiator crushed as it slid to the right, toward the edge of the cliff. Then the front fender caught and the car stopped. Gravel and dust began to fall around him, blackening the snow. The German soldiers began firing. And then, from close by, came the chatter of return fire. The windshield of the patrol car exploded into tiny shards that danced like snowflakes in the sunlight.

But Anders' attention was now riveted on his own car. Birgit was still inside, and under the impact of the explosion, the car had jostled a few feet closer to the tip of the ledge. He had to get her out.

He crawled quickly through the mud, kicking the limp body of the dying driver. The door fell open as soon as he pulled on the handle. Birgit slid out into his arms.

"Stay down!" he shouted at her. "They're firing at one another."

The words were still on his lips when a new blast of gunfire shattered the back window of their car. He threw himself over her to protect her from the fragments.

"Get away from the car," she told him with no hint of the panic he expected. She pushed him away and began crawling toward the bushes, below the feet of the three German soldiers who were returning fire beneath the protection of their patrol car. "Keep moving," she ordered without breaking her pace.

They were rocked by another explosion, this one seemingly under the outside edge of the car they had just left. The automobile bounced violently to its right. The fender that had been locked into the tree tore away like a sheet of paper. The car slid, rolled over when its side caught the bushes, and disappeared over the edge of the cliff.

And then there was another explosion, this one sending a flash of light under the patrol car, which bounced into the air and landed back on its four wheels.

One of the German soldiers screamed, rose up to his knees, and then fell over backwards. Anders turned to help him, but the man—really a boy—rolled down to the edge. The body that came to rest had no hands and no face.

"Jesus!" Anders screamed. He wretched until his forehead was pressing against the snow. Birgit's hand tore at his coat collar.

"Keep moving," she yelled. But, instead, he pulled away from her grasp.

"We have to stop this," he shouted at her. He tried to stand, but his feet began to slip. He started up toward the road, half crawling and half running, screaming for them to stop shooting with all the breath he had left.

A khaki-clad figure darted up to the edge of the road in front of him, and pointed a gun that seemed to explode in his face. At the same moment the German soldier to his right began firing. The khaki figure snapped backward, shaking from the vibration of the weapon that was still firing. It was at that instant that Anders felt the bullet tear through his left arm. The impact spun him on his heels and he began falling toward the slope of the hill.

Still another explosion hit the patrol car, this time jolting it sideways. The German soldier, whose shots had saved Anders' life, tried to roll away, but the car slid over him, drowning his scream in the roar of crushing metal.

Birgit crawled to where Anders was struggling to get back up on his feet. She threw her arm around his neck and dragged him to the ground.

"Stay down," she begged, now pleading rather than ordering. Her eyes darted up to the edge of the road, expecting to see another figure in khaki with a blazing gun. Their defenders were dead, the mangled bodies scattered beside them. They were at the mercy of the attackers.

And then there was a new roar of gunfire, coming from further up the road in the direction they had been heading. Other guns began firing directly above their heads. Birgit buried her head against Anders' coat to escape the deafening chatter, but pulled abruptly away when she felt the warm flow that was spreading in a giant stain across his sleeve.

The gunfire stopped, suddenly replaced by a dead silence that seemed just as threatening. Birgit and Anders lay together, almost afraid to breathe.

There were voices—commands being shouted in German. Then there was the sound of running footsteps. Birgit looked up. A German soldier in a gray uniform appeared at the edge of the road.

They were led carefully up and over the crest of the road's shoulder. A German officer rushed toward them as soon as they reached the paved surface. Without speaking, he unbuttoned Anders coat and jacket, and slid them carefully off his shoulders. The sleeve of his shirt was stained dark red and matted against his arm.

"We'll get you a doctor," the officer promised. Then he ordered one of the soldiers to bring the car that was pulled to the side of the road a few hundred yards away. As the soldier broke into a run, the officer tore Anders' other sleeve from his shirt, rolled it into a strip, and began to tie it above the wound in the bleeding arm.

"Do you want morphine?" he asked as he worked.

Anders shook his head.

"You will," the officer smiled.

But Anders wasn't paying attention to his wound. His eyes were wandering up the road, counting the slaughter that was all around him.

The chassis of the first patrol car was smoldering in the center of the road, perhaps fifty yards ahead. There was a blackened figure draped over its outline. Two gray uniformed bundles were piled to his right. Another German soldier was stretched out on the ground, being helped by one of his comrades.

Directly ahead was a khaki figure, a carbine lying by one hand and a red beret close to the other. Another form in a red beret was sitting quietly in the bushes across the road, his head thrown back and his mouth open. And there was the body of the attacker who had shot him, lying where he had fallen, just behind where Anders was standing.

"Who are they?" Anders asked.

The officer pulled tight on the knot he had made. "English commandos," he said as he examined his work.

"Here?" Anders was stunned. "What were they doing here?"

The officer looked up and shook his head at the naivete of the question. "Trying to kill you, of course."

HECHINGEN — *January 6*

Anders opened his eyes into a gray haze. He blinked, but the haze wouldn't go away. He tried to focus. A dark shape came into view and gradually narrowed until it became the tall post at the corner of his bed.

Then the outlines of his room appeared. He could make out the other bedpost, and beyond it the washstand with its porcelain basin and pitcher. He rolled his head slowly, and blinked again at the light that was pouring in through the window. Then he saw Birgit, sitting in the chair, looking toward him and smiling.

"Are you feeling better?" Her words came from a great distance and were drowned in their own echo. He tried to answer, but the effort seemed impossible. It was easier simply to close his eyes.

She watched him as he drifted back into his drugged sleep. Since the moment when the military car had returned them to the inn, he had never been out of her sight. She had stayed in the room while the doctor cleaned and dressed his wound.

"It's nothing serious," the doctor had said. "Just flesh and perhaps a bit of muscle. But we should take him to the hospital. He will be more comfortable there."

She had protested. They had given him morphine, and he might need more if his pain continued. She was afraid of what he might say while under the drug.

"He's better here," she had decided. "His associates will want to consult with him."

The doctor had shrugged as he replaced his instruments into his bag. "It really doesn't matter. I'll stop by and look at it in a day or so."

As she sat in the silent room, watching over his sleep, she tried to assemble the confusion of the pieces. They certainly were British soldiers, unmistakably identified by the patches and badges that they wore. And there was no doubt that Karl was their target.

She had been confused over that point at first. The scientists always left together in the morning, in a caravan of automobiles with armed soldiers in escort cars. The British couldn't have been sure which car Karl was riding in. More than likely, they were simply attacking the entire group.

But then she had remembered the telephone call. It had come in just as they were boarding the cars and had clearly separated Anders from the others. The delay in connecting the call had caused the other cars to go on ahead. And then, when there was no party on the other end, Anders and she had set out alone. It must have been the English calling. The number of the inn was in the telephone directories of the surrounding towns. They could have placed the call anywhere, even a building across the square from which they could have watched Anders leave the group and walk back into the inn.

The Germans had claimed that there were four commandos. They had been spotted several days before by home guardsmen, dressed as Italian conscript workers. Only three had participated in the attack on the car, so it was probable that the fourth had been in Hechingen placing the phone call. He was still free, but the

Germans had sealed all the roads and were conducting house-to-house searches. They expected to capture him at any moment.

So, it had been no accident. The British commandos had come into Germany to kill Karl Anders. But why? Why murder an agent who held the key to their victory? What did they know about him that he had never shared with her?

She had heard hints of British assassinations. But they had always involved double agents—people the British thought they controlled, but who were secretly in contact with the Germans. And she had been told of the suicides. Agents carried cyanide capsules that they were expected to use if they faced capture. But Anders certainly wasn't a double agent. She had lived so intimately with him that she could guess his thoughts before he even spoke them. And Haller had never expected Anders to offer himself up in suicide. There had been elaborate plans made to kidnap him if his cover began to unravel.

Perhaps it had been a botched kidnap attempt. Of course! The shot that had hit him had been sprayed wildly by a wounded commando who was falling to his death. Perhaps he never intended to shoot Anders.

But then she remembered the explosives that were tossed towards the cars, and the blast of gunfire that had shattered the windows. The attackers were trying to destroy everyone. Protecting Anders' life was certainly not part of their orders.

It had been the Germans who had saved his life. She remembered her joy when the soldier who appeared above them was dressed in gray rather than in khaki. And she remembered the concern of the German officer who had just risked his own life and those of his men to fight his way through to Anders' side.

Could the British think that he had turned? They had probably heard about the medal that Himmler had sent, conveying the personal gratitude of the fuehrer. Did they believe it? Was it possible that they thought Anders had become so involved in demonstrating the reactor that he was now laboring for its success instead of its destruction?

The possibilities overwhelmed her. Birgit had to try to clear her mind so that she could start from the beginning.

Anders groaned and tossed restlessly. She crossed to his side and rearranged the blankets. Then she stepped back to her chair.

Through the window, she could see the soldiers that the Germans had stationed to protect their prize scientist. There was an armored car parked in the center of the square, its turret bolted down and its twin machine guns scanning menacingly. Pairs of armed soldiers were stationed at each corner of the inn, and patrol cars were pulled across each of the streets that opened into the square. Clearly, they were expecting that the British might try again.

It was absurd. All their fears had focused on the Germans. Now, it was the Germans who were their protectors. They had thought of rescue by the British as their final hope. Now it was the British who were trying to murder them.

What had changed? Birgit slumped into the chair and began to travel the whole excruciating ring of logic all over again. Why would the British kill him? Perhaps, if they thought the Germans were on to him, it would be the only sure way to keep him from confessing that he had ruined the reactor. But if the Germans were on to him, why was there a company of men stationed in the square to protect him?

The German sentries were proof that the Nazis still regarded their Swedish scientist with the utmost importance. Which was exactly what Haller had hoped for. Why had Haller suddenly changed his mind?

Anders slept through the night, unaware that his colleagues had tapped softly on the door to ask about his progress. But he was fully awake in the morning, his mind cleared of the morphine and the pain in his arm more annoying than crippling.

He dressed, with Birgit's help, fully expecting to join the others for the day's tests. But Diebner wouldn't hear of it. He ordered a holiday, and laughingly threatened to have guards posted at his door to keep Anders in bed.

They walked in the square, and when they were out of earshot of the soldiers, Birgit told him her worst fears. The attack had been a British effort to assassinate him. He nodded at her statement and agreed without emotion to her conclusions.

"There hasn't been any correspondence," he explained. "We've been cut off, either by the British or the Germans. I guessed that the Germans might be on to us, but I didn't figure on the British tidying up their loose ends."

She gestured toward one of the sentries that they were passing. "But the Germans are protecting us."

"The dead commandos obviously didn't think that they would," he answered.

"Then what do we do?"

Anders smiled reassuringly. "Exactly what we came to do. We make damn sure that the reactor never runs."

"And then. . . ?"

"Then we're on our own. I don't think we'll be welcome here. And we sure as hell aren't going back to England."

WÜRTTEMBERG — *January* 7

Haller could move only at night, and then only for very short distances.

He had guessed that his cover as a telephone lineman had been compromised and so he had abandoned the truck and begun his escape on foot in civilian clothes. He had found the roads alive with German patrols, certainly searching for the fourth commando. They knew how many linemen had passed the bridge and how many commandos had been in the raiding party. They had all the roads covered, were patrolling the open ground in the surrounding forests, and were conducting detailed searches of every house and structure in the area. The darkness of night was his only protection, and even then he had to avoid the roads and keep his distance from lighted windows.

He had left the radio in the truck, choosing to carry a warm jacket, a blanket, and a change of socks in addition to his assault rifle. It had been a good choice. There had been a heavy snowfall the first night, and the jacket and blanket had saved him from freezing as he cowered in a wooded undergrowth during the next day. That night, trudging through knee-deep drifts, he had broken through the ice of a ground stream. The socks had saved him from crippling frostbite.

On the second day, he had rolled into the blanket in a small open patch, hidden by a dense thicket of trees. Moments later, he had heard the sound of a small engine echoing above the treetops, and moved out to the edge of the woods to get a clear view of the countryside. A German Stork reconnaissance plane, moving slowly with its nose canted into the wind, was coming straight toward him, following the tracks he had made in the snow during the night. The plane turned abruptly over the trees, seemed to hover for a moment directly over his head as it came full face into the wind, and then headed off toward the west. The observer, peering down through the bulged windows, might have seen him. But even if he didn't, he had certainly seen the tracks and radioed his report to the German patrols. Haller had rolled his blanket quickly and pushed on further into the woods, in a direction away from the abandoned farm that he was trying to reach.

His destination was the same house where British agents had left the truck. When he reached it, he planned to keep a distance, observing it until one of his people made the scheduled visit. Then he would leave with the agent, trusting the sympathizers who were infiltrated into the area to provide him with cover and get his report back to England.

Now he crouched at the edge of a clearing, the broken barn clearly in sight a few hundred yards away. The house, with its empty window frames, was in total darkness. The damn detour, forced by the patrol plane, had cost him too much time. If the British agents had checked the house, he had missed them, which would mean another day of hiding out in the open. And if they were in the house, he couldn't see them. He would have to wait and watch, and hope for some sign that they were already inside.

On the distant road, he could see shrouded headlights moving—probably German patrols kept active to cut off his escape from the forest behind him. German troops, alerted by the plane, had most likely moved into the forest to search. He guessed that he was trapped between the troops behind and the open ground that lay ahead.

His best move was to double back into the forest. With the cover provided by the dense trees, he might be able to slip past the pursuing Germans. But to what? The battered house was the only rendezvous point he could reach. He would have to return the next evening when the area might be alive with patrols. Besides, his chances in the forest weren't that good. Everywhere he moved, he would be leaving tracks in the snow, which would make him easy to find once the sun came up. And he might not survive another night in the forest. He was cold, his feet numb and his wet trousers frozen against his legs. He hadn't eaten in two days and he had been able to sleep for only a few broken hours. He didn't know how long he could keep moving, and once he stopped, the cold night wind would prove as lethal as any German bullet.

Haller looked longingly toward the house. Even with windows out, the walls would provide a wind barrier. The wet hay in the barn could serve as a warm blanket. The Germans probably wouldn't be searching deserted houses in the darkness of night. If his contacts were waiting inside, then they could make their escape under cover of darkness. And if they weren't, he could leave the house before dawn and return to his vigil at the edge of the woods.

He checked the clip in his rifle, and then crept forward, dragging the blanket behind him in hopes of erasing the footprints. Every few yards, he dropped down on his belly, looking for any movement around the house and listening for any sound. He moved to his right, keeping away from the sightline to the open door of the barn.

As he moved closer, he was suddenly aware of the sound of his own breathing and of the dull crunch of the snow beneath his feet. He waited until he was able to get the exhausted panting under control, and then he started again, setting each step slowly and carefully.

He reached the back wall of the barn and was able to look in through the spaces between the weathered siding. At first, he saw only blackness, but after a few moments he was able to make out the shapes inside. The hay, which had hidden the truck, was scattered in a thin carpet all across the floor. Someone had been inside, and they had searched thoroughly before they left.

Haller sighed in relief. There was no reason why his agents would have searched for anything, so it must have been one of the German patrols. If they had already been here, it might be several days before they would return.

He left the shelter of the barn and crossed the open space toward the house, leaning low to stay beneath the sightlines of the windows. He crept around to the back and raised up to one of the window frames. Through the blackness he could make out the interior of an empty room with traces of snow on the floor directly beneath the window. He pulled himself up to the ledge, threw a leg over the windowsill, and settled noiselessly inside.

The flooring creaked beneath his feet as he crossed the room, and he stopped to listen. There was no return sound. He moved to the door and lifted the latch carefully. Then he pulled back the door and peered into another shapeless space. Slowly, he moved into the main room of the house.

He had taken only one step when his foot kicked into something soft and heavy. Instinctively he glanced down, and saw the outlines of an unrecognizable shape. When he heard the sound behind him, he began to wheel and duck in one motion. But his reflexes were slowed by his ordeal in the cold countryside. He saw something firing toward him out of the darkness, felt the explosion at the side of his head, and sensed that his legs were collapsing. He was already unconscious before his body crashed against the floor.

When his senses returned, he was lying flat on his back, his feet raised on top of something that was lying near him. His hand slipped as he tried to push himself up to a sitting position. He thought he heard a voice, but it was either whispered or coming from a distance. He couldn't make out the words.

When he opened his eyes, there was a flickering light in the room, and he saw the small gas torch that was burning on a bare table. His eyes scanned and found a uniformed German soldier, standing behind his head. The pencil-thin hole of a machine-gun barrel was pointing into his face. The soldier yelled something in

German, and two other soldiers moved into the glow of the lamp, each with a gun pointed toward him.

Again, he tried to push himself up, and again his hand slipped from under him. He looked down and saw that he was resting in a large stain of blood that was oozing from the crumpled form under his feet. His eyes focused. There were two bodies stretched out on the floor, one under his legs and the other beside him. The open-mouthed face that was looking toward him was one that he had seen before.

Suddenly he was being lifted to his feet, held by the soldier who had been standing behind him while the others kept him covered with their rifles. As he was dragged toward the door, he pieced together what had happened. The German patrol had surprised his agents who were waiting in the house. They had shot them, and then simply waited in their place for his arrival.

He was pushed, face down, onto the floor of a car that they had summoned. Two of the soldiers climbed into the seat with their feet on top of him and the muzzles of their rifles pressed against his back. The engine started, and the car bounced off the siding and onto the road.

Haller knew the horrors that awaited him. But for the moment, at least, he was warm.

LONDON — *January 10*

Even the war stops on Sundays, Air Marshal Ward thought as he entered the communications center. The skeleton weekend crew that was covering the desks didn't seem particularly busy. The teletypes were strangely quiet and the constant stream of visitors and messengers was noticeable for its absence. The traffic from all over the world that kept the center frantic, day and night, seemed suddenly to have quieted.

But Ward was interested in only one message, and that message was long overdue. He had received two reports from Haller since the major had parachuted into southern Germany, and he was anxiously awaiting the third.

The first message had confirmed that an air attack on the castle church was useless and that a sneak attack by a small raiding party was now out of the question. An airborne division would be required. Ward had responded that the German breakthrough made the assignment of airborne units unlikely for the foreseeable future. He had suggested that Haller concentrate on his alternative plan.

The second message announced that Haller had located Siegfried, and promised that the mission would be completed within a week. "Will report results immediately," Haller had signed off.

But the week had passed, and with each new hour, Ward became more certain that something had gone terribly wrong. Haller would have notified him of any change in schedule. He would have asked for additional support if it were needed. And if everything had proceeded on schedule, he certainly would have sent a "mission accomplished."

Ward tapped on the door of the coding room. The clerk who opened the door had obviously been napping, and he tried to stuff in his shirttail while he snapped to attention.

"Anything for me?" Ward asked softly.

The clerk rushed back into the coding room, buttoning his collar and pulling up his tie as he searched the message boards. He returned with a half dozen signals, none marked for priority handling, all absolutely routine.

Ward took them, walked to his darkened office, and tossed them in his mailbox. They could all wait for the next day.

He opened his desk drawer, lifted out a bottle of Scotch whiskey, and poured a splash into his teacup. Then he leaned back in his chair to weigh the possibilities.

The attack on Siegfried had succeeded, but Haller and his men had been killed. Reasonable, he thought. In that case he would never receive confirmation. The Germans weren't likely to announce that they had lost the one man who could save them. But they would have absolutely no doubt that Nils Bergman was genuine. And if Siegfried had estimated his reactor design accurately, then the Germans would waste the rest of the war trying to operate an impotent reactor.

The attack had failed, and Haller was dead. Then he would soon hear of German boasts that they had foiled an assassination attempt on their valuable scientist. And Siegfried would still be in place to see the reactor to its destruction.

Haller had been killed before any attack could be launched. If the Germans realized why Haller was in Germany, then Nils Bergman's credibility would be enhanced. But if Haller had never gotten even close to his man, then the mission was wasted and the Germans would still harbor suspicions about Bergman.

Haller was on the run. That would explain his failure to report. The third message might still arrive.

Haller had been captured. Unlikely. He wasn't the kind of man who would ever raise his hands over his head. But still, it was possible. And that was the possibility that the air marshal feared most. A man who knew what Haller knew, in the hands of the Germans, would be a disaster for Siegfried and his plans to sabotage the German atomic bomb program.

Ward sipped the Scotch and realized that he knew absolutely nothing. Was Haller dead or alive? Was Nils Bergman a hero or a traitor? Would his reactor fail or succeed? He didn't even know how much time he had to get the answers. Would the Allies be stalled at the Rhine until a spring offensive? Or would they follow the retreating Germans right into the heart of the Reich?

His odds looked good if Haller had made a convincing attempt to get at Siegfried. They turned into a long shot if he had not been able to get close to his target. And there were no odds at all if Haller had somehow been captured.

HECHINGEN — January 12

Birgit felt her breath catch the instant she saw the officer climb out of the sedan in the street below her window. He was wearing the black cap and black leather coat of the SS, and the way he raced up the steps of the inn, taking them two at a time, told her this wasn't a casual visit. He had come with a purpose, and since she was the only one at the inn, his mission had to involve her.

She rushed to the table where she had been preparing Nils Bergman's correspondence with the university, coding in still another message for Haller. She closed the folder and pushed the papers into the leather briefcase that had become Bergman's traveling office. Then she stood by the foot of the bed, waiting for the knock on her door that she knew would come.

"Miss Zorn?" he asked, and then he acknowledged her with a casual salute that was more like a tip of his cap. "I am ordered to ask you if you would join us at our headquarters. We will require just a few minutes of your time."

"SS headquarters?" She heard the fright in her own voice, and watched the officer smile at her response.

"Yes, if you don't mind. There has been an incident that requires your attention. Professor Bergman will be joining us there."

Birgit nodded. "Yes, of course. My coat is downstairs."

The officer stepped back and waited while she locked her door. It was a silly gesture. The old bolt lock could be broken out of the door frame with one kick of his boot. If they wanted to search her room, the oversized iron key that she dropped into her jacket pocket wouldn't be any barrier.

"How far is it?" she said, as she walked down the stairs beside him. "I didn't know that there was an SS unit here."

He took her coat and held it for her while she slipped her arms into the sleeves. "Just a street away," he told her, as if to be reassuring. "It's just a temporary headquarters. Our people arrived only yesterday."

That wasn't completely true. There had been a constant stream of SS officers visiting the construction site. But they had come from Berlin and had used the inn as their base of operations, dominating the conversations with war talk when they joined the scientists for meals. What was frighteningly different was that they had apparently established a permanent headquarters in Hechingen. They would be constant companions from now on.

The driver held the door while Birgit slipped into the backseat. Then the officer climbed in next to her and waved the driver to his post behind the wheel.

"You are Swedish?" he asked as soon as the car began to move.

"Yes, from Stockholm."

His eyes toured from her extended ankles to the hem of her dress, which was just above her knees.

"I am very fond of Sweden," he allowed. "I visited there often and always found it enjoyable. I hope you are enjoying your visit to Germany."

"I liked it better before the war," Birgit answered. His eyes narrowed in disapproval, so she explained, "I was in Berlin, working at the Kaiser Wilhelm when it was bombed."

The officer nodded. "Working on a very important project for Germany, I understand."

She turned away in confusion. Was this the beginning of an interrogation? What had the SS learned about her and Nils Bergman?

"I'm not allowed to discuss my work," she answered.

She heard him laugh, mocking the innocence of her response. "We already know all about your work," he said. He leaned back into the seat and began slapping the gloves he held in one hand into the palm of the other.

The car had circled a block of small houses that leaned one against the other. It was now heading down a street that led back toward the inn. As Birgit looked ahead, she could see two black sedans that were pulled up onto the sidewalk. The car slowed, jumped the curb, and stopped behind the parked cars. Then the driver rushed around and opened the door.

They entered a private home, stepping up from the street through the front door. Immediately to the right was a small sitting room with stuffed chairs backed against flowered wallpaper. The two windows looked out onto the street where the cars were parked.

"We will wait in here. My commander and Professor Bergman will be arriving in just a few minutes." Birgit sat on the edge of one of the chairs while the officer paced slowly back and forth, slapping his gloves in his palm.

"Do you know what this is about?" Birgit tried.

He stopped his pacing and looked offended by the question. "I'm not allowed to discuss my work," he said, mocking her earlier comment. Then he settled into the chair across from her, slouching back in contrast to her rigid, concerned posture. "But you will know soon enough."

She felt herself beginning to crumble under his self-satisfied smile and unwavering stare, and glanced absently around the room. It was a private house with a family Bible resting on one of the tables, and photographs of grim parents in stiff clothing hanging on the wall. Probably the SS had picked it at random, told the inhabitants to move in with neighbors, and simply taken it over. No one in Germany would dare to quarrel with the orders of the SS.

But they didn't seem to be planning to stay long. The radio equipment and the file cabinets that were fixtures of the elite military force were nowhere in sight. The Nazi flag had not been draped over the door and the requisite photograph of the fuehrer had not been hung. They had arrived quickly, and they were leaving quickly.

But why? The regular army troops that guarded the castle church and that had surrounded the square after the British commando attack were more than adequate. Certainly, the small SS detachment wasn't here to safeguard against another raid. There were no problems at the reactor site. Construction was right on schedule. The SS officers who had visited had promised that they would return laudatory reports to Himmler. There was nothing happening in Hechingen that would command the sudden interest of the internal security forces.

The correspondence, Birgit suddenly realized. She had been coding messages into Bergman's regular correspondence even though there had been no return mail from Stockholm. Had the SS broken the code and read the progress reports that were being sent through Sweden? Both she and Bergman had been summoned, the officer had told her. Could their real identities have been compromised?

She looked back at the officer, who was obviously enjoying the fear that she was beginning to radiate. Did the bastard know about her and Anders? Was he musing over the brutal interrogation that they were about to face? His eyes roved up and down her body as if it would soon be his to enjoy. Was he one of their professional torturers, or was he just a messenger sent to bring them back to Berlin?

Birgit found herself hoping for the sound of the car that would bring Anders. If they had been discovered, she knew that she should be praying for his escape. But her fear of the silent, smiling Nazi was growing into terror. The seconds were stretching into interminable hours that she couldn't endure alone.

She heard the front door open, and the confident, casual officer was suddenly braced at attention, his arm extended in salute. Another officer, in the same leather coat, with the silver insignia on his black cap, strolled into the room, waving a return salute. Karl Anders followed at his heels.

"Tell them we will be down in a moment," the senior officer ordered, and Birgit's tormenter clicked his heels and rushed out of the room. Karl stared blankly at Birgit. Each could tell that the other had no idea of why they had been brought here.

"Please be seated, Professor Bergman," the commanding officer offered. There was no threat in his voice. Anders slipped onto the sofa next to Birgit.

The officer took off his coat and tossed it casually on one of the chairs. Then he reached into his pocket, withdrew a silver cigarette case, and offered it first to Birgit and then to Anders. They refused with gestures as they waited for his next word. But he was in no hurry. He carefully selected a cigarette, closed the case, and then tapped the cigarette against the cover.

"I'm afraid I have some very distressing news for you, Professor Bergman."

Anders and Birgit waited while the colonel searched his pocket for his cigarette lighter and brought the flame to his cigarette.

"We have positive information . . ." he broke his thought while he inhaled deeply and watched the cloud of smoke rise above his head, "that the British plan to assassinate you. You were the target of their foolish attack last week, and since they failed, we can expect them to make further attempts to reach you."

Anders looked at Birgit. She feigned shock, even though she had already told Karl her suspicions. Then he turned back to the colonel.

"I had assumed that they were after the entire team. There are many well-known scientists, and our work has military applications."

Before he was finished, the officer was dismissing his comment with a wave of his cigarette.

"No, it was definitely you. We have captured one of the British infiltrators, and his orders were to kill you. It was to be a cold-blooded murder of a neutral citizen in violation of all the rules of war."

"Only me?" Anders asked. "Not the others? Why?"

"They think you are essential to our success. They tried to recruit you themselves, didn't they?"

He nodded. "Over a year ago. Before I came into Germany."

"So! They appreciate your value to us, and they want you dead," the officer said. "Reichsfuehrer Himmler is outraged. He has notified your government of this violation of your neutrality and he has ordered the man shot. He has ordered that you and Miss Zorn are to be present for the execution."

Anders recoiled from the suggestion. "I am to be present at the execution of a British soldier?"

"He is not a soldier," the colonel snapped. "He was wearing

civilian clothes in violation of international law and has none of the rights of a soldier. He is a murderer."

Birgit looked down at her hands. "I don't think I want to be present for an execution," she whispered.

"You must be," the colonel snapped. "The reichsfuehrer has ordered it. Several brave Germans died to protect you. Now you must honor their sacrifice."

Anders moved his hand on top of Birgit's. "When will this occur?" he asked the colonel.

"Immediately. They are waiting in the basement."

Anders couldn't hide his shock. "Now? In a basement?"

"The man acted like a rat. He deserves to die like a rat." He crushed out his cigarette as he pronounced the sentence and snatched his coat from the chair. "Come with me. Now!" It wasn't a request. It was an order from Himmler.

Anders held Birgit's hand as they followed the colonel to the back of the entrance hall and turned down the narrow wooden steps that were built against the stone wall of the cellar. A single bare lightbulb hung from its electrical wire at the foot of the stairs, illuminating the young officer who had accompanied Birgit. He turned, and led them through the shadows, past a wooden coal bin to a planked door under the front of the house. He opened the door on a lighted storeroom and stepped back.

The colonel walked in and Birgit began to follow. But suddenly she gasped and stopped dead. Her hands flew to her face, and then she turned and tried to push past Anders in flight out of the room. But Karl was already in the narrow doorway, and the young officer behind him blocked his retreat. He caught Birgit in his arms, but before he could comfort her, he caught a glimpse of the sight that had horrified her.

A mutilated body, spattered in its own blood, was fastened with wires to the opposite wall.

The fingers were missing from the outstretched hands. The toes had been cut from the feet. The torso had been beaten to red broken welts, and the penis and scrotum had been hacked away.

"This is your assassin, Professor Bergman," the colonel announced contemptuously. He nodded to a muscular figure in a rubber apron who was standing proudly beside his work. The man stepped to the body, grasped the matted hair, and threw the head back.

It was Haller, his face spared by his tormenters so that he could witness the horror of his own dismemberment.

At first, his eyes rolled aimlessly, bobbing in their sockets as if they were floating in a jar. Gradually, they steadied, and the blank, mindless stare began to focus. They settled looking straight ahead, right into Anders' face.

The young officer pressed from behind, forcing Anders and Birgit into the room, and closed the door behind them.

Anders looked pleadingly toward the colonel. "This is horrible," he gasped. "You have no right to bring us here."

"Horrible?" the colonel demanded. "Do you know what his bombs did to the soldiers who defended you? This is what you would have looked like if he had gotten close to you." He reached out and spun Birgit away from Anders' grasp so that she was facing Haller's mutilated form. "This is what his bullets and grenades would have done to you."

He nodded to the young officer who immediately unbuckled the holster he wore at his side, and withdrew his pistol. With a quick motion, the officer pulled the bolt and let it snap forward, loading a round into the chamber. Then he turned the pistol and held the handle toward Anders.

"Reichsfuehrer Himmler has ordered that you be the one to shoot him," the colonel said.

Anders fell back a step away from the pistol that wavered in front of his face. He shook his head slowly. "I can't. I don't know how," he begged.

The colonel was angered at Anders' protest. "You refuse to honor the soldiers who died to save you? You value an English life more than theirs?"

And then Anders understood. He was being tested. The reichsfuehrer's sick mind had devised a final test of his identity. Would he strike back at his own murderer? Or was the assassin really his ally? Would he build the bomb that would mutilate thousands of bodies? Or was his loyalty to the Nazi cause a pretense? If he couldn't kill one Englishman—one who had made an attempt on his own life—how could they believe that he would work to kill thousands of Englishmen?

His hand raised slowly toward the pistol.

"Fire into his stomach," the young officer advised. "He should suffer for his crimes."

Haller's eyes searched Anders' face as Karl's fingers reached for the gun. Then they locked on Birgit. He couldn't suffer any more. He was pleading for her intervention.

He never told them, she realized. They cut him to pieces, hour after hour, and he never betrayed them. And now they were forcing Karl to inflict still more agony.

She took one step forward, reached out, and snatched the pistol before Anders' hands could reach it. She held it in both her hands and pointed it straight into Haller's face.

"Murderer," she hissed.

Birgit pulled the trigger and sent a single round through the center of his forehead.

The body slumped peacefully while the deafening sound was still echoing through the room.

She turned the gun around carefully and handed it back to the young officer whose mouth hung open in astonishment. Then she turned to Anders, whose hand was still extended as if reaching for the pistol.

"He tried to kill us," she explained defiantly.

Anders nodded. Then his face turned slowly to the colonel.

"Please tell the reichsfuehrer that we have done our duty."

BERLIN – *J a n u a r y 2 1*

Heinrich Himmler had picked the date on which the world would end. June the first. By then, everything had to be destroyed.

He leaned back into the upholstered chair, carefully removed the wire-framed glasses, and pressed his fingertips against his weary eyes. There was so much to do, and the Allies were leaving him with so little time. They were already in the Reich, the Russians in Prussia and the Americans and British lining up against the Rhine. His armies of children and old men couldn't hold out much longer. His air force no longer existed. His submarines were being hounded to surrender all over the Atlantic. The incessant bombers were pounding his cities to rubble. He had to prepare for the end.

On his desk were orders to his SS loyalists on dealing with deserters. Any soldier leaving his post was to be treated as an enemy of the Reich and shot without trial. There were orders to the guards of the underground factories. Shoot the sick and the weak, use those who could work to destroy machinery and blueprints, and then shoot those. There were orders to his concentration camp commanders. Kill everyone, then destroy the gas chambers and the ovens, leave no evidence. And there were orders to the thousands and thousands of bureaucrats who had made the Reich function. To industrialists, to mayors, to judges, to police chiefs. To the engineers who ran the power plants and the clerks who ran the railroads. Kill all conscripted workers, burn all records, break all machines.

He would leave nothing for the Allies to conquer and no one for them to rescue. And he would leave no legacy to the German people who had proven so unworthy of the fuehrer's magnificent leadership. Everything would vanish in the Gotterdämmerung.

As he leaned forward over the mountains of papers that waited on his desk, Himmler wondered how one man could be expected to accomplish so much. What he had built over a decade had to be destroyed in just a few months. Destruction was no simple matter. It required resources, just as building the Reich had required resources. He needed bullets for all the executions, and ammunition had become scarce. He needed petrol to burn records, and there wasn't a drop left in the country. He needed explosives to destroy the gas chambers, and his munitions factories were gone. He needed bulldozers to bury the corpses, and there were none to be found.

And yet, as he lifted his pen and began signing the orders, the reichsfuehrer was not without hope. There were still a hundred rockets, hidden on their launchpads, fueled and waiting. There was still the processing plant buried under fifty feet of rock, waiting to build the uranium bombs. And under the castle church in Haigerloch, his atomic reactor would soon go into production.

It would work. Of that, he was certain. All his lingering doubts about the loyalty of his scientists had vanished with the report of the SS colonel he had sent to Hechingen. The British had jumped to his bait and tried to kill Nils Bergman. Bergman and his woman had executed the English major. The man and his work were genuine.

"Without doubt, Reichsfuehrer," the officer had assured him, standing at ramrod attention across his desk. "The British officer was certainly telling the truth. Our interrogators were most thorough in their work. Toward the end, he was volunteering information that we hadn't even asked for."

"How did they learn about Bergman?" Himmler had asked.

"Exactly as you predicted, Reichsfuehrer. One of their agents compromised an official at our delegation in Switzerland."

Himmler had allowed himself a brief smile of satisfaction. "And Bergman showed no sympathy for the British officer?"

"To the contrary, Reichsfuehrer. Of course, he and the woman were momentarily taken back by the procedures of the interrogation. Certainly they are not familiar with some of the necessities of war. But when they were offered the opportunity to perform the execution, both of them reached for the pistol."

When the colonel had left, Himmler had spent a moment wondering why he should have ever been suspicious. Bergman hadn't forced his way into Germany. He had been invited. No one had seriously questioned his work. Even Werner Heisenberg, who was usually reserved in his praise, had called the man a genius. The woman was certainly genuine. She had been observed in Bergman's office at the university, and had positively identified the man she met in Berlin as her lover. The tests of Bergman's work had been successful, and the production reactor was progressing ahead of schedule.

But he had learned to be suspicious. There was no one that he trusted completely. The final test of Bergman's loyalty, before he was allowed to take control of the production reactor, had been a sensible precaution. And Bergman had passed the test. Now, at least, there was good reason to hope that the crumbling Reich could be saved.

But nothing was certain. Even with the combined genius of Bergman and Heisenberg, something could go wrong. Perhaps the new, incredibly explosive element would prove difficult to separate. Perhaps the Allies would destroy the rockets on their launching pads before the warheads could be fitted.

Himmler continued signing the orders. He hoped they wouldn't be necessary. But it would be prudent to have them ready. If the super weapon didn't work, then the Allies would meet in Berlin by the first of June. So that was the deadline by which everything had to be destroyed.

HECHINGEN — *February 15*

Birgit had begun working regularly at the castle church the day after she shot Haller, unable to face being alone with the chilling memory of his hanging corpse. Each day, she rode quietly beside Anders to the reactor site and climbed down the circular metal steps that led from the church to the reactor vault. She donned a blue laboratory jacket, and lost herself in the comments and notes that Anders dictated as he inspected the construction. She filled her time assisting the scientists in their most trivial needs, and she packed her mind with the calculations and dimensions, the pressures and the temperatures that were the vocabulary of the program. Her biggest fear was an idle moment when she might see Haller's pleading eyes turning toward her.

The scientists knew she had killed the English soldier. She could tell by the way they turned their faces when she approached and by the blank gaps in their conversation whenever she was close enough to hear. "She shot him. Grabbed the gun from the officer's hand, cursed at the English soldier, and shot him right between the eyes," she imagined them saying. When she heard them laugh, she could guess at their jokes. "I'd be afraid to sleep with her. She probably keeps a pistol under the pillow."

But they said nothing. They censored their conversations to avoid any hint that they even suspected what she had been capable of doing and, as a result, their words rang false. At dinner, the sounds of glasses and tableware filled the long voids in the conversation. And the voices gathered around the fireplace were whispered and conspiratorial.

Even Anders said nothing. In their walk around the square, when they tried to reason why the English might have turned against them, neither of them used Haller's name.

"They can't know," Anders said, referring to the Germans. "If they knew who we were, we'd both be dead."

"But if we're not compromised, then why would the English want to eliminate us?" Birgit countered.

They tried every possibility. Perhaps this was the British way of covering the original kidnapping of Bergman. When the war was over, they might not want to explain how they had botched the illegal seizure of a Swedish citizen. Better to let the University of Stockholm think that Nils Bergman had died in Germany. But wouldn't they wait until after the reactor had failed? How could they be so sure that the faults Anders had designed into the graphite would prove fatal?

Maybe they believed the propaganda about the medal. Maybe

the English thought that Anders had become so involved in the scientific discovery of the century that he was actually working for its success. Could they really think that he had turned and was working for a German victory? They had question after question, but there were no answers. All the answers had died with the single shot that Birgit had fired.

Haller was between them in their bed. Anders felt the coward for not having the courage to take the pistol. It was his responsibility to serve as the executioner that the Germans required. He should not have left the obscene work for her. How could he make love to a woman he had failed so terribly? And Birgit knew that the cold-blooded murder had violated every understanding that she shared with Anders. He was a man who detested violence. He was risking his life to spare the world from still another method of slaughter. He could not take the pistol that the Nazi officer had held out, but she had hardly hesitated. Could he ever understand the pleading she had seen in Haller's eyes and forgive the willingness with which she had fired the shot? She felt as if she had been discovered in a shameless adultery. Night after night, they tried to console one another with lovemaking. But their words stopped at their lips. Their kisses were brief, and they seemed to recoil from one another's touch.

She could find peace only in her work and in the obscurity of disappearing among the other blue-coated technicians. When there was nothing for her to do, she separated herself from her colleagues, climbed the iron steps and sat in the church, bathed in the colors that flooded from the stained-glass windows. She had destroyed everyone—Gunther, Bergman, Haller. She had even destroyed the frail moment of love that had blossomed amid the decay of the dying nation. In the church, she could admit that to herself. The glowing faces of the angels in the windows wouldn't reproach her. Perhaps they would even listen to her prayers and save Anders from the death sentence she was certain that she had brought down on his head.

As they ran the final tests of the reactor, she began to understand what Anders was preparing to do. Everything was checking out perfectly, and the scientists were becoming more and more excited over the certainty of their success. She wondered how his design could possibly deceive so many of the world's best minds in fission physics. How could it fool Werner Heisenberg? Or the ever-suspicious Fritz Lauderbach? If they were all so confident that the graphite pile would run, why was Anders growing more and more certain that it would fail?

Then, one morning, she listened while Karl outlined the start-up procedures to his colleagues. She heard him review the power curves he had predicted when he first arrived at the castle church. And suddenly, she had understood. He had designed a reactor that would perish in the inferno it would cause. But it would begin to burn only when it was pushed to its full power. Karl was planning to stay at the controls to see it to its death. When its insane heat overwhelmed the cooling water being pumped from the river and broke through the graphite walls, it would spread white fire throughout the cave. Karl would be in the cave, standing at the control panel, when the Reich's last hopes went up in flames, one more victim to her involvement with the German atomic bomb.

Tonight, when the dinner had been cleared and the scientists were gathering around the fire, Birgit had started for their room, but stopped suddenly at the foot of the stairs. She reached for her coat, which was hanging inside the door, and stepped outside into the cold night air. Anders watched her form move past the frosted windows, then jumped up to follow her.

He caught up with her as she turned the corner of the building and was starting down the snow-covered path toward the edge of the river.

"Can I join you?" She nodded and took his hand, and they walked silently past the guards who were patrolling the area.

"I should have sent you home," he said, breaking the deathly quiet of the night. "Back in Berlin, when we first discussed it, I should have insisted. If I had, none of this would have happened to you. You'd be safe."

She didn't answer.

"But if I had, I don't think I would have survived," Anders added. "If I had been alone through all this, I think I would have gone crazy."

Birgit was still facing the river when she spoke. "I had to shoot him. He had suffered all that just to protect us and they were going to make him suffer more. I had to put an end to it."

Anders grabbed her shoulders and turned her face toward his. "You didn't have to do it. I did. I'm the one who should have pulled the trigger. And I can't forgive myself for letting you do it for me."

"But you didn't have to be here," she protested. "I could have stopped you the first day we met. Gunther didn't have to help that girl. Jesus, he didn't even know her. And Haller? I don't even know why he came after us. But still, I killed him."

He shook her shoulders. "You didn't kill him. You didn't kill Gunther. The Nazi bastards did, just the way they kill everything that they touch. And if I don't make it out of here, it will be the Nazis that stop me. Not you. All you've done is try to put an end to their madness. You said once that you didn't want to get involved. But that wasn't true. You did want to get involved. You saw something evil and you tried to stop it."

"But I've killed you," she cried. "I know what you're planning to do."

"You haven't killed me. You haven't killed anyone."

She wasn't listen to him. "You're going to be there when the reactor catches fire. That's the only way you can destroy it, and I'm the one who sent you here to destroy it."

"No," he snapped back at her. "I can stop it. I can run it until it destroys itself and then I can shut it down. It doesn't have to kill anyone."

She pushed him away. "I've heard you. I've listened to you and the others. I understand what you're saying. You had to make them believe you, so you didn't leave yourself any room for escape."

"There is room," he insisted. "I have a few seconds to start the shutdown."

"A few seconds? That's all the chance you're giving yourself—a few seconds?"

"It's enough," Karl argued. "It's the only way. It has to be destroyed."

She stood facing him, her eyes looking angrily into his. Then she nodded slowly. "Yes, it has to be stopped." She turned away from him and walked a few steps toward the bank of the river. "But it didn't have to be you. And I didn't have to help it be you."

He walked up close to her. "You didn't pick me. I did. And don't give up yet. We still have a chance."

"What chance?" she asked. "Even if you escape the reactor, the Nazis will come after you. And who will help you? Haller is dead. I killed him. There's no one you can turn to."

"I'm turning to you." he answered. "In a few days, there will just be the two of us. But that's all we need. I swear to you, Birgit, we're going to make it. We're going to beat them all."

She buried her face into the collar of his coat and he held her tight against the cold.

"I need you," she told him.

"No," he answered. "I need you."

HAIGERLOCH — *M a r c h 3*

"Then we're ready," Kurt Diebner said. "Ready to begin production."

The scientists gathered at the side of the reactor looked to one another. There were no objections. They had completed all the tests and verified all the design parameters. All the subsystems were operating. The first fuel rods hung in their packing cases just inches above the flat, black top of their graphite mountain. The control rods were already inserted. In the control room, each of the dials and gauges had been tested for accuracy. There was nothing more to be done except take the reactor critical and begin the continuous chain reaction that would convert a small portion of the uranium oxide to plutonium.

Diebner smiled broadly. "Tomorrow, gentlemen, will be a great day for science. And a great day for Germany. Tomorrow a new age begins."

Lauderbach began the applause, which quickly died self-consciously. They were all tired and, despite the bravado, secretly apprehensive. Some of them had been present when Heisenberg's primitive reactor had overheated. All of them had watched Bergman's test reactor come within a few degrees of destroying itself. The dark, silent machine before them was a hundred times larger than Bergman's first small pile. They couldn't begin to comprehend the energy it might generate.

They climbed the stairs to the castle church, and filed toward the main door where their cars were waiting. Anders was standing on the steps with Birgit when he heard the great church organ groan, and then drift into the first notes of a song.

"Heisenberg," he smiled. Then he asked Birgit if she would go on ahead with the others. "I need to speak with him. Alone. This may be my best chance."

He turned back into the church, expecting to hear the complexity of Heisenberg's beloved Bach. Instead, the lofty space was filling with a simple melody that seemed to bypass his mind and flow straight to his heart.

It came from the woodwind keys, unadorned by the horns or the bass. A folk song, Anders thought, but there was no sense of spirited celebration. Instead, the notes spoke of a quiet joy, and evoked the peaceful pleasure of a child's smile, or the touch of a familiar hand.

He listened as he climbed the steps to the choir loft, certain that he had heard the piece before but unable to remember where. When he reached the top, Werner Heisenberg sat with one hand on the keys. There was no music spread before him.

He smiled at Anders while he finished the piece, then turned on the bench to face him.

"It's an old German hymn. A prayer, set to music. I used to sing it as a boy, but I forget the words."

"It doesn't need words," Anders said.

"No, it doesn't," Heisenberg agreed. "And this seems like a good time to pray."

"For the success of the reactor?" Karl wondered.

Heisenberg shrugged. "For God's will, I suppose. I don't know what success would be. Maybe we're going where we have no right to be. Then we should pray that God would stop us before we get there. Maybe our greatest blessing would be if the damn thing didn't work."

Anders smiled. "I wouldn't ask Kurt Diebner to join you in prayer."

"No. I don't think we pray to the same God. Mine doesn't wear an armband."

Anders settled into one of the choir pews. "Play it again," he asked. "I think I'd like to pray with you."

Heisenberg turned to the keyboard and extended his hand. But then he let the hand fall into his lap and turned back to face Anders. He sat silently for a moment, his head tipped in curiosity as he stared at his fellow scientist.

"Who are you?" he finally asked.

The question seemed to knock the wind out of Karl's chest. His eyes widened in shock.

"Who are you?" Heisenberg repeated. "I have to know."

"What do you mean? You know who I am."

Heisenberg's head shook slowly. "No. All I know is who you aren't. I know you're not Nils Bergman. I knew that back in Berlin when you first joined us and demanded that we change all the graphite. I read Nils Bergman. I knew how his mind worked. Your equations were interesting. But they didn't come from Nils Bergman's mind.

"Then I saw your test reactor design. I was amazed. Page after page of brilliant work all building inescapably to a reactor that couldn't survive its own heat. This man, I said to myself, is absolutely brilliant. Too bad he's an arsonist instead of a physicist."

Anders found himself smiling.

"It was wonderful," Heisenberg continued. "All my colleagues were congratulating themselves on the genius they had shown in working out their little pieces of the puzzle. None of them saw that, when you put all the pieces together, you had a disaster. I watched you sitting at the end of the table and I was certain that you knew exactly what you were doing. This man has come to destroy us, I told myself. Who in hell is he?"

"But you approved the design," Anders reminded him.

Werner nodded. "By then I had decided that I didn't want Diebner's God to have any more lightning bolts.

"I remember watching the temperature climb when we started the test reactor. I thought we were all finished. I wasn't frightened because, as a German, I was finished long ago when I let the lunatics take over my country. But you knew you were about to die, and yet you stood there with your hand on the controls and turned up the power. Who is this man? I kept asking myself. I decided you were British, and for a moment I wished that I were British too so that at least I would be dying for something.

"And then the damn thing stabilized. I was amazed because all my figures—your figures really—said it wouldn't work. I thought, for an instant, that I had been wrong. Maybe you knew exactly what you were doing. But then I looked at you and you were as surprised as I was. You really wanted that reactor to fail, didn't you?"

Anders nodded.

"I knew it," Heisenberg said, slapping his hand against his knee.

"It should have gone right through the roof," Anders admitted. "But as you had warned me, we were dealing with unknowns. I still don't know why it worked."

They sat for a moment shaking their heads at one another in admission of their foolishness.

"And then came your construction drawings. Truly genius. I knew they had to be faulted, but I couldn't find the errors. I walked around each new page for hours. Where is he taking us? I kept asking myself. When I finally figured it out, I laughed until I had tears in my eyes."

"No one else saw it?" Anders asked.

"Fichter," Heisenberg answered. "He walked in one day with a few pages of equations and said he thought something was wrong. His logic told him that this wasn't an exact scale up of your test pile, but he couldn't explain the differences. He wanted to call a review meeting to check everything all the way back to the beginning."

"What stopped him?"

"I did," Heisenberg roared. "I said, 'Fichter, you ass, if you delay this program for even an hour, I'll get you a rifle and have you sent to the Russian front.' He reworked his calculations and decided that he had made an error."

"Then you put yourself at risk to save me," Anders observed.

"You're the only thing around here worth saving," Heisenberg answered.

"I had it all figured out. The real Nils Bergman is probably still in England, I reasoned. This is probably one of our own physicists who fled Germany. Plastic surgeons have changed his face, and the English have sent him back to haunt us. Then I decided that you were probably a Jew. One of the Jews kicked out in thirty-four. And that was truly funny. I could have wet my pants at the thought of that asshole paperhanger sending a medal to a Jew who had come back to destroy the Reich.

"But then the English tried to kill you. That really baffled me. Why would the English kill their own agent? So I know you can't be English. And I know you're not Nils Bergman. I even know that you're not one of the famous members of our fraternity. If you were, I would have recognized your work in an instant.

"So who are you? And just so I can have some hope that justice eventually triumphs, please tell me that you're a Jew. I could die happy if I knew that our fuehrer had sent a medal to the Jew who had destroyed him."

"An American," Anders answered. He told Heisenberg about the coincidence of his resemblance to Bergman, and the months of study that had made him Bergman's alter ego. Heisenberg's smile grew broader as he absorbed the details.

"And Bergman? He was pulling the strings? Telling you what to say?"

The smile vanished when he learned that Bergman had died.

"I always looked forward to his papers and articles," he said. "His work was . . . elegant. Beautifully precise. But if he was dead, then this work I have been seeing? It was all yours?"

"My efforts to sound like Nils Bergman," Anders said.

Heisenberg nodded his congratulations. Then he reached into

his jacket pocket and took out a long, thin envelope. He tapped it against his hand as he spoke.

"I thought you would probably be leaving abruptly. When you're great achievement goes mad tomorrow, our colleagues will tear into your work like sharks. You'll want to be gone before they understand what you've done. You'll need these."

He passed the envelope to Anders.

"There is a set of orders, to me from Himmler, entitling me to travel to Celle. Also, my German passport. You will have to replace the picture."

He reached into his pocket and took out two keys on a small chain. "I have an automobile for my private use. It's the one next to the inn with the government identification plates. I'm supposed to be going back and forth between here and Celle but, unfortunately, the Thousand-Year Reich seems to have run out of petrol." He handed Anders the keys. "Perhaps you will find a way to use it."

Anders balanced the envelope in one hand and the keys in the other. "What about you?" he asked. "When Himmler learns what has happened, things could get difficult, even for you."

"I'll say you must have stolen them. I'll be outraged. Besides, I have my bicycle. I may just climb on it one morning and pedal my way home. My house is in Bavaria. Believe me. Our reichsfuehrer is going to have bigger problems in the months ahead."

Anders slipped the envelope into his jacket and put the keys in his pocket. "The English are trying to kill me, and a German is trying to save me. I don't think I understand the world anymore."

"Nothing is certain," Heisenberg answered. "Not even your reactor. You know, your changes are very subtle. Have you thought that when we start it up tomorrow, the damn thing may run perfectly. You may not have to flee. You may be a national hero."

"It will run, but only for a few minutes," Anders answered. "And I won't be a national hero." He tapped the envelope. "I'll need these."

"Then it will overheat. You're going to melt it down."

"I'm going to try," Karl said. "Just enough to put it beyond repair."

Heisenberg's eyes narrowed. He remembered a conversation they had shared once before. "You may not be able to stop it. You realize the risk, of course. It's possible that nothing will be able to stop it."

Anders nodded. "That's what I came to tell you. I want you to find a reason not to be there tomorrow. I was going to lie and tell you that, in case anything went wrong, it was important that one of us be able to carry on the great work. But you know what I'm going to try. I don't want to be putting you in danger."

"Thank you," Heisenberg answered. "But I wouldn't miss it for the world. Maybe we can help each other to survive. That's what you're all about, isn't it? Trying to help the world survive."

He turned back to the keyboard and began the simple melody of the hymn. "I wish I could remember the words," he said to Anders. "I think we may need to pray."

Anders sat silently and listened until the last notes of the piece settled quietly on the empty castle church.

"It doesn't need any words," he said.

SPRING

1 9 4 5

The Americans crossed the Rhine at Remagan, marching boldly over a bridge that the Germans had been unable to destroy. Now they were marshalling their tanks for a crushing assault through the heart of the Reich. The Russians were at the gates of Berlin, massing their cannons wheel to wheel in an arc that swung from north of the German capital all the way around to the south. The end of the Reich was at hand. Within Germany, madness had replaced any pretense of order. Citizens became refugees as they fled the advancing Allied armies. German soldiers deserted the battlefields. And the Nazis turned on their own people, determined to punish them for the defeat they had suffered.

HAIGERLOCH — *March 8*

They kissed quickly at the door of the inn, but as Anders tried to turn toward the waiting car he felt her grip tighten on his arms. Her eyes repeated what she had whispered the night before as they embraced in their bed. She wanted to go with him. She couldn't survive the day alone, wondering if he was going to return.

He drew her back into his embrace and kissed her again softly, fighting back the thought that it might be the last moment he would ever spend with her. Then he broke out of her embrace and darted down the steps.

It was the only way, he reminded himself as the car followed its armed escorts toward the river road. She had to stay behind. If the reaction within the graphite pile slipped out of his hands for even a few seconds, it could turn the cave into a hellish inferno. He couldn't let her become one of its vanished victims. Or, if things went as he hoped, and the reactor itself was the only victim, then they would have to begin their escape immediately. Birgit needed every second that was left to plan their escape.

She had to make certain that the German officer fueled Heisenberg's car. Anders had waved the orders to Celle under his nose the night before, explaining that he had to be ready to leave on a moment's notice. The officer's eyes had widened when they reached Himmler's signature, and he had added the suggestion that the battery should probably be replaced.

They needed road maps. Anders knew that the owner kept several maps of the area in his office. Birgit would have to find them. They needed warm clothes. She would have to select a few essentials and move them secretly to the car. And they would need food and water for their journey. Birgit had the run of the kitchen.

They had to play separate roles if their fragile hopes of escape were to have any chance. Yet neither of them could accept the thought of being apart. She would have no way of knowing what dangers he was facing at the castle church. Dangers from the reactor he was determined to destroy even at the cost of his life. Dangers from the Nazis, who might punish the failure of their super weapon dreams the instant that their failure became obvious. And he would have no way of knowing what was happening at the inn. If the officer checked up on the orders he had been shown, then their escape plan would be immediately compromised. Or if her interest in maps was noticed, she could be arrested on the spot. He couldn't let himself think about the interrogation that would follow.

They were both at risk, and the dangers would grow throughout the day with every tick of the clock. Both Birgit and Karl could endure the threats directed toward themselves. But neither could hold down the terror they felt for the other. "I have to be with you," she had whispered. But they both knew their only hope of escape was in acting separately, no matter how frightening it was for each of them.

Anders could hear the dull drone of the diesel engines when he entered the castle church, and the sound grew louder as he turned down the iron steps that led to the vaults below. The preliminaries had already begun. Cooling water was being pumped up from the river and through the pipes that latticed the graphite mountain. The cadmium control rods had already been lowered into the pile. When he reached the reactor, the technicians were in the process of lowering the uranium fuel rods to the top of the graphite.

Kurt Diebner immediately rushed toward him, escorting the small party of dignitaries that would witness the event. Colonel Hartmann, the stone-faced SS officer who had been his first interrogator, was accompanied by a young captain. They responded to the introduction in unison with heel-clicking salutes to the fuehrer. Anders remembered Heisenberg's rude dismissal of Hartmann's credentials as a scientist. He would certainly be no threat to Anders' plan of running the reactor to its destruction. He wouldn't even understand what he was seeing. But his role could become deadly once he realized that the Reich's last hope had been destroyed. There was a civilian in a dark trench coat, who brought greetings from Goebbels and the entire Ministry of Information. He explained that he would write the official record of the day's events so that it could assume its proper place of importance in the chronicles of the Reich. Behind him was a short man, adorned with leather film cases and carrying a press camera.

"Almost ready," Heisenberg said in greeting, as Anders entered the control room. "Everything has been checked. The fuel is nearly loaded." Anders looked down at the bank of motionless dials that reported the lifelessness of the graphite. In a few moments, they would begin to climb, at first slowly and then with incredible momentum until they roared past the danger lines. His only hope, at that point, was to shut the reactor down. Quickly enough to prevent its melting into an unquenchable mass of fire. But slowly enough so that the captured heat would warp its shape and fracture its foundations.

The fuel rods were partially inserted. Once the reaction began, he would press on its accelerator by lowering the fuel still further into the pile, and then raising the control rods. At some point, according to his figures and diagrams, a stable balance would be achieved. But that point, if his secret theories were correct, would be well above the heat limitations of the structure.

"Let's begin," he said softly. The scientists pushed up to the console. Just outside the door of the control room, Diebner and his guests turned to face the black wall of the reactor.

The neutron source fired, its activity scarcely perceptible on the gauges. There was no response from the uranium fuel, so the rods were lowered further into the pile. One of the needles flickered.

A nod was the only order that Anders needed to give. The process had been well rehearsed, so one of the scientists touched the control that lowered the fuel still further. The control console began showing signs of life. As the needles quivered, Anders held up his hand. Another scientist activated the motors that began to withdraw the control rods.

The gauges responded immediately, showing the neutron count within the pile as it increased. Anders watched the needle until it swept past the highest output of the neutron source. The fuel was beginning to fission. Neutrons were breaking free from uranium atoms and firing off into the vastness of their graphite universe. Some—an imperceptibly small number—were colliding with other uranium atoms and shattering their structures. More neutrons were then breaking free. He switched off the starter. The gauges never noticed the loss.

"It's on its own," he said. But the announcement that had brought excitement in the Berlin bunker now brought no response. The scientists had seen the test reactor achieve a self-sustaining reaction. They had never doubted that they would get this far. Their concern now was controlling the reaction on such a vast scale.

The counters began to drop. At Anders' gesture, the fuel was lowered still further while the control rods were raised. The neutron count leveled.

"We'll hold here for just a moment," he said, and the hands pulled back from the controls. The pile was stabilized in a low-level reaction, almost like a car engine running at idle. The only sound was the distant roar of the diesels, and the vibration of the pipes that delivered the cooling water.

"Temperature is steady," Heisenberg reported, staring at the gauge that measured the heat of the water. "We could stay right here forever."

They could, and if they were still working in a laboratory, that's what they would choose to do. They were demonstrating the transformation of heavy metals, a theory that many had doubted could ever be proven. If, after a few days, they examined the fuel, they would find traces of the new material, plutonium. They were succeeding in the transformation of matter.

But this was not an experiment. They needed more than traces of plutonium. Their goal was to produce the wildly unstable material in quantity. At their present operating rate, that would take a year. Anders nodded. Hands reached for the controls, and the fuel rods began to drop further into the pile. The needles responded immediately, climbing to higher readings.

"Temperature is moving," Heisenberg chanted. There was no need to say in which direction. Faces turned toward Anders, but he made no response. Under the chatter of the overhead motors, the fuel rods continued to descend and the cadmium control rods continued to rise. The movement of the needles began to accelerate.

"Let's check it," Lauderbach advised. Anders nodded his agreement. The motors stopped.

They watched the indicators, hoping that they would immediately settle. But all the gauges continued to climb. The reaction was taking control of its own destiny.

Anders ordered the control rods lowered, and once again the reaction came to rest. But now the process was running at a higher speed. They had reached perhaps ten percent of the reactor's capacity, nowhere near the level at which they hoped to operate. But still, there were smiles of satisfaction. They had shown that they could control the reaction, at least at its lowest levels.

Birgit watched the officer slide behind the wheel of the car.

"Give it plenty of choke," he advised, pointing to one of the knobs on the dashboard. He touched the starter button and the engine groaned as it turned slowly.

"The oil is frozen. This will take a few tries." He hit the starter button again and again, but all he could produce were the same labored groans.

"Will it run?" Birgit asked. The German threw up his hands. "It should. If not, I'll have one of my men look at it."

He had delivered the petrol directly from the tank of one of his trucks, backing the truck alongside and siphoning the fuel into the automobile. They had tried to start the car, but the battery was dead, and so he had returned with a fresh one. "I hope it's not the electrical system," he explained. "I don't have any parts."

He hit the starter again. This time the engine coughed, belching out a blast of white smoke. But the sound died immediately.

"When will Professor Bergman have to use this?"

"I'm not sure," she lied. "Whenever he's called to Celle."

The officer shook his head. "It could take days for us to get parts." He tried the starter again, but the engine wouldn't catch.

"I'll send over a mechanic," he offered as he climbed out and closed the door behind him.

Birgit smiled her thanks. Then she went back into the inn and slipped into the kitchen where she began to slice cold cuts and cheese onto thick slabs of dark bread.

Anders watched as the control rods rose slowly. Once again, he was pressing gently on the accelerator, increasing the rate of the reaction. The gauges responded.

"Textbook," Lauderbach said to Diebner, who was pressing into the doorway of the control room, his dignitaries peering over his shoulder. "Everything is exactly according to plan."

At Anders' signal, the fuel rods were lowered still further, sending the needles on the gauges to their right.

"One eighty," Heisenberg reported from the temperature gauge. Anders ordered the fuel rods stopped.

"We'll hold here," he told the scientists. No one dissented. They were reaching close to an overheat situation, with the reactor still running at less than half its theoretical capacity.

He lowered the control rods. The neutron counters began to settle. The heat held steady. Again, they could maintain the reaction, but the plutonium production would be too small to be useful. They needed to push their machine to a higher speed. Right up to the boiling point of the cooling water.

The housekeeper walked into the kitchen just as Birgit was wrapping the sandwiches in a white towel. Birgit looked up and smiled, and continued calmly with her work. "I was going to ask you to prepare these," she said. "But I know how busy you are."

"Why do you need sandwiches?" the woman asked.

Birgit explained that Professor Bergman might have to leave for Celle as soon as he returned to the inn. The woman seemed satisfied with the explanation and pleased that someone had noticed how busy she was. "If I can help you . . ." she offered.

"Perhaps you can," Birgit suddenly realized. "I believe there are road maps in the office. Do you happen to know where they are?"

"Of course. Do you think they could find anything around here without me?"

She dashed off to the office, anxious to demonstrate her value.

Through the window, Birgit saw an army patrol car pull up next to Heisenberg's car. Two soldiers climbed out, and one of them lifted the hood of the sedan. She squeezed her eyes shut in a momentary prayer.

"Let's move ahead," Anders decided. He began raising the control rods while lowering more fuel into the reaction. If the faults he had designed into the machine were accurate, the heat would soar rapidly. The reactor would begin to self-destruct before they were able to shut it down. If he were wrong, then the system would begin to stabilize at a higher operating level, with the water temperature just below boiling. In that event, he would trigger its total destruction. He would take the controls and drive the fuel all the way into the core while simultaneously pulling the control rods. There would be a moment of confusion while the scientists tried to comprehend what he was doing. Then there would be screams of protest.

They might rush forward to tear him away from the throttles. Or in the moment of hesitation, they might see the needles jump off their scales and realize that the rush of power within the graphite had become irreversible. Then, instead of attacking him, they would run for their lives. He couldn't know how they would react. But he was sure that once he seized the controls, his life would be over. Probably from the fireball that would sear through the graphite. But probably even more quickly from the bullet that Hartmann would fire into the back of his head.

"One ninety," Heisenberg told him.

The dials were pushing toward the right, indicating that the reaction was racing ahead. More and more atoms of uranium were splitting, increasing the number of neutron bullets that were seeking still more targets. The pace of the reaction had reached two thirds of its theoretical limit.

"I'll settle for seventy-five percent of capacity," Anders said. The scientists, becoming alarmed at the water temperature, instantly agreed.

"We may not get there," Lauderbach shouted. "The water temperature is at two hundred." He looked from Anders to Heisenberg. "Cut it back," he screamed at Werner.

Diebner pushed up to the controls with Hartmann right at his side. "Begin shutdown," he told Anders.

"Not yet. It should stabilize," Anders lied. Diebner's head snapped toward Heisenberg. Werner's expression was confident. Almost serene.

They were right on the edge. To save the machine, Anders knew he should begin shutdown immediately. To destroy it, all he had to do was let the reaction carry itself to a higher level. He only had to wait a few seconds. But if he waited too long, there would be no way of stopping it. They would all become victims of its furious heat.

Birgit heard the motor cough, and then the car seemed to disappear in a cloud of white smoke. She rushed out through the kitchen door. The engine sound was uneven, but at least the motor seemed to be running.

"It will be fine," the soldier told her. "In this weather, you have to run the engine for a few minutes everyday."

The rasping sound turned into a smooth, throaty hum.

"Let it run awhile," the soldier said, slamming the hood closed. She promised that she would and thanked them for their trouble.

The two men started back to their car, but one stopped and turned back toward her. "When are you leaving?" he asked.

"Perhaps tonight."

He nodded his approval. Then, in a low voice he told her, "Stay off the roads during the day. The American planes are everywhere, and they shoot at anything that moves."

"Shut it down!" Lauderbach shouted.

Anders hands reached for the controls. The temperature gauge was at the boiling point. If he pulled back, there was still a chance that the reactor would respond and begin to slow down. If he pushed forward, he was dead. His hands hesitated above the switches. Another few seconds. That was all that he needed.

The engine was running at a quiet hum as Birgit packed the sandwiches under the seat. She slipped the road map that the housekeeper had brought her into the pocket on the inside of the door. Then she turned the engine off.

She waited a few moments. There would be no soldiers to start the car for them when they left in the middle of the night. She had to know that the battery was charged and that the electrical system was working. Birgit mumbled a silent prayer. Then she touched the starter. The engine rattled and coughed a few times. Then it sprang into life. She shook her head thankfully.

The neutron counters tipped to the right. The temperature needle jumped all the way to its stop. Anders' hands hit the switches to begin shutdown.

"It's out of control!" he shouted. "Everyone out of here!" But Diebner had seen the sudden turn of the gauges. When Anders looked up, he was already in full flight with Hartmann and the SS captain battling him for the doorway. The scientists were right at his heels.

"I'm staying with you," Heisenberg said. There was no trace of fear in his voice.

"There's nothing you can do," Anders snapped back. "Get out."

"There's nothing more you can do, either," Heisenberg answered. "It's finished. It's destroyed."

"I have to be sure."

They stood together, watching the glowing fuel rods climb out of the graphite into the lead-shielded cases that Heisenberg had designed. With the heat of the rods, the lead would quickly soften and begin to melt. They heard the sound of steam breaking loose inside the graphite pile. Pressure valves popped open along the pipelines that traveled back to the river. Jets of steam rushed into the cave with a deafening roar.

Heisenberg grabbed his shoulder. "It's done for. Let's go."

They spun away from the searing heat and rushed through the door of the control room. But suddenly there were flashes of blue light, and a shower of sparks blocked their escape. The heat from the rods had set fire to the power lines that fed the overhead motors. The electrical circuits were shorting. Behind them, they could hear the explosions as the steam pressure broke through the seals in the graphite. Ahead, the metal steps to the safety of the church were disappearing in the jets of steam from the piping.

And then the lights went out.

Birgit sorted silently through their closet, selecting warm sweaters, gloves, and their knit winter hats. She rolled them together and pushed them under her coat as she started back toward the car. They would leave the rest of their things behind. When people came looking for them, they wanted a full closet and their suitcases to be found as indications that they would soon return. She pushed the clothes under the passenger seat, next to the sandwiches.

Now all she could do was wait. And hope. Hope that the Germans weren't checking the orders that Karl had shown them the night before. Hope that the housekeeper didn't boast to the owner that she was the only one who could have found the maps. Hope that Karl was still alive in the cave beneath the castle church.

They held hands so that they wouldn't become separated in the darkness as they dodged the jets of scalding steam that were cutting through the plumbing. "This way," Heisenberg shouted, more familiar with the turns that led to the steps. "Just a few more feet." He was reaching out, groping for the iron railing when he suddenly began to gasp for air. The cave was filling with fumes from the smoldering electrical insulation. Time was running out on them.

"Shut the door," Hartmann ordered to the scientists who were reassembled in the aisle of the church. He could see the trace of acrid smoke that was beginning to seep up from the cave. "Seal it off."

"But they're still down there," Fichter protested. "We have to help them."

"Close it," Hartmann screamed. The captain jumped forward and slammed the metal door.

"Over there," Anders said. He began pulling Heisenberg toward the sound of the slamming door he had heard above their heads.

"I can't make it," Werner answered weakly. Anders plunged forward in the darkness and slammed against the steps. He swung Heisenberg in front of himself and began pushing him up the stairs.

The smoke thickened as they climbed higher, and Anders began to feel the weight of his own limbs. He was nearly carrying Heisenberg, who was now racked with coughing.

"Keep going. Just a few more steps."

Heisenberg sprang forward with the last burst of energy he could gather. His head struck against the door at the top of the stairs.

"It's them," Fichter yelled. He broke away from the scientists and rushed back to the door.

"Don't open it," Hartmann said, but Fichter ignored the order. He pulled the door open and jumped back from the cloud of smoke that exploded into the church. Werner Heisenberg staggered forward and fell into his arms. Then Anders appeared, sucking eagerly at the fresh air that suddenly surrounded him.

They closed the door behind them, and then helped Heisenberg down the aisle and out into the open air. In a few moments he was breathing easily.

In the cave below them, the smoldering insulation quickly burned itself out. The diesels shut themselves down when their controls sensed the loss of water pressure due to the ruptured plumbing. The engineers were able to restart the ventilators, and begin pulling the smoke out of the cave.

"What went wrong?" Diebner questioned, while they waited for the air to clear so that they could go back into the reactor vault.

"It wouldn't stabilize at high power," Anders said, explaining the obvious. "We'll have to recheck the calculations." Then he shook his head slowly. "We must have missed something. Something in the equations. Werner and I were able to shut it down. But it's badly damaged."

Colonel Hartmann pushed past Diebner. "Can it be fixed?" he demanded, already formulating his report to Himmler.

"Of course," Heisenberg lied. "Perhaps a few days. Maybe a week. We'll have to wait until it cools down, and then we'll inspect it. But it works. That's the important point. You can tell the reichsfuehrer that his reactor is a success."

But the scene that they found when they went back into the cave put an end to all pretense. The control rods were fused into their ports. The graphite would have to be shattered with jackhammers in order to pull them free. The lead casings had melted against the fuel rods, and dripped lead into the fuel ports. The new rods of uranium oxide that were waiting to be processed wouldn't fit into their ports. And down in the well, at the base of the pile, dark water was oozing out through the seams. A murky pool was rising against the side of the reactor like an incoming tide.

The photographer's camera flashed as he made the official recording of the reactor. Hartmann immediately demanded the film holder, which he slipped into his pocket. Then he took the camera and smashed it against the stone wall.

"The reichsfuehrer will want your report in the morning," he told Diebner. "And your estimate as to exactly when the reactor will go back into operation."

"Of course," Diebner promised. But the scientists could only look vacantly at one another. The estimate should be obvious to anyone but a fool. This reactor would never go back into operation. It would have to be completely rebuilt. And that work couldn't even begin until they had reviewed every calculation, every page of drawings, and discovered why its heat had climbed so drastically. The officer was talking in terms of hours. But the scientists knew that the answer would have to be stated in terms of months.

When they were alone in the car, returning to the inn, Heisenberg nodded his congratulations to Anders. Anders accepted the compliment with a weary smile.

"I don't imagine that you will want to wait until morning to hear Diebner's official report," Heisenberg whispered.

"I hate to miss it," Anders said.

"Don't worry," Werner smiled. "I'll take notes. I'll tell you about it, the next time we are able to get together."

WÜRTTEMBERG — *March 9*

They left at night, slipping noiselessly through the dark halls of the inn, each carrying just one small valise. Most of their things, and the rest of their luggage remained in their room, disguising the fact that they would never return. They waited until the Germans were changing the guard so that the sound of the truck motor would hide the noise of their engine. Anders drove across the square that they had often walked and pulled to a stop where one of the guards was blocking a street. The soldier took the orders to his officer, and when the two returned, the officer simply saluted without questioning the documents. The raven insignia on the letterhead and Himmler's signature at the bottom carried their own authority.

They drove slowly through the street, its windows darkened, and turned onto the same road that had brought them from the airfield months before. It was only when Haigerloch had disappeared behind them and Anders had brought the car up to speed that either of them dared to breathe.

"We made it," Birgit said, folding the orders into their envelope. "Where are the armies that were supposed to be protecting us?"

"On the Rhine," Anders speculated. German broadcasts were still talking about the heroic defense of the fatherland. But they had listened to British news broadcasts that reported an Allied crossing. It made sense that, if the Americans were across the river, the Nazis would be throwing the few tattered armies they had left into a counterattack.

They were driving northward along a two-lane road that had

been occasionally plowed. There were white banks to either side, and patches of blacktop showing through the hard-packed road surface. The small sedan held traction, and Anders was able to ease up to a decent cruising speed, outrunning the dull glow of the masked headlamps. He wanted to make all the distance they could before they turned eastward onto the narrow roads of the Swabian mountains.

Headlamps approached in the distance, and he backed off the accelerator, expecting the car to turn and block his path. But the open military truck, with armed soldiers on the back benches, ignored them, flashing past and quickly disappearing in the darkness.

"They're not looking for us yet," Anders allowed.

"Why should they be?" Birgit answered. "They won't know we're gone until morning. The officer who checked your orders didn't suspect anything."

The road turned, and suddenly there was a red lamp flashing ahead. They could make out the shape of a parked truck with figures moving around it. Anders braked the car to a gentle stop.

He rolled down the window as an officer approached the car, and held out the orders that Birgit had passed to him. The officer used a flashlight to study the document.

"You are Herr Doctor Heisenberg?"

"Yes," Anders replied, and handed over the passport that Heisenberg had given him. His own photograph replaced the original. The flashlight darted from the photo to Anders' face, and then flooded inside the car to illuminate Birgit. She handed over her passport.

The officer made detailed notes on his clipboard, and then passed the papers back into the car.

While the truck was backing out of their way, Birgit noticed that they were at an intersection with the road that led into the mountains.

"Do we want them to see where we are turning?" she asked.

"We have no choice," Karl said. "We have to turn here."

He pulled past the truck and swung onto a narrow road that was marked only by the trees that grew up to its edge. He accelerated cautiously, steering into the ruts that had been pressed into the smooth, icy surface of the snow.

"This is hardly a road," Birgit commented. They could feel the rear wheels slipping and the back end of the car swaying gently from side to side.

Anders remembered the Wisconsin winters when the roads were forgotten and people laid up their cars in their barns.

"It's going to get worse. Probably the only cars that use these roads are the army patrols. They can't be in good shape."

Birgit leaned over the back of the seat and retrieved a jar of black coffee that was wrapped in a towel. "We should drink this before it gets cold," she said. She poured the coffee, still steaming, into a metal measuring cup that she had taken from the kitchen, and passed it to Anders whenever he was able to take one hand off the steering wheel.

The road began to climb, narrowing further as it stretched up into the slope of the mountains. Anders pressed gently on the gas pedal, increasing the speed as far as he dared. They were moving briskly, the speedometer needle settling close to 65 kilometers. He began calculating how far they would travel if he could only maintain his present pace.

In about fifteen minutes he would intersect with a road that ran to the southwest, doubling back past Hechingen. Once he made the turn, it would take about two hours to reach the Danube at Tuttlingen. That would be their greatest point of danger. They had to cross one of the Tuttlingen bridges before the Nazis began looking for them.

The Danube formed a hard barrier against Germans escaping to the south, and there would undoubtedly be checkpoints at every bridge. They wouldn't be able to use Heisenberg's orders to Celle because they would be crossing in the wrong direction. They would have to count on their Swedish passports to get them across. But that would mean announcing that he was Nils Bergman. And if the Nazis had been alerted to their escape, it would certainly mean their capture.

Once they crossed the Danube, they had about thirty miles more to the Swiss border at Schaffhausen. Again, there would be

Nazi officials along with the border guards. But here they would need visas and entry papers along with their passports. They had decided not to attempt to cross legally. Instead, they would drive into the country outside Schaffhausen, abandon the car, and attempt their crossing on foot. Once inside Switzerland, their passports would give them full legal protection. At worst, they would be detained until they could be shipped back to Sweden.

They reached the intersection with the road to the south, and they were relieved to find it unguarded. But hardly had they made their turn when a new obstacle appeared. A light dusting of snow began to fall onto the windshield. Within minutes, they were pushing slowly into a blinding snowstorm.

The ruts in the road that had served as their guidelines began to disappear in the heavy white powder. They were driving in the darkness without being able to see the turns that they were navigating. And the frail wipers that hung down from the roof weren't up to their task. As they packed snow to either side, the opening that they were clearing on the windshield became smaller and smaller.

Anders hunched forward over the steering wheel, blinking into the dull glow of the fading headlights. His speed was down to a few miles an hour, the car groaning in its lowest gear. And even that speed was terrifying with the road ahead hidden. As he eased into the turns that were marked only by the indentations of the drainage ditch at the roadside, he was aware of the steep drop to his right. The road was built into the slope of a mountain, with a hill to one side and the land falling away to the other. Should he miss the turn, he would slide well down the slope, probably until the car tangled in the underbrush or struck a tree. There would be no hope of getting it back up to the road.

"We should pull off," he mumbled to Birgit. "We could run the engine for a few minutes at a time to give us a little heat."

"Keep going," she answered. "We may drive through this."

They had to keep going. Every minute they lost made it less likely that they would reach the Danube on time. And even when the snow stopped, the road would still be impossible. Plowing the back roads had become the last concern of the Thousand-Year Reich.

The wipers stopped, jammed against the snow that they had pushed aside. Anders let the car roll to a stop, then jumped outside to clear the windows. When he got back in and put the car into gear, he heard the back tires whistling as they spun freely on the ice. He tried rocking the car to find traction, but the wheels only dug themselves deeper into the mounting snow.

He climbed out, letting Birgit slide across the gearshift and into the driver's seat. She tried to ease the car ahead gently while he pushed from the outside. But his feet slipped out from under him and, for a moment, he thought the car was going to roll back on top of him.

He found branches, and packed them in under the back wheels. Then he ran around the car, cleared the snow from the headlights, and once again freed the wipers. While he pushed, Birgit nursed the gas pedal. The car broke free. Anders ran next to it until he could jump into the passenger seat. Then he crouched over the inadequate heater, trying to warm his frozen hands and feet.

Birgit was a more daring driver than he, and she pushed the car to a higher speed. They were rolling at about 30 kilometers, only half the speed they needed to stay on schedule, but still more than the road wanted to allow. The car swayed abruptly as the wheels found ruts and potholes that were buried under the blanket. As they carved into turns, the rear wheels slid toward the edge of the road, then seemed to catch traction at the very last second.

"I think you should slow it down," Anders advised at one point when a back tire had spun madly before catching and pushing them forward. Birgit seemed to bite down harder on her lip and lean closer to the wheel. Instead of answering, she added more weight to the accelerator.

He knew what she was thinking. And he knew she was right. Reaching Tuttlingen before the alarm was sounded was their only hope of escape. To slow down was to surrender, and Birgit was determined to keep fighting as long as there was any chance left.

But they weren't driving out of the storm. If anything, the snow was falling more heavily. The headlights were dimming, and once again the space cleared by the wipers was narrowing.

"I can't see," she finally announced, long after Anders had real-

ized that he had no visibility beyond the car's circular hood orna-
ment. She waited until they had labored to the top of a long
incline and then she braked to a sliding stop.

Anders rushed out and cleared the lights and the windshield. It
seemed a useless gesture. The snow began to build the instant he
had wiped it away. But this time the car started easily, rolling
down the hill until its tires were able to gather traction. Once
again Birgit pushed the speed, correcting each skid with unerring
pressure on the steering wheel.

"How much farther?" Birgit asked, her eyes fixed ahead. Anders
opened the map even though he knew it wouldn't help. They
hadn't seen a single road marker. He could only guess at the speed
they were making and how much time they had lost at each of
their stops.

"Maybe forty kilometers. Fifty at most. No more than two hours
if we can keep going," he concluded.

The road seemed to be straightening, indicating that they were
breaking out of the foothills and into more level country. Birgit
was tempted to push the speed still higher, but now the buildup of
snow was a more serious problem than the turns in the road. The
wheels were plowing their own path, and the engine was clearly
laboring under the strain.

Anders broke open one of the sandwiches she had prepared, but
Birgit shook her head at the suggestion. He tried to eat, but found
he couldn't swallow.

"We'll have to stop again," she announced. "The damn snow is
burying us." This time it was Anders who took over the driving,
and he was surprised to see how greedily Birgit devoured a sand-
wich and a cup of cold coffee as soon as she was free from the
responsibility of controlling the car.

She had the cup raised to her lips when the rear tires broke free.
The car had plowed into a drift that left the back wheels spinning
too fast. The rear end slid by them, caught momentarily in the
drainage ditch, and then dropped off the road. The coffee splashed
wildly as the sedan spun and plunged backward down the slope.
Anders spun the wheel furiously, trying to straighten the car while
it still had momentum. There was a moment of hope when he was

able to point the car back toward the road. But then the rear end broke free again, and they slid further down the hill. The car crashed into a row of bushes and came to rest on a steep angle, its nose pointing back up toward the road.

Anders climbed out and took a quick tour around the sedan. One of its back wheels was completely buried. The other hung in midair. The snow was up to the running boards on both sides of the chassis.

He shook his head when he climbed in beside Birgit. "Impossible," he told her, describing what he had found. "We'll never get traction. All the power will go to the wheel that's off the ground."

"They'll open the road in the morning," she said. "Or at least an army truck will come by on patrol."

"We should try for the nearest town," he argued, unfolding the map. But he had no idea where the nearest town was. He didn't know where they had crashed off the road.

They ran the engine for a few minutes at a time throughout the night, raising enough heat to keep them from freezing. Birgit was able to lean against him, wrapped in her coat, and fall asleep. He promised to wake her in an hour so that she could watch while he slept. But when the hour was up, he let it pass. She was sleeping peacefully, as beautiful as she had been when they first slept together under the lenses of Himmler's cameras. And he knew that he wouldn't be able to even close his eyes.

He saw the snow stop and the stars appear overhead. And then he watched the pale blue morning silhouette the tops of the hills that they had driven through. In his mind he weighed the few alternatives that they had and fixed his plan.

He had to get to the nearest town as soon as the sun came up, even if they had to guess at a direction and begin walking. They would try to find help to pull the car back up onto the road. But time was their most dangerous enemy. If they couldn't find help quickly, then they would have to take a ride on anything that was moving. A bus, a truck, or even an army vehicle. They had to keep moving in order to cross the Danube before the Nazis came looking for them.

He heard the sound of an engine in the distance and woke Birgit immediately. Then he climbed out of the car and pulled himself through the snow until he reached the road. He waved frantically at the army truck that was moving slowly toward him.

There were two soldiers in the cab, and two more huddled with their rifles on the benches in the back. They rolled to a stop and jumped down, seemingly pleased at the diversion from their dreary patrol. One of the soldiers ran down to the car, poked around it, and returned, shaking his head.

"We can pull it out," he told the sergeant who seemed to be in charge, "but it won't run. The springs on the back wheels are broken. They have to be fixed."

Birgit had followed the soldier up the hill and heard Anders ask, "Can you get us to the nearest town? We have to get a car or a bus. We're on a very tight schedule."

"Do you have orders?" the sergeant asked. "All transportation has been taken over by the army. You can't travel without orders."

Birgit took the envelope out of her pocket. "We have to get to Celle," she explained, as she handed the papers to the sergeant. He examined the document carefully, his eyes narrowing.

"These are SS orders," he noted. He looked from Birgit to Anders. "You must be very important."

"It's an urgent mission," Karl tried.

"But you'll never find transportation," the sergeant said. "If you have to get to Celle, we'll have to take you as far as we can."

The men agreed.

"That's not necessary," Anders protested. "If you can just help us get to a town where we can find help."

"The SS have roadblocks on the road to Stuttgart. We'll take you in that direction until we find one of their control points. Then they'll be able to get you to Celle. Believe me, it's the surest way. The SS can get anything done. If they need a train, they'll steal one." He laughed at the thought and the soldiers joined in his amusement.

Anders and Birgit watched helplessly as the sergeant ordered one of his men to retrieve their belongings from the useless car. Then he squeezed Anders and Birgit into the cab beside him, leaving three of his soldiers to ride on the benches outside.

"You're lucky we came along," he explained as he shifted the truck into gear. "We almost called off the patrol because of the roads. You could have been left out here all day."

"If we could just get to a town," Anders nearly begged.

"Nonsense," the sergeant roared generously. "It won't take us long to deliver you to the SS. They're everywhere. And with orders signed by Himmler himself, who knows? I might even get a medal."

They roared off over the roads that Birgit had driven so dangerously the night before, heading back in the direction that they had been trying to escape. With each minute, the Danube fell further behind. And they drew closer to Himmler's elite troops, who were probably waiting with orders for their execution.

Birgit reached over and squeezed Anders' hand. They had done all that they could. And, at least, they were facing the end together.

They had driven for over an hour, slowly at first while they plowed through the snow in the mountains and then at decent speed when they connected with the highway north of Hechingen. All the while they sat in silence, scarcely listening to the sergeant's monologue, which counted the details of Germany's collapse.

"You could have been there for days," he repeated as a constant theme. "We have only two trucks that we can use, so we can't patrol even half of the roads in our area. And then only when we can get our allocation of petrol.

"There are no parts. We have to pirate some of our trucks to get the parts we need to keep the others running. Even simple things. Would you believe that one of the trucks had to be taken out of commission for a fan belt? Of course nothing could get it running now. We took its radiator for this truck, and two of the tires for the other one. It's the same way all over Germany. Once something breaks, it gets torn to pieces for spare parts. I swear, if I sprained my ankle, someone would take my rifle and strip off my clothes."

He laughed raucously at the thought. "And they won't admit that everything is gone. I call for a fan belt and they tell me to fill out a requisition. Everything gets processed with carbon copies to my commanding officer, to the supply depot, and even to the factory. God knows why! The factory was bombed last year and the depot a few months ago. But still, everyone stamps the copy and files it carefully. The only thing we haven't run out of is requisition forms. We have enough of those for the whole thousand years."

Again, the laughter, this time punctuated with a despairing wag of his head.

Anders felt Birgit's grip tighten on his hand. He glanced up and saw the roadblock ahead.

"I knew we'd find them," the sergeant said smugly. "You can't drive anywhere without being stopped by the SS." He pushed the truck into a lower gear and rolled to a stop in front of the striped barricade that had been lowered across the road. The soldier who approached with a machine gun hanging at his hip wore the dreaded black uniform. The sergeant raised his hand casually. "Heil Hitler!" The guard returned a stiff-armed salute.

"Civilians travelling under SS orders," the sergeant said, nodding toward his passengers. "Their car went off the road in the snow. They have to get to Celle immediately."

The guard held out his hand. Anders passed the orders and their passports to the sergeant who handed them down. The guard examined them briefly, then walked toward a small farmhouse that stood near the barricade.

Anders and Birgit exchanged anxious glances. It had been ten hours since they had escaped through the back door of the inn. By now, they could well be fugitives.

The guard marched out of the house, escorting an SS officer who was buttoning his leather coat as he walked. The officer exchanged salutes with the sergeant whose upraised arm was now more proper.

"Get your things," he ordered Anders. "You will have to wait with us."

They climbed out of the truck and took the small valises that the soldiers handed down from the back. As soon as they were clear of the running board, the sergeant threw the truck into reverse and backed into a turn away from the roadblock. He pulled away, leaving Anders and Birgit, their luggage in the snow at their feet, alone with the SS officer.

Anders bent to pick up their bags, but the officer's order stopped him. The soldier slung his machine gun, took the valises, and marched off ahead of them. It was a hopeful sign. Both of them guessed that SS troops didn't carry baggage for fugitives.

The house had been recently confiscated. The furniture in the parlor was pushed to one side, making room for a radio transceiver and a table with two typewriters. The small dining table served as the officer's desk with a Nazi flag hung on the wall behind it.

"There is a car bringing my replacement down from Mannheim tomorrow morning," the officer explained. "I will be returning in it. You can ride that far with me."

He tossed the orders and the passports on the table in front of the radio operator. "Tell them we have two priority passengers for Celle," he said. "Direct orders from Reichsfuehrer Himmler." Then he circled behind the desk. "There's a train from Mannheim to Kassel. It runs at night, after we've repaired any damage to the tracks. So we can certainly get you that far. There may even be a courier flight that we can get you on. We'll make every effort to get you to Celle as soon as possible."

Anders forced a "thank you," but he was desperately hoping for an alternative. It was obvious that Heisenberg's orders carried enormous authority. The SS would hand-deliver Birgit and him into the heart of Germany, perhaps even directly to Himmler's office.

"If we could use a car," he tried. "Anything. I don't think we can afford to lose an entire day."

But the officer was already shaking his head. "Even if we had a car, we couldn't spare any petrol. Everything is needed at the front." Then he gestured toward the hallway. "There is coffee in the kitchen. And the lady can use the bedroom at the top of the stairs. My things are already packed. I'll have them moved out so you can have some privacy."

Birgit nodded her gratitude. They had no choice. They were houseguests of Himmler's killers.

BERLIN — *March* 9

"Four months," Himmler said absently, as his manicured fingers turned the page of the report. "Four months from the date when a new supply of graphite is delivered to Haigerloch. That would mean that the earliest date for restarting the reactor would be—"

"Early July, Reichsfuehrer," Colonel Hartmann prompted. "Herr Diebner is confident that, if materials deliveries can begin immediately, they will have the damage repaired by early July."

The weak chin nodded in the light from the desk lamp. "Herr Diebner is confident . . ." The pages turned slowly.

"The design did not anticipate the extreme temperatures at acceptable operating speed." Himmler read. "Who came to this conclusion?"

"It was the general consensus of the scientists," Hartmann answered. "They reported that everything was as anticipated at low power levels, but that temperature quickly got out of control when they advanced to production levels. Herr Diebner suspects that there may have been a slight miscalculation in the graphite cross sections."

"Herr Diebner suspects . . ." Himmler said idly. He rose slowly from his chair and disappeared into the shadows behind his desk. When he spoke again, his voice came from the darkness.

"Tell me, Colonel, do you recall Herr Diebner suspecting any 'slight miscalculations' in the test reactor?"

"Certainly not, Reichsfuehrer. He was completely confident that all the theoretical problems had been solved."

"Completely confident," the disembodied voice agreed. "So the 'slight miscalculation' must have occurred in scaling up to the production reactor. That should have been a fairly simple part of the program, wouldn't you agree?"

uniform jackets over their work pants. They passed a procession of
women and children, carrying parcels and suitcases as they trekked
wearily toward the south. The SS officer's eyes fixed on each scene
of despair, but he said nothing. Anders and Birgit could only look
away.

When they entered the city, the streets were blocked by long
lines of civilians, old men, women and children, who shuffled
toward tables that the SS had set up on the sidewalks. The terror
they shared had broken down all social barriers. There were men
in dark topcoats wearing solemn homburgs, pushing against farm-
ers in rough jackets. Gracefully shaped women's hats with tall
feathers bobbed next to woolen stocking caps. On the ground,
alongside the lines, were fine oiled valises standing next to bundles
of clothing tied in a bedsheet. The officers at the tables carefully
reviewed the refugees' identity cards and travel orders. Some were
allowed to pass to continue their flight into the south, but most of
them were being turned back.

SS troops moved slowly through the columns, then darted
quickly to seize their targets. Boys, hardly in their teens, and
white-haired men who still had the strength to stand tall, were
pulled from the lines to the screams of the women who tried to
hold them back. They were handed uniform jackets, and marched
toward the waiting trucks.

The car stopped at a checkpoint and the officer handed over his
papers to a saluting enlisted man. Birgit and Anders surrendered
their passports and waited in deathly silence while the soldier
checked their names against long printed lists.

"Deserters and other traitors," the SS officer said to assure them
that they had no cause for concern. Anders watched the soldier's
eyes dart back and forth from the lists to their passports. He turned
through several pages, then handed back the documents without
ever looking up.

As they turned through the barricades and began to accelerate
out of the city, Anders saw the time on the driver's wristwatch. It
had been over thirty hours since their escape. By now, the alarm
had certainly been sounded. Their names would be on the next
list.

*   *   *

The road was clogged with columns of soldiers marching north and, on the other side, streams of civilians escaping to the south.

Most of the soldiers were on foot, their line interrupted by an occasional truck dragging a field piece, or by an armored car with soldiers sitting on its roof and clinging to its sides. The uniforms were ill matched. There were browns and grays, and occasionally civilian garb topped with a bouncing steel helmet. Some had rifles slung over their shoulders and others machine guns cradled in their arms. There were shabby boots and civilian shoes, all caked with mud in contrast to the high shine on the black leather boots that the SS officer stretched out in front of Birgit.

The civilian procession was just as shabby, the attire and the luggage just as varied. Nearly everyone walked, with an occasional horse-drawn cart topped with furniture and bundled children. Some pushed wheelbarrows loaded with trunks and bundles. One cart was pulled by an old man and a woman, their household bouncing precariously each time a wheel dropped into a rut.

"The Americans have crossed the Rhine at Remagan," the officer explained casually. "Everyone seems to be panicking." Then he added, "Senseless. We'll drive them back into the river in a matter of hours." He tapped a cigarette on his silver case, and leaned back to enjoy it. But the assurance was hollow. The troops staggering along the side of the road were not a force that could mount a counterattack. They were no more than fodder that might slow the treads of a tank.

If we could just get out of the car, Anders thought. Their path of escape was right outside the window. If they could break free from the SS officer and driver, they could easily disappear in the line of faceless refugees. He had no idea where they would go. Perhaps they didn't have to go anywhere. If they could just find a deserted building or a half-collapsed barn, they could simply hide and wait. It was obvious that the Nazi empire was collapsing all around them. It could only be a few days—a week at the most— before American troops would overrun the area.

But the car kept moving. The motorcycle, roaring on ahead, kept a path open through the sea of humanity, and the car, with its

SS markings, earned salutes from each officer that it passed. No matter how crowded the road would become, there would be room for them to proceed. They were important people, travelling under the protection of Germany's rulers. Nothing would be allowed to delay their passage into the center of the country.

They were passing a cluster of trucks, when the grim procession suddenly turned to panic. The trucks pulled to the side of the road, and the soldiers began rushing into the woods. The civilians abandoned their carts and luggage and fled into the trees. And then their driver veered sharply, taking the car bouncing across the drainage ditch.

"Get out!" the officer screamed. He charged across Birgit's legs, threw open the door and dragged her behind him as he ran for cover. Anders lifted his door handle and followed in confusion.

He was still running when he heard the whine of aircraft engines. The American Thunderbolts were in a diving turn, swinging toward the west in order to line up with the road. Soldiers on top of the trucks were frantic, trying to bring their machine guns to bear. The planes became silent as they leveled off just a few feet above the treetops. Then their engines roared as they flashed by. Anders could see the bombs as they fell away from the wings, traveled beneath the planes for a few seconds, and then curved down toward the trucks. First there was an earsplitting blast as the center of the road erupted, and then a flash of light as one of the trucks burst into flames. A second truck exploded, hurling bodies to both sides of the road, and then a third lifted into the air and cartwheeled onto the siding.

On both sides of him, soldiers climbed to their knees and began firing at the flat-nosed airplanes. But the Thunderbolts ignored them, rolling into turns and quickly climbing out of range. They swung into a new arc, again bringing them back in line with the road. This time it was the machine guns in their wings that sparkled with life. The bullets raised a cloud of dust as they dug into the siding where the German troops were cowering. The soldiers broke from their positions and turned toward the cover of the trees. But the gunfire cut them down before they could find safety. Bodies danced, jerked, and then spun to the ground on top of one another. Another truck burst into flames as the machine-gun fire found its gas tank.

Anders raised his head. The soldiers to either side of him were dead, one nearly cut in half through his waistline. The road was nearly invisible through the cloud of choking smoke. He could easily make it across the road while the planes were etching another of their sweeping turns and while the German troops were retreating into the forest. He turned his head. Birgit was about 30 feet to his right, stretched out on her stomach, her head raised to follow the flight of the fighters. But lying with his arm half over her was the black-uniformed SS officer, protecting her from the attackers with his own body.

Anders reached out and pulled the rifle from the fingers of the dead soldier beside him. He pulled the bolt and watched a live round fly from the chamber, but saw another round stripped from the clip and pushed into the chamber. Then he rose to his knees and elbows and began crawling toward Birgit. He could hear the Thunderbolts turning into another dive. In a moment, their guns would tear up the line of German soldiers, scattering them in confusion. As he crawled, he kept the muzzle of the rifle pointed toward the officer.

The planes' guns exploded again, tearing up the ground at the roadside. Some of the soldiers held their positions, firing toward the flashing fighters. Others rose up and ran toward the safety of the trees. Anders crawled to within a few feet of the officer. Then he lifted the muzzle of the gun out of the ground, and pulled the trigger.

Nothing happened.

He squeezed again. The rifle didn't respond.

Then the officer jumped up, still holding Birgit by the hand and dragging her behind him back up toward the road. Anders pulled the bolt of the rifle, tossing out the dead round. But before he could load a new round, he felt a hand grab the back of his coat. He was nearly lifted to his feet by the driver, who pushed him into a run toward the car. He looked up and saw that the planes had broken off their attack and were heading toward the west.

The car had been hit. Its back window was shattered and there were two dented holes through the roof. But it roared to life as soon as the driver touched the ignition. A moment later, they were weaving through the burning debris of the shattered trucks, and bumping over the bodies that were tossed like rags on the ground.

They reached the Rhine to the west of Heidelberg, and could see Mannheim only a few kilometers ahead. Again, the entrances to the city were clogged with civilians waiting to have their papers checked so that they could begin their escape to the south. Word had spread of the American forces that had crossed the Rhine only two hours to the north. The entire city was in chaos.

The car stopped in front of a large, brick schoolhouse, and the guards ran down the steps to open the doors. They marched beside Birgit and Anders as they were led into the building, then up a curved staircase to the second floor. An SS major was waiting in a small administration office.

"Papers," he demanded as his only greeting. He held out a gloved hand until Anders could assemble the two passports and the orders that had been issued to Heisenberg.

"You are Werner Heisenberg?" he asked.

"That's correct," Anders answered.

The hand moved like a flash, slapping the papers across Anders's face. "Liar!" the major shouted. His face twitched with rage he was making no effort to control. Then his hand fired again, slapping Anders face in the other direction.

"Your name?" he demanded once more.

"Werner Heisenberg."

The major looked down at the papers for an instant. When his eyes turned up, they were locked on Birgit.

"Who is this man?"

"Werner Heisenberg," she said. "Traveling under the personal protection of Reichsfuehrer Himmler."

He clenched the papers in his fist. "Liar!" The fist shot out and smashed against the side of her face. Birgit's knees buckled, but the guard behind her caught her arm and held her up as a limp target. The major cocked his fist for another blow.

"Nils Bergman!" Anders shouted.

The fist stopped in midair.

"We are Swedish citizens. Neutrals, trying to return to our country." He reached into the pocket on the inside lining of his top coat and produced the passport he had been saving for the Swiss border. The major snatched it from his hand without taking his eyes from Anders' face.

"We know who you are. And we know what you are. You are saboteurs who have destroyed important German weapons. You have no rights as neutral citizens."

"We are scientists—" Anders started to argue, but the hand holding the passport slashed across his face.

"Silence," the officer commanded. His face reddened as he screamed, "You are saboteurs under sentence of death! I am ordered to bring you to Berlin so that Reichsfuehrer Himmler can witness your execution. But if there is no transportation, I will execute you here. With the other traitors and deserters."

He grabbed Anders' shoulder and hurled him toward the window. At his nod, the guard pushed Birgit across the room next to Anders, and pressed her face to the glass.

In the courtyard below, a row of naked bodies hung suspended by their feet. Each had been garroted with piano wire so that the blood would run down over the face and soak into the uniform that was piled below. Birgit gagged and tried to turn away, but the guard caught her hair and held her face against the window.

"Deserters!" the major screamed. "They die more painfully than they would have died in battle. You will join them shortly!"

He waved to the guards who dragged Birgit and Anders away from the window and pushed them through the door. They staggered down a corridor with the soldiers' hands in their backs.

They stopped short at the sound of a boyish scream that seemed to echo through the building. A door ahead of them opened and was immediately filled by two soldiers dragging a uniformed figure. As they struggled past, Anders could see that the prisoner was a boy, perhaps twelve years old.

"Don't let them hang me!" he screamed toward Birgit. Her hand moved toward him, but then a push in the center of her back sent her falling forward as the boy's cries disappeared behind her.

They were forced into the room. A dozen soldiers, all half-uni-

formed and none more than fifteen years of age, stood facing the
far wall. At the end of the line were three men in civilian clothes,
one with his jacket torn down the back. Two SS soldiers stood at
the opposite wall with machine guns resting against their hips.

"More traitors," one of the guards announced, and Anders and
Birgit took their places next to the civilians. They heard the door
slam shut.

LONDON — *March 10*

"You may be interested in this, sir."

Air Marshal Ward set down his morning tea and reached for the
typewritten messages that his communications officer was offering.

"They were broadcast in the clear on an open administration
frequency. Probably exchanges with field units that have no en-
cryption capabilities."

Ward fixed his glasses and read the first sheet. It was a priority
request for transportation for two civilians, Werner Heisenberg and
a Swedish citizen, Birgit Zorn. He glanced at the time of receipt,
almost twenty-four hours earlier.

"Why didn't I see this?"

The officer shuffled. "We weren't copying for Heisenberg, sir.
You requested copying for Nils Bergman. I'm afraid our people
didn't make the connection with the Zorn name until they picked
up the second message."

Ward looked to the second message that had just been received.
It was an arrest report on Nils Bergman and Birgit Zorn with a
request for instructions.

He understood immediately. They had decrypted a message two
days earlier reporting damage to the "Castle Church facility."
Ward had been overjoyed. It could only mean that Anders' had
been correct in predicting that his design was doomed to failure.
He had phoned the prime minister to report that their long-shot

effort to deny the Germans an atomic bomb had succeeded. The prime minister had responded with a prayer.

But then, yesterday, there had been a reply from Berlin, broadcast in the clear. Nils Bergman and Birgit Zorn were to be arrested. The lack of any information on Major Haller's mission had left Ward uncertain whether Anders was dead or alive. Now the all-points message announced that Siegfried was still living and had somehow escaped from Hechingen. Ward had immediately ordered a commando squad to stand ready for a jump into Germany to assure the safety of two civilians. And then he had asked for the radio watch to pick up any traffic concerning Nils Bergman.

The first message told him how Bergman had escaped. He had assumed Werner Heisenberg's identity. The second message told him that the cover had been broken. The Germans held him and Birgit, and knew exactly who they were.

"This originated in Mannheim," Ward said, noting the information on the top of the message.

"Yes, sir. Less than ten minutes ago."

"They've asked for instructions," Ward thought aloud. "So, if Jerry is on his toes, there should be a response message within the next hour."

"We have a man sitting on that frequency," the communications officer assured.

"I want to know the instant you pick up anything," the air marshal ordered. "As soon as it starts to come in."

He was already reaching for his telephone and demanding a connection to the airfield in Reims where his commando raiding party was headed. Within a minute, he was patched through to the Red Devil commander who was leaning over the radio desk on board a twin-engined Wellington.

"Your target is Mannheim. Keep this line open and report when you are in the area," he ordered. "I hope to have something more specific for you by then." The "roger" came back in a crisp, confident voice.

Ward took his tea to the enormous map of Europe that dominated one of his office walls. His gaze found Mannheim imme-

diately. The original order had called for the return of Bergman to
Berlin. If that order stood, then there was a straight line between
Mannheim and the Nazi capital along which he would have to
attempt his rescue. The problem was how Himmler's prize prisoners would be traveling.

He doubted they would use a plane. There was no Luftwaffe left
for protection, and the roving Allied fighters were shooting down
anything that managed to make it into the air. He knew about the
night train runs from Mannheim to Kassel. The Typhoons and the
Thunderbolts blew the tracks everyday. But somehow the Germans
had the railroad back in operation at night. If he could get his
commandos to a deserted stretch of track, or stop the train and
drop them down on top of it, they might be able to save the passengers. Or, they could attempt to reach Berlin by a car traveling
at night. It was an eight-hour journey, but the car could detour
around bomb-damaged intersections. With the German transportation system in shambles, the SS might decide it was the surest
way to travel.

He needed to be ready to do three things. Intercept a flight leaving Mannheim and force the plane to turn to an Allied-held airfield. Attack a train, and escape cross-country with two of its
passengers. Or, drop his commandos somewhere along the most
direct road to Berlin, probably the auto highway that followed the
northern bank of the Main River.

The Red Devils were already moving toward their potential target area. He turned back to his desk to alert his air crews of the
possibilities.

Ward knew his chances of saving his two agents were almost
nonexistent. It would take a tremendous stroke of luck to find
them and intercept them in the chaotic vastness that was the
crumbling Reich. And even if he made a perfect attack, there was
nothing to prevent an SS guard from putting bullets into their
heads in order to keep them from being rescued.

But he did have one thing in his favor. The Germans would
issue meticulously detailed orders on the delivery of the prisoners.
They would notify every roadblock, or every train station of their
progress. The thoroughness with which they documented every de-

cision and every movement had often proved to be their undoing. It might prove to be the perfect way of tracing the movements of Anders and Zorn.

It wasn't much of a chance. But it was at least as good as the odds they had faced in infiltrating the Nazi reactor program. And that chance had paid off handsomely.

MANNHEIM — *March 10*

The door blasted open and two SS guards stepped into the room. All of the prisoners, lined against the wall, closed their eyes. Then there was the sound of boots striking the wooden floor in a slow cadence as the guards walked to the end of the line and began pacing toward their next victim.

The agonizing ritual had been repeated several times. First, they had stopped behind one of the child soldiers, who began crying as they led him out to the courtyard. On their next visit, Birgit and Anders had listened to the footsteps as they walked past the soldiers and stopped behind two of the civilians just to their left. The men had left smartly, flaunting their unbroken pride. The SS guards had returned again, this time walking to the end of the line, turning slowly behind Birgit, and then walking back to the center, where they suddenly pounced on one of the soldiers.

Now the footsteps grew louder, moving closer in a measured tempo, tormenting each victim with a pause before the next foot fell. Even without seeing them, Anders knew they were enjoying their power. They had mastered the science of terror and had learned to make the waiting for execution more excruciating than the slaughter itself.

The sound stopped behind the civilian to his left, a moment calculated to make Anders hope that the man next to him would be selected. He fought down the instinct.

"I'm Nils Bergman," he announced to the wall. "If you're looking for me, you've found me."

A furious hand grabbed the back of his collar and dragged him out of the line. The other guard took Birgit by the arm. They were pushed toward the door.

In the corridor, Anders extended his arm and Birgit took it in defiance of the gun that poked into her back. She pulled close to Karl, and they walked together at a quick pace.

The SS major was waiting in his office, a smile indicating how much he was enjoying the sentence he was about to impose. "I am ordered to bring you to Berlin. Directly to the reichsfuehrer. He is arranging a special ceremony in your honor." He paused to let his threat take effect.

"The reichsfuehrer doesn't trust you to kill men," Anders said to the major. "Children are all you can handle."

The smirk disappeared from the officer's face. He rose on his toes, coiling for a murderous blow. But then he stopped and settled calmly back to his heels. The threatening smile returned to his face, and his hand reached out gently to touch Birgit's cheek.

"You will enjoy watching what we do with her. We may even give you a few hours to think about it before we start on you."

They were marched down the steps to the front door where two sedans were waiting. The civilians who had been selected before them were seated in the first car.

"I don't want to reach Berlin," Birgit said to him as they were led toward the second car.

"We won't," he answered. "I promise you."

Birgit was pushed into the front seat, next to the driver. Anders was squeezed into the center of the rear seat, between an SS soldier and the major. Two motorcycles pulled into position in front of the first car. An open patrol car with three soldiers and a mounted machine gun closed in behind them. The officer waved a gloved hand through the open window, and the procession began moving slowly away from the building through the evening shadows in the streets. It was nearly dark when they turned next to the train station.

They were led to the single passenger carriage in a short train made up of boxcars and flatcars. There was a rapid-fire antiaircraft gun mounted on one of the flatcars, and a machine-gun nest built

on top of the passenger carriage. Their compartment had two facing benches, with a door on one end that opened out onto the
station, and another door that led to the passageway. An armed
guard was standing in the passageway, his back pressed against the
glass. Birgit and the SS officer sat on one bench, facing forward.
Anders shared the other bench with an SS soldier who was armed
with a machine gun.

Whistles sounded as soon as the officer had secured the door
from the platform. Steam hissed, and there was a metallic clanking
as the locomotive strained against the couplers. Then the train
began to move slowly from the station, picking up speed as it
crossed through the switchyard.

Death was all around them. In the labored shuffle of the soldiers
who trudged toward boxcars for a journey to a front that was coming to meet them. In the gaunt, blank faces of the refugees waiting
on the platforms, who could not flee from the west without rushing toward a destruction that was coming from the east. In the
warehouse buildings that had been blown open to the weather. In
the signal towers that showed no light. And then, as they sped out
of the station, death was visible in the deserted barns where hay
hung through the siding above the heads of starved animals. In the
roads that ended abruptly at ditches and in bridges that had fallen
into streams they were intended to cross. In the telephone lines
that dangled from the stumps of shattered poles. In station houses
that had been gutted by fire. All Germany was in its death agony.
And its masters, in their funereal uniforms, were determined that
the death should be slow and painful.

"You think we are beaten?" the SS major taunted, when he
noticed Anders staring out at a column of refugees. "There are
super weapons we are about to launch. Weapons so powerful that
they will bring victory in a single stroke. Those who are fleeing can
flee all the way to hell. We will have no need for them when we
rebuild the Reich."

Anders nearly laughed at the mention of a super weapon. But
he wasn't interested in the mad boasting. He was studying the passing posts and listening to the wheels as they clattered over the rail
joints in order to gauge the speed of the train. He was waiting for it

to slow down for a sharp curve or a damaged roadbed. Then he would keep his promise to Birgit that they would never reach the executioners in Berlin.

He needed the machine gun that the soldier seated next to him had rested across his knees. The sling was around the man's neck and under his arm. His hands rested on the stock and along the short barrel. There was no way of taking the weapon from him. But all he needed was an instant's surprise. Grab the weapon. Force its muzzle up toward the back of the guard who stood outside the door. Pull the trigger. Pull up on the handle to open the outside door, grab Birgit, and leap. And then everything would be uncertain. Could they survive the fall? How long would it take the soldier to recover and swing his machine gun to the outside, or the major to clear his pistol from its holster? Would the gunners on the roof of the car see their escape? Were they ready to fire?

Would they have time to disappear into the countryside and lose themselves in one of the processions of fleeing civilians? Or would the Germans stop the train and have search parties after them before they could even begin an escape? There were no sure answers. All he knew was that, if the train slowed and he could get his hand on the gun for only an instant, they would never have to face the reichsfuehrer's rage.

"We will reduce London to ashes in a single explosion," the major was intoning. "Whole armies will be annihilated in an instant."

The soldier's hands seemed to be relaxed. He sensed no hint of danger. But the train was hammering ahead at a steady speed, much too fast for him to think of jumping.

There was a flash of light that brought the shapes of the trees out of the darkness. Just as Anders heard the crash of the explosion, he felt the car shudder, rock from side to side, and then smash to a stop. The major came hurtling out the seat, flying toward Anders, his head slamming into the wall next to Anders' face. Birgit flew forward, ramming into the chest of the soldier. An instant later, the countryside lit up with gunfire.

The guard in the corridor staggered back to his feet. The soldier next to Anders threw Birgit from on top of him, and raised the machine gun with one hand while he pushed Birgit back into her seat with the other.

Anders grabbed the gun and dragged it toward him, pulling the soldier's head onto his shoulder. His finger jabbed under the trigger guard, squeezing down on the soldier's finger. The machine gun exploded.

In the blinding light of the muzzle flash, he couldn't see the rounds that punched through the roof. But he heard the shattering of glass as the muzzle swung across the door to the passage and cut a row of holes through the back of the guard's uniform.

Anders saw the major fall backward onto the floor, his cap flying away. But even as he was falling, his gloved hand was clutching at the handle of his holstered pistol. Karl kicked out with all the force he could gather and drove his heel into the man's face. The head snapped back and the pistol toppled to the floor between his feet.

Karl still gripped the machine gun, which was now pointing silently toward the roof. To his right, the soldier struggled with the sling that was twisted around his neck. Across from him, the SS major, his forehead split and already flowing blood into his eyes, was trying to reach the pistol.

Anders let go of the machine gun, and hurled all his weight against the officer, driving him against the door. Then he pulled up on the handle, and with another thrust of his body, drove the officer out through the door.

Birgit had lunged back on top of the soldier who was fighting her off with one hand while he tried to straighten the machine gun that was twisted behind his shoulder with the other. The man's arm was around the stock of the weapon, and his fingers were groping for the trigger.

Karl spun around, lifted the officer's pistol from the floor, and pressed it against the soldier's uniform jacket. With the roar of gunfire all around them, he never heard the sound of the pistol when he pulled the trigger.

Birgit fell back into her own seat. The soldier toppled against the compartment wall, then stood unsteadily, his fingers still clutching for the trigger. Anders raised the pistol in both hands, pointing it straight into the rolling eyes. But the man's arms fell to his sides, the gun hanging harmlessly from its sling. Then he slumped into a heap at Birgit's feet.

Karl grabbed the machine gun and swung the strap over the dead man's head. He gave Birgit the pistol and then, without saying a word, pulled her arm and led her to the open compartment door. They looked down into the darkness, and jumped together, sprawling out on the ground when they landed.

They were lying on the slope of the roadbed. The passenger carriage above them was off the tracks at its front end, pressed against a boxcar that was compressed like an accordion. The car ahead of that was a twisted steel skeleton. The rest of the train had disappeared. The explosion he had seen had blown the train in half.

From beneath the wreckage, and from the gun emplacement on top of the carriage, the German soldiers were firing out into the darkness. Return fire from the muzzle flashes along the side of the track was raking the steel sides of the crippled train. There was no trace of the Nazi major who had fallen through the door ahead of them.

Karl took Birgit's hand and began crawling away from the tracks. At first he moved slowly, almost afraid to break the crust of the snow that covered the ground, as if the sound could give them away. Then he began running, his body still bent low. And finally, when they reached the cover of a thin stand of trees, he ran as fast as he could. They were a few hundred yards from the train, with the sound of the guns fading behind them, before they were overtaken by their terror and exhaustion. They slumped to the ground, and dragged themselves into the low bushes that had grown up between the trees.

He could watch the progress of the battle. The Germans, visible in the pale lamps that still burned at the ends of the wrecked cars, were better targets than their attackers, who were hidden in the night. All the screams of pain came from the tracks as one soldier after another was picked off by the surrounding marksmen.

And then the attackers emerged from the darkness, one or two at a time. Each man seemed to run a short distance and then dive to the ground. Another suddenly rose and ran past him without making a sound. Anders watched in dumb fascination as they closed in on the ragged form of the train, then poked cautiously from car to car. At one point, one of the attackers fired a short blast into the wreckage and, after a moment, probed forward to examine his work.

He could hear voices as the men exchanged shouted whispers and, in the sudden stillness of the night, he was terrified by the words. They were speaking in English.

"Bergman," he heard a soldier call into the compartments of the carriage. He felt Birgit's grip tighten on his arm.

"Bergman. Zorn."

They were the target, not the Nazis. The English who had tried to kill them in Hechingen had come back. Why? What were they afraid of? Why couldn't they allow him and Birgit to reach Berlin?

"Bergman. Professor Bergman." The English were beginning to search the woods on both sides of the train.

"Miss Zorn. Birgit Zorn."

"We've got to get away," she said, starting to climb to her feet. He pulled her back down and raised his fingers in front of her lips.

"Stay still," he ordered. "They won't find us."

What difference could it make to them if he reached Berlin? Even if they believed that he had turned to the Germans, how could he possibly help them now? And then he realized. The British didn't know that the reactor was destroyed.

"Bergman. Professor Bergman."

They don't know, he concluded. They think the program is still alive. They think I'm building a bomb for the Nazis. There was no other explanation.

"Miss Zorn." The voice was fainter. The hunters were moving off in another direction.

Still he didn't move. The train had traveled for about half an hour. That meant it would take the Germans time to get here. A half an hour at least to fire up another train and get troops aboard, and then another half hour to get their rescue party to the scene. He could wait a few more minutes until the voices had disappeared. Then he and Birgit would begin moving in the opposite direction.

But where? He looked into the sky and was able to identify north. He should probably move to the west, but that would take him back in the direction he had come from, toward the Germans who would be coming to the rescue. And he had seen how the Nazis were cutting off the escape of their own people to the south.

They were fleeing south because the Americans had broken across the Rhine to the north. If Birgit and he could move in that direction and just find a place to hide, it wouldn't be long before the Americans would set them free.

He didn't know what they would find to the north. More German patrols? More SS death squads searching for deserters? They would have to avoid main roads and even small villages. They would have to disappear into the mass of homeless refugees. They would have to flee from anyone who might ask for their papers and travel permits.

But at least they had a chance. And he would be keeping his promise to Birgit that he would never allow her to be brought to Berlin.

"Let's move," he told her. They rose cautiously, and began to walk slowly, keeping the railroad tracks to their right. Then, when they were out of sight of the wreckage, they rushed quickly up the siding and dashed across the silent tracks. They were well into the open country to the north when they heard the distant sound of the Nazi rescue train rushing past them.

FRIEDBERG — *March 11*

They found a deserted back road that wove to the north, stepped up onto it cautiously, and began walking through the cold night air. At first they were afraid to be out in the open, away from the cover of the trees. But it soon became obvious that road was little more than a tractor path, scarcely used in the winter months and certainly not at night. It wasn't a likely target for roadblocks, and if it were patrolled, they would hear an approaching car long before it came into sight. They would have all the time they needed to take cover to the side.

Their real enemy was the weather. The temperature was near freezing and even the light breezes were icy. The ground was covered with crusted snow, packed down along the paths that passing trucks and cars had cut, but ankle-deep in the center and to both sides. Their topcoats and plain street shoes provided little protection.

They passed the outbuildings of truck farms that were cut into clearings, and toyed with the temptation of taking whatever shelter from the wind and cold they might provide.

"Let's keep going," Birgit decided. Even though they had no idea what they would find ahead, it seemed safer to put as much distance as possible between themselves and the ruptured train they had fled. The English were searching for them, and when the Germans understood that Himmler's prize prisoners had escaped, the SS would organize its own hunting parties. Hopefully, the Nazis would begin looking toward the south, since that was the direction that they had originally headed. But for Himmler, they would search everywhere.

They had to keep moving. But as the temperature dropped, and the winds roving through the hills became stronger, they both realized that they couldn't keep walking throughout the night. Birgit's feet were already numb, and her hands were pressed against her ears to hold down the biting pain.

"We have to get in out of this," Karl told her.

She nodded. "We can go a little further. Let's try to make it for another hour."

Anders carried both of the weapons, the machine gun slung from his shoulder and the pistol pushed into the pocket of his topcoat. There was a curved clip hanging beneath the chamber of the machine gun, but he had no idea how many rounds it held. He had fired the pistol once, and guessed that there were five or six cartridges left.

He would use them against anyone who tried to take them, English or German. If it were the British, he would keep firing until the guns stopped. The English had no reason to hate them. They would simply make sure that they could be of no further help to the Nazi secret weapon. But if it were the SS troops that cornered them, he would save at least one round in the pistol. He would not allow Himmler or his worshipping madmen to satisfy their vengeance with Birgit's body.

They stopped dead in their tracks at the groan of a distant engine. Anders looked back and could see pinpoints of light blinking through the trees behind them. He grabbed Birgit's hand and crashed through the low snowbank at the roadside, pulling her into the cover of the trees.

The noise grew louder, and the masked headlights became clearer. It was a truck, winding up the road behind them, struggling with the slight upgrade. Its engine was coughing, uncertain whether it should keep pulling or simply shut down and rest.

"It can't be army," Anders speculated, even though he couldn't make out its shape. The sound was too laboring for a modern engine. He eased out toward the edge of the tree cover to get a better look.

It was a small cab with a large, open bed, probably a farm truck used to cart vegetables into the cities. The truck bed was filled with irregular shapes, some towering over the top of the cab. As it came closer, Anders could make out furniture, a household piled on the back between the open slat siding and tied into position. Someone, probably a family, was trying to escape into the vastness of the countryside.

He jumped from his cover and ran toward the center of the road, waving with one hand while he tried to conceal the machine gun behind his back. The weak headlamps illuminated his feet, then rose to pick up the color of his face. The truck groaned to a stop.

Karl walked cautiously toward the cab, peering through the windshield at the forms inside. There was a man in a peaked hat and a rustic, woolen jacket, and a woman who wore a heavy scarf wrapped around her head. As he reached the side window, he could see faces that reflected the same fear he was feeling.

"There are two of us. My wife and myself. Can we ride on the back of your truck?"

The driver looked cautiously at the woman beside him, then turned back to Anders. "You're not . . . fugitives?"

Karl shook his head. "No. Like you. We're just trying to find a safe place."

"Where are you going?" the driver asked.

"Anywhere. North. East. Just away from the front."

The man looked toward the woman.

"Please," Anders said. "We'll freeze if we keep walking."

The woman leaned across her husband and studied him suspiciously. "We're not going far," she said, trying to discourage the stranger. "Just a few miles to my brother's house."

"Anything will help," Karl begged.

"You're not wanted? The SS isn't looking for you?"

"No," he lied. "Please."

The woman nodded to her husband. "Climb up on back," he told Anders.

Karl ran back into the headlights and waved toward the dark roadside. Birgit ran toward him and he helped her climb up into the truck bed. The engine, which had been popping idly, roared as the truck was dropped into gear. Then, with a violent lurch, they began rolling, picking up speed as they headed to the north.

They were still out in the open. But, by pressing against the stacked furniture, they were able to escape the wind. The parcels of clothes and bed linens served almost as blankets. And they were able to huddle together, wrapping their coats up over the tops of their heads.

The truck gathered speed on the downgrade and its engine sounded more in command. As the minutes passed, one mile and then another passed under the bouncing wheels. They had traveled perhaps half an hour before the truck rose into another upgrade and their speed slowed to a crawl.

"We'll have to get off soon," Karl told her. "There have to be some patrols. Maybe even a roadblock. We've been lucky, but we're stretching it thin."

"When we see a shelter," Birgit answered.

It appeared almost immediately. To their left, set back perhaps fifty yards from the road, a tall barn came into view. The house, with the glow of an open fire in one of its windows, was another fifty yards from the barn. They pushed to the back of the truck until their feet were hanging over the edge. Then they both jumped down.

Even at the slow speed, they fell as soon as their feet hit the ground, sprawling onto their backs and sliding on the packed ice. Karl scampered up and found Birgit already climbing to her feet. They watched for a moment as the unlighted mound of furniture moved away from them.

They started toward the barn, Anders swinging the machine gun around to his side so that his finger fitted around the trigger. They angled first toward the south until the blank wall of the barn came between them and the house, and then moved toward the giant swinging doors that were open only a crack. As they came close, he told Birgit to crouch low and wait. Then he went ahead, pushed against the door until he could squeeze through the opening, and stepped inside.

Half the space was cluttered with farm implements and an antique tractor with spiked metal wheels. He moved slowly around a large hay rake designed to be pulled behind the tractor, past a wheelbarrow, and through a stand of rakes and scythes. There was a pile of wooden crates, some filled with ancient harnesses, others packed with vegetables and apples. The room was empty.

But he could hear heavy breathing from behind the boarded walls of the stalls that were directly ahead. He moved silently, then turned into the stare of a swayback horse, who studied him without making a sound. Two boney milking cows, standing in the next two stalls, ignored him. Anders turned slowly. There was no one else in the room.

He climbed slowly up the steep steps to the loft, keeping the weapon pointed ahead of him. He knew that there wouldn't be soldiers waiting for them. But the countryside was alive with deserters and refugees. There could easily be others hiding in the room overhead, crazed by their flight and determined to defend their sanctuary.

He raised his head above the floorboards and saw the stacks of baled hay. Slowly, he crept around them, examining every space in which someone might hide. But the building was empty. It was theirs.

As soon as he pushed back through the door, Birgit came running toward him. They climbed into the loft, broke open one of the bales, and spread it as a quilt. Birgit collapsed into the straw. Anders moved to the loft door, high above the swinging doors they had entered, and pushed it open a crack.

He had a commanding view of the road and the open field that they had just crossed. With the machine gun, he could slow down anyone who tried to approach from that direction. He crossed the loft to the back of the barn. In the gaps between the planking, he could see the house and the packed footprints that led from its front porch to the back door of the bar. With Birgit watching in one direction and he in the other, there was no way that anyone could take them by surprise.

But Birgit was already fighting against sleep. And, if they were lucky, they might be hiding here for a long time. They couldn't both stay awake forever. They had to risk a few hours of rest. He decided that he would take the first watch, moving back and forth to check both the road and the farmhouse. Birgit's protests were easy to ignore. She was already curled into the hay. For the moment, at least, all her fears had been put aside.

Anders found himself laughing at the irony. They had started at the Kaiser Wilhelm Institute, the Valhalla built to house the gods of science. They were ending in the loft of a dilapidated barn, built to house horses and cows. Their mission had been to unleash the incredible heat energy of matter. Now the heat that sustained them came from rotting manure and the decaying apples in the crates below. And he had begun as an objector in conscience to even the thought of killing. Now he carried a machine gun that he wouldn't hesitate to use.

As he moved between his two observation posts, he wondered at all the things the German scientists might have built. Were there medicines that could end disease, or chemicals that could make even the deserts fertile? Surely, locked in that same matter, were untold benefits for the Earth and its inhabitants. Instead, they had devoted all their talents to discovering the primeval explosive, the ultimate force of destruction. And that search had brought their own destruction.

Their cannons and their rockets, their unstoppable tanks and agile jet fighters had served them poorly. The great German Reich had become a wasteland with all its monuments to achievement shattered and truncated. The Master Race had become slaves to its own leaders, wandering endlessly in a country from which there was no escape.

What might they have imagined, the Heisenbergs and the Lauderbachs, the Krupps and the Messerschmitts? What might they have achieved? But instead they imagined eternal power and glory. And what they built was total devastation and everlasting shame.

Perhaps he and Birgit were the only ones in Germany who were truly alive, the only ones with even a wavering glimmer of hope. Certainly they were more alive than the assassins who had been sent from England to seal a secret, or the SS madmen who were determined to kill anything that would not join in their suicide.

He checked the bolt on the side of the machine gun and examined its curved storehouse of destruction. An ugly device, he thought. But he would use it if he had to.

He heard the noise before he was awake, a loud, repetitive pounding that echoed like a kettledrum. His eyes opened slowly and blinked into angular shafts of light. For an instant, he was lost like an insect on the floor of some giant forest. The noise seemed to be an ax cutting into the trees that were overhead.

He sat up abruptly and found himself in the hayloft, leaning against one of the bales, the machine gun resting across his lap. Halfway across the room, Birgit was still curled into a pile of hay. But her eyes were wide open, filled with apprehension at the noise that had awakened her.

He had fallen asleep. He had been sitting beside the loft door, keeping watch over the road. He must have closed his eyes for just an instant. Now it was dawn, and someone was hammering against the side of the barn.

Birgit started to get up but he stilled her with a gesture. There was someone in the barn below. The slightest movement could creak the old, worn flooring or perhaps drop a shower of hay into the chamber below. He lay perfectly still and listened carefully.

The banging was from the other end of the building, a door swinging in the breeze. Another sound was coming from directly below where someone was digging through the crates of apples and vegetables.

He turned his head slowly, looking out toward the road. There was no one in sight, no car or truck pulled over to the side. Soldiers, he guessed, would have come from the road.

It had to be the farmer who had come from the house, leaving the back door open. He would take what he needed and then leave, closing the door behind him. If they stayed perfectly still, if there were no reason for the man to climb the ladder to the loft, then they might not be discovered.

There were footsteps below, and then the banging stopped. Birgit began to move, but again he motioned for her to stay in place. They both listened to the sound of crunching snow.

Anders sprang up, cradling the gun in his arm, and dashed across to the back wall. Through the boarding, he saw an old woman wrapped in a long coat and scarf, shuffling back toward the house. He watched her carefully until she disappeared onto the covered porch. Then he sighed in relief.

"Who was it?" Birgit asked, rolling onto her knees.

"A woman. From the house."

She walked carefully toward Anders and peered out into the empty yard. "Did she see us?"

"I don't think so."

"Should we leave?"

He shook his head. "There's no telephone line. Even if she knows we're here, she can't call anyone. We'll watch. If anyone leaves the house, then we'll have to get out."

They took up their positions at each end of the barn, Anders guarding the road and Birgit watching the farmhouse, envying the smoke she saw rising from the stone chimney. She could almost feel the warmth of the fire and taste whatever the woman might be cooking. The cold seemed to have penetrated to her bones and there were gnawing hunger pains in the pit of her stomach. But still, she knew, they were fortunate. The barn walls provided a windbreak and the hay could be used as a blanket. There was food below. They could survive for days in the loft. Perhaps even until the advancing Americans pushed the front lines past them.

But it was dangerous to pause in one place for too long. The British were looking for them and the Germans were looking for them, fanning out from the train wreck that was probably no more than a few miles away. How long would it take them to reach the barn? Perhaps only a few more hours. Certainly sometime before nightfall. And the old wooden structure was an obvious refuge. No one would pass it without searching it thoroughly.

They had to keep moving toward the north. But they couldn't use the road in daylight. There would be German patrols and SS checkpoints, all alerted to their escape. And even in the warmth of the sun, how long would they last trudging through the frozen forests?

She left her post and walked carefully to where Anders was crouching by the open crack in the loft door.

"We can't wait here all day," she said. "I think I can make it through the woods."

He touched her coat. "Not very far," he answered, "unless we can find you something warmer. And a better pair of shoes. I've been thinking that if we could just get into the house. There might be something that you could wear."

"Do you think the woman would help us?"

It was the question he had been asking himself. The Nazis had turned on their own people, and the woman might have more sympathy for civilians in danger than for the Nazi cause. But like all Germans, she was probably terrified of her own soldiers. She would be writing her own death sentence by helping enemies of the state. It would be terribly risky for them to force her to make that kind of a choice.

They could just take what they needed. He was armed with a machine gun, and as far as he could tell the woman was alone. They could cross quickly to the house, steal clothes and food, and then escape into the forest. Even if she reported them, they would have a head start, with a chance of surviving in the open country. But against a defenseless woman, the gun would be nothing more than a prop. He certainly wouldn't use it. He probably couldn't even make a convincing threat.

"Let's wait a bit," he suggested to Birgit. "If she leaves the house, we can break in and take what we need. We can be gone before she gets back."

"How long?" she pressed.

He shrugged. "Maybe the English have given up on us. And the SS probably has bigger problems. Maybe no one is looking for us."

They waited. Birgit kept an uneventful watch on the house. Anders had one fright when he saw two trucks winding up the road from the south. He drew Birgit to his side and steadied the barrel of the machine gun through the crack in the door. But the army vehicles groaned past. The few ragged soldiers hunched in their cargo bays weren't even looking out.

They heard aircraft engines droning in the distance and then suddenly growing louder. With a roar, two silver fighters, marked with American stars, flashed past over the road and disappeared toward the north.

"There's nothing for them to shoot at," Anders told Birgit. "Maybe the Germans have pulled back from this area."

There was quiet all around them. No sound of gunfire. No military traffic. No parades or refugees. Their hopes began to climb as the sun climbed into the noon sky. Was it possible that the Nazis finally understood? Did they realize that, with the destruction of their reactor, their last hopes of victory had been destroyed? Had someone finally decided that surrender was a better choice than death?

Karl left Birgit watching the road. He checked the house through the openings in the back wall and then climbed down the ladder. The horse in the stall watched him as he crept toward the front and searched in the crates, where he found potatoes and turnips, and began wiping them against his coat.

"Karl."

It was Birgit's shouted whisper from above. And then he heard the distant sound of an automobile engine.

He dropped the vegetables and rushed back to the ladder. He could hear the engine sound growing louder as he climbed furiously up the steps. Through the crack in the door he could see the patrol car racing up the road from the south.

They waited silently as the car made its last turn and moved directly toward them. He squeezed her hand reassuringly as it held its speed, seeming to be rushing toward some distant destination. And then, directly opposite them, exactly where they had jumped from the truck during the night, the car screeched to a stop.

Three SS soldiers jumped out and spread out along the road, their rifles at the ready. Then the officer stood up in the car and shouted orders that Anders couldn't make out. But he didn't need to hear the words to know exactly whom they were looking for. When the officer tipped back his cap, Anders recognized his face. It was the SS major who had been bringing them to Himmler.

The soldiers began moving forward toward the barn, each in turn advancing a few yards while the other two kept their rifles aimed at the barn. They weren't searching. Instead they were moving toward their target confident of what was inside.

"How could they know?" Anders wondered aloud.

"The people in the truck," Birgit whispered. "They must have seen us jump."

He weighed their choices. They had no chance of escaping from the barn. The soldiers were spread out enough so that at least one of them would be able to see them no matter which direction they took. And even if they could make it as far as the house, the SS attackers would still have them cornered.

He could let them come closer. He was no marksman, but eventually one of them would charge toward the door below. At that moment he could push the gun barrel through the loft door and fire down at point-blank range. He could certainly get the first one. But he had little chance of winning a gun battle with trained soldiers. And once they locked him into their sights, what would happen to Birgit?

Or, they could wait in silence with their guns aimed at the top of the ladder. Only one soldier at a time could climb into the loft. And he would be completely vulnerable for the first instant when his head appeared above the flooring.

He had to decide quickly. The first of the attackers was already halfway across the field, dropping down on one knee to cover the advance of one of the others. And the major had left the patrol car. He was walking slowly toward them, behind the protection of his soldiers. In his hand he was carrying a coiled spool of wire.

"Don't let them take us," Birgit said. It wasn't a plea, but an order. Karl looked at her quickly and found no hint of fear in her expression. Her eyes were clear, angry rather than anxious. Her lips were set. She had watched the Nazis destroy her world and murder people she loved. Now she wanted to fight back, even to the death.

He remembered the bodies dangling naked in the courtyard under the major's proud gaze. That wasn't the way that Birgit had chosen to die.

"They won't take us," he told her. He took the pistol from the pocket of his coat and handed it to her. "You cover the ladder."

One of the soldiers had advanced to within twenty yards of the barn door. Anders held himself back from the opening, out of sight, and waited.

"Bergman," the major's voice shouted. "I know you're in there. You're surrounded."

The distant voice was tempting. Karl wanted to rush to the door for one chance to empty the machine gun at the SS commander. But he hung back, knowing that his best chance was against a close target.

"Come out, Bergman. There is no escape."

The voice echoed, and then there was silence.

Karl couldn't see to either side. Soldiers might be advancing right up to the barn. But through the crack in the loft door he could watch the ground directly in front of the building. One of them, he prayed, will try for the front door.

He heard the snow crunching, and then a black-uniformed figure flashed through the space below. He bolted forward, the gun
thrust out ahead of him, and hit the loft door with his shoulder.
The soldier, his hands already on the barn door, snapped his head
upward. Anders squeezed the trigger. The snow swirled up in an
instant storm, and the soldier dropped into its cloud.

Anders pulled back just as the door shattered inches away from
his face. He rolled away from the opening and heard the blasts of
rifle fire from outside. Huge chips of wood broke away from the
door frame, and gaping holes suddenly appeared in the planking
on the front side of the loft. The firing continued for almost half a
minute, shredding the wall. Then it stopped, its faint echoes ricocheting through the countryside.

He raised his head as much as he dared. He could see the officer standing in the distance, his leather coat thrown open in a
defiant pose. There was no chance of reaching him. Then he
heard unseen voices close by. The two soldiers that were left were
right up against the side of the building.

He looked back over his shoulder. Birgit was stretched out on
the floor, holding the pistol in both hands, its muzzle pointed
toward the top of the ladder.

He heard running outside, and almost at the same instant there
was a rattling sound from the room below. Something had been
tossed through the crack in the barn door and was bouncing across
the tops of the crates.

He leapt toward Birgit, wrapped her in his arms, and rolled her
into the hay where she had slept through the night. Then the
grenade exploded with a deafening crash.

The floor seemed to jump and smash against them. There was a
searing flash of heat that ended almost the instant it burned against
them. And then a roar as the boards along one side of the barn fell
away, opening up a huge hole to the daylight. The floor creaked
and began sloping toward the open hole. But then the motion
stopped with the floorboards tilting toward space. The smell of
cordite was nearly choking.

They lay motionless, blinded in the smoke and deafened by the
ringing inside their heads. Then, as the smoke cleared, they could

look down through the wrenched openings in the floorboards and see something moving in the space below. The soldiers had come back for their body count.

Anders groped around for the machine gun. He raised his head cautiously and saw it back near the loft door where he had been pinned down by the gunfire. He had dropped it in his rush to save Birgit from the grenade.

He heard a boot strike the first step of the ladder. One of the soldiers was climbing up to the loft. Karl tried to move noiselessly, avoiding the openings that would expose him to the soldier who was waiting below. He heard the boot strike the next step and then the next. But the machine gun was still several feet away, too far for him to reach without jumping up and running. And if he did that, he would be shot before he could get the weapon into his hands. He looked back toward the ladder. The black dome of a steel helmet was edging into view.

Birgit raised her hand slowly out of the straw. The gray steel of the pistol emerged and then panned toward the ladder. The helmet rose up and then two cold eyes cleared the floor line and fixed on Anders. At that instant, Birgit fired.

The helmet jumped to one side and the eyes widened. An open-mouthed face rose for an instant into view. Then it dropped from sight with a clattering sound as the body tumbled down the ladder. But that sound was lost in the explosion of gunfire from below. Holes exploded in a trail through the flooring as the last of the soldiers made his escape, firing blindly up into the loft.

Anders knew what would come next. He rushed back toward the machine gun, ignoring the rounds that were cutting through the floor around him. He snatched up the gun and dove toward the opening that had been left by the loft door. Immediately below him, the soldier had stopped his retreat. He was pulling the pin from another grenade that he still held in his hand.

Anders fired without aiming, the rounds stirring up another snowstorm. But the soldier in its midst took the handle of the grenade in his hand and cocked his arm over his head. The hand had already started forward when the shower of bullets found their mark. The soldier dropped on his back, the hammer-shaped missile falling to the snow beside him. At that instant, the gun stopped firing.

Karl had turned back toward Birgit when the grenade exploded. Its force threw him forward, sprawled out on his face. The already shattered front side of the barn buckled inward. The teetering loft dropped into the debris below, and a second later the roof with its heavy beams came crashing down on top of them.

Anders never lost his awareness. He felt the loft floor shake and then fall out from under him. He saw the bales of hay begin to topple inward. He watched Birgit roll violently away from him and disappear into the dense cloud of dust. He crashed painfully, realized that the shadow of the roof was closing down on him and heard the roar as the planking fell all around him. He braced against the crushing pain that would surely follow, but felt nothing. The rafter above him had caught against the crumbled siding. A large section of the roof flexed a few feet above his head.

He thought of Birgit and began crawling in the direction where she had vanished, reaching blindly into the dust that seemed to be rising everywhere.

"Birgit," he called into the haze.

There was no answer.

He saw her hand and reached out for it. It did not grasp at his fingers. He saw her hair sprayed out across the fallen planking. But the rest of her was hidden, buried under the roof boards that had crashed down on top of her.

He pushed at the boards and they broke free. Then he saw her face, bloodied by a gash on her forehead, ghostly white and silent.

Anders picked up the gun that was lying next to her fingertips and began backing away from the tight space that held her prisoner. He was able to turn in the open area where he had first landed and then find an opening out from under the slope of the fallen roof.

When he stepped out into the sunlight, the SS major was still standing in the field, halfway between the wreckage of the barn and the parked patrol car, still holding the coil of wire in his hand. He had watched his men enter the barn, heard the shots, then seen one rush out and turn to throw a grenade. The machine-gun fire from the loft had been his first evidence that his victims were still alive. Then he had seen the explosion, and watched the building buckle and collapse.

Could they have survived? Should he follow his orders to the letter and walk into the wreckage to identify the bodies of the traitors? Or could he assume they were dead and return to his car? The major was still debating his choices when Nils Bergman's form stood up uncertainly from the wreckage, perhaps a hundred yards ahead of him. The traitor had lived. His duty was clear. He dropped the wire coil and reached for the pistol in his holster.

He had taken his first step toward Anders when he realized that the man was no longer fleeing. Instead, his prisoner was walking directly toward him. He stopped, stunned by the audacity of the man. Then he saw the pistol that swung freely in Karl's hand.

Anders saw the officer draw the gun from his holster. But it didn't matter. He had nothing left to live for, and the madness had to be stopped. He thought of the flattened buildings he had seen outside Berlin, and the slaves who labored like gnomes in the cave factory at Nordhausen. He saw the frightened faces that had surrounded him while the bombers pounded the Kaiser Wilhelm to rubble. He remembered Haller's hideously tortured body and the children soldiers hanging naked by their feet. And mostly, there was the image of Birgit's bloodied face. Someone had to stop it. The madness had gone on long enough.

They were fifty yards apart when Anders saw the officer raise his pistol. He heard the cracks of three shots squeezed off in quick succession. He ignored them all, walking relentlessly toward the savage who seemed to be responsible for all the agony. The gun still hung from his hand, the muzzle pointed toward the ground.

The major's pistol flashed again, and Anders heard two more shots. One tore up the snow at his feet, but he never broke stride. Then, when he was thirty yards from the Nazi, his own hand began to rise, tilting the muzzle up toward the black uniform in the leather coat.

Suddenly, the German felt panic. He had fired too soon, well beyond the accurate range of his pistol. He tried to steady a hand that was beginning to shake. Then he fired again and again.

Anders didn't hear the last shot. The round hit his left shoulder like a fist, knocking him off balance. He struggled for an instant, but regained his footing and continued his march directly into the face of the SS officer.

The Nazi fought to steady his pistol as he waited for his victim to close. Then, when Anders was only twenty yards away, he squeezed the trigger gently. The gun clicked harmlessly. He looked down long enough to fumble with the slide. When he looked up, Anders was only fifteen yards away, still moving toward him. The pistol, which had faltered when Anders was hit, was once again rising into his eyes.

The German backed up a step or two, then wheeled abruptly and began running toward his car. He stumbled in the icy snow, crawled a few feet as he scampered up from his knees, ran a few more steps, and then slipped again. When he glanced back in terror, his victim was still walking calmly behind him, closing in with the pistol raised to fire.

He struggled up the shoulder of the road, grasping at the sides of the open car as he again began to slip. When he turned, Anders was still only fifteen yards away, closing the distance. The arm with the pistol was fully extended.

The Nazi hesitated. He didn't have time to make it around the car. And even if he did, the barrel of the gun would be pressed against the side of his face before he could get the engine started. He looked uncertainly from side to side, and then into the eyes of the man who was only ten yards away. He raised both hands into the air in a gesture of surrender.

But Anders shook his head. "No," he told the Nazi. "It has to stop."

He fired slowly and methodically, shot after shot, until the pistol stopped firing and the bolt locked open. Then he blinked his eyes at the black uniform with its silver ravens, slumped against the tire of the car. His arm dropped down to his side. His hand opened and the pistol fell into the snow.

He turned and began walking back toward the barn, unaware of the blood that was running down the back of his hand and trailing red spots onto the frozen ground. Somehow, he had to lift the rafter that had pinned Birgit's body. He had to free her so that he could take her with him. He could never leave without her.

He stopped dead when he saw something move inside the shell of the barn. He blinked his eyes, then saw a second figure rushing from the farmhouse, low to the ground and cutting back and forth in a haphazard path.

Soldiers! There were more troops, perhaps two or three of them closing in on the wrecked structure where Birgit was pinned helplessly.

"No!" His scream cracked through the quiet. He dropped his head and began running with all his strength toward the fallen building. "No. Don't touch her!" He rushed into the wreckage.

A khaki figure jumped up in front of him, caught him in a hug and wrestled him to the ground.

"Professor Bergman."

He was staring into eyes that looked back from beneath the edge of a red beret.

"Don't touch her," Anders begged.

"She'll be all right," the voice assured in perfect English. "We're pulling her free. Then we have to get the two of you out of here."

"She's alive?" He couldn't believe what he had heard.

"She's talking to us. We'll have her out in a minute."

He felt the powerful arms that held him relax. Then a strong hand reached down and helped him to his feet. He looked around and began to understand that British commandos hadn't come to execute them. Two of the Red Devils were crouched behind their rifles, keeping watch over the surrounding fields. Four others were lifting the beam that had trapped Birgit.

"It's all over for you two," the soldier said. "We're taking you home."

SUMMER

1945

The Thousand-Year Reich had died in May, when the Red Army and the United States Army met in the heart of Germany. British scientists had entered the cave beneath the castle church of Haigerloch and found the ruins of the German reactor. Like everything the Nazis had built, it was lifeless. The war still raged, but now the battles were on the other side of the world. Japan's island empire was vanishing, and the fleet that had once roamed uncontested from India to Hawaii now rested at the bottom of the Pacific. All the world waited for the final assault on the Land of the Rising Sun. But there were a few scientists who understood that no assault would be necessary. They had been present at the testing grounds in the American desert for the instant of triumph that had been denied to the Germans. They had seen the full fury of hell.

LONDON – August 8

Werner Heisenberg was stunned by the news.

The Americans had just dropped an atomic bomb on a city in Japan, a bomb that they boasted had the explosive force of nearly 20,000 tons of TNT. The city and most of its population had been incinerated in a flash.

"It could have been ours," Lauderbach whispered, his fists clenched on the conference table. Then he pounded the table in frustration. "We were so close."

"We were ahead of them, weren't we, Werner?" Fichter asked.

But Heisenberg didn't answer. His thoughts were locked on the American scientist who had hated the idea of a bomb as much as he had himself. "He knew," Heisenberg whispered to himself. "He knew, and he used me."

The German physicists had surrendered at Hechingen to the first Allied patrol that had entered the town. Heisenberg, who had escaped on a bicycle to his home in Bavaria, waited until the final collapse of the Third Reich. Then he simply identified himself to the occupying forces. The German atomic team had been gathered together by the British and brought to London. Now they were sitting through cautious meetings with the English scientists who were hoping to involve them in a combined research effort.

"How heavy was the bomb?" one of the Germans asked their English hosts.

"How was it triggered?"

But the British physicist who had interrupted the meeting to read the historical announcement was already waving away the questions. "All we know are the facts that I have just read to you." He held up the news release that the Americans had issued. "It was a single bomb, dropped in daylight from a B-29 bomber, and exploded in the air over Hiroshima."

"Enriched uranium or plutonium?" a German pressed. The Englishman pointed to the paper he held in his hand. "It doesn't say. It simply calls it a nuclear explosive."

Heisenberg pushed back his chair and walked to the head of the table where Frederick Lindemann was presiding.

"Please, I need a minute with you. Alone."

Lindemann excused himself and led Heisenberg into an office that adjoined the conference room.

"When did they begin processing fuel?" he asked as soon as Lindemann had closed the door.

"I have no idea," the English physicist started. "All we know is what the Americans—"

"Please," Heisenberg interrupted. "This is most important to me. Personally."

Lindemann looked at him suspiciously. He had the greatest respect for Werner Heisenberg. There was more to the question than professional curiosity.

"Early in 1944, I believe."

Heisenberg nodded. The Americans were already building bomb material when their agent had come into Germany. So it was just a military game. He was delaying the Germans so that the Americans could build the hellish weapons for themselves.

"I would like to meet with Nils Bergman," Heisenberg said. Lindemann's eyes widened at the suggestion.

"He came into Germany—to the Kaiser Wilhelm—in the winter of forty-four. We worked together."

The Englishman shook his head. "That's impossible. Nils Bergman was dead by then. He died tragically in an airplane accident."

Werner nodded. "Not the real Nils Bergman. The American who impersonated him. I don't know his real name."

Lindemann looked flustered. "An imposter? Someone impersonating Nils Bergman?"

"Please," Heisenberg begged. "Someone in England knows about him. British commandos tried to kill him. It's important to me that I see him. Only for a few minutes."

The British physicist walked slowly from the door where he had been standing and crossed to the window. For a moment he looked absently out into the first peaceful summer that his country had seen in five years. "No, that's quite out of the question," he said. Then he turned back to Heisenberg. "We know nothing of someone impersonating Nils Bergman."

Heisenberg seemed to slump as he accepted the decision. "I helped him," he told Lindemann. "I thought it was the right thing to do. Now . . . I feel betrayed."

"I'm sorry," the Englishman answered. "I can't imagine who he might have been."

The meeting dragged on for three more days. The Germans pressed their English hosts for more information on the American program, but the British had no answers. In turn, the English looked to learn whether the Germans could help them overcome the American lead. They concluded that their best hope was to wait for the Americans to share their atomic secrets. Heisenberg offered little contribution to the discussions. He had no interest in atomic bombs, no matter who owned them.

He was in his quarters, his bags packed for his return to Germany, when a military guard knocked on the door and handed him a note from Professor Lindemann. A car would pick him up within the hour to take him to a special meeting. He was asked not to discuss the meeting with any of the other German scientists.

An RAF officer sat silently beside him as they drove out of the city to the Fighter Command base at Gatwick.

"What's this all about?" he tried, his curiosity building with each passing mile.

"Haven't the slightest idea," the officer said. "Just orders. Pick you up here, and make sure you get there. That's all there is to it."

"Will Professor Lindemann be waiting?"

"Lindemann?" He shook his head. "Never heard of him. Is he stationed at the air base?"

They were saluted through a narrow gate, and directed along one of the runways to a closed hangar at the end of the field. A Wellington bomber waited on the tarmac, its crew lounging under the wing.

"In there," the officer said, reaching across Heisenberg and pushing the door open. "I'll be waiting when you're finished." Werner walked uncertainly toward the building and pushed open the office door.

"Bergman!" he said, as Anders rose from a desk chair to greet him. "You are real."

"And alive, thanks to you. But my name is Anders. Karl Anders."

Heisenberg framed him comically with his hands. "And looking very well. You've lost weight. You've even lost several years. What kind of man is it that grows younger instead of older?"

"I had to grow older to be Bergman. Now I'm trying to be me. It's a harder role to play."

The levity passed into an awkward silence.

"You have heard the news?" Heisenberg asked, switching to the subject that was torturing him.

"About the American bomb? Yes. It's news all over the world."

"You knew your country was working on it?"

Anders nodded.

"You knew you were ahead of us?"

"I thought so."

Heisenberg turned away and walked to the opposite side of the room. His shoulders slumped and his voice weakened to a whisper. "I suppose it was naive of me. I guess I knew that with all the best physicists gathered in America, you would certainly build a bomb. But I thought . . . I hoped . . . that you might find some way of avoiding it."

"Everyone thought that we needed it," Anders explained. "We were afraid not to be the first."

Heisenberg turned slowly, weighted by a truth he had just confirmed. "Then I'm a traitor." He looked up into Anders' face. "I should have turned you in the moment I became suspicious."

Karl's eyes showed his shock. "I thought we understood each other," he said.

Werner's head shook slowly. "When I accepted your errors, I wasn't trying to give America the lead. I swear, I was really trying to keep the damn thing from ever coming into existence. I hoped no one would be first. I thought you were hoping for the same thing."

"I was," Anders protested.

"But you knew your country was building it. So it was just a war game that you were playing. Slow down the enemy so that you can be first. It was just a war game, and I helped you win it."

Anders walked across the space that separated them and put his hands on Heisenberg's shoulders. "You know better than that, Werner. You and I know that neither of us won. We're all losers."

"But you worked for them," Heisenberg protested.

"No. I never worked for them. They asked, and I said no. They came back twice more, once to appeal to my patriotism and once to threaten my career. Both times I said no. I told them I would never have anything to do with the bomb they were building. And then they asked, if I wouldn't build an atomic bomb, would I help destroy one?"

Heisenberg eyed him suspiciously.

"We're both traitors, if you like," Anders went on. "You tried to stop your country and I tried to stop both our countries. But damn it, Werner, who did we betray?"

The German smiled. Then he reached out and embraced the American. "It's good to see you again. I hoped against hope that you had escaped."

"It was close," Karl began. As they settled into the crude wooden chairs that furnished the hangar office, Karl told him the details of the escape. Heisenberg roared when he heard that the SS had been driving him around Germany while Himmler was screaming for his head.

"And your companion? Birgit Zorn?"

"My wife, now," Anders smiled. "We were married just three weeks ago."

He described their flight to the barn and the attack by the SS soldiers. Karl omitted his cold-blooded murder of the SS major, but remembered how he had gone back into the rubble to die with Birgit.

"The British were looking for us. We thought they were going to kill us, and we escaped from them once. But they found us in the barn and dug us out. Birgit was hurt badly. One of the rafters had broken her leg. The Brits carried her for miles until we got to a safe house, and then flew us out the next night. We were here in England for a month while they fixed her leg. And then we went home."

"To America," Heisenberg guessed.

"No. To Sweden. I have a teaching position. Not with Bergman's status by any means. But it's a start."

"You chose Sweden?"

"They don't have any atomic bombs," Anders explained.

Heisenberg nodded. "I was right. We do understand each other. And since we are neighbors, we will be able to see each other often."

Karl's lips tightened. "Not officially. The English want me to keep a distance from Germany. It wouldn't help their image as gentlemen if the Swedes ever put us together and figured out that His Majesty's government was forging Swedish passports."

"But, the English arranged for us to meet," Heisenberg said, gesturing around the room that they were sharing.

"Just this once," Anders said. "They flew me here just so that we could say good-bye. And they'll fly me back as soon as we're finished. The last thing they need is for Nils Bergman's look-alike to turn up in London."

"Then I've lost you as quickly as I found you. Surely we can meet 'unofficially.' By accident, if you like."

Anders smiled. "How can they stop us?"

"Then where? When?" Heisenberg was already excited by the prospect.

Anders tried to think of a suitable place. Then his eyes brightened. "In Haigerloch, at the castle church. In one year. On the anniversary of the American bomb. We'll meet in the choir loft. And we'll sing that hymn together. You remember? The prayer you were playing on the organ. The one with no words."

"It has words," Heisenberg said with growing enthusiasm. "I looked them up as soon as I reached my home. I'll bring them with me."

"What are they? Do you remember them?"

Heisenberg nodded. "The Lord is praised in simple words. The Lord is seen in simple things."

"Hardly the motto of the Thousand-Year Reich," Karl teased.

"Or of your bomb builders," Heisenberg countered.

They held each other and laughed in joy.

"Maybe if we sing well enough, there will never be another atomic bomb," the German said.

"Maybe if we sing *loud* enough. I can't sing well. I have a terrible voice."

They were filled with hope when they parted.

The next day, the Americans dropped an even bigger bomb, made with plutonium, on Nagasaki. The city and most of its population were incinerated in a flash.